# THE ]
# & FALL
# OF
# DEREK
# HAFFMAN

# M.J. NICHOLLS

Sagging
Meniscus

© 2024 by M.J. Nicholls

All Rights Reserved.

Set in Williams Caslon Text with LaTeX.

ISBN: 978-1-952386-74-9 (paperback)
ISBN: 978-1-952386-75-6 (ebook)
Library of Congress Control Number: 2023942609

Sagging Meniscus Press
Montclair, New Jersey
saggingmeniscus.com

*"Sometimes people mistake the way I talk for what I am thinking."*

*–Idi Amin*

# Contents

# THE FALL & FALL OF DEREK HAFFMAN

# I

# THE MALIGN ALP

D EREK HAFFMAN PUCKERED his unkissed lips and puffed three smoke rings towards the TV where Oliver Reed, sweat streaming from his brow, sat milking his alcoholism for chuckles on the Parkinson show. Lounging on a king-size in a Premier Inn with his shirt four buttons free, Cuban cigar tweaked between thumb and index in imitation of a Texan Oil Magnate, Millie Currigan from experimental rock band Forerunner Hammer Precision slumped at his side in a soignée curl, Derek was 5′11″ and aroused. He slithered his left hand towards her uncased thigh. Noting the unwanted appearance of these opportunistic digits, she rebuffed his lustful plea with a stern northeasting of her pupils, choosing not to acknowledge the hillock of penis inside the parallel trews.

"You reek of cabbage," she said.

"You reek of Lidl perfume," he said.

"Oliver Reed never recovered from the 1960s," she said, taking a toke on the Cuban. "He was the living embodiment of that roaring arse who wants to keep the party alive when the entire room is unconscious at 11am."

"He started out in Hammer horrors and sex comedies. Most people remember him for soiling himself on prime time," Derek said.

"Top trivia, Decca."

Millie made to manoeuvre her leg from the fumblesome fingers. Derek claimed a victory of thigh by massaging a pinkie along the skin below her hideous maroon skirt. As a digit of seduction, the pinkie was pathetic—as erotic as a breadstick or toothbrush—however, a full-fingered invasion of her pubis might provoke a narked uncuddling or even worse, one of her matronly knuckle-slaps, so the pinkie had to suffice. She continued not reacting for minutes, more minutes, and further minutes as Oliver Reed blabber-belched inebriant anecdotes, until her patience with the pinkie-rubbing wore thin and she sat up to stub out the cigar. Derek's unappeased throb asked:

"Millie, is tonight the night I might breach the Chinese firewall of your knickers?"

"No. You're volcanic with lust. That won't work." A mirror assessment followed. She tugged at the periorbital puffiness below her eyes, re-tousled her pre-tousled hair of the flame-red variety, and scrabbled in her bag for a range of de-ageing unguents. Derek unzipped his flies and began fingertipping the shaft.

"When might I have the privilege?"

"You have further to travel, Derek Haffman. You must arrive at a place beyond lust. If this is to be meaningful, then haste is not our friend. We have time. Anyhoo, I've to go to Glasgow tonight. We're headlining at the Barrowlands," she said, painting her unkissed lips the colour of marmot blood.

"You're not. You're on at the Rotten Carcass. You know, that hole beneath the Cessnock underpass?" Derek replied. She made a quizzical moue, tapped her head with her forefinger and welcomed the bathroom.

The beer-fattened face of Reed, the sudden bathrooming of Millie, the frustration with sexual frustration, and the bars from Beck's 'Loser' that had boogied in his brain since breakfast, was making masturbation a chore. He teased the shaft some more and spidered towards the sac where the pinkie nicked his right nut. Recalling the pinkie seduction failure several minutes earlier, he felt acute revulsion towards his pinkie, towards Reed's pinkie, towards Beck's pinkie, towards Millie's pinkie, with that smudge of unpicked black varnish still lingering on her nail, and towards the pinkie world in general, especially the stupid word 'pinkie'. A tiring and pointless war to remain erect inside these thoughts was not something he was willing to wage.

Millie had brought the footage of Oliver Reed to the hotel to illuminate her latest mantra. *Controlled delusion. Controlled delusion. Controlled delusion.* It was her contribution to the ongoing betterment of Derek's crumbling, blundering presence, a sloganistic salve for a deeper existential arseache. As a Member of Scottish Parliament so unpopular with his constituents that an online petition to replace him with a bag of sawdust had topped 2000 signatures, she suggested a programme of willed self-delusion to help him vault current woes. "You are staring at reality with unblinking eyes, Decca, and inviting reality to shit on your nose," she'd said. "Why sniff faeces when you can engineer your own reality through controlled delusion. Picture yourself as popular. There! You're popular. Picture yourself as a pioneering MSP introducing a new bill that houses three thousand homeless. There! You're a hero. But remember to keep the delusions within a controlled framework. This will not work if you self-inflate too much. Look at Reed. A helpless alcoholic with the self-poise and confidence of a younger, richer, more handsome man. He is controlled delusion in the flesh." He'd nodded along in the hope she might let him suck on her knees.

It occurred to him that he was uncomfortable. That the bed was rock-hard, that the headboard had been stuffed with flight feathers, that the duvet was soldered to the mattress with industrial adhesive, that the room smelled like that bleach murderers use to cover up the stench of their murderings. It occurred to him that he was sitting upright in a bed in which scores of single men had fingered themselves to climax, that he was slumped in the fraid of a million miserable wanks, flaccid and unpleased. Millie exited the bathroom in a retro leather coat and ripped denims—a retro not part of a present fashion trend and so matching the proper definition of retro—and snatched her bag in readiness to scarper. In the pall light of the room, she resembled a young Glenda Jackson, a fact that softened Derek's lust even more.

"You're almost there, Decca. You need to delude yourself into functioning. It's a matter of extreme cognitive discipline, and I know you are capable," she said, fucking off with no parting balm of a smile.

"Yeah, I'll . . . lard your ludicrous idea into my inner being until I sweat merriment," he mumbled. He had an acute craving for a plate of poached eggs and no motivation to reach over and order one.

Three months past, Derek met Millie at a New Year's Eve shindig at the pied-à-terre of Paul Thomson, percussionist from noughties art-rock outfit Franz Ferdinand. Leaning on the arm of an Edwardian davenport, supping botanical cider through a paper straw, pouring endless pseudo-philosophical waffle into his open ears in her shrill Dundonian trill, mixing Ram Dass with Tadeusz Kotarbiński, Eckhart Tolle with Mikhail Bakhtin, she had fluttered her long fingers across his shoulder, transporting him to a lost teenhood of the light and the profane. Her enthusiastic babble and willingness to spend more than fifteen minutes at his side in a roomful of sexier, sportier, snappier mortals, sparked an instant infatuation, and an arrangement to meet on the QT on a semi-regular basis to exchange cosmic notions and, on his side, attempt to instigate a consensual union of orificies.

She was keen to create a conceptual distance between them for "brain betterment", referring to their mutual occupation of a two-star hotel bedspace as "mere organisms in alignment through the confluence of chance". To her, this was the "template" of an affair, and to proceed toward meaningful humping required intense mental pairing as with radio waves—a kind of cerebral bluetooth—through processes even she could not understand. Although experiencing acute distress at unappeased arousal, this process allowed Derek to respect the wife that occupied his house, who expected him not to poke around in the bodies of pale-skinned rock starlets as part of their unspoken marital contract, and to avoid a scandal in the Scottish tabloids and a clichéd end to a career aspiring to cliché.

When this consummation was to occur was unclear, though those lilting Millieian adverbs made an occurrence sound inevitable, whether this month or a month in 2040, provided the correct incoherent conditions that neither he nor she understood were to form themselves through conversations about Emil Cioran and Oliver Reed. In the meantime, she used sex repellant techniques, such as rubbing her breasts with haddock, coating herself in expired perfumes from warehouse skips, leaving her legs and armpits unshaven, smoking cigarettes, cigars, and cigarillos, and mentioning her mother's vericose veins whenever the erotic impulse twitched. "I have no interest in crushing a marriage," she'd said, failing to explain how prickteasing him bi-weekly in a Premier Inn constituted concern, and made a series of cutting conclusions, referring to the wife as an "overforked spud" and a "wilting legume" while Derek described their dwindling sex life in an attempt to mention sex as often as possible to will sex into happening—a failed use of controlled delusion that Millie found "hellarious".

Clearheadedness was not a-coming. He was an MSP, and the time was 4.19pm, and a speech was to be sluiced from his throat towards schoolchildren in precisely forty-one minutes. The topic was the power of salad, or the power of running, or the power of kale, or the power of not inserting lard and marshmallows into one's maw, or something an intern had cribbed from the NHS website on the scourge of fatness. He twirled a hot strand of chest hair and, for the fourteenth time that week, imagined the consequences of not moving from the bed. The buzzsaw of the bedside Huawei, signalling the panic of a St. Mungo's RC department head in her formal pumps, placating the impatient pupils made to linger behind for an extracurricular harangue.

7

The perplexed email from a ministerial upper, seeking 'splain for the no-show, begging for a template of apology from the 2019 *Handbook of Excuses for Buggering Off to Tank Tequila and Nap.*

The temptation to sleep.

The temptation to eat poached eggs in your pants.

The temptation to take your member in hand and make him right dishonorable.

The longing for freedom.

The longing to bonk Millie in a pricier king-size in a sunnier climate.

The longing to no longer inhabit a 54-year-old corpse, lusting after a 27-year-old loon who imagines herself into triumph using the age-old technique of having several zillion screws loose. Temptations and longings, crushed under the merciless boot of a Google reminder. He worked towards sitting up. Socks, shoes, shirt buttons. The stomach howling "fill me with risotto, asshole!" The rain outside, promising to soak the shit out of whatever non-waterproof coat was worn in error in the overcast morn.

Last week after FMQs, Bill Howeth had called him a "pusillanimous pennyfarthing poser" in the bar. The remark was intended to slap down the sort of working-class peacock who waddled through the chambers acting like a high-muck-a-muck choking on his airs, when genetic accident required of him humbleness and obedience. He had been trialling a new stride, one with more purpose, and Howeth, who loathed men from the Lothians for reasons unknown (one notion floating around was that a lustful barmaid at The Black Bitch had refused to roll her tongue along his hairless pate), caught Derek's stride in an unrefined state, mistaking a simple experiment in perambulation for a pompous swagger intended to puff up a poor lad's status in the annals of Dame Government.

In the bar after, where the alcopops flowed and acid tongues unrolled, he called Howeth a "slaphead of stupefying arrogance", a remark that reached Howeth at the other end of the room. He retaliated by exposing his boyish buttocks to encouraging whoops from the sort of Conservative members who consider Terry-Thomas the pinnacle of British culture. It was added to Derek's Roster of Revenge, a clothbound book of snide remarks awaiting riposte, with two columns, one for the remarker and remark, i.e. Helen Ringwald, MP for Woking—"as politically astute as Mark Morrison with none of the Mack"; David Oakie, MP for Clapham South—"a harmless bacteria awaiting flushment from the body politic"; Ronald Grate, MP for Birmingham Yardley—"puts the bad in fucking terrible useless fucking MP"; Charles Poll, MP for Kensington South—"a little Dettol will sort that out"; Fiona Butteridge, MP for Ebbw Vale—"the human equivalent of the Suez crisis"; and so on.

He tried to make himself as unobtrusive as possible at Holyrood, maintaining a substanceless nodding presence in the background, taking to his feet to ask a question on zoning permits when the Red Bull kicked in. It was impossible to pass through the corridors without making enemies, whether for loitering in the wrong corner, taking the last salami in the cafeteria, having the chutzpah to want to represent the inhabitants of a Lothian town that most of the opposite benches wouldn't even deign to pronounce, or suggesting that Grieg's Sonata No. 3 in C Minor was of equivalent scintillance to the Lyric Suite. It was best to keep quiet, or to be so outspoken that no one could keep track of what remarks were attributable to you, allowing you to claim credit for any notable wit.

"The speech begins thus," he addressed the mirror, straightening his tie. "You are overweight because the sugar and salt industries are sick-headed horrorshits who pack their revolting food with built-in heart attacks, and your cashless parents cannot afford a butternut squash or sprig of coriander to save you from their manicured, strangling tentacles." He combed his tuft of brown head-fuzz. "And another thing, kids. Millie has beautiful breasts that I would like to caress with these wrinkled ol' hands. Because kids, I am entering the slow decline of a short, unremarkable life, and I still haven't found a better thing than having sex with a woman called Millie with beautiful yet teensy breasts. Questions?" He slung on the non-waterproof. "Yes, little girl. I am a repugnant pig. Next?" Booked a cab. "Yes, I am pathetic, unimaginative, and a stupendous bag of walking awks." And out. "Eat a carrot, little fockers."

There was no time for a beer or two to calm the nerves. His nerves never came from fear of public speaking, more from fear that people might see his complete lack of interest in whatever prewritten blather was coming. That someone might expose him and snuff his last remaining purpose as an MSP (as a mouthpiece for the ideas of interns with positive, hopeful messages on some topics and stuff) was to crush him entire. Denied his right to exist as a mere mouthpiece, there was nothing left. "You could seal yourself in the hotel room and order seven curries, nine Chineses, twelve fish suppers, and takeaway yourself to death," he said to the stair carpet. "You could seal yourself in the hotel room and write the longest suicide note in history, a million pages of sneering at protons."

A Venn diagram?

A PowerPoint?

Straddle a chair?

Breach the childwall?

"No, better stand in the centre of the room and maintain a yawny monotone," he said to the revolving door. "Avoid questions after."

Into the taxi with controlled delusion. Picturing himself the Winston Fucking Churchill of lecturing wee porkies. The Keir Fucking Hardie of patronising underprivileged urchins at one of the worst schools in the Lothians into liking broccoli in spite of their prehensile palates pre-programmed to loathe broccoli like the science said. The Tam Fucking Dalyell of standing upright in a suit in a room thick with asbestos while a bored teacher checked her phone and imagined with a lour the oncoming commuter traffic. It was a source of constant surprise to him how the simplest things never ceased to torment. How sometimes you lay awake in bed, watching yourself standing up in several minutes' time, and how the act of standing up might cause your stomach to erupt in a butterflutter of panic at the responsibility that standing up, and staying upright, and taking part in the process of motion, ALL DAY, entailed.

Onto the motorway with controlled delusion. The total respect shown for teachers and the teaching profession. The near religious reverence towards these valorous altruists moulding young minds. The borderline erotic appreciation at their command of the classroom and understanding of the fragilities of the teenage mind. Yes, these were the sorts of deluded positives that Millie had in mind.

"Mind if I crank up The Shamen?" the cabbie asked.

"What?"

"Move Any Mountain. A 1991 rave classic."

"No, that's all right."

It wasn't all right. The cabbie had elevenned the stereo, putting Mr. C's inane rapping front and centre in Derek's mental ticker. Although the lyrics shared the same motivational sentiments Millie was trying to impart—"I walk so tall ascending I stand so high"—Derek was unable to appreciate the E-fuelled togetherness of the Aberdonian electrobeats and lost control of the controlled delusions.

"Turn it down," he said.

"You said it was fine, mate!"

"Not that loud."

The delusions dwindled, opening up a chasm of cynicism. He was en route to a school suffering under the current non-budget for education where, etched into each child's face, was a neediness he had the scantest power to change. He would see, carved with a bloodied hatchet, the lines on the faces of overworked teachers, whose sagging skin told a million tales of weeks and months without resources, of a curricula not updated since the late nineties, of babysitting children on their paths to dope-dealing and dole-dwelling. And into this class-room would walk a liar, Derek Haffman MSP, a man wheeled in to lecture vulnerable children seeking a little happiness in the tingle of sugar on their tongue, in the sparkle of saturated fats, on the value of replacing this little world of happiness with the tasteless, bourgeois assault of cabbage, cauliflower, and broccoli. All to deflect from this parliament's failure to invest in the poorest communities, who waste their monies polishing a statue of Donald "who?" Dewar.

He should stand there courting abuse. He should be nothing more than a magnet for hatred and resentment. He had nothing in common with these kids. He was raised in a time when education was prized. When teenagers aspired to become businessmen, laywers, doctors, or politicians, not makeup vloggers, meme artists, or urban rap sensa-tions. He hated what the world he had helped to build had done to the young. He hated that they could not see that he had helped to build this world and that his words were hollow. The right thing for him would be to drop to his knees in tears, shooting apologies from his nostrils and encouraging the teachers to flog him with warm towels. You patronising cunt. You supercilious, patronising cunt. You super-cilious, hypocritical, patronising—

"Hey, you're that MP? Derek Hoffnung?"

A welcome intervention from the cabbie.

"Yes. Haffman."

"Where is it you MP again?"

"Linlithgow," he said.

"You remember when that Billy Howeth came here? Got that five-head o' his licked in The Black Bitch."

"That happened?"

"Yeah, mate. Fiona Birkinshaw it was, tongue like a tube-lipped nectar bat."

"I need to tell kids to stop poisoning themselves."

"Crack?"

"Crisps."

"The old MSG, eh?"

"Yeah."

"Must Stop Guzzlin'!"

The cabbie was tickled at his improvved rebranding of the abbrev. Derek smiled along with a tolerant air, knowing as soon as the Mondeo vanished along the M9 to Polmont, the line would conclude his talk.

"Here we are," the cabbie said, still pink-tinkled.

"Keep the change, friend."

"Thanks, pal. Best of luck, Crispsnatcher!"

Derek regretted the tip after this remark. An allusion to Thatcher was not how to win an MSP over. The Mondeo departed and the school insisted. A mere slab of floors with rooms, poured into the landscape with rectangular respect, the establishment combined the best of Scottish school receptions—soulless concrete pillars, moth-caked overhead strip lighting, and fox-mauled foamless sofas. A trio of crisp packets whooshed inside, a cosmic reminder of the anti-nutritive nemesis, the foil-sealed foe ruffling the future of these tough kids, and that he hadn't eaten since breakfast, and that a packet of crisps would sate the rumbling beast and taste so sweet. As reception was unwomanned, he poked around in seek of a vending machine and, locating one tucked into the tuck shop, raided soaked pockets for a pound to release the delicious salt and vingear brand from the claw of snack.

Nothing.

An unkempt pupil ran past, shirt untucked. Derek pictured Gus Rosen, his teenage rival, now working as a barrister-at-law in Swindon, running past him at Drumcoll Academy, shirt untucked and hair unkempt, a distinct look of sauce on his mug. Ten seconds later, Carol Hessian, who bossed his wet dreams like a Trump, appeared in a similar state, red-cheeked from kissing the lips of smug Gus Rosen.

"Slow down!" he snapped at Gus.

The Gus-a-like slowed as the no discernible welcome continued. Then:

"Hellooooo!" from a crevice. The headteacher, a tall woman with Balkan features, appeared in an unexpected tracksuit from the same route as the Gus. "You're here for the talk?" she asked and kept walking and made come-come movements with her endless fingers, taking Derek toward the room wherein the kids.

"I'm covering the after-school dodgeball," she said.

He thought of no response.

"Several kids threw too hard and bruised their calves."

No response.

"We wrote to the council about less leathery dodgeballs."

A response expected. None came.

"Here we are! Thank you for coming along Mr. Haffman."

"You're welcome."

As he entered, an unwanted flashback came to the time he referred to a persistent PTA campaign as "the meddling of liquored-up, unfucked housewives" in earshot of several PTA members. Then another, to the time he accused the schools minister of "upskirting economic prudence to sniff the beaver of benefit" in earshot of the schools minister's sister. Then another, to the time he referred to PE teachers as "brainless bonobos with half a GCSE between them" in earshot of a bonobo at the zoo. Then another, to the time he referred to politics teachers as "fustian lechers with a fondness for underage shank" in earshot of a former politics teacher convicted of molestation. Then another, to the time he referred to Scottish schools as "needle-strewn sinks of iniquitous kvass" in earshot of an attender of Scottish schools. The unwanted downlowds kept coming.

Another, to the time he referred to school meals as "plates of mush passed through several generations and microwaved" in earshot of two dinnerladies. Another, to the time he referred to RE classes as "pope-sanctioned brainwashing of the bumfucked masses" in earshot of the

Bishop of Motherwell. Another, to the time he referred to the talent show as "a wilful strangling of the creative imagination" in earshot of an under-ten Shakespeares Sister cover act. Another, to the time he referred to art departments as "pretending Cubism never happened" in earshot of a famous Cubist-inspired art teacher. Another, to the time he referred to school trips as "herding sour-faced tweens into busses to ignore landmarks" in earshot of a coach driver. Another, to the time he referred to LGBT lessons as "exercises in titter management" in earshot of a pansexual semi-woman. If words were to emerge from the frothing heck of his mouth at all, a miracle would be upon him.

The class was void.

"Oh."

He ambled the corridor, thankful for the cockup. He could bail now, legitimate. The wrong room. He waited for fifteen minutes, no kiddies here. His apologies. He has a heaving schedule and will not be free for weeks, perhaps never. No one even offered him a cup of tea or a pack of crisps. Regrettable. Around the corridor, another teenage sulk, shirt untucked, fingering feeds on a phone, no notable awe at a suited man's arrival.

"Been excluded from class?"

"Nup."

"Reason for loiter?"

"I called Harriet Beecher Stowe overrated."

"That explains things. Casting aspersions on America's pre-eminent female novelist's virtue is worth an unseating. I was caned once for slagging George Gissing. I called him a whingeing bottom-feeder in hock to sluts. A better class of mindless insult in them times. Right. Is there a class there?"

"Huhn."

"An affirmative huhn."

It was one of the principal pleasures of adulthood, mocking the primitive vocatives of illiterate teenagers—a truth that reflected ill on adults and teenagers—and Derek took a moment to savour the minor lording.

In fact, this room too was kidless. A teacher, at last, was visible, a bearded male spooning in custard and fingering feeds faster than the excluded scruff. The messiness of this operation was beginning to needle now. He had cancelled a coffee/muffin with Ian McWhirter to appear at this school. The will to persist with a task that had required an enormous mental heave tantamount to self-abduction at knifepoint was never in his arsenal. Now he was expected to have patience with a screwloose comprehensive, where the headteachers taught dodgeball in schemie tracksuits, the receptionists were nonexistent, and the teachers sat with overgrown facial hair spooning in custard. He was tempted to lock arms with the Stowe-slating kid outside and hotfoot it towards the offie, knocking back several tinnies and unleashing Nazi hell on the walls of a hospice.

"I need help," Derek said.

"Oh! Mr Haffman?" He had the brass to first spoon the custard pot clean.

"Yes."

"The talk on health foods? Next door. The class was handpicked based on bmi. Most of them are calm. Two of them might attempt to blind you with rubbers," the unself-introduced teacher said with no smirk.

Condoms or erasers?

"I understand. If one of them talks smack, I have a police-issue taser in the old back pocket," Derek said. No smirk either, deadpan the thing.

"Steer clear of impromptu pile-ons. Happened to Alex Salmond when he came to talk about woodland conservation in the age of fracking. His shins never recovered from the heft of Bobbie Henderson."

"Are you sitting in?"

"No. You'll be all right. If one of them starts humping your leg, that's a sign of affection."

"Thanks for your help."

Into the class, at last. And howdydoody, chubsters! A row of red-hued blimps from readymeal households, their massive arms folded atop the realms of flab stowed under the desks, staring at Derek from their shrunken pupils, telescoped into the underpuff around their face-consuming cheeks. A room of wanton parental and societal neglect, the product of slack-assed government no-marks like himself, failing to prevent crisps and soda corroding their little teeth and rotting their little livers, failing to fling himself into a campaign of intense cauliflower appreciation, failing to stop the heartless corporates from trepanning MSG into the sleeping brains of these neglected little sods. The scene made him sick, or the hunger at lack of crisps made him sick, or the task ahead made him sick. Whatever, he had to concentrate on not being sick all over their wanting, engorged kissers.

"Hello, children. I am Derek Haffman MSP."

"Whatssat?"

"Questions after. I am here to speak to you on healthy eating."

Yes, these children, with their bitter memories—memories of supersize cokes and pepsis, of frenzied nougat-scoffing in the woods, of hurricane farts on buses, trains, and planes, of struggling to stand upright in PE, of bullies hoisting up their shirts and ventriloquizing their fat, of scales shooting into the red, of GPs imploring stubborn mothers to serve parsnips and kumquats, of sallow, cancer-sick skin, of permanent exile to a sort of social Siberia . . . this was their childhood.

"Your childhoods are over," he should've begun. "Your lives henceforward will consist of successful and failed attempts to reshape yourselves, physically and mentally. You will be at permanent war with your paunches, weighing the existential ramifications of each sweet transgression. You will strive to make peace with the third-class state of being open to you, of life within a caste system determined by the size of your gastric band." Instead, he said: "Lettuce is not your enemy." He stood soaked in the bilgewater of the remark. A real human man in a £100 tie, up to his knees in oratorical bilgewater in front of a gloomful of kids, having failed to even glance at the speech beforehand. Haffman, you disgrace.

"My name is Derek. I'm the MSP for Linlithgow," he said, pretending not to have begun one sentence ago. "I minister for the constituents of the town of Linlithgow, in West Lothian."

And?

Lettuce, you were saying?

Hello?

Scrummy, yummy lettuce in my lardy tummy?

Then . . .

He Widdecombed. He pictured the withered flesh of former Conservative MP Anne Widdecombe, a sexless Victorian governess peddling freeze-dried views of an imagined England in a shrill condescending whine—a lump of suet dredged from the larder, thrown into plus-size shoulder pads and made to spout the opinions of landowning luddities from the monocultural spasm of horror—Maidstone, Kent. Even worse, he watched the Widdecombe remove her clothes with a mixture of upbraiding and excitement, and lost himself in the terror of her senior torso—her downcast breasts, unlicked and unmilked, her love handles unloved and unhandled, her untended pubic hair in ruffle above her unpenetrated vagina. He hadn't experienced a Widdecombing this visceral since 2014 while addressing the Linlithgow Knitting Circle, where she ambushed him in lederhosen and caramel pumps, whispering lines from Goethe's *Iphigenia in Tauris* in a Germanic burr.

The phenomenon of Widdecombing was common to most MPs, catching them at vulnerable moments and tenpinning them with horrorfaced holograms of their political nemeses at times when their careers were on the precipice. It had happened to Derek Hatton in 1987, when Militant was careening towards oblivion and Cecil Parkinson, that crumpled fartbag of a human being who spurned his own disabled lovechild, appeared with Pozzoesque panache, riding crop in hand with a slave strapped to his left ankle, spitting in the wind. It was thought that the speech Hatton made that afternoon buried him as a political force forever. Another notable example was MSP Claire Arnock, who once visualised Denis Healy, the former Tory Chancellor with hornèd eyebrows, in a state of wild arousal while attempting a potent address on abortion rights. The speech collapsed into throat-clearing and platitudes, and spoiled one of the most significant chances to inflame the media towards her caring face. This Widdecombing, Derek knew, was a mere foretaste of further, more wounding Widdecombings to widdecome.

"Is there something wrong?" a child asked.

"No, sorry," he mumbled. Widdecombe rotated to reveal the malign alp of her arse. If he failed to focus, she would begin a series of pornographic flexes, crouching on soft furnishings to expose her jewels.

"So, salad!"

He vaulted octaves.

"I am here to speak about healthy eating. You might not believe this"—she shoogled her arsefat with vim—"but there are thirty-nine grams of sugar in a can of coke"—and ran a wet finger along the crack—"which is more than your recommended daily intake"—blew him a bent-over kiss—"and crisps, as far as crisps are concerned"—then parted her cheeks a little more—"there are more calories"—

It was becoming intolerable. He went rogue. "Look, I could read this speech my researcher prepared, or I could speak to you as someone who struggled with their weight as a child," he said. Widdecombe stood up, intrigued. "I used to weigh seventeen stones. I used to eat eclairs for breakfast." She covered her nipples with her palms, surprised. "I had pepsis all afternoon and seven fillings before the age of nine." She went to fetch her pants. "Then I noticed I was having a hard time, with—um—um—um—the lardiness." She smiled and shook her finger at this comment, exposing his extempore bluster as sheer MSP cant. As punishment she wet her index finger and inserted—

"Lettuce! Look. Lettuce is nice. On an aesthetic level, lettuce is verdant and mercurial"—he was becoming desperate—"and brings to mind what Keats called the season of mists and mellow fruitfulness, although lettuce is a plant not a fruit"—and there was no more evasion possible, as Widdecombe, straddling a desk, parted her labial lips and began pleasuring herself with several fingers, highlighters, and a stapler. He buried his face in the printed speech and read the Wikipedia pastings of a researcher who, in twenty minutes, would find his or herself in deep disciplinary doodoo.

"D'you eat lettuce?" asked a triple-chinned cherub.

"Thanks for the question—" He left a space for the cherub to insert his name. The cherub was unfamiliar with the upward inflection seeking the insertion of a forename, coming from a council estate, raised on chips, beans, and QVC, where people never used such a conversational prompt. He blinked at Derek.

"I prefer broccoli," he replied. "And spinach. Both are chockful of Vitamin B. When I say 'chockful', I am not referring to chocolate!"

Nothing.

The room's mouth hung open.

Widdecombe was moving with the aid of two paperclips towards a breathless orgasmic finale.

He needed a poo, he wanted a nap, he craved a pie.

He began to question his skill at making impromptu speeches. If he were to leave the room with a smidgen of self-like, the situation called for an Oscar-nominated rousing improv, so he assumed the ministerial pose.

Legs an equidistance apart.

Hands in contemplative clasp.

An intense expression that suggested thoughts were swarming towards him like a flock of carrier pigeons, bringing wisdom and insight.

A Blairesque pause.

A thought-clearing.

And off.

"It is integral, as the next generation, that each of you set an example to your younger siblings that high-protein calorie-quaffing is the path to pain. You must stop loading up on chips, pizzas, burgers, and fish suppers. Now, I am not suggesting that you ask your parents to rustle up tagliatelle au gratin in béchamel sauce every friggin' night. These are straitened economic times. All I am suggesting is that you put the Playstation to one side, hit the streets for an hour or so, and shovel in some more vegetables. Skip the sweets. Make no more appointments to see Dr. Pepper. You have this chance to, to—you have this—" His attempt careened into a buffer, 360'ed in mid-air, and rolled into a bog. Anne came hard with a long shriek and a vast outpouring of widdecum, trickling down the table legs.

"Enough. Thanks for your time."

There was still the cabbie's MSG line. Should he?

"Remember, when—"

Anne writhed on the desk, displacing a calculator and several jotters.

"—someone says MSG, think Must Stop Guzzlin'!"

All that remained was to make a dignified beeline for the exit. The bearded teach had cracked open more custard, the Head was still bruising calves on the dodgeball court. He was free. The first place he headed was Burger King where he ordered one of those burgers with several patties storied between limp lettuce ceilings, spanning three human mouths; a carton of oversalted fries with extra salt sachets included; and a large coke inside a plastic cup with a plastic lid and a plastic straw, triple middlefingering the planet. Having never found a workable method of tackling such a robust meat edifice, he flattened one edge, forcing a backsquirt of ketchup, and made a minor imprint in the bap. There were no arguments to be made against this stuff. The planet had no chance of surviving another millennium. The reduction of meat production was a means of postponing our inevitable end, reducing the little pleasures we had left to us while suffering inside an uninhabitable sweatbox. People like him had no right to lecture the poor little fuckers who had caused none of these problems on not stuffing their faces.

It was becoming harder to serve the unvarnished truth to the people. Hope had left the building around 2002, somewhere between the release of Coldplay's second album and the invasion of Iraq, and he had been elected to peddle hope. People expected politicians to erect a strong scaffolding of hope to save them from falling into reality, i.e. a bottomless chasm of despair and doom. A politician was a sticking plaster on a slashed throat. A splodge of cortisone on a gangrenous leg. A scented candle in a morgue. Rather than confront his constituents with the sensible revulsion he felt towards most things, he served up prechewed sentiments on the niceness of stuff, like those volunteering at foodbanks, those picking up litter for free, or those who ring the RSPCA about a wounded rabbit, rather than hellmouthing hard on the fucking madness that folk have to attend foodbanks in the sixth richest nation in the world, that we have such a problem with wealth-hoarding, immoral thundercunts that politicians are powerless to make a single fucking difference unless these fuckers are lined up against the wall and machinegunned to mush and their riches buttered across the poor.

A rot was setting into his character, turning him into the sort of prick who instigated an affair in Premier Inns with a rock starlet, who patronised oversize teens into supping kale smoothies, who lied to old ladies on the power of communities to make a real change to stuff and something and someone somewhere. It was time for a Nigel call. MSP for Thurso, Nigel Granger was his oldest confidant, a level-headed voice of chill, on hand to offer Caithness calm whenever Derek was picklepussed to fuck. He completed the first assault on his burger, leaving a tepid tower of sinew for later, and called.

"Haffman. Good afternoon," Nigel said.

"Have a chinwag window?"

"I was about to ram a spoon into the smooth contours of this coconut ice-cream. But I suppose the onset of diabetes can wait for an old friend."

"Magical."

"What's Haffmanning?"

"You first."

"You called me, Decca. You forgotten how to chinwag?"

"I'll listen to your soothing tones for a moment. Lay on me your latest woes, you saucy Highland rogue."

"Decca, I represent the people of Thurso. There are no woes. The worst that happens here is that a tourist loses her nanosim in a crevice, then after a second-long police-sweep of the chair, that nanosim is returned uncracked to the suicidal Yank."

"Can we swap seats?"

"Never. I won this cushie seat with sheer pluck."

"I've come from a talk on healthy eating at a school. I'm sitting in Burger King."

"Is that all? Your silence is sinister. Let me guess. You accidentally included stills from Deep Throat in your PowerPoint? You wore your lamé leotard instead of your pinstripe? You broke into a number from the Beyonce catalogue in a desperate effort to be yoof? Oh God. Decca, you didn't piss in a little girl's mouth again?"

"Worse. I Widdecombed."

"Wow. You . . . total Widdecombe?"

"The whole floorshow. This was noughties Anne, with the black bowlcut, the blimp-sized bmi, powerdressed and unimpressed."

"Sweet Jehu."

"You want to hear about the paperclips?"

"No, I don't want to hear about the paperclips."

"I'm shaken up."

"Relax, Decca. It happens to us all. You remember when I Widdecombed at a Stop the War march in Dingwall? I was limbering up for a blistering attack on Rumsfeld when I noticed her sour features, made up like a Fassbinder whore, in the front row. She stood to unpeel the leather bodice that was stuck to her skin in the heat of the hall. I let Rumsfeld off the hook with a few muttered oaths."

"I was there. You went the colour of horseradish."

"I can still hear that squelch when sweat met the resistance of leather."

A pause.

"Can I ever make a single honest utterance as an MP, Nigel?"

"That's not the sort of question for six o'clock in the evening. That's a seven scotches later sort of question. You can't solve the greatest political conundrum in the universe over a whopper and coke."

"It's not a whopper, it's two whoppered together."

"Pardon."

"The argument we are hostages to our own choices is bullshit when there are twelve Burger Kings, nineteen pubs, one hundred vaping shops, and two million coffeehouses on each street corner, and maybe one place in a basement selling peas and water, if you live in a city. I should be teaching these kids to tell capitalism to fuck itself."

"Why not?"

"Because I'm tired. I need a poo, it'll take a week for this food to escape my arteries, and I'm trying to have sex with a punk."

"Wow! That's the bombshell I craved, Decca."

"I haven't finished this topic."

"Too late. Explain the punk."

"She's the singer in a band called Forerunner Hammer Precision."

"Uh-huh."

"She has nice hair and I want to fuck her."

"Decca!"

"Apologies, Nigel. I pardon your northern prudishness. This is all part of a larger existential rot. She's convinced she can save me from the spiral into vice and sin that I'm willing into being with a series of demotivational Kafkan monologues. She's suggesting she will have sex with me if I overcome this spiralling tendency, as though extramarital sex is a moral exemption."

"What sort of punk are Forerunner thingie?"

"Have you heard Melt-Banana?"

"Nope."

"Have you heard The Slits?"

"Nope."

"Have you heard The Hives?"

"Decca, the last CD I bought was the Best of Sting. And I still haven't removed the wrapper."

"A wise decision. I forgot your musical education ended when plainchant went electric. I refer you to a brief review from rock blogger Alex Magpie: 'a heinous putsch on the ears.' And another, 'if Yoko Ono met Kat Bjelland in the Hadron Collider, the resulting noise would be an improvement over this shite'. And another, 'the sort of no-wave squall that leaves one begging for a mere whiff of melody'."

"That meant nothing to me."

"Loud and terrible."

"Got it. Your attraction to this caterwauling babe is merely physical?"

"No. I'm drawn to her fragility, her illusion of control. I feel like she might shatter with a few stern words. She must have father issues, mother issues, or brother issues to allow me into her sexual orbit. I have a horrible urge to break her. She is a symbol of the youth that our belligerent generation have rendered so weak and helpless, and with one fatal, killing blow, I could shatter the entirety of youth."

"You're such a laugh, Decca."

"Either that, or I have some hidden desire to protect something young and precious. I have some noble aspiration to atone for the havoc caused by the deregulating planet-fucking baby boomers. If I can save Millie, I can save the world."

"That doesn't sound like you."

"Precisely. She's enigmatic. She's like a infinite slice of Viennetta, a skyscraper of Jenga in the form of a skinny woman from Coatbridge."

"Practice caution. Remember Colin Coover? Started an affair with a waitress. She started posting selfies of their sextime on Instagram. Him sleeping in his boxers. Him sleeping next to a box of Durex. 'Chillin' with new squeeze, MSP for Dumfries xxx', she wrote. Make sure this one isn't a total moron."

"She has social media nous."

"All right. I think this chinwag is winding down."

"Concur."

"Keep on keepin' on, Decca."

"Incredible advice."

"Hmmph. Well, look at this. Most people form their opinions on politicians based on the most ridiculous and arbitrary things, like their tortoiseshell spectacles, their elegant salt and pepper hair, something overheard on the radio about free parking for single dads said by another politician, a misattributed quote from a tabloid, a viral video from 2006 of them speaking on a topic that no longer interests them, the proverbial cut of their proverbial jib, a limp-fingered handshake on the doorstep . . . and people pledge fierce loyalty to these complete strangers, the contents of whose minds are as unknowable and unwanttoknowable as any other random bystander with a big mouth. They hold these people responsible for the shape of our civilisation based on these random, tenuous threads."

"You're going to say it, aren't you?"

"They get the politicians they deserve."

"There we are. Fortunately, all the people of Thurso need is a man to rescue their sheep from hedgerows, reassure the moribund residents that Islamists are not planning to invade Caithness, and schlepp to Holyrood every other month to whinge about farming subsidies."

"I'm their man."

"Thanks for the wag of chin, chum."

"Tread lightly, Decca."

In the Burger King toilets, Derek performed a smooth bowel clearance. He thought about becoming a race-baiting populist tubthumper, a sinister maverick in a long coat who came on stage wrapped in a Union Jack to the sound of Big Black. He could become the acceptable face of the muddled misanthropic masses, convinced that immigrants were responsible for raping their sisters and bludgeoning their babies, and persuade them to start loathing themselves instead. Having won their love and respect through calling brown people bottom-feeding no-hopers clinging to the coattails of an empire that gave them life, he could convince them to confront the enemy inside themselves, i.e. themselves, and after a sustained campaign of morale-sapping messageboarding, make the braindead racist masses immolate themselves en masse, like a more entertaining Tiananmen Square.

Or, he could take a micro-interest in each constituent, inserting himself into the lives of those Linlithgow inhabitants with issues, working to resolve each crisis personally, moving into that person's house, spending intimate hours with them to tackle the root of their anxieties, and offering them moral and emotional support, whether that involved kissing them all over their lonely bodies, punching their mirthless bosses, physically clearing up their bins and recycling in a rented van, or crawling into the sewer to unblock the drains. He could transform himself from a mild-mannered penpusher of astonishing mediocrity into a selfless crusader for a perfect world, and become a worldwide example of the sort of altruistic lunatic willing to smother their own needs for others the world badly requires.

For now, the train home.

Back to the ten-year marriage with a woman in a house. Back to the scent of sandalwood and conifers in the hallway, the unpocketing of a text-tingled phone, the removal of a coat, the hellos and heys and howareyous and howwasyourdays. It was, all of it, fucking brilliant, each nostril-tingling scent, each pocket unburdening, each casual expression of interest in another warm-bodied and loving human being and the loving love from that loving human being. The house, the hallway, the pocketemptying, the greetings, these were the things worth dragging oneself towards a school and patronising plus-size teenagers for.

"And do you believe that, Mr. Haffman?" a man beside asked. A pockfaced sneer in a goatee was showing him a headline that read 'Scottish Government on Course for Crime Targets'.

"Yes. We're murdering crime in the face."

"I'm not sure, Mr. Haffman. I heard seven new crack dens opened up last night in Gorgie, and that a known paedophile took over a crèche in Wester Hailes, and that more mothers are being knifed in the shins than ever before." The sneer tugged his goatee in triumph of a well-articulated sentence.

"It is true that more mothers have been the victim of stabbings in the last year."

"And?"

"Nothing. It is true. But fewer cars have been stolen, fewer kittens lit on fire, and fewer post offices have imploded. Crime targets are down."

"But—"

"And if you will excuse me, I have emails to check."

The sneer retreated.

He had no emails.

From the train to the cab.

"Mind if I fire up the wireless, mate?" asked the driver.

"S'fine."

The radio said:

🔊 Mike in Cirencester, what is your solution to the school shooting problem?

🔊 Hello Iain. Hear me out on this. The NRA issues each pupil with a Kalashnikov to use on unstable school shooters. It is kept under each desk and the teacher presses a button to release the submachine guns whenever a shooter is about to unload. Now, I know what're thinking. There might follow problems with the catch mechanism upon locking and loading. This often stems from underuse, causing the mechanism to suffer from low-temperature oxidation. It should be recommended that each pupil use their Kalashnikov on a regular basis, ensuring that this partial rusting process is not at the result of pupils' lives. I recommend a special round of target practice, perhaps in the mornings when the mind is most alert. Because if the mechanism fails at that crunch moment, and tens of pupils are massacred, this could lead to a serious spike in their confidence to tackle future offenders. Also, if the teacher is not in class, the pupils must be able to defend themselves.

🔊 What if the teacher isn't in class to press the Kalashnikov release button?

🔊 A Head Boy or Girl would have releasing privileges.

🔊 Right. And what if a misbehaving pupil accidentally shoots another pupil during target practice?

🔊 Then their parents should be notified.

🔊 Is that all?

🔊 No, I have another suggestion. The introduction of predictive snipers in schools. These are snipers with complex motion recognition technologies inside them to map the movements of each pupil to detect whether their body language mirrors that of the average school shooter before a massacre. The sensors would react to fear and anxiety, predicting whether a shooter was preparing to tool up, and assassinate him before he could begin. Of course, this might backfire—excuse the pun—if the snipers accidentally assassinated pupils who were afraid and anxious that the snipers might accidentally assassinate them. This could lead to a classroom of pupils too terrified to move, unable to complete their reports or answer questions in class, for fear putting one's hand up is seen as a Nazi salute, and the sniper blows their brains out.

◀)) Thanks for the call, Mike.

◀)) I have another—

"On second thoughts," Derek said, pressing his skull between his indices in the hope of pausing that part of the brain that dealt with awareness of sounds, sights, and emotions, "I'd prefer to have silence."

The cabbie dropped Derek outside his refurbished Georgian domicil in the New Town, one long-winded speech away from the surrealist clam of Holyrood. Inside the home was a wife, her name Camilla, the sort of name no Scottish wife tended to have, who wielded a strong face, the sort of face that suggested she might solve all the things that were wrong with the world with a single furrow of her forehead, if she could be bothered, and auburn hair with all the bounce of boutique shampoo and conditioner. She worked as an executive at a leading manufacturer of unisex moisturisers.

"I'm back now, in the house now, I am back," he said, brogues kicked into the shoe corner. The sensation of sock on calico was the sensation of home, comfort, shame, frustration, repulsion, and rage, so he moved onto the kitchen tiles.

"My stomach has been waiting," she said from the living room. He remembered he was supposed to be cooking a simple king prawn, garlic, and chilli linguine for her, and made a wince audible in the next house.

"I have tinnitus from that wince."

She appeared in leggings and kept herself three paces apart. The evenings of welcome air-kisses, shoulder-rubs, back-cuddles, and endearments had long been macheted in the chin and buried in a copse.

"About this meal rota. I reckon we should reduce our formal dinners to two a week. We can pour a packet of crisps and a box of biscuits into a bowl in the week then at the weekend devour several generations of cow."

"Is this a response to your three-star shepherd's pie?"

As part of their campaign of humorous mutual baiting—a campaign that had long moved from humorous to crushing, from baiting to taunting—each meal was rated out of ten on the fridge after eating. To prevent fierce consumer feedback, Derek kept his ratings at a tepid five or above, even her tasteless Mexican paella with cauliflower rice (a wretched sludge of tilapia fillets and saffron threads) while she waged a continuous attack of twos, threes, and fours, even for his stellar Mongolian meatball ramen (a mouthwatering fusion of low sodium chicken broth with panko breadcrumbs).

"Like all rotae, this has become a sweltering oven of oppression," he said.

"This scheme, which was yours, was intended to make us raise our culinary games, with the rating system a kind of electro-shock performance-shame to make us braise our cabbage to a higher standard," she said.

"Correct. Although a series of low ratings, with no recourse to an independent ombudsman when these are in contention, has caused a serious morale sap. Those roasted carrots with Israeli couscous were rated a four, when the tumeric tingled on the tongue, and the fresh mint offset the heft of paprika to perfection."

"Hmm. I tasted a series of sopping carrots, unevenly sliced, with kale strewn across the plate like a twelve-car autobahn pile-up."

Her low ratings were in curious correlation to whatever verbal offences Derek had made that morning, i.e.:

"Your sister's incapable of even glancing at me with the teensiest kindness"—Moroccan Fried Liver and Onions, 3/10;

"A walk-in closet is a signifier of bourgeois indifference"—One-Skillet Bratwurst and Onions, 5/10;

"Being found in possession of a Bettie Serveert album is a fine excuse for waterboarding"—Scottish Oat-Crusted Fried Herring, 4/10;

"Your brow wrinkles like a rhino when you whatsapp"— Roasted Fennel with Parmesan, 3/10.

"Face it, you despise Belgians because one Belgian pinched you on the ass when you were twelve"—Mediterranean Baked Sweet Potatoes, 2/10;

"The shoes are nice, but donating the cash to Greenpeace would have been nicer"—Pan-Fried Hake with Lemon and Herb Butter Sauce, 1/10;

"I warn you with peace and love, if you say *à la mode* again, I will puncture your neck"—Quick Stewed Squid with Tomatoes, 0/10;

and so on.

In addition, a form of ingredient-tampering-as-passive-aggressive-provocation had been taking place—for example, an erroneously inserted piece of kumquat in a liver and onion stew as a red flag for some deeper, unspoken beef in their relationship. The insertions had been mild so far, with Camilla trying to push Derek towards emotional catharsis in the form of four Polo mints in her Ugandan bouillabaisse, a lump of lamb shank in her Albanian vegan risotto, and a sprinkling of chilli powder in her Eritrean low-fat roulade. It was his turn to retaliate that evening, although his provocations were on the whole milder, uneager to trigger the inevitable marital screaming and shouting explosion from a rogue lobster claw in a bowl of Ghanian rice pudding. Last week, Camilla had secreted a blackcurrant Fruit Pastille into a casserole, a lemon Starburst into a chilli, and a smattering of shortbread crumbs into a ratatouille.

As she sat in the front room reading the new legal thriller from Vaughan Stitcher, *The Chechen Hacienda*—a Cold War tale of incest and talmudic transgression set in a kibbutz—Derek emptied a pasta sauce into a pot and measured two halftablespoonsful of custard for insertion into the completed meal. He chopped a pepper, liberally bathing the occasional slice in the waiting custard, then four campari tomatoes, liberally dunking the odd slice in the waiting custard, then half an onion, liberally coating every slice in the waiting custard, and mixed the vegetables into the saucepan. Once the sauce had been sizzled to readiness, the two measured portions of cold custard were worked through with a weariness that almost caused Derek to weep into the ultra-boring meal he had made.

Last week, he had manufactured a sophisticated custard stroganoff like an artist. He carved apertures into selected beef chunks and, with the aid of a pipette, exacted droplets of Ambrosia into the waiting meat, and sealed the burrows with a nest of coriander and oregano. As the beef saturated the strong fort of stroganoff, he fork-tendered the chunks to open up their custard-pocked pores, allowing the substance to sweat into the sour cream sauce until the mushrooms took on a subtle xanthous tinge of Ambrosia. The tiniest tingle of satisfaction at this culinary hoodwinkery had long passed. Now, he would neglect to scrutinise her seventh bite to check for a wince of recognition.

"Pasta ahem!" he called. She completed the paragraph on p.229 while standing and walking and sitting and chair-tucking.

"The rabbi of Urus-Martan is snogging his auntie," she said.

"This is a novel set in the thriving Hebrew faction of the Chechen Republic?" As he peppered her pasta he noticed an icteric pallor to the sauce at three o'clock on her plate.

"Correct. A barrack of blind siddur thieves has overrun the hacienda to extinguish the spurious Talmuds of the Urus-Martan Yahweh."

"You're speaking in semitic tongues," he said, mixing his sauce in the hope she might follow. It was obvious that the sauce had a hue approximating the #ffff00 hexadecimal. It was not obvious she would rise to the provocation.

"I applaud novels that invent Jewish communities in administrative centres of Chechnia." She pressed a piece of pasta with the back of her fork, sending a minor spurt of custard-rich sauce into the puddle of liquid tomato forming a moat between two hillocks of conchiglie. For a mo, Derek feared her remarking on the obvious oddness of the odd hue. If she wouldn't remark on this obvious oddness and initiate the first brawl in series of protracted marriage-mangling brawls, she would never make the first remark and initiate etc. She too was afraid to begin hacking at the tether of contentment that kept them bound in their comfortable Costorphine bubble of warm carpeted rooms with spacious hiding places.

"I Widdecombed somethin' fierce earlier," he said, returning to a calmness that aided digestion.

"While addressing the fat kids?"

"Yes. I was trying to talk up the virtues of broad beans when she appeared in her vintage pomp and let rip a bovine cabaret of illegal proportions."

"No better advertisement for avoiding crisps than Anne Widdecombe."

"Indeed."

"You stumble through all right?"

"Not especially. I couldn't work up enough bullshit to promise these kids a future. All I saw in their doughiest cheeks was the callous, uncaring hand of a brutal civilisation built on cowing the bodies of children with sugars, salts, unsaturated fats and MSG, and adulthoods of consumption and self-loathing."

"What'd you do after?"

"I went for a Burger King."

"Of course."

"I often think as ministers our role is to prevent people from swallowing unpeppered facts whole. It's the reason the US want to torture the pants off Assange. If we stood on a soapbox and explained to people the various thousands of little strategies that exist to control our behaviours dreamt up in backrooms by psychotics who love profiting from killing people with their products, no one would ever vote for us again. We simply deal in disappointment management. We keep the really insidious, fucked-up realities from upsetting the populace enough so they can work and consume the products that are killing them. We are nothing more than a means to appease the populace by offering bland reassurances that things can change while finger-fucking our overlords under the table so nothing budges a squirt. What a pathetic little riddle of a world we have made."

"But other than that, it went well?"

"Textbook, babe."

Their marriage had relaxed to the extent either of them could announce a sudden departure into the night without fear of pique. "I'm meeting Callum to talk trade initiatives and ting," he said to the nodding unconcern of Camilla's head. She had been absent the previous night until around three in the morning at the opening of a proto-menninst exhibition in Cowcaddens, sinking peach schnappses with her boho acquaintances. It was his turn to vanish into the night in nebulous terms and a coat of Harris tweed.

His destination was the Burst Lothario subbasement on Legion Street, a subwoofer Abu Ghraib where Forerunner Hammer Precision were stencilled in as headliners for an evening of untamed skronk menace. Millie's fellow non-musicians were a mishmash of art college sleep-ins who never submitted their Riefenstahl-inspired antiwar shorts, their collages of G-list celeb cellulite snipped from tabloids, or their pictospasms of smashed mobiles and tablets to scrape their HNCs. The group had formed in a fireball of fume at these non-awards, a response to the heartless cacocracy of the Scottish Qualifications Authority. They sought to merge the talentless amp-abuse of late '70s no-wave to the one-chord monotone of vintage drone.

This was the unaesthetic intention. The result was less concrete. Millie based her stage persona on spindle-shanked beatnik Patti Smith while the bassist fingered the strings in imitation of Jah Wobble. The lead guitarist had a fixation on Duane Denison of The Jesus Lizard, while the drummer was inspired by the minimal rhythms of Gideon Alorwoyie from the Afrikania Cultural Troupe of Ghana. These ambitions collided in a sound one critic defined as "madness without method". Their belief that the mere holding of their instruments in an ambient room while waiting for a wisp of afflatus to spur them into organic and mature compositions of supreme experimental magnitude was unaffected by the fourteen published reviews in blogs, hand-stitched zines, and police reports that emphasised the complete lack of afflatus in each eardrum-bursting microsecond. Her band was controlled delusion pulled into the musical realm and tethered to three unwitting instruments.

In the cab, Derek read the most recent review on his phone, from the *Morningside Metalhead*:

> Down at the rock and roll club in West Kilbride, the scene was set. From the hormonal plague pit of the Busted Tabernacle, a former strip joint responsible for spawning such arrhythmic abscesses as The Cracked Turnips and The Cypriot Burglar Boys, teetertottered Millie Currigan, a.k.a. Queen Warble, sporting tight cheekbones and an anti-stomach as if anorexia nervosa was still in vogue, limbering up for a night of chronic tinnitus. Unwashed streaks of blood-red hair like the demonic mane of

Alice Cooper's favourite horse arced across her shoulders as she took to the mic in scissor-slashed slacks and a T-shirt bearing the slogan This Pigeon Aesthetic Is BS, and thrust an upturned thumb across the fourth wall, as though summoning a ride to a place where sound is valued and a second chord is sacred.

"You sure you have the right venue?" the cabbie asked.

"Burst Lothario," Derek confirmed.

"Sure thing."

Pete McCann's (a.k.a Double F's) cigarette-burned strato-caster simulates a buzzsaw inside a beard of bees, as if Shellac, Off Richard, and The Goddamned Biscuits had been booked to perform at the same kindergarten. Steve Rubic appears be-mused at the string-like things on his bass that make a bum-bum sound. The drummer, known as The Ant, is a shirtless hobo who appears to have been promised a shirt on the pro-viso he pummels two tomtoms with the violent spasticity of a man pulled from an underpass and thrown on stage without a shirt. Millie, a walking advertisement for the power of choco-late brownies fried in lard, somehow produces noises from her diaphragm that resemble Tom Waits coughing up catarrh in an echo chamber, snatches of which sound like this: "Carrie, lap the blood! / Refugee fisting in a clotted iron prism / The death of Situationism / Oh, Suki Webster!"

Rest assured, readers! At no point within this frantic protest against talent and the pentatonic scale, appear the passé concepts of melody, rhythm, synchronicity, or motor skills. This outfit manages that unmanageable feat, a feat not even achieved by the persistent Lydia Lunch—playing skronk badly. Forerunner Hammer Precision are four people you wouldn't want pointing you toward the Rawlplugs in your local DIY em-porium. You wouldn't cross the street to avoid these people—you would have the entire neighbourhood napalmed several times over, and then yourself napalmed, to end the unspeak-able pain of existing within the same spatial orbit as them. I would not recommend this band.

Derek would soon inhabit a room enveloped in the factual heft of these three paragraphs. Rather than lounging on a £1000 couch with foam-packed armrests snoozing at the Bergman boxset he had still to remove from the plastic, he was heading for the bowels of aural hell to mingle with one hundred scowling sweat glands. He had evaded a critical opinion on the FHP oeuvre (one EP had been ransomed onto cassette) so far, telling Millie that "modern rock sounds ain't in my wheelhouse", or "my musical explorations ended with the second Cocteau Twins EP".

The Burst Lothario was in the fine tradition of sinister underground Edinburgh venues that kept their pavements outside broomed and sick-free, in contrast to the long trails of fermented urine and revellers with sewn-up lips carving a path to iniquitousness in Glasgow clubs. The venue was a rubber-bottomed square-inch positioned two violent lunges from a small plinth crenellated with barbed wire and rat-chewed amp cables. On the backwall on a small shelf was a vial of GG Allin's sweat surrounded by the furious scrawlings of long-dead acts, intent on carving their place into underground indie history with a knife borrowed from their mother's Bruntsfield kitchen. The Scabbed Granddad, circa 2002, had written "the man who invented fire burned his babies in the gazebo" in a 34-pt font, forming the unofficial slogan of a subbasement that was sometimes used to store deckchairs.

Millie clocked Derek at once, figure-of-eighting past the huddles of ex-bands there to fix their faces to snarl, fart a lot, and mutter "derivative" under their breaths. If there was one reason for Derek's presence, aside from the fruitless pursuit of passionless sex, it was the strange kinship with people content in their flattenedness, people like cardboard boxes hard-stomped for placement in blue bins, in wait for a new life as recycled human beings. She had changed into a long black dress with a mesh-like fabric, corrosive to the touch as both an antirock statement and preventive measure against the 4AM mental unshelling of manqué rapists.

"This is a surprise," she said.

"I am nothing if not spontaneous."

"Hmm."

"I am nothing."

"You saw the five-star review of our Busted Tabernacle show? There was one sentence in there that made me oooh. 'The best thing since Sliced Bread.' You know, the post-punk sextet from Swansea?"

"I haven't heard that particular sextet."

"You chose the perfect night for a spontaneous showup. Our amp imploded so we're acoustical. At some point I'll perform 'The Dildo in Vicar Trousers' on the bouzouki. No, hang on. Pete sold the bouzouki. I'm not sure it was a bouzouki, to be honest. Might have been a bazooka."

"Is that the song where the Pope is sodomised with a menorah?"

"You remembered!"

"A classic of nonuple anal rape."

"You should write our PR. I'll squeeze in 'Horro-Politico' too. I wrote a new verse where I kidnap Dennis Quaid and make him suck the fat from Roger Ailes's corpse."

"Exceptional."

She thrummed her fingers along his shoulder, either showing affection or practicing keeping time in 4/4. He experienced a fluttering sensation akin to balancing on a highwire ignited at either end.

"Some turnout. 12,000 people, a packed house."

Then the resistance, the need to woo this woman on sane terms, the niggling need to call a spade a pish-soaked subbasement populated by people rotating online personas with Kekistan avatars.

"Hmm. I see flotsam of the grunge revolution fading like the last few organisms before the end of everything."

"Derrrrrek. You were doing well. Remember. Wallpapering. Blindfolding. Hazmatting. Make a little paper militia of people holding hands singing 'Shiny Happy People'. Controlled delusion.

Controlled delusion. Remember that song 'Eugenics on Toast'? 'One malignant cell infects the others / the die is cast on our sisters and brothers.' Those were the words. Have a think on that, Derek. For us."

"This isn't the venue for another evaluation of your theory, one that flies in the face of the entire history of psychology, psychotherapy, and psychoanalysis. If I adopted it in parliament and made pronoucements of epic insanity, I'd find myself plastered across the pages of the Scottish Sun and the Daily Record with words like loony, nutbag, and screwloose captioned below the image of my sweating face in mid-brag about the millions of Linlithgow urchins I have rescued from poverty, smallpox, and nonspore-forming rod-shaped bacteria of the genus aureobacterium."

"Or, having freed yourself from a prison of self-disregard, you might suddenly flourish with brilliant notions about saving kids from bacteriums, or whatever."

"Hmm. I would—"

The exchange ended when Double F, the guitarist, approached in ochre spats and a cardigan besieged with badges promoting and condemning Bolivian rooster farming practices, forcing Derek's face towards his unpert, unshining, unmoisturised same. He resembled a six-foot marmot, having shaven his hair the previous month, and maintained an eight-stone waistline through a strict regime of carrots and cibophobia. His particular brand of controlled delusion involved still taking an MA in Philosophy that had ended (in failure) seven years past, permitting him licence to misquote Heidegger to fill awkward silences and strike a laissez-faire attitude toward hoovering up handouts from his divorced parents. (Primarily, to fund a habit bagging Mission of Burma bootlegs on Ebay). He pretended the cosmos was made of fudge, told people he was a mere traffic cone on the M25 of existence, and that his middle name rhymed with orange. He sometimes performed under the *nom de stage* Flavour Flavine, named after his favourite heterocyclic ketone and clock-sporting East Coast rapper.

"Make him scarper using words," Derek whispered to Millie.

"All right, man?" he asked, raising his right hand at a tilt in anticipation of a reciprocated hand to bro-slap.

"Yes, thank you." Derek kept his hands in an insecure clasp while Double F recast the bro-slap to a bro-tap, left shoulder.

"So Mills, I was thinking"—Derek released a sarcastic expulsion of air—"we should launch the set with a twelve-minute rendition of 'Horsewhipped by a Hasbeen Teen Poet'. It's a song that imagines the wilderness years of Arthur Rimbaud, when he ran slaves in the Horn of Africa. There's an electric kazoo solo."

"An underused instrument in rock."

"Precise."

"What's your nickname again?"

"Double F, or The F-F, The Man Called F Twice, F + F, The Geezer After E Before G."

"Or Peter William McCann," Derek said. Millie scowled at the attempt to make Double F confront the pedestrian as the stage beckoned.

"Come on, F-F, time to slice the universe's fundament," she said.

"You mean perform?"

Millie stuck out her tongue at the D.

Forerunner Hammer Precision loped toward the stage with undead élan. Their drummer, The Ant, liked sleeping and snoring after transferring his primal torment through the medium of the kit. An amiable simpleton whose foibles included coating equal slices of toast with pre-tallied baked beans, repairing mangled sieves with scrap mesh, and counting backwards from minus twelve, his lone composition was 'Turbulent Fromage', a snare solo inspired by a French yoghurt that once served as a laxative on a trip to Lyon. The Ant arrived in a pair of sports slacks with a T-shirt that read 'Is Albania Real?'

"Double vodka, please," Derek asked.

The barman blinked and moved not.

"Double vodka?"

The barman blinked and moved not.

"Vodka vodka?"

The barman blinked and moved not.

"V-V?"

The barman blinked and moved not.

"The Drink Called Vodka Twice?"

The barman poured something into a tumbler.

"Merci."

The set commenced with 'Dadaist Pickup Truck'. Derek shoved the industrial silicone earplugs further into his canals as the sheet-metal scraping sent the audience into raptures. The screeching travelled from his neuroreceptors to his teeth and sent a stinging pain into all crowns and fillings, simulating root canal treatment sans anaesthetic. He checked that blood wasn't pouring from his mouth. This was the 'acoustic' set. This was the acceptable face of sadomasochism. These people, these backroom haters, these tormented trolls, these bedroom nihilists, rather than receive the high-heeled humiliation of Madame Ouch, the nipple-searing of a leather-clad ringmaster, or the rectal cat-o'-nine-tails of a retired schoolmarm, preferred their pain from these aural torturers. A pain that made them feel alive, a pain that punished them for the pain in their childhoods, a pain that permitted access to the world of feeling. For a moment, Derek was envious of their access to this fuss-free feeling, to this purgative world of pain. His ragbag of anger, boredom, and melancholia was unreliable and misleading. To experience real howling, aching, searing pain was at least a certain thing: it fucking hurt, this fucking *hurt*. Sheer hurt was better than a list of opaque feelings in some unindexed emotional miscellany.

As a performance technique, controlled delusion had merit. The band were wacko simpatico, mauling their instruments as though present at the birth of punk and stunning the skinheads with their warped kinesis. In their minds, this music was as significant as the Sex Pistols Free Trade Hall performance or the first Velvet Underground set at the Factory. It was a means to contrive a rock revolution every evening, a form of group-think that might have worked after several years spent learning their instruments. As it stood, it was thump, screech, howl, thump, screech, yowl, thump, screech, hell.

Watching a forty-three-year-old man in the crowd strip to his knickers, leap to the stage on his knees, and thrash his head around as though possessed by the spirit of hair metal, Derek sank into a contemplative depression mingled with a lust for Old Testament retribution. He felt the air expel from his body like a rubber lover deflating and opened a deckchair, slumping into the fabric with the sigh of an escaped soufflé. A swirl of menacing thoughts commanded his mental tickertape:

I would like to stab Double F

I would like to cudgel Millie in the nose

I would like to hurl Camilla into a ravine

I would like to force-feed these rockers anthrax pasties

I would like to set fire to The Ant

I would like to snip the barman's balls

I would like to lob faeces into the fat mouths of those fat-ass children

I would like to arson up the Scottish Parliament

I would like to yank the First Minister around on a chain

I would like to shoot most people in the head

Yes, it was that time. It was Time of the Quiver time. Also known in political circles as Quiverification, this was a process whereby an MP, having failed to improve a single life, having failed to enact a single positive change, having been little more than an occupier of a chair on £63,000 per annum, turned so contemptuous of themselves and the world, their morals slithered down the plughole into a nest of vipers. It was a relief for most failed members to fall into the warm hellmouth of careless fuckofferie. That little voice of reason and kindness, clinging to the cliff-edge of truth with scabbed fingernails, at last, could receive the firm stomp of leather-brogued decision. This was no time for YES WE CAN. This was the era of NO WE CAN'T. The era of NO, YOU CUNT. It was time to say, "Let me be clear. I cannot stand your whining faces. I have and will continue to do nothing for you, for nothing is what you all deserve, as you scurry along ratlike in your fruitless lives in sad ignorance of your utter nothingness."

"The polar icecaps is leaking / our leaders are misspeaking / the planet's on fire / as profits surge higher," Millie howled in her excruciatingly underinformed eco-rant 'Power to the Motherfucking Penguins'. Derek escaped to the chill Legion Street pavement to bleed the distortion from his pores and scan his notebook for vitriol on colleagues. The words took on a special shimmer in the moonlight:

> Aaron Mitchell, Tues 3 Mar, 3.50pm. A snide remark was passed on spelling errors in the points-based immigration proposal I wrote. Mitchell reminds me of that bottom-feeding flatfish that buries itself under the sand and shits in its own mouth for nutrition.

> Helen Horson, Fri 12 Mar, 4.33pm. A snub in the chamber. No hello. No polite smile. Horson is a thistle-mouthed fishwife with the spatial awareness of a drugged rhinoceros, stomping into lobbies with her monstrous thighs and massive, waddling arms.

> Bill Grappel, Thu 19 Apr, 11.54am. No applause at the conclusion of my address on the modern slave trade. Grappel is a fertiliser-sniffing farmhand with the vocab of a Mongolian peasant. The walking embodiment of manure, Bill Grappel is manure in man form.

"Beautiful," he said.

Back in the club, Millie was performing self-origami, standing on her hands and spreadeagling her legs in mid-air over a repeated $G^7$ chord and a balloon-popping snare assault. She thrashed her legs around and squealed as though running from a killer on an inverted backroad, nodding her head in agreement with her own lunacy. Her wire-mesh dress enveloped her upper half, exposing her pants and long legs, securing a whoop from the unsexed contingent of the crowd, i.e. the whole crowd. In an unwise move, she began hand-walking toward The Ant, hand-tripping on a cable, and catapulted herself into the kit, sending drums, cymbals, and limbs into a graceless crash against the backwall. The sound of something snapping was inaudible under the unending $G^7$ chord and the shriek Millie made was interpreted as an epic vocal climax to this piece of artistic self-sabotage.

As her shriek resembled the one from 'The Rumbling Opium-Trinket' on the *Muddles & Puddles* EP, some muttered "unoriginal", while others echoed her pained shriek with vein-popping commitment. Observing the look of proper, uncontrived pain in Millie's face, Derek pushed the shrieking morons aside and rushed on stage. Double F and the bassist were frotting their guitars to prolong the climax and paid no attention to the fact their singer had broken her leg. "Phone a fucking ambulance!" Derek shouted.

"Phoneafuckinambulance! Am-bu-lance! Am-bu-lance!" the crowd chanted.

"No, you sweaty fuckers, phone an actual fucking ambulance!"

"Am-bu-lance! Am-bu-lance!"

"Fine, I'll call one myself."

"No, Derek! I can turn this into a show-stopper!" Millie objected. "I'll plant a swarm of locusts in their pants. I'll hop-sing 'Father Carmella' with a snapped leg hanging loose in the magical night." She made a noise resembling a banshee backing into a motorcade.

"The ambulance is coming. Controlled delusion, Millie. Pretend your leg ain't all snaptwigged to Belgium."

"Yes. It's fine, it's fine. I'm a biped strolling along slabs with two legs in a piston-like motion and I'm moving I'm moving I'm moving—"

"Look at me, Mills"—as Derek said this, The Ant arose from the heap where he'd been micronapping under a cymbal—"I'm a buckled exhaust pipe. The slope I'm on isn't slippery, it's a buttered ice rink with bonus banana skins"—The Ant was shooed off with an authoritative waft that sent him running to the coatroom for a snooze—"so I've made a semi-conscious decision. I'm going Full Quiver. No more weeks and months and years holding the crumbling pound cake of fact together with the wholewheat of lies. It's melon-in-a-microwave time, honeyface. It's head-on-the-train-tracks time. It's time to pedal full-pelt toward the White Cliffs of Over and salute Nihil, the God of Nothing as I plummet into the subfusc with a big-ass boner."

"You're that MP, hey?" a man with hair asked.

"Shit off, peasant," Derek snapped.

"Caw!" The man with hair walloped Derek's side-of-face with his front-of-fist, prompting a skirmish involving Derek stomping around with an amp lead and wrapping the rubber cable round the man's throat while the man returned weak blows to Derek's chest, making further bird noises like "squaw" and "nak-nak" until the ambulance crew arrived and attention was re-directed toward the woman mumbling fantasies of movement into the burning hellscape of the airless, fart-scented room.

The parademics manoeuvred Millie onto a stretcher, impervious to the hooting clumps of boozed-up dunderwhelps, taking the sort of charge that Derek was looking forward to relenting. He followed his stretchered non-lover to the ambulance, continuing his adrenalised monologue. "As a minister, I warn people about to step into puddles of snakes and rats to rethink their notion of stepping into puddles of snakes and rats. A minister is supposed to permit people space to hold their sumph-pated opinions of cackling thickness and nod along with tolerant simpers. I intend to mangle this mumpsimus. How are we supposed to progress if our elected representatives cannot call people tongue-tarnished linguafucks whose sub-hominid minds are incapable of the merest squeak of rational thought?" Needles were inserted into parts Millie never knew she had. "As a so-called liberal, I'm supposed to champion enlightened thinking. Somehow, this championing has become entwined with cockamamie notions of excessive politesse, where liberals have to respect the verbal slurries of factless ninnies." The soothing fluids swirled round her frame, bringing the numb. "If the liberal mind is to triumph over the sewage-soaked onslaught of right-wing screamers, we have to call a spade a gormless sheep. A sheep who enables the agendae of career incontinents, splashing their verbal piss-streams into the thankful mouths of the rage-filled masses, desperate for something to kick in the head."

"She's skipping through Elysian fields of morphine, mate," the paramedic said.

"I know. I have to finish this monologue. If there exists a raft of bent illiberals, building meat casinos on the graves of burned children, there can exist a raft of bent liberals, using crooked and amoral methods to correct the world's wonkiness with whatever loopholes are needed to blowtorch far-right bollocks. You can't fight evil with kindness. You fight evil with evil and kindness. Liberals are missing the evil. I want a new political beast to emerge: the moral corrector, a liberal running on spite, willing to plunder the same shitpits as the sickos. If your opponent is in the sewer, you can't fight him in the Ritz."

"Is it possible to counterpose kindness and evil?"

"Good question, paramedic."

"Maurice."

"Good question, Maurice. People are a burst condom of contradictions. The fact the Left smothers their frothing rage in a fireblanket of inclusivity, snubbing racists, and taking the moral high ground is insane. We should lather up in the cesspools of the country, and pummel the teeth from these sad losers."

"Hmm."

"First, I need to taste evil's zesty lips. I have kindness. I have resentment, frustration, irritation, and incoherent lust. I need to alchemise these into evil if I am to fight evil with evil and kindness," Derek said. He went quiet until the ambulance reached A&E. Reflecting on his brushes with aberrant behaviour, he rated past half-hearted frolics as feeble. Strolling through the Red Light District with Lembit Opik as he wolf-whistled the window whores. Purchasing twelve umbrellas when blotto and throwing nine of them in a skip. Driving semi-drunk through Gorgie with Finlay Quaye blasting from the stereo. Stealing half a kiev from the plate of a blind diner. Forwarding Alex Salmond the link to a teen chatroom. Napping throughout the 2013 Linlithgow Over Nineties Lawn Bowls Final.

"You coming?"

"No, I'll leave her in your capables. I need a night mull," Derek said. He crawled along Craigmillar, slow-shuffling north toward Holyrood. His thoughts led him toward an embezzlement scheme, creaming the misdirected government monies (for things like rampart buffing on castles) into more worthwhile avenues, like forming an underground movement of moral correctors, blocking noxious policies through a hivemind of sinister ministers. There must be shock, awe, illegality, political and social upset, and humiliation. The Left could no longer retreat to the corners when the Right bared their blood-soaked claws.

10.59pm was the right time to hone the evil. He found himself in a newsagents, purchasing a can of the lemon-and-lime-flavoured fizz sensation known as Sprite. He opened the can and approached a sitting man at a bus stop thrumming Desmond Dekker on his knees, and tipped the contents over the man's blonde locks. The sitting man spasmed in surprise, pushing Derek wallwards as the lemon-and-lime fizz continued to froth over the rim towards the raging and confused man, whose bus had arrived. "Get your bus, you soggy smeghead," he taunted. "Look at you, all sopping with Sprite." The man barked unformed swears at the night, choosing the bus over a fist-fight. Derek emptied the rest down his collar and the man received this liquid with no protest, ordering a ticket as the driver looked on bemused. The evil act had been performed. He felt no relish. He felt ludicrous and callous. These feelings would be suppressed.

"How about this," he said to himself. "I round up the raggediest rebels in the chamber, and together we pickpocket the credit cards of members after Scottish Questions to fund the sort of undefined guerilla activities percolating at present in the cappuccino-frother of my mind." He thought this a tremendous idea. "I need the backbench outliers who bask in the waft of their own brain-trumps. I need the attention-starved campaigners who use cancer walks, Ebola marathons, or mental health struts to promote the loving beaming kindness of their own roseate faces. I need the utter crackpates who lurk in the lobbies listening to Dinosaur Jr. on Walkmans, pretending not to be elected MSPs. I need the balding unsexed septuagenarians still tailing women up stairs for furtive knicker-peeps, their liver-spotted hands a festival of frustrated fumbles and gropes in cupboards. Those are the species of slime I must harness."

The criteria established, names came to mind. Francis Tuckwell was a pint-sized timebomb, known for frothing at the mouth if criticised and Tourettish outbursts whenever opposition MSPs spoke on trans rights. He had lost two wives to his choleric approach to post-60s cultural changes, still waging the war on addressing blacks as coloureds. He had been instructed to shut up on 379 separate occasions, too senile now to stare down the hostile, booing faces of the right-on powermongers. Liam Hossmoth was a Scots-hating Scottish MSP, living in Berwick-Upon-Tweed in protest, lobbing parodic edicts into parliament such as "no shoes in town centres after seven except diamond-encrusted pumps". He had tried for years to remove the strong Shetlandic twang from his accent and failed, speaking in a glottal mash of Geordie, RP, and Norn. Having to work in Holyrood was a source of constant physical anguish for him to the extent he took showers throughout the day, complaining that "the spores in the Scottish air are killing me", and wore a St. George's flag in the lining of his suit as a form of comfort blanket or flesh-protector. Another contender was Tom Killoche, who had been arrested twice for throwing hot mochas over mutts in groggeries, and wrote a 300-page proposal for the liquidation of urban canines that earned him a lifetime ban from the SSPCA.

Seeking immediate snooze, Derek switched from feet to cab. Back home, he found Camilla still engrossed in the page-turning properties of her sizzling semitic thriller. She uptilted her pupils in presence-acknowledgement as he released his body from the burden of man-made fibres. On his phone, a text from Millie: *Tnx for hanging round :( :( :(.* He replied: *Hope leg is better. Had breakthru. Speak tomorrow.*

"How's the rabbi of Urus-Martan?"

"Garrotted at a seder," she replied, bookmarking the page. He observed the stunning woman in a silken nightie—sparkling wit, whip-smartness and strength hewn into her well-moisturised phiz—and wondered what satanic forces made him fear initiating sex with her. The fact he had been permitted to stand in the same room as her used to be a cause for pan-dimensional celebration. Now, the vision of writhing around on top of her for over a minute made him wince. The propsect that someone could become tired of such a stunning, intelligent, and supportive woman in favour of fucking a delusional, snap-leggèd weirdo from Coatbridge was proof that man was a thing of infinite pity.

At that moment, which was then, when he should have inserted remarks about where he had been and what he had done, he inserted no remarks.

"I could use a new tie," he said, removing his trousers.

"What sort?"

"Perhaps a Pingu tie. I could celebrate the anniversary of devolution through the medium of British-Swiss stop-motion claymation."

"It'll bag you the preschool vote."

"You know, Camster, the reason we no longer fuck? Because, in the words of caustic French novelist Frédéric Beigbeder, love lasts three years. In three years, you spend every mote of passion, you exhaust every spontaneous romatic gesture, you acclimatise to the niggling unnewness of your partner's patter. Your attempts beyond expiry to contrive similar are mere dumbshow. Your entire union has expired, and what remains is tolerance, impatience, and the inevitable spiral toward separation," he said not.

"Remember when Gordon Brown kneecapped me with a five-iron?" he said in fact.

"Best thing Brown ever did."

"I was thinking if I were to snuff it tomorrow, I would be remembered for that one thing. I would forever be the MSP kneecapped by a former Prime Minister. I would have to, you know, reverse climate change while rimming Leonardo DiCaprio to change that narrative."

"You're overselling the accident. You walked into the path of the five-iron. He had no idea who you were, and what you were doing standing there."

"Sometimes you stumble unwittingly into the spotlight."

"Yes, although you knew that was Gordon Brown and you had deliberately approached him to share your ideas on improving morale in the health care sector by offering free tickles for nurses."

"Still an underrated idea."

"And afterwards, he never apologised. One of his aides sourced a bandage to halt the bleeding and carted you back to the car, threatening you with the wrath of Alastair Campbell if you leaked to the Record."

"That's Gordon."

"Hmm."

Scrubbing all crevices, loofahing the loneliest middle-aged nooks with pomegranate cleanser, Derek contemplated Mrs Romfold. The prime kvetcher at his MSP surgery, she had fresh nark for a new dawn. Her lowlights included a lament on the spread of bollard vandalism—the sharpied epithets of a lurid nature left on their stainless steel semi-domed foreheads, secreting coded messages to bigcheeses in the thriving West Lothian underworld. She hated the silent menace of windfarms and felt that her contributions to the world entitled her to retire to a cottage without having to see a wafting turbine from her bedroom window somewhere in the middle distance. She had a problem with the proliferation of bananas from Dutch greenhouses and the third-rate fruit that was being shipped from continental Europe without proper quality checks. Derek liked to picture her head as a balloon he could burst several times—the wondrous mash of her popped pate brightening his desk.

He found the term 'surgery' revolting. He was somehow expected to extract society's tumours, to contain the civic diseases causing such unhappiness to the Mrs Romfolds of the world, using the mere tools of reading and speaking. A surgeon had a near decade of training in intricate healing procedures. The MSP had nothing. The MSP had the skill of reading reports and speaking in rooms packed with people who had no interest in curing these ills, and sat taking minisnoozes on the benches while the people-who-gave-a-single-finger-licking-fuck made impassioned speeches that made for fine viral fodder and caused no substantive change. It was as if a surgeon, having been presented by the stark facts of the tumour in the patient's lungs, took note, then presented another point of view. "On the one hand, letting this patient succumb to their ailments might send a more positive message to other tumour-sufferers, that one needn't let these things weigh them down. It might help people to empower themselves into wellness and prevent further strain on our NHS."

He awoke to a wifeless bed and a craving for a chocolate brownie in custard. His breakfasts were lapsing back to those of the bachelor—whipped cream on chocolate Digestives, Coco Pops in chocolate milk, a hot chocolate with a bag of marshmallows for dunking. Rather than risk the twelve o'clock sugar burnout, he located a mango and nibbled while preparing himself for the call to Francis Tuckwell.

"It's ringing," he said to the mango.

"Tuckwell?" Francis answered.

"You always answer the phone querying your own name. It makes you sound unsure of yourself as a corporeal entity."

"Who the fuck is this?"

"Derek Haffman em-ess-pee."

"You're that miserable chit from Backwater Region with the snooty missus?"

"She's called Camilla. That doesn't make her an heir to the Duke of Buckinghamshire."

". . ."

"Hello?"

"I'm waiting for you to approximate a point."

"I have a scheme to pitch that might be up your alley, you grumbling behemoth. If you have anything planned for the next ten minutes, shove that plan in a napkin and discreetly place that napkin under the table."

"Proceed with your scheme."

"Thank you, Francis. Now, as you know, neither of us should be allowed within a five-mile radius of Holyrood or Westminster. We are shiftless vagaboys who woke up one morning and found ourselves in suits hurling nouns around an important room on things about which we don't particularly care-a-toss. We are windbeaten purplepeopleeaters, we have chronic constituenteriasis, causing us mental squits of the worst kind. In our hearts, we long to set the parliament on fire, burn the whole slackocracy to hell and start anew, with fewer iron-shod platinum-plated rumblecunts in charge of the whole shebang."

"Still listening."

"Right. Last nicht, I was in a subbasement listening to my wannabe mistress's skronk unit Forerunner Hammer Precision when I had a moment of hmm. We need to unleash the Quiver at a moderate-to-severe lick. You see, there are politicians in this world who are satan-kissed shit-kickers, midnight marauders of suffering on a thirdreichian scale who profit from pumping pain into all fourteen electoral orifices. These people are using their evil *for* evil. There are no people using their evil for kindness *and* evil. There are no people, for examp, kicking the tramp's head then placing a $5K cheque in his cup. No people, for examp, stealing the sewing machine to cross-stitch two hundred shawls for freezing urchins. No people smashing the windows then paying for a complete renovation of the entire extension. No people cutting in line at the checkout to treat all shoppers to a bottle of Bollinger. No people slapping their kid then treating them to a slap-free childhood of endless love and care."

"So politics should be an abusive, manipulative relationship?"

"Not such. I propose a secret organisation based on this proppo. For our first strike, we swipe the wallets from all the trashtalkers in parliament to fund some sort of inverted counterinsurgent organisation."

"Vague! I love vague criminal schemes. The best kind."

"Once we have the monies, we can pull together a committee, taking votes on the best use. The funds should be used to plug our failures as parliamentarians, to counteract the sort of wasteful arsewisp that we blow the budget on."

The line went silent as Francis made a long rasping sound of asthma and incredulousness.

"Still there?" Derek asked.

"Yes. I'm wavering between slamming the receiver or keeping you talking while I text the Crime Prevention Agency."

"The problem with liberal-intentioned rebellions is their rule-bending reluctance. Taking the moral high ground when the opposition are shitting into the mouths of the rule-writers is not a wise move. We have to become experts at scheming criminality, using our knowledge of the law to pack our opponents' poopholes with loopholes, to circumelectrocute their asses with Jardycian whomp. You dig?"

"No clue, mate. You want to fuck over some twats?"

"In a nutshell, oui."

"I'm on board. I haven't fucked over twats for months. Makes me hanker for the times I put turds into the pockets of feminist MPs. Made me chuckle to watch them reach for a chapstick then emerge with a claw coated in schnauzer cack. Hilarious! Then there was that time I called in a bomb scare to a care home for a brilliant photo op of me consoling bewildered codgers at the fire assembly points."

"Your career highlights."

"I'll think on't."

"Thanks."

"You recall the last time we spoke?"

"Yes . . . ?"

"I'm waiting."

"For . . . ?"

"Fucking sorries to pour from thine lips like liquid caviar."

"You mean the Cornershop clash?"

"You're not telling me you still consider *Handcream for a Generation* their opus maximus?"

"No, Francis."

"Because the range of riddums of *When I Was Born for the 7th Time* are immense. The sunshine pop of 'Sleep on the Left Side', the swirling instrumental 'Butter the Soul', the Hazelwoodian ballad 'Good to Be on the Road Back Home Again', the Allen Ginsberg cameo

'When the Light Appears', and the immense sitar-pluckin' epic 'We're in Your Corner'. You're not about to whine about the so-called filler material again?"

"No. I respect your strong feelings."

"Is that it? You're not about to say how 'Chocolat', 'What is Happening' and 'Coming Up' are non-tracks, and that the Casio keyboards on 'Funky Days Are Back Again' are an assault upon your delicate aesthetics?"

"I'm saying nowt."

"Because the repetitive dance sound of *Handcream* is pap. Sheer aural pap. You're not telling me that the organ-funk on 'Wogs Will Walk' is some kind of step up from the utter transcendence of 'Brimful of Asha'?"

"It's a weak album."

"Liar."

The receiver received a thorough ramming as Derek entered clothes and speed-dialled a taxi toward the shed-sized office behind a kebab shop where he kept two desks and chairs. There arrived an unusual sensation that the immediate future might hold some sort of promise. It was a feeling specific to 1988, when Charlie Kennedy had taken his hand and told him "sunshine, the future is spreading her legs to the light of Scottish politics." The promise was tempered when the sheen of the silver brooch clipped to Mrs Rutherford's handbag made Derek start back to the irritating normalness of the moment about to happen in a room. She was part of a quintet of spinsters known erstwhile as The Furious Five, renamed The Furious Four after Mrs Birkinshaw collapsed face-down in a plate of patatas bravas when she heard Barack Obama had been elected for a second term.

The protesting pensioners met in a cottage to cook up solutions for improving the sinkhole that was millennial Britain. To help increase the potency of their wrath the ladies would schedule a quarrel with their partners or least-loved children that morning, provoke checkout assistants encountered in the course of their village recces with unPC zingers, or tank two espressos to bring themselves to the requisite pitch of pique. To the soundtrack of men on scaffolding hammering stuff Derek simpered at Rutherford. His blitheish spirit soon fizzled to a spiritless hump under her unwelcome face, BBQed to a sausage-brown hue under Suzie McStein's sunbed.

"Morning, Mrs Rutherford. Been shopping I see?" he asked, slapping her with the first in a series of inoffensive, tedious, bait-refusing remarks.

"Hence the bags," she replied.

Her humorless, acidic expression said "I haven't read a book since school" and her hostile stance said "and even then I skipped the middle bits" and her frothing lips said "I listen to right-wing talk radio, like, ALL DAY" and her polite stepping forward said "I consider myself an elegant female being" and her flared nostrils said "I haven't changed the views I have never fully thought through in three decades" and her narrow stare said "I am the pure embodiment of rational thought and all attempts to pose an opposite view are like suppressing a cancer drug" and her cardigan said "I might be an old woman but that doesn't mean I like people to perceive me as the intolerant brainless old shit-stirrer I have become".

"What's on your mind?"

(The room smirked).

"That lopsided road sign," she said. "The recent storms have blasted the sign downwind by approximately 5.7 degrees. In two months, we are looking at a road sign that will scrape the tops of lorries and buses and cause multiple pile-ups. You will be personally responsible for the deaths of hundreds of people for choosing to ignore these warnings. You will be causing a public scandal on a par with Grenfell."

"The road sign is still embedded in the concrete, however? There's no risk of the pole itself being uprooted by bad weather?"

"Mr Haffman, that is not the point. Don't pretend to be an expert on the strange ways that physics and metereology interact"—she had been reading from notes—"as my nephew drives a truck which has a high centre of gravity, around thirteen feet and four inches from the base to the top at the last estimate, and I could imagine him in an absent-minded moment misjudging the sign and ploughing straight into the danger. The sign might snap off the pole and crash into the windscreen of my nephew's truck, stabbing through his head like a carving knife through a watermelon. My nephew is not an intelligent man, Mr Haffman. But does he deserve such a pointless and cruel death?"

(The room thought about that).

"And don't forget bikes. Those travellers who attach bikes to the tops of caravans. Can you imagine the chaos flying bikes would cause on a motorway?"

He was about to make an inoffensive, tedious, and bait-refusing remark when he stopped himself. He recalled the man on whom he emptied a can of lemon-and-lime fizz the other night and the no consequences that followed. It was time to progress into the world of necessary bastardry, right there, in that room. He heard the words of Jon Bon Jovi: "All I have is this guitar, these chords, and the truth."

"Mrs Rutherford, we are living in end times. Your nephew having his skull sliced open by a lopsided road sign will soon sit in your memory as the sort of light-hearted fluff we used to laugh about in a kinder era. You will have more pressing concerns, like swarms of tethersnapped citizens smashing up shops, banks, and supermarkets, torching public parks, leaving mounds of excrement on the lawns of the rich and complacent. When the vile charade of free market capitalism collapses, when the working classes awaken to the shafting that has taken place over several generations, and storm the fortified castles of the elites, then heads will roll. And it is bothersome, petit bourgeois doilies like you, Mrs Rutherford, that will be hanged on your washing lines and left for the vultures to pick clean. Blood will flow like wine as the new world order is established."

"Mr Haffman, I—"

"I haven't finished. Of course, the elites will not surrender without a holocaustal conflict spanning decades. These power-mad despots will ship in Colombian guerillas to protect their estates and use the latest drones to bombard the masses with napalm death. But the British army will revolt on the side of the people and take back vast swathes of the land cordoned off by aristotwats. There will be mass genocides of working men from Workington, common men from Clapham. Some leaders might pull an Assad and wipe out entire cities of their own people in order to keep their seventeen palaces and harems. But we will succeed, for there is no world without the working man."

"Mr Ha—"

"Because, Mrs Rutherford, our real problem, the only problem, is ourselves. The only problem is the essential blood-throated cuntishness of the human plague. We are the problem. And it starts here. It starts with a simple complaint about a lopsided road sign. Here you are, living in peacetime, with all the cake and vodka you could possibly need, sitting miserable in your cottage overlooking the River Avon, when our future is prising dead babies from piles of rubble, our future is parched rivers, lakes of blood, and swarms of locusts. And you dare to come to me and complain about metal improperly embedded in concrete by a trunk road. You should hang your head in shame."

Rutherford treated these remarks as sheer impertinence, having understood not a word.

"You finished?"

Fear frissoned along Derek's clavicles. He must crush her. He must take the essence of Rutherford and pound that essence into paste with the pestle of profanity. He must snap this woman in two, squeeze her blood and organs into a bowl, and blenderise them into a Victory

Smoothie. If he failed to annihilate this simple sap of a woman then how could he take on the supercontinental axis of eejits?

"You know your estranged son? Yes, Kenneth D. Rutherford? He sent me an email after reading about your campaigns in the West Lothian Courier. He said that he had thought about breaking the 28-year-long silence and meeting you for a coffee. That enough troubled water had flowed across the rivers of time and that he might build a bridge back to your affections. That he could see a future where he could open his battered heart to you again. That perhaps he could rekindle that bond you had when you were young and unbothered by the sins of George McGork. Then he reconsidered. He remembered that time you slapped him on the scruff when he wanted to show you the litter of newborn frogs by the pond. You were having a stern word with George over his fingering of Nellie Sutter. You had no time for your sun-faced son. He was so excited to see those little frogs, Mrs R. This was his first experience of the magical dynamism of the natural world and for ten seconds, he needed you to bask in the wonder of this moment with him. But no, you were too busy. You were angry, and you chose to express your anger on the back of your son's head. His heart splintered that day. His heart softened and sank like a sodden cookie. You lost him that day. He will never forget the callous disregard you had for the condition of his scruff for the rest of the day, either. You were too wound up in where George had put his penis. Your son was before you, crying tears of rage and disappointment, crying away his childhood innocence, and the whereabouts of George's penis was your only consideration. And for that, he will never forgive you. He said, Mrs Rutherford, that you are a shrivelled old shrew and the sooner you choke on your own neglect, the better. I hate to say this, Mrs Rutherford. This is not easy for me to relate. I am afraid he wrote that he's looking forward to shitting on your grave. He added that he will gorge on laxatives on the evening of the funeral so the shit flows in a

furious geyser across your cheap little headstone that will simply read
RUTHERFORD. CUNT."

She wept, she shivered.

"Now, I want to be honest. You people whine that politicians are
never honest. Well, let me be clear. I am fed up looking at your repugnant chin. I'm in the process of Quiverifying. I'm in the process
of becoming an absolute shitshower for your sake. The only way I can
affect any change in this world is through scheming and cheating. So
I will. And for you, Rutherford. I hate you. I hate everything you are.
But I hate more the people who unload oil kegs on penguins. I hate the
polluters, the taxdodgers, the exploiters. So I must walk among them.
So, if you will indulge me, let me tell you what I want now. I want
to crawl up inside my lover's young pussy. She is lying in a hospital
bed, having snapped her leg off playing skronk, and I wish to crawl
between her delicate legs and taste the sweet cuntade that pours forth
from her womanly slit. That is what I want. I want to fuck this skinny,
mental bitch. Now, please get the heck out of my office, you withered
old knuckle from Hades, West Lothian."

She wept, she left.

He pictured Rutherford returning to her cottage, bawling on her
bed, stumbling through tears to the medicine cabinet for the aspirin.
He saw her swallowing two packs, running to the river in a mackintosh
with stone-packed pockets, and leaping into the icy waters for the last
time. Deader than her living form. He pictured her blubbing face, her
bubbling mouth filling with weeds and algae. The whole scene made
him chuckle, smile, and look forward to stuff. Perhaps the thought
of the most vindictive, pathetic people lying dead on slabs is the one
true pleasure in life. The serotonin that rises up whenever we watch
a villain's brains splatted on the wall in action movies. We crave violent, vengeful solutions to our problems. He must continue this move
from bad-tempered unigrouch into a multidimensional slimeball like

Sir Geoffrey Howe—an überprick in the mould of great Thatcherite brown-nosers from the 1980s.

"A proper affair with Millie, not this feeble template, is the perfect fillip I need to launch the überprick persona," he said to the chair on which Rutherford had wept. He spent the rest of his surgery formulating a plan for his scam using storyboards on Microsoft PowerPoint, wondering whether a fourth person would be required to avert failure. The MSP for Bo'Ness Norman Ginseng came to mind. Ensconced in a third mid-life crisis and sexting court case, he would be perfect for the scam, if his alcohol abuse remained below Charlie Kennedy's concept of "a wee dram" and he could pause the dt's during the actual pickpocketing procedures. His working title for the caper was The Artful Dodger Experiment. He texted the three would-be accomplices to attend his premises that eve.

After strikethroughing a one-to-one with a trade union manager ("have the shits mate, soz"), he went to visit Millie in hospital. He loathed talking to the managerial classes with their salt-of-the-earth poseur, texting their caddies under the desk to saddle up their clubs for a 4.30 quickie. In turn, trade union managers and workers found Derek a confusing and strange customer. He had been quoted on the record describing the working classes as "a coarse obstruction to progress in Primark pants and furskinned toques" and the middle classes as a "raft of semi-educated piddlebrains who think their 2:2 in Medieval History permits them lifelong access into the realm of the clever". No one knew whose side he was on.

He found Millie with her leg in plaster, riffling through a *Kerrang!* from 2004, reading the article on FHP below a panning of the latest Manics LP, where her legsnapping was lauded as the catalyst for an artistic rebirth on a par with Dylan's motorbike crash or Mark E. Smith's public assault at Brownie's, NYC.

"Bob returned with *John Wesley Harding*. A tender-hearted portrait of the downtrodden American underclass and one of the finest folk albums ever recorded. The Fall entered their revitalised phase with *The Marshall Suite* and *The Unutterable*, two thunderous classics that begat a hit-streak spanning eleven albums."

"Hi Millie."

He went straight to her face and kissed her on the lips. Her sleep-less, sedated appearance—sweatslicked hair, cracked makeup, and pocked skin—was the closest to vulnerable she had ever seemed.

"You brought me nothing, Johnny Sunshine."

"Correct. The logic being that no one wants to eat grapes even if their legs aren't broken. Chocolate provides unexpendable energy. And making patients in hospital beds responsible for watering and arranging flowers is imbecilic. Someone has to end these traditions."

"Sharp. I'm reading Paul Morley's take on last night. He describes the evening as 'the most breathtaking spectacle since Iggy garrotted himself with a mic cable and brought himself back to life by squeez-ing the oxygen cylinder in his anus'. He then called us the most vital live act since the Dawn of Man. You know, the freak-funk band from Regina?"

"Yeah. They started as that tribute band Saskatchewham!"

"You're on form this morn. I went into a trance last night," Mil-lie said, staring at the uneaten scrambled egg on her breakfast plate, "and imagined myself chasing raccoons with Thom Yorke as the world was burning. Nothing seemed to matter except trapping these skit-tish mammals as the flames charred our skin. Thom had that intense, pained expression he had in the nineties when belting out The Bends."

"That's interesting. But I need to talk about me. I've been squat-ting on this controlled delusion for longwards. I understand. You want to prevent an Oliver Reed moment. To prevent me staggering into Wogan sans trews and saluting the end of a short and piddling career. To stop me melting into Morrissey, pinning Britain First badges to my lapels while massacring Roy Orbison. To stop me from threatening to overrule him, from threatening to overrule him, from threatening to overrule him, from threatening to overrule him. We can park that for the nonce. I have something new to—"

"Decca, I—"

"Hold on. Listen down. Most politicians practice controlled *confusion*. Disaster artists, tossing their word salads around the studios and newspaper offices of this land. Their intention is to produce the least meaningful statements their mouths can muster and to bemuse voters into not voting. I intend to practice something called controlled *repulsion*. I intend to commit one of the cunningest schemes—"

"Decca, I'm not sure you should"—she burped—"be telling me this. Cool your vibes. You send that list of questions of mine to Sturgeon?"

"You mean the questions like whether Rapeman attained greater extremes of punitive scrimmage than Black Flag? If the Bowie mix of *Raw Power* diluted the screaming grandeur of Ron Asheton's Gibson? If there was a single post-Smiths Marr recording worth listening to? If the Tindersticks were the least irritating band from Nottingham? If the ebbing of Beck's talent was a sinister plot from the scientologists to bring him back to the church? If two-tone had ever evolved from the Skinhead Moonstomp? If Liz Fraser had been working in a shoe shop in Howwood when the Cocteau cheques stopped coming? If the duet between Kelly Osbourne and Andrea Bocelli had been suppressed? If the monophonic synth that Portishead used in place of a theremin had sold for ten million at auction? If Krist Novoselic forgot how to play the bass for twelve post-Nirvana years? If Lulu invented hummus?"

"Them's the ones."

"In the post."

"Brill. Let's talk about your new scheme later. I need to nap. I'm having visions of Melissa Auf der Maur prancing around in knee-high boots to 2Unlimited." She slumped flat and yawned herself asleep.

✵

A new email read:

> Dear Mr. Haffman,
>
> It has come to my attention that you have made foul and in-
> sulting remarks towards my mother, Andrea Rutherford, at a
> recent meeting. She claims that you invented a story about her
> son (my brother) Kenneth, knowing the two have not spoken
> for years. She phoned me in a state of dismay, saying that she
> had lost the will to live—

"Yes!" Derek yes!sed.

Further emails flooded the inbox in shrill textual puddles. Having
faced the worst humiliation in a week, Rutherford rallied her network
of indignant working mothers and message-board malingerers towards
the Official Channels of Complaint. In under two hours, a band of
furious fogies would congregate outside his surgery waving placards
and chanting uninspired slogans like "sack this man". The wrath of the
righteous retiree with nothing to do was coming to a village near him.
She had phoned the President of the Scottish Protection for the Rights
of Elderly Women's Association and assembled a posse of women eager
to funnel their hatred into the latest youngish male vessel.

In the past, he might have cancelled MP surgeries for a few weeks
until the protest blew over, citing old classics diarrhoea or haemor-
rhoids as the reason for cowardice. This time, he would tackle the
hostiles head-on. If the last decade of Conservative rule had shown
anything, it was that if a politician started apologising for one massive
public cockup, the apologies for massive public cockups would never
stop pouring forth in a bitter stream of insincere mea not culpas until
everyone forgot what cockups were still left to apologise for. He had
attracted scorn from feminist figureheads in the past, telling a professor of gender politics once to "loosen up" at a debate on the gender pay

gap, which earned him a few ignominious column inches in *Mslexia*. His subsequent explanation, where he described the incident as an "erroneous malapropism" and that he had meant to say "slacken up", had led to twelve weeks of apologetic emails to all offended parties in the United Kingdom and Her Overseas Virgin Territories.

This time, no apologies. Double down on the offense. The response:

> Dear To Whom,
>
> I make no excuses for my remarks. I said what was necessary for your mother to accept reality. I did not become a minister in the Scottish Government to placate the imagined concerns of vengeful, carping busybodies from safe, untroubled backwaters.
>
> Yours, etc.

His cohorts clomped into the hall around supper, scowling toward the faux-rococo so-so study, where printed plans awaited on a surface of shiny pinewood. Liam Hossmouth was live via Google Hangouts from Berwick. His sunburned pate loomed from the laptop screen like a malevolent egg as the others shed coats and selected seating.

"You've eaten?" Derek asked.

"No," Francis Tuckwell said.

"Shame. I'd have Camilla serve a cache of chips in limeade or a cheeseboard smeared in beef pâté, but she's out."

Norman Ginseng sprawled on the antique armchair, tugging loose threads from the rest with an expression of bespoke impatience.

"This room has never seen such audacious bastardry," Derek said.

"You've never been in your own study?" Francis asked.

"Can you turn the camera? I can't see anything," Liam moaned.

"The last real wheeze of mine was in 2007," Francis said. "I exchanged ballots with Doug Ankel who was on track for a landslide in Nuneaton and wanted to escape into the private sector. I spent the entire campaign trolling. I set fire to the saltire in public, shouting 'Bannockburn the lotta yous!' in a Scouse accent. Classic. I made a two-hour speech on Thatcher's handbags, praising the luscious leather sourced from the finest buffalos and alligators, and her poise in handling the soot-black peasants of the coalmines. I introduced a trouser tax for the poorest people, forcing old men to waddle to the shops in their skiddies. The look on their faces when my landslide was announced. They had a collective stroke!"

"That's nothing. In 2012, I booted up a national campaign to make pregnant women leave the house in duffelcoats," Norman said. "I had that slogan 'Ban the bump!' that resonated with millions. I wanted an end to the unwritten rights that pregnant women had like seats on trains and buses and access to expensive epidurals. Of course, I couldn't have foreseen the escalation of fellow feeling that followed. Soon pregnant women were singled out for abuse, with armies of narked barrens chanting 'Punch a preggo!' on high streets and low lanes. Milk cartons were hurled towards bumps, replica placentae made from corn starch and ketchup were posted through letterboxes, some women were pushed into trolleys and wheeled downwind toward canals. The rise in pre-partum depression was immense."

"I forgot that was you," Liam said. He corkscrewed a pinkie into his left nostril, scraping a clique of mucus free from the caverns of his choanae.

"You're on camera," Derek said.

"Right well," Liam replied, skimming over the error, "those are impressive feats. But what if I told you I once shot a man in the anus? I was hunting on a grouse moor in Caithness with a tabloid editor. He was telling me that four hundred and twelve lies appeared in his newspaper in that month alone. I knew this was the one chance I had to make this entitled prick experience real pain. I pretended I was having problems with the shotgun and made several terrible shots towards the grouse. Then I took the initiative and aimed towards the wide load of the gasbag and shot him in the anus. It was one of the happiest moments in my life, watching him howl in the weeds as blood seeped from his moleskins. He recovered after two weeks of surgery, but needs special cushions when sitting at all times now. Hee hee!"

"That is a perfect example of what I propose. Gentlemen, welcome."

Derek poured Pepsi from a two-litre bottle into three scotch glasses for sláinte purposes.

"Scotch was replaced in the Waitrose order."

"Where's Camilla?" Norman asked.

"She's seeing an adapation of *Measure for Measure* at the Playhouse. It's one of these socially right-on versions from the Simon Mayo Production Company, set in a rough comprehensive showing the plight of T-square abuse in woodworking lessons."

"I only ask as I've always wanted to shag her. MSP wives are a mixed bag of shrivelled stoics, embittered shrews, and surprising superbabes, and I put Camilla into the last category."

"I'll pass on the compliment later, if she's struggling to vomit."

"What's the masterplan, maestro?" Liam asked.

"As we all know, the political world in which we were whelped is dead. We live in a realm of smarm-charming Falstaffs and sexless Iagos in Top Shop menswear. We have tried to improve the world with wit and erudition. We have sweated rivers attempting to communicate basic truths to our lumpen-headed contwituents. We have sat through long tedious debates on how to prevent the masses from falling into manholes in an infinite loop of walking and manhole-falling and walking and manhole-falling. We have lost. As we were working hard buffing clauses in backrooms, a new breed were reading Sun Tzu in their bedrooms, plotting their ascent. These bargain-bucket Bolsonaros have a thousand strategies for bombing and back-stabbing and not a single clue as to how to make things work."

Norman sneezed.

"As we watched their ascent, we sank into moral torpor. Some of us more than others. We absorbed their corruption in fruitless, stupid ways. Having affairs. Creaming a quid or two from building schemes. We behaved with the muddle-cocked mischief of the eunuch who awakes with a bulging sac and a triple-shot of testosterone. We must school ourselves to use our moral torpor in tandem with our lifetime of political experience in a scheme that wields evil for kind results. Let's crack on. We swipe the credit cards. The technique is simple sleight of hand. Stun, swipe, conceal, and retreat. Once we have their wallets, we max out the credit cards on expensive purchases, then sell them on. The profits will be funnelled into our special bank account. Once we have the funds, we can begin."

"Begin what?" Liam asked.

"I haven't thought that far."

"So we're to risk our political lives and personal freedom to funnel cash into an unspecified criminal scheme that might somehow improve something for some people somewhere at some unspecified point?" Francis wondered.

"Yep. Who's in?"

The evening unfolded in a miasma of philippics, polemics, and piffle. There was risk of a long prison sentence. There were simple methods of catching fraudsters in place at all banks. The female MSPs kept their purses in their bags. These were the most pressing concerns, aside from the consensus was that the scheme was the most insane, desperate thing that anyone had ever pitched. Derek went full Don Logan. Suggesting that the lads perform the scheme for the sheer fuckoffness, for the sheer fuckitallness, for the sheer fuckyouness. No promises were made. Francis fell asleep, Liam lapsed into a ten-second lag, and Norman continued to praise the calves of Camilla in a leering manner that made Derek swell with uxorial lust.

69

✵

Derek met Camilla at the door, stumblefooted and mojitoed, praising the merits of Davie Graham's Vincentio. A surge of machismo upon seeing her sexyfaced and steaming. Like that other king-size Don, Don Draper, he craved the freedom to take his wife where- and whenever, and have his dalliance on the side with a 6′4″ blonde lattice of a secretary. He longed to charge at Camilla and launch her onto the settee, rip off her skirt with bucksfizzian fervour, and make an assault upon her sumptuous sex parts. He commanded the hallway with the stately paunch that said "kneel, woman", as though expecting her to melt into a frothing puddle of lovejuice, until she pushed him aside: "Move, heffalump, I need a shit."

In the time-honored tradition of bowel references killing lust stone dead, Derek's lust was killed stone dead. He headed to the bedroom, hoping to reignite the hallway hotness with thoughts of Camilla appearing scented in a nightie—her tanned, toned calves, her petite titties caressing the fabric—when she appeared in her *Frozen* pyjamas, yawning and hiccuping toward the bed where she rolled under the sheets and fell into a deep snorting sleep. He allowed his thoughts to wander to erections of the past and wondered whether it was better to walk around having constant sexual thoughts with constant erections or to have constant sexual thoughts with no erections or to have no sexual thoughts and spontaneous erections or to have erections when prompted by the warm form of a female. Reaching no conclusions, he changed for bed and went to sleep without an erection and sank into a mental collage of potential revenges on his MSP colleagues. He would now be free to

🔎 persuade George Adam that his left leg is on fire, lunge for a fire extinguisher, totally foam up his dry leg, then upload the results to Instagram;

- lure Clare Adamson into a vat of peanut butter, make her roll around like a sow in muck, then airlift her between two enormous pieces of bread;
- feed Alastair Allan cheese toasties for two months until he forgets how to feed himself, then stand back and watch him fumble with pasta sauces, cereals, chocolates, and apricots, until he collapses to the floor in a puddle of milk and tears;
- instruct Arthur Tom to vegetate in a pool of lugubriousness;
- install Jackie Baillie as a waxwork at Madame Toussaud's then complain at the unlifelike rendering;
- involve Claire Baker in the smuggling of opioids across the Ugandan border, then convince her to become a tooled-up druglord in Kampala;
- perform regular bottom-kissing on Jeremy Balfour until his cheeks become dependent on the imprint of loving lips, then withhold all kissing privileges to the point he bares his unkissed arse in public, begging strangers to plant a fat one on his fat ones;
- tell Michelle Ballantyne that her caustic remarks on split peas are not welcome here;
- praise Claudia Beamish for her slaughter of seven wasps with a hard textbook thwack;
- beat Colin Beattie the brat with a baseball bat (oh yeah!);
- make Neil Bibby read Elaine Kraf's *The Princess of 72nd Street* and say "See! Told you!";
- encase Bill Bowman in bubblewrap for a week, encourage people to pop along until the bubblewrap is over, then encourage them to keep popping anyway, at which point strangers start popping warts, blackheads, and other sebaceous bumps, leaving him a bleeding and purulent mess, staggering around the streets of Angus begging for plasters;
- read Sarah Boyack a sweet bedtime story, then plant seeds of dread into her ears as she sleeps, so her waking life becomes riddled with

paranoia and angst, her one salvation your sweet bedtime stories, then charge her £4,000 per night for each tale;

- make Miles Briggs eat part of Colorado;
- paint Keith Brown a shade of Keith brown;
- cure Arnold Burrett's chronic piles by removing his anus and replacing his anus with a picture of an anus drawn by a child who loves saying anus;
- call Cameron Donald a strutting sowskin;
- strap Aileen Campbell to a chair and make her watch Jim Carrey's beard in *Dark Crimes*;
- make Jackson Carlaw smoke a pack of fags while wearing a newborn-nooked papoose;
- remove the anvil in Finlay Carson's mouth and release him at last from the rictus;
- explore Peter Chapman's ageing torso with a lust on par with the oestrus of ostriches;
- compare Willie Coffey to a Corinthian order column and see how he likes it;
- recommend Alex Cole-Hamilton for a promotion to First Minister with a long effusive letter bristling with praise from William Hague, Lana Del Rey, David Miliband, Steven Moore, Terence Stamp, Iman, Vivian Leigh, and Gordon Brown, then write a correction the next day, "Sorry, I meant Willie Coffee";
- scold Angela Constance for the mortar she accidentally dropped on Tobin Sprout;
- wheel Maurice Corry into A&E, persuade the staff to remove his torso and stitch his head atop his genitals, then stand back and laugh as he spends a lifetime failing to self-fellate;
- accuse Bruce Crawford of promoting hemophobia in hospitals;
- invite Roseanna Cunningham to a bat mitzvah then shower her with a stream of anti-semitic abuse on a par with a Labour party meeting;

- tickle Ruth Davidson until she begins to sweat the blood of the righteous;
- take Ash Denham to dinner, serve her lobster bisque and curried scallops, take her on a long moonlit stroll along the promenade, have a romantic kiss in a bandstand, then ask her if she has heard of the Kalergi Plan;
- crawl around Graeme Day's legs like a mutt, bark ferociously when he calls the police, then bite hard on his shins as the officers drag you away;
- bung Bob Doris a few bob for the bus;
- promise James Dornan you will never betray him in a million years, then immediately betray him by selling him for scrap;
- sleep with Fergus Ewing in a Renault then reveal that you are secretly sleeping with Fergus Ewing in a Renault;
- accuse Annabelle Ewing of promoting tachophobia at racetracks;
- reassure Linda Fabiani that her bill to prevent bilgewater being pumped into schools is safe, then pump twelve metric tonnes of bilgewater into every classroom in the country;
- call Mary Fee a blithering bungpeg;
- smuggle Neil Findlay into the cinema, then reveal that the movie showing is *Good Will Hunting* (!!!);
- snare Jack Finn in a honeytrap in a hotel room, literally encasing him a thick gloop of honey, then send the pictures to his boyfriend;
- stab Joe Fitzpatrick for suggesting the twelve-minute opener on Shellac's *Terraform* is a "repetitive threnody";
- accuse Kelly Forres of running a brothel in Lochaber without adhering to basic sanitary conditions and using half the profits to fund her habit for ormulu clocks;
- persuade Murdo Fraser to donate his pinkies to the British Heart Foundation;
- convince Jeane Freeman that standing is better than sitting, and watch her legs wobble and snap three hours into parliament;

- pierce Kenneth Gibson with the acid-tipped rapier of your hilariousness;
- urinate on Jane Gillie for twelve hours until she becomes so thirsty she opens her mouth and swallows some of your wee;
- tell Mike Gorgie if he continues to slap his children with such viciousness, he will not be able to continue his hand-modelling career;
- love Mairi Gougeon like no other man can't;
- have a quiet word with Christine Grahame that if she continues to trash the last two R.E.M albums on her music blog, when the band managed to recapture the excitement of their late-80s pop masterpieces on songs like 'Hollow Man', then she would receive an unpleasant package through the post;
- have a word with Rhoda Grant, that word being "euphuistic";
- swallow Iain Gray whole, watch him flail around in the tumult of your stomach, then excrete him back into being;
- cross paths with Jamie Greene, i.e. walk along the pavement marking 'X' in chalk;
- round up all the Ross Greers into a pen, mix them up, then ask their mothers to identify the Ross Greer they whelped;
- accuse Mark Griffin of promoting pteromerhanophobia in airports;
- ask Jamie Halcro Johnstone the reason for spoiling his alliteration with a pompous, pathetic middle name;
- book Rachael Hamilton in for a Friday sac wax;
- recommend that Emma Harper stop bragging about her skill at bending her knee above her neck and her left foot over her shoulder bones, and come up with some policies to prevent the relentless lamb burning in South Scotland;
- persuade Alison Harris not to;
- launch Patrick Harvie into a brand new career as an elected Scottish Member of Parliament;
- spit venom at Clare Haughey, then apologise for mistaking her for a predator;

- accuse Jamie Hepburn of promoting wiccaphobia at a ritual burning;
- ask Fiona Hyslop for a crisp, even though she is allergic to you;
- sign up Daniel Johnson as the face of Strepsils;
- lure Alison Johnstone to a torture chamber, replete with swords, chains, and ballgags, then make the only form of torture the anticipation at what form of torture she will have to endure;
- sweat on James Kelly until he likes it;
- bribe Liam Kerr into saying "frothing fields of Asian cum" in a speech;
- make sure Bill Kidd is all right before you set him on fire;
- contemplate Johann Lamont like a slab of neorealist art, including the hmms and mmms such contemplation requires;
- ask Monica Lennon if she eats shaved fish;
- realise that Richard Leonard is mortal, and that a sustained campaign of rocket fire on his children is not called for;
- kill Gordon Lindhurst in the most mundane way, such as force-feeding him rye bread;
- mansplain Richard Lochhead;
- open Dean Lockhart like an ottoman, revealing the unwanted frill of sheets and pillowcases therein;
- remember that Richard Lyle is a metaphor for something unmetaphorisable, then wonder if that word is real, or if you are skidding into a linguistic buffer;
- remind Gordon MacDonald, Lewis Macdonald, Angus MacDonald, Fulton MacGregor, Ken Macintosh, Derek Mackay, Rona Mackay, Ben Macpherson, Joan McAlpine, Liam McArthur, Mark McDonald, Ivan McKee, Christina McKelvie, Stuart McMillan, and Pauline McNeill that appending a Mc or a Mac to their surnames does not make them any less terrible at Connect Four;
- place Ruth Maguire in the wrong list with the Macs and Mcs then move her to here in the edit;
- invite Jenny Marra to your region for a while;

- persuade Gillian Martin to collapse into mathematics;
- inbox John Mason for later reading;
- kickstart the busted carburettor that is Tom Mason;
- strap Michael Matheson into a trebuchet and launch him into the flaming maw of his own hubris;
- bequeath Margaret Mitchell a tractor, then threaten to repossess the tractor until she uses the tractor, then watch as she tries to operate a tractor along residental streets while weeping into her plaid sweater;
- cull Edward Mountain;
- share parts of Oliver Mundell with the assembled;
- accuse Alex Neil of promoting cacophobia next to Edwina Currie;
- convince Gil Paterson that he is a small cottage, and ask a refugee couple to move into him rent-free for as long as it takes for them to settle into the country, so that Gil Paterson spends a year of his life carrying Syrians around on his shoulders like two traumatised humps;
- know Willie Rennie like your closest kith to the point you disown him forever, then make a teary attempt at reaching out in your late seventies, as you ponder the lymphoma eating you from the inside;
- force Shona Robison to vaunt a bollard in her undies;
- turn Gail Ross against grass, so that she curses and rants when passing lawns or parks;
- turn Alex Rowley against concrete, so that he curses and rants when passing streets or roads;
- test to see if Mike Rumbles;
- impound Mark Ruskell for a few years until he rusts, then reclaim him at half the price;
- cross swords with Michael Russell, i.e. inking an 'X' on their blades;
- remind Anas Sarwar that trouble is his middle name, or possibly Clarence;
- bulldoze John Scott's pied-à-terre;

- accuse Graham Simpson of promoting microphobia at the miniature museum;
- wobble along the route like Elaine Smith;
- persuade Liz Smith to shave her head to raise £2,000 for sepsis, then laugh at her baldness while pissing on a child with sepsis;
- neglect Colin Smyth to the point he leaves this here town;
- sprinkle some Shirley-Anne Somerville on the seedlings;
- accuse Stewart Stevenson of promoting octophobia at Isobel's eighth birthday party;
- remind Alexander Stewart, David Stewart, and Kevin Stewart that having the same surname does not make them besties;
- swap Nicola Sturgeon for an actual Nicola;
- accuse John Swinney of promoting entomophobia at the antfarm;
- xerox Todd Maree then bin the original;
- ask Adam Tomkins if he can keep a secret, tell him the secret, ask him to repeat the secret back to you, accuse him of making up lies about you, then hire a legal person to sue him for slander;
- send David Trance on a one-way trip to the beating heart of Innsbruck;
- shout at Maureen Watt repeatedly until she turns down SL2 on her boombox;
- beg Annie Wells to stop fat-shaming in the middle of the pie-eating championship;
- concentrate so hard on Paul Wheelhouse until a single one of his utterances makes sense;
- lament the pocket billiards of Sandra White;
- squeeze Brian Whittle into light;
- call Andy Wightman an aseptic gnoofe;
- accuse Beatrice Wishart of promoting gamophobia at the altar;
- leave Humza Yousaf alone;

or stuff like that there, and fell asleep.

# II

# THE ARTFUL DODGER
# EXPERIMENT

THE NATION's elected representatives sat in the debating chamber, snug in their shrine to medium density fibreboard. A roll-call of third-rate TV presenters, bolshie ex-councillors, preening Pecksniffs, and loudmouth idiotlogues, all awaited their turn to prattle under the menacing iron struts and artless beams zigzagging 'cross the ceiling like a human spellcheck. Their bodies rose and fell like whackamoles over three uninspiring hours, a timevoid of smug partisan points and semiliterate speeches on the rising damp in underfunded Bronze Age kirks. A roomful of failed middle managers and insipid mehbots, their minds engaged on the shrimp parfait that awaited them at the five-star bistro.

Among them the kindhearted sods, the D:Ream set who had never recovered from the nineties, living for long-diluted manifestos, their frowns frowning toward their nipples, long stomped into complacence and exiled to the corners for ease of panic attack management. Reduced to the shadowiest nooks, streaming 'Nick the Stripper' into their bluetooth buds, silently mouthing "insect!" as rivals stood to intone incorrect opinions. Derek was at home among this contingent until that morning, their mirthless faces rustling up a bee in his well-stung bonnet. "You self-loathers are more contemptible than the conmen . . . you allowed the smart-tongued spivs to bulldoze your idealism without so much as a bareknuckle carpark brawl to the death," he said to his sleeve often. "You skulk around the foyer in your inexpensive slacks like the last superfan seeking a peep of Pete Cunnah and co. I hate you mostly."

Meanwhile, two wasps, locked in a protoplasmic embrace in the backscalp of Miles Briggs, made whoopee as the member for Lothian extolled the virtues of free laptops for crims in sink estates as a means of encouraging entrepreneurship.

It was the morning of the Artful Dodger Experiment and the four participants sat clicking their pens and shifting in their chairs, their pants packed with chiggers, flitting their pupils in expectation of the SWAT team crashing through the roof with laser-sighted rifles trained at their bald spots. Over the last month, the four MSPs had met for booze-free practice sessions, schooling themselves in the art of pocket-snatching until their hands were well-trained wallet-seeking automatons that lunged for pockets without their owners even realising. The technique followed a simple credo—drift, swipe, conceal, retreat—and in an hour or so, the ruse would commence.

"Picture shoals of offenders receiving their laptops spurting into action with e-businesses that change the world. Our future dream is a housing scheme," Miles continued as the entire room pictured shoals of offenders selling their free laptops for a hundred quid and blowing the wad on skunkbags.

Throughout the speech, Derek had been listening to L7's *Bricks Are Heavy*, the Butch Vig-produced riot grrl album from 1992. Millie had recommended them last month "to upset the trivial", following a long recounting of Donita Sparks thrusting a tampon from her vagina into the crowd at the Reading Festival. Gazing at Ruth Davidson's imperious mug, Derek pictured her performing a similar act, lobbing a pessary towards Dean Lockhart's yawning mouth. The thought then inspired a series of revolting tableaux such as Gordon Lindhurst mounting the table, breeks down, urinating into the open mouth of Christina

McKelvie, culminating in Kenneth Gibson sodomising a conga line of MSPs, his enormous one spearing through their throats and their mouths into the anus of the next recipient, until the entire parliament was a kebab skewer of Cunninghame North cock.

His accomplices kept themselves in a state of upright headlight-trabbited über-alertness. Liam sat nearest the front, wearing a fearful expression akin to the time he was caught slapping a 300% tariff on South Korean whelks. Norman had been too nervous to shave, snowing skin flakes on a ring binder of regulations on Dutch defibrillators. Francis teased microdrops from a long-drained Vittel bottle.

"I have a wee dream," Miles said. More like a wee dram, replied the room. "Picture Easterhouse as the next Silicon Valley. Picture that fatherless ned, slithering into flats with bags of dope, transformed into the next Mark Zuckerberg, channelling the same can-do attitude into world-changing earth-shaking technological innovations that change the future of us. Picture a flat block on Lochend Road morphed into a hotbed of fibreoptic revolution. Yes, our free laptops might be water-damaged stock from a warehouse in East Kilbride, but they could transform Dunfermline into the new Tokyo."

Applause, a smattering, sarcastic.

The dullness of Miles's speech acted as the perfect soporific for the aftershow attack. The MSPs left the chamber staggerbottomed with tiredness, a Mexican yawn moving through the kvetching clumps that formed in the vestibule, four or five per clump. The Artful Dodgers moved into their diamond formation. Having wambled towards the centre, a casual exit would be made with the spoils.

Liam, north diamond. He approached the clique known for killing bills for the LOLs, Bills Corpse, named after Bill Gravelaxe, former independent who'd voted for nothing in over two decades in parliament to ironic whoops. The clique was a mix of stock right-wingers and out-of-stock left-wingers whose conniptions had conniped them toward the right of the left-wing and the left of the right-wing. First, the drifting phase—hands in backclasp, legs in nonchalant ambling motions, lips in poutication of a whistle, merging into the fold like a parasitic bacteria in an organism reeking of Old Spice. "I think you should rename this clique Kill Bill," Francis said, using the micro-huh? of pop-cult perplexism to swipe the wallet from Ken Gibson and Pat Harvie's pockets in a brave twofer, concealing the spoils in his own spacious blazer. For the sake of storage, the linings of their pockets had been cut through to allow the wallets to circulate to their backs. "Tarantino," he clarified.

Retreat.

Norman, west diamond. The clique, Frownland. Known for their sourpuss expressions, equatorial wrinkles, and frothing maws, the clique comprised crusaders on lost causes like equal pay, taxing the rich, and providing children with adequate food, in a permanent froth at the Number 10 chokehold on their freedoms to change whatever the fuck they wanted in their own country without an Oxbridge cunt's approval. He sidled up to the clique, checking the steadiness of his hands. "I sent the foreign sec like a million texts," Rhoda Grant said, "on the infected penstocks of Ouagadougou. No response from the fart-hearted wombat-fucker." The slow unfizzling of this remark was the perfect moment for swiping a wallet and a bolus of lint from the blazer of Fergus Ewing. To explain the friction, Norman lobbed an "excuse me" into Ewing's conch in the two-minute lingering period.

Retreat.

Liam, east diamond. The clique, My Human Gets Me Blues. Known for their intolerable rationality, their all-night pecking issues to the clean skeleton of fact, an on-the-other-handism that sent fans of impulsive decision-making based on whims and fancies into tailspins of frustration. Liam inclibued himself, earing up a convo on newish tweaks to the Strang Amendment, allowing for the inclusion of therapy dogs in swimming pools. "Our main concern are the strands of hair that fast swimmers might swallow, leading to an increase in chlorinated hairballs," Linda Fabiani said. The phrase chlorinated hairballs was ripe for a swipe, which Liam performed on the wallet of Cam Donald, transplanting from blazer pocket to blazer pocket with Las Ramblas speed. He scratched his leg below the wallet, touching Cam in mock-error to throw him off the scent of the nab.

Retreat.

Derek, south diamond. The clique, Wild Life. Known for shaking up the quo of status, whether sporting Zappaesque facial hair, purple streaks through blonde bangs, or releasing wasps into the chamber to disperse the dullest speakers, the clique had a thousand schemes for not reading 800-page dossiers on fiscal prudence. Derek made an awkward introduction to the pack. "Rights for cannibals," he said. "Human rights for people who eat humans, right?" The clique popped this conundrum on their mental turntable for a spin while Derek tweezered Bill Bowman's leather thingie into his own concern.

Retreat.

On, centreward.

Trouble swooping across the prodigious beerbump of Iain Gray to the pocket resulting in an awkward backstep and "whoopsie!"

"If burkas were fitted with a moisture-wicking fibre this might stop liberals worrying about overheated Muslim wives," said Bill Kidd as £200 exited his pocket with a finger-tinglin' sideswipe.

The problem—*choo!*—with Ivan McKee's—*choo!*—allergies, causing a frustating—*choo!*—swipus interruptus—*choo!*—and the testing of Norman's nerves—*choo!*—and the dilemma whether to—*choo!*—wait for a larger sneeze—*choo!*—or use a smaller one—*choo!*—when the others weren't staring—*choo!*—to make the move—*choo!*—or whether to abort and move to another—*choo!*—clique—*choo!*—and the impact retreat might make—*choo!*—on his nerves—*choo!*—and whether this might ruin his focus—*choo!*—leading to a botched swipe—*choo!*—and ruin the whole scheme—*aaaaaaaaaaccccccccccchoo!*—then a sign from God when the wallet came loose with a mere thumbtweak.

"If Maggie Thatcher were exhumed and repainted human, the people of Moray would vote for her," said Tom Mason, unaware that his credit cards were no longer nooked in the sweating orbit of hisself.

The grammar of silence. The arms unfolding, the stances reconsidered, the round-the-room peeps, the unbearable realm of throat-clearings, saliva-swillings, soft sniffs, and big breaths. The thoughts caught en route from brain to mouth in a form of uttersputtermuttering limbo, nixed or freed as "hhhmmnn".

"Your first idea is always your best. All subsequent ideas are strained attempts to better yourself, resulting in an hour-long squeezing of umpteen artless turds that invariably lead to you returning to your original idea," said Mike Rumbles, losing a Polaroid of Francine Grolsch in her lilac undercrackers plus wallet.

The excuses for contact.

"What's that fabric? Feels like heaven!"

"Thought I noticed a spider crawling into your pocket!"

"Hands, eh? Where to put 'em!"

"Got a tissue? The old nostrils are fretting!"

"Step aside, old man!"

"Pardon me. I forget what a rhinoceros I am!"

"Oops! Hashtag Me As Well!"

"Arms, huh?!"

"I could never be an octopus!"

For a micromo, Derek caught sight of something sticking from the handbag of First Minister Nikki Sturgeon, that impenetrable fortress of straight-up reasonableness, that Bastille of British politics, that pink-suited pocket-size one-woman monument to candour begging to be stormed. Each time he conversed with her, he saw the sort of politician he should have been—one unkeen to lasso their personal grievances with human idiocy into their conduct, one who shouldered their responsibility to the millions of poor sods walking along the train tracks of life who needed nice, ordinary, smart people to help them avoid the splatter of an oncoming train—he saw this politician and experienced shameish shivers. He simultaneously loved and loathed her integrity, her refusal to daub the walls of parliament in her warm excrement, her skill at not sounding like an android when she spoke. He observed her purse protruding left corner, half-nooked and half-available, and made a slow sidle towards.

Then she caught his gaze.

In that two-second eyelock he read an invitation.

"C'mon, Haffman! You think you can take my purse, prick? You think your arthritic hands can take my imperial, imperious purse, prick? Look at you, with your pickpocketing prowess based on two months of YouTube videos, actually entertaining the thought that you could. C'mon on then, Haffster."

Retreat.

Liam, north diamond. The clique, The Dust Blows Forward 'n the Dust Blows Back. Known for their world-class can-kicking skills—taking an issue and brownbroguing it into the longest of long grasses until the issue was lost in the fronds, lawnmowered under time's rotors, slithering back snakelike to sting their careers. Brian Whittle had brought a Happy Meal and nestled the fries in his blazer pocket while munching the Mac (hand left) and slurping the Coke (hand right). "I know that smell, Whittie! I'm famished. Can I pinch a chip?" Derek asked. "Sure, help yourself." Whittle, in no rush to devour the showcase of fries, took one every twelve seconds, forcing Derek to snatch the carton from his pocket and offer them to the others, taking a risk with second-hand sharing— mock-assuming that the chip offer extended beyond himself. For the sake of politeness, Whittle nodded along, narked at the depletion of his chip quota while resenting the proxy kindness. Derek chose the moment while hands were reaching for free fries to swipe the pre-blocked wallet. He waited until the fries had ended before—

Retreat.

Norman, west diamond. The clique, Sugar 'n' Spikes. The youngest MSPs, a mix of naïf helots and acid-tongued reformers, known for hatetweeting far-right mouthpieces and making right-on noises in terfwar threads. Playing the elder statesman card, Norman sidled up to Ross Greer. "Can I retweet a snapchat?" he asked. "Or even snaptweet a rechat?" The late millennial clump warmed to this sweet ludditism, safe in the nous that the parliament soon was theirs and old customs would vanish with the unstoppable oneclick of modernity, and explained the difference between snapchats and retweets as though talking to a zygote. Norman nodded and whip-snapped the whippersnapper's wallet, keeping up the Grandpa routine even though he'd spent four hours chatting to JoBean292 last night, watching her soap her budding buds via webcam in a paddling pool for more profit than he made in a year.

Retreat.

Liam, east diamond. The clique, When Big Joan Sets Up. The nucleus, Joan McAlpine. The neutrons, her followers who came to absorb her insights and epigrams, agreeing with acute whiplash. As no one paid attention to anyone except Joan, Liam could simply circle the clique, poaching each wallet without even trying, ending with an arse-slapping flourish on Dean Lockhart before—

Retreat.

Derek, south diamond. The clique, Old Fart at Play. The toughest clique to penetrate, known to contain the utter shitheads, the moaning amoral cuntlets, the friendless clodpates, the brainless old humptynumpties, long unputbacktogetherable. Reaching into the pocket of Patrick Harvie, the hypersensitive Green MSP, reacting to Patrick's reacting to his hand, Derek pushed him on the shoulder as a distraction. "Fucking wind farms," he said.

"What?"

"You ruined the countryside, you tree-licking amateur."

"Shut up, you old hack."

"Come on, then! Take me. You too weak? Not enough Vitamin D, Swampy?"

"I could pulp you into papaya."

Catching Norman's northwest no-no-no, Derek fireblanketed the situation with a retreat, glowering at the furious face of the Green as he moved to the next clique, sort of covering up the mistake with random spite.

Having swiped clean the cliques within their demarcated zones, avoiding immediate suspicion, but behaving with such obvious weirdness to make the later suspicion more immediate, the foursome exited the building one after t'other, waiting two minutes betwixt, meeting atop Calton Hill to exchange spoils. Staring at the sullen skyline toward the pickpocketed parliament, the men stood a second to think on the mad thing that had happened in that place and on the mad people they had become, a madness that was now irreversible, having happened over two mad calculated months, performed with such mad precision that sanity clearly had no place any longer in their maddish minds.

"Right. Unleash the lucre," Derek said.

Francis: "Fourteen."

Liam: "Twelve."

Norman: "Nineteen. Plus a pen."

"I have twenty-four," Derek said. "Count the cash."

Francis: "Total sum, £25."

Liam: "Total, £10.06"

Norman: "Total, £34.80."

"I have £45.45," Derek said. "Right. So the total amount we have from forty-nine stolen wallets is £115.31?"

Silence.

"After months learning to become PhD-level Fagins, planning the most audacious pickpocketing scheme in the history of world parliaments, having sweated blood for an hour pocketing wallet after wallet after wallet with our hearts battling tachycardic eruption, our career ruin a mere slip away, a mere pause away, the sum total accrued would not even foot half the bill for a lunch at The Honours?"

Silence.

"I'm going home."

That undefined political something that would form itself in the act of theft had not formed itself in the act of theft nor after. That assault on the complacence of the political elites that would bring on some universal rebuffing of politics and force politicians to do politics better was the soppiest, muddiest, scuddiest, twiggiest, mulchiest, scummiest of pipe dreams. Derek sat in the taxi like a man slapped awake from a long daydream into the pullulating cunt of reality. The whatsapps inflamed.

WHO'S LOST THEIR WALLETS??!!

WHAT?

ME TOO OMG

OH GOD YES

WTF AYE ME AN AW

WHATS HAPPEND

FKS SAKE

I HAVE TOO!!!, Derek wrote to avert suspicion.

The radio said:

🔊 Wilbur in Stockton-on-Tees, what would you like to say?

🔊 Our government controls the clouds. Have you ever noticed when there are protests or marches, the clouds accumulonimbulate, or whatever the meatylogical term is, and the rain comes down Old Testament. In the week, the rain is concentrated on Mondays or Tuesdays, when no one is shopping or dining or beaching. Then at the weekend the sun appears like presto to send us into the streets to shop for alcohol and tampons. The government could make the sun shine in winter, but the neuro-programming algorithm that controls us makes that impossible. It is in their interest to make the weather cold in the winter, to keep the public depressed and docile, to make us plan our brief escapes in the spring and summer, to prevent us making ourselves richer and happier. To keep the economy spry in winter, they crowbar in Halloween and Christmas and New Year and Valentine's Day.

◀)) It's been raining the last three weekends.

◀)) It has. That's to throw us off the scent. No weather pattern is the same, but their seasonal algorithm remains fixed.

◀)) Thanks for your thoughts, Wilbur. Next we have Rylan in Staines.

◀)) Listen. When the European Union tell us how much sunlight we're allowed in one of their directives, when Angela Merkel phones Emmanuel Macron to split their massive allotment of nice weather, and palms off the UK with rivers of rain to flood Hebden Bridge, and when the world's scientists are ordered to ramp up the 'climate change' rhetoric, they take us for utter morons. When the European Union flood our towns and cities with relentless rain, they hobble our economy on purpose to maintain supremacy over us. This climate change thing here is nothing more than a power game, nothing more than the Krauts and Frogs ruling us. We're taking our weather back!

"Turn that off," Derek barked.

Cabbie complied.

Thinking with amazement on how he had managed to pull himself through five decades of existence, how he had managed to construct ever more nebulous reasons for not sautéing his noggin in an oven, and with even further amazement on how his ancestors had managed the same without white chocolate Twixes, the music of Warren Zevon, or access to crisis helplines, he flipped through David Trance's wallet and retrieved a post-it note listing each and every pin and password to his financial accounts. Lost in a stroboscopic fuzz of utter poopdom, a horror-montage of oblivion featuring human repugnance's Greatest Hits—babies on bayonets, mass extinctions in gas chambers, the songs of Marti Pellow, the shooting of unarmed black children outside American schools, etc.—Derek needed two minutes to heed the significance of the post-it for his own prospects.

"Thick cunt's passwords," he said at last.

"What?" Cabbie asked.

"Where's the nearest bank?"

Santander-bound, plans continued to elude. There were seven potential Dereks.

D$^1$: Bounding thru the streets with post-Scroogian pomp, showering florins upon the pox-ridden, lobbing stuffed turkeys towards soot-faced urchins, solving wealth inequality in Dickensian fashion thru ad hoc philanthropic whims.

D$^2$: POLITIX TWO-POINT-OH. A new, sexier politix sans the scumbags. A politixal partie with coolness, awesomeness :D :D, and CH-CH-CH-CHANGAEYS, starring Tuppence Middleton and Tom Hiddleston, bringing lust and seXXX to politix to make ppl vote for things that matter, like more $$$ 4 stuffz an' 'ting.

D$^3$: Fuck y'all. I'm takin' a hike to Tahiti.

D$^4$: "Ladies and gentlemen, welcome to our first meeting. As per our literature, you will observe that our organisation's first task is simple. We must murder all right-wing journalists tomorrow. As you will see, once we have completed this genocide, all right-wing newspapers will fold. We can then begin to participate in a country where a semblance of truth is communicated to the masses. Free uzis at the back."

D$^5$: Yeah, I have a million freakin' pounds, so what? What has a million pounds ever changed? Who ever rocked up with a million and said, look here, with this pot of piddling pounds, I'mma shake up the whole political situation wid wicked skills right? What's the point, when the only solution is to out-billionaire the billionaires, and to become a billionaire, you have to have a black festering chasm of filth and pus where a heart should be? Why not make like The KLF, and burn that million?

$D^6$: Put the cash in an account until I have a semi-workable idea for reinventing British politics.

$D^7$: "Millie, here's ten thousand pounds. Please touch my penis."

"Bank. £12.50," Cabbie said.

"Here's £20. Keep the change."

"Naw, mate. I'm no a charity case, take your change."

"Fine."

If he paused for even a second at the door, his brain would make an heroic helter-skelter toward his lumbar, split in two, and seize his legs for a sprint of retreat toward the nearest bedspread. That being so, he powered into the branch with the post-it curled in his palm for furtive pin peepage, lining up in a four-strong queue, looking on the random placement of red sofas in fear at their massive redness. The advent of online banking was a blessing for those who loathed the prison-visit atmosphere of branches, where clients stood to have one-to-one conversations through thermoplastic with their own money. Proving to their own money they owned their own money, making redblazered spinsters and pimpled college flunks chatelaines of their hard-won incomes.

Queue fatigue. Time to wonder if David Trance had cancelled his cards already, if Scottish prisons offered en suite rooms. The Muslim woman in niqab, failing to make herself clear to the twerp named Filo through her layer of cloth. The man who at close of his first transaction retrieves a bag of coins for deposit, $1/3^{rd}$ of which are pesos from 1993. The amnesiac in an anorak resetting yesterday's reset passwords from yesterday. The natterer with a cheque deposit who hasn't mastered the deposit machine in eleven years. The man stood there since last week who sends the clerk back and forth to a backroom for inexplicable reasons and requires the CEO of Santander to clear a suspect £1.98 transaction. These folks, ahead in the queue, in all banks, for all customers, at all times, forever. "How about two lanes," Derek said to himself. "One for those with a contempt for time who still barter in salt and human skulls, one for those who know how banks work so want to leave the fucking bank as hastily as humanly fucking possible."

Queue fatigue. Time to recall the richest people he'd known and their duncical diddling of funds. On loathsome sports cars with enfattened wheels and bonnets to be powered along country roads, their superior overtaking skills a metaphor for how amazing they are at life. On spacious top-floor apartments in a permanent state of showroom blankness, all signs of lived-in-ness mopped up by Małgosia on Mondays. On plates of tempura shredded through the gills of a Mexican tequila splitfin over quarter-glasses of vino at £300 a sip. On shindigs for the similar featuring a set from a famous comedian who roasts them for an hour so they feel better for having been prodded from their perches . . . retiring to the ballroom to waltz in their tailored fineries to have the time of their weeks to the tune of a bazillion.

Queue fatigue. Time to recall the resentment from constituents he had tried to help. Mr Tennant whingeing in that rasped tone that politicians were crooks and swindlers while the politician before him was literally helping him to feed and house himself. Mrs Gradie ranting that the politicians never deigned to help their constituents with hands-on work while the politician before her was literally scrubbing the outside bin shed himself. Mr Finton who complained that he had received no help from the council about the harassment from his next door neighbours when the politician before him was literally talking to his neighbours with the police about their behaviour. Mrs Swinton who bemoaned the lack of accessible parking spaces at her local community centre when the politician before her was literally creating four new disabled spaces with a bucket of paint. Hundreds of them. People who complained that their everlasting happiness was too long and too perfect and that politicians never helped make them fucking miserable for balance. People who held him personally responsible for their own incurable self-loathing who believed if the calibre of their MSP was stronger, their own spitting hate might mellow.

Queue fatigue. Time to recall the unreported scandals he should have exploited. The one where Robin Cook made a pantless cameo in the 1970 Swedish sex comedy Rötmånad under the name Rodeo Mike. The one where Jack McConnell made love to a prostitute with such vigour her neck detached a little, requiring £50,000 surgery at the taxpayer's expense. The one where Michael Matheson was caught invaginating a hibiscus at the Falkirk Flower Festivus to steal second place with a below-par halberd-leaf rosemallow. The one where Brian Adam sneaked lime cordial into the tap waters of colleagues at parliamentary soirées, causing the entire plumbing to be uprooted for no reason at the taxpayer's expense. The one where Ross Finnie lost his rag while on hold to Virgin Broadband and slaughtered a hectare of squirrels at various West Scotland parks in one twelve-hour killing spree that spoiled a decade of conservation. The one where Rhona Brankin sang The Libertines at karaoke to such applause, she spent a lost weekend in Shoreditch snorting drugs with Kate Moss and showing her tattooed arms to passing strangers at the taxpayer's expense. The one where Stewart Maxwell made a mixtape of Charles Manson recordings and sent that mixtape to the widow of a murdered man for the ROFLs. The one where Nanette Milne took to licking babies' heads when canvassing for re-election, tonguing their hairless pates in a salival circumference that caused fear and agitation in the parents, leading to £388,999 in hush funds at the taxpayer's expense. The one where Euan Robinson introduced penalties for excessive coughing at classical concerts, causing seven people's tracheae to burst from their throats at the close of Dvořák's No.7 in D minor. The one where Maureen Watt claimed to have invented the parsnip, contra to all historical references and proof of pre-Watt parsnips, and brought buckets of parsnips to parliament to showcase her invention, forcing her colleagues to send her for a strenuous mental scrubbing at the taxpayer's expense.

Queue fatigue. Time to recall monies wiff-waffed up the wall across his career. £200,000 on buffing the tops of bollards after Morningside residents complained of unample buffage. £783,000 correcting misplaced apostrophes on signs after a vicious smear campaign from The Grammar Grannies. £102,182 for excess postage on a postcard to the Qatari embassy. £1,829 to sate the First Minister's craving for salted caramel and almond cups. £29,000 to use a png of Sean Connery on the SNP website. £3,000,000 on investing in a prototype for a hamster-powered car. £67,000 on a firework that exploded in the shape of Donald "who?" Dewar's face for the New Millennium. £28,829 to Michel Houellebecq to open the refurbished Cardonald Library. £2,000,000 in bribes to farmers to be nicer to ramblers. £3,000,000 to suppress revelations about Walter Scott's unpublished manuscript *Scotland the Cesspit: Why I Damn to Hell Scotland and All Jock Shits For Eternity*. £1,000,000 per annum in free dope for Edinburgh residents during the festival month. £500 on the manservant to drain Karen Whitefield's foot ulcers.

The queue depleted. The clerk was a svelte, cheekboned youth with Radiohead eyes. His clippered hair, longing to irrupt into spikes of post-rock revolt, spoke of a generation for whom rebellion was not an option. The consequences of lagering up and rampaging across Ireland on a tricycle for a year after college were too stark. That CV chasm sending employers into frenzies of fretting suspicion.

"Sir?"

What happened to a generation whose spirit was smothered from teenhood?

"Sir?"

When was the anger, the rage, the rowdiness of youth released?

"Excuse me, you're up."

When that generation exploded, what was next?

"Right." Derek snapped alive. "Hello there. I would like to check the amount in a savings account. Mine, the savings account of me."

"No problem, sir. Pop your card into the machine for me."

Then the tap.

"Scuseme?"

Tap two.

"Scuseme?"

Tap three.

"Scuseme?"

The unignorable tap of recognition.

"Yes?"

Derek turned to a Peter Falk lookalike holding a Lidl bag.

"I know you."

Yes, the first ever public recognition. At the worst possible time.

"Uh-huh?"

Karma's KO.

"You're a MP."

No name. No name. No name.

"Yes."

No name. No name. No name.

"Which one?"

"David Trance, nice to meet you," he said, turning back to Kid A.

"You have £3,028,819 in your savings account."

The room blinked.

"No, that's not it," Peter Falk said.

"I'd like to withdraw the lot," Derek said.

"Maximum withdrawal is £5,000," Kid A said.

"You're Derek something," Peter Falk said.

"Excuse me, I'm trying to transact here," Derek said.

"Maximum withdrawal is £5,000," Kid A said.

"Yes, I heard," Derek said.

"Derek . . . Hofflicks?" Peter Falk said.

"I think I know my own name," Derek said.

"Maximum withdrawal—"

"Yes, I heard the seventh time. Manager, please."

"Could've sworn—"

"Sir, I know my own name. Please stop disturbing me."

"One second, sir."

"All right. Touchy, are we? Problem with the public, eh?"

"No, a problem with one public."

"You MPs, two-faced scumheads. You can't even speak to the people politely."

"Sir, you're—"

"Don't sir me, scumhead."

"You're trying to tell me what my own name is when I'm talking to the cashier."

"He isn't here now, so tell me, Hofflicks. What's your problem with the proles?"

"I have no problem with the proles, as you call them. I have problems with berks carrying plastic bags trying to tell me my own fucking name."

"Oh! You hear that! You're a liar, Hofflicks."

"What?"

"A liar. You're all liars, cheats, and scumheads. You deserve to swing."

"I agree. We're a barrel of nauseating spunkbeads. But you're worse. The electorate. You're pathetic. You have one chance every five years to vote for politicians with integrity, those born to plaster the cracks in democracy, to throttle the silver-spoon Murdoch babies. But you don't. You sit there jeering on your couches at the corrupt scumheads on screen, fisting their nanas for power, and you toddle off to the ballet box and vote for the one who ran on a manifesto of setting cancer patients on fire for the LOLs. Because somehow the opposition are too idealistic. They are too ambitious. They are too weak. They are too soft on terrorists. They are too spendthrift. They are too unstable. A vote for the minority parties is a wasted vote, or whatever you tell yourself to mask your sorry self-interest. So, you toddle off and vote for the people who want to rape your mothers and drown your babies, and somehow feel democracy has spoken. You read your right-wing papers, convincing yourself you are smart enough to see through the shitewash and cuntruths harming your delicate eyes for years and years. You listen to bozos, hecklers, and morons, and admire their chutzpah, even when their policies have you licking their shitty brogues and sucking their scurfous cocks. You are too lazy to actually read the manifestos, to research the policies and issues on independent non-partisan fact-checking sites. Still, you have the time to phone into radio shows to vent your spleen on politicians and issues you know nothing about and parrot soundbites. You sit in the pub yelping opinions spoon-fed to you by snide aristos in country estates who would have no problem shooting you and your children in the head for an extra truckle of caviar. All that is required from you is to pay attention for one fucking minute, to challenge your worldview and think for once in your life with logic and reason, not fear and coercion. And you fucking blow it, every time, every time, every flippin' time. And you have the stones to call *me* a scumhead?"

"Mr. Trance, the manager will see you now. This way, please," Kid A said.

"Liar! Liar!! Liar!!!" Peter Falk continued to shout, having spooled the tirade ear-to-ear, bypassing the brain.

The manager was classic backroom—Uriah-like accommodatingness with a whiff of basement debasement. An ambiguous musk suggesting evenings spent cuddling his wife over *Planet Earth* repeats, other evenings spent cuddling the cum-soaked fishnets of the dominatrix thonging his anus. Classic backroom.

"Mr. Trance, I understand you requested a complete withdrawal of your savings account. As you may know, we have strict limits on how much our clients can withdraw and at one time, and as your account—"

"Fifty grand."

"Excuse me?"

"You can have fifty grand if you bypass the legal bollocks and have my money in an off-shore account in under twelve minutes."

Then, a thing unexpected. Wetness on the seat, there appeared. An assumption of spilled water sated for two seconds. Then the wetness trickled calfwards and shoewards. Unavoidable. He was the victim of unsolicited self-soiling on a red felt chair in a bank manager's office. The manager turned his everyman smile into a sinister simper, from family man to pathetic little worm in one facial realignment.

"Bribe?"

"Seems."

"Right."

"Glassawater?"

"I'll bring one for you."

Derek regarded the sopped slacks.

He thought he heard sirens.

He thought he heard bars rattling.

The manager returned with the water.

"In two minutes, I walk. Make up your mind," Derek said.

"Mr. Trance, you have to understand some things. Firstly, I'm a man respected in this community, trousers free from bungs for two decades." He stood and pulled the purple lining from his pockets. "Not a sou to be seen. Secondly, the processes involved in squirrelling millions are costly, complex and criminal. As you will have observed from the quality of my trousers, those are costs impossible."

"I'll cover those expenses."

"I accept your offer."

"I'll take £75,000 in cash myself, right now."

Now was the time to spill water over the sopped piss and make "oopsie" motions and to accept the tissues and mop the stain. Then was the time to demand a satchel and watch the manager, who had also wet himself, move towards the room with the bundles of bucks in vaults, so that happened. Then was the time to walk to the vaults and watch the manager handyshakedly wobblekey in the code and unlock a lorra wonga with passcodes and access codes and precodes and postcodes and plop the thousands on a table and stagger off in search of a satchel and finding no satchel wrap the thousands in a black bag and pocket the £50,000 plus an extra £25,000 for the commission to the crooks and shake Derek's hand from one pant-wetting makeshift criminal to another, so that happened. Then was the time to bumblestumble to the pavement with the loot in a bin liner and walk across the road towards a thing and walk across the road to another thing and zigzag across a zigzag and loop-de-loop round a loop-de-loop and bump into him and bump into her and bump into them and bump into a wall and a window and a wall and answer the phone who said

"Derek?"

Being Francis.

"What?"

"Is—"

"Callyouback."

Stood with arms wrapped round a lamppost, Derek shook himself into coherence, remembering important things like name, address, email, self. If strolling along pavements with bin liners stuffed with illicit monies was not the Full Quiver, then what in the blinking blink was the Full Quiver? The Full Quiver had arrived and was here, tickling his toes *c'mon, Dezza, you piddling amateur* and caressing his ailing feet *head up high, look to the sky* and kneading his fat ankles *spit in the Lord Jehu's eye* and lathering up his legs in soap and water *cometh the hour cometh the legend* and tonguing with love his testes *there's no honour among thieves* and lovingly fellating his bulbous tip *but there are* bags of thousands and oiling up his torso *and off-shore bank accounts on South Atlantic atolls* and working on the knots in his shoulders *and the sort of notoriety that makes you even richer* and frenchkissing his mouth red raw *and enshrines your place in the pantheon of history's inglorious basterds* and ruffling his lustrous hair *and ensures people will remember your name forever . . . people only remember the crooks, the plotters, the chancers, and the brave liars, so c'mon, Dezza, hail that cab, and embrace me, embrace The Full Quiver!!!* Goshdamn siree, these vultures have been after me since the '60s and never landed a single punch. Remember that old bespawler Harold Sparkley, trying to make out I'd fiddled expenses at the INT Convention! Pshaw!!! That heffalumping monstrosity needed mummykins to tie his shoelaces! Honestly, that man couldn't clean a sieve with the world's foremost sieve-cleaning implements!!! I remember once seeing him hunched over his Oxfords, shoelaces tweezered between thumb and index, wearing an expression of sad-eyed befuddlement, crying out inside "HWELP ME MUMMM-MEEEEE!!!" HA HA HA AND HO!!! And you'll remember, Dezzybabes, that incident in 1975 when some stinking Canuck accused me of pinching a trio of slacks. I remember the cop's white afro and pimply chins, stuttering out accusations as I stood there in my pomp, totally unwilling as always to tolerate smelly cumberworlds, shooting him my finest HOWTHEVERYDAREYOU expression and watching his wee legs retreatertotter to the squad car. I had simply left the store forgetting I had placed three expensive slacks in a carrier bag. We've all accidentally walked out of slack shops with three slacks, us people with schemes and scandals on our minds! Sometimes I feel I am the only rational man in this universe, orbiting our planet like a God who knows the shit from the shinolae. Next came the worst of all, that mimsy driggle-draggle Christine Cornell (anyone see her bestselling novels besting the bookshelves of millions of homes across the land?) who accused me of pinching a plot from her shitey story, her meagre slit of a storyette, and frankly, these useless sorts should be pitching me their stories and begging me to turn them into bestselling brilliance, paying me to take the plots and alchemise them into utterly compelling narratives! Dezza, let me warn you away from loose women. You *remember that raggabrash hoor Sharleen Porter, now a mere footnote in the epical sprawl of my unbettered existence? Remember that lawyer, persuading the jury to look upon my angel Sally, asking them why with a foxy filly like that, with a succulent twot like that waiting for me at home, why I would seek solace in the mound of a scragglecunted bint like Sharleen Porter? Ah, the look in Sally's eyes, that saintly halo, those plebs had never seen a piece of regal pussy like my Sally . . . no way they were sending me downriver! Libel, libel, DAMN LIBEL, Dezza! My whole life, the wolves of libel have been chewing at my face, those jealous snarling wolves, and never once have they managed to tear me from my towering heights! I know what you're thinking, D-Man, that I was eventually caught by those fustilarian losers, those frantic fopdoodles desperate for a scoop, when I attended Wandsworth Prison having been found guilty of perjury in 2004. Sally's charms having faded, she was unable to convince the jury, and frankly, Dezza, I was pleased for the chance to explore the prison system as a method-writer. Some have said that I orchestrated my imprisonment on purpose for literary triumph . . . the quality of the books that followed will attest to that! And speaking of the books, GOODHEAVENSWHATANEMBARRASSMENTOFRICHES! Some gnashgabs claim that I have absolutely no imagination whatsoever, that my novels are utterly predictable potboilers, that my titles are merely a succession of recognisable clichéd phrases like finders keepers red sky at night hindsight is a wonderful thing it never rains it pours and so on, tailor-made to appeal to an illiterate public who think that's clever because I was once a politician and I sue people regularly (can't start the morning without a lovely lawsuit!), and so I must be clever, and therefore my books must be smart, even if they merely recycle tired old genre tropes constructed for the biggest financial payoff, but they are all lying quisbies, D-to-the-H. You think forty-nine trillion copies sold makes me a bad writer? Let me tell you, writers of the world, you insult the very people you are desperate to have read your pathetic little novels. All the chesty literary novelists are the arrogant ones, thinking anyone cares about their descriptions of technological doodads or whatever the youths are writing these days. The people want two things, A PLOT and A CORPSE, and they want them together, like bacon on a Big Mac. Yeah, I'm the Mc-Donalds of fiction. I'm fucking popular and irresistible!!!* and sent Derek in a confident strut towards a taxi, hailed and entered, vroomed and vamoosed.

✿

Principles, in freefall. *What're principles? Those pliers for extracting Georgian babies?*

How can I be free in thought and deed without morals? How can I avoid falling in with the sick-hearted cliques, the sewers of human excreta with their sociopathic narcissism, and end up, as Bukowski said, one of "the dead fucking the dead"? *Derek, you don't have to take up coprophilia as a criminal. I've been in prisons and courtrooms and never once had the horn for a well-embalmed corpse.*

How can I ever speak with conviction on a single issue of ethics again? *Bad heavens, D-Man. You even* met *a politician? First question at politics school: can you look a starving orphan in the eye and promise him fresh food, a new mommy, and a castle all to himself, moments before he's hosed down and packed off to the paedophile ring? If yes, you're in.*

If I spend my career sweating lagoons to make the world a better place, will I have a restful conscience, a more serene outlook, and peace of mind as I pass? *Man, you're a morbid mopebucket. You can't make the world a better place. The world is populated by rabid wolves and flesh-chewing monsters called human beings. You see, you're working hard not to "help" people, but to appease that caustic critic calling you a loser. Take that critic and stamp him underfoot like a newborn chick.*

I cannot lose sight of the original aim. To become a bastard and use that skill for nice purposes. *Hoooo! That was painful. You think once a man has bloodied his hands, once a man has driven the bayonet into the guts of his rivals, that man returns with knightly notions of morality, that man can somehow harness the evil that has clotted inside him and make that evil a handpuppet of goodness? No offense, me Scotch mucker, that is the thought of a third-class lubberwort. Good and Evil can never be civil partners, on-off lovers, no-frills fuck-buddies, or it's-complicateds, Good and Evil are two starved tethered mongrels straining at the leash to snack on each other's necks and emerge victorious. There is no nuance in this world, Derrykins. There are unequivocal shitheads and people too hung up on morals, consciences, kind-nesses, and appeasing their own Catholic guilt to simply throw in the towel and come to the Inevitable Side, with the money, the postmorals, the massive country estates, the sex-on-tap, the freedom from a veneer of civilisation that acts as if we're not the same primitive who-fucks-wins beasts that we have been since our earliest ancestors began clubbing each other over a piece of bark.*

Is the world a mere slave to chaos, where nothing matters, morals a mere tether on our natures? *You said right, My Dizzle. Let's stop with this nicey-nicey. You know that the decisions we make are 99% for ourselves. The 1% of kindness we practice to appease that little voice that says "selfishness bad". What a load of arsecrack. If we wanted as humans to eliminate self-ishness, we would be living in socialist utopias where we are all financially equal. But no system in history has ever been able to contain the essential cuntishness of our natures. There is nothing we can do to hold back the tide of our repugnance as a species. Stop fighting it. There's no hope for our kind. Take the fucking cash. Grab that little slit of yours. Get the hell out of this country. Go smoke a stogie or two and live your life before your bleeding heart bleeds all over your one shot at real freedom.*

If I leave Camilla, leave my home, leave my country, will there be anything new to live for wherever I end up? *No idea. But you can't stay, not with that swag bag and the camera footage of you stealing funds from an account and the inevitable arrest of that gillie-wet-foot of a bank manager. It's not like Interpol will be chasing you round St. Kitts & Nevis for a mere three mil. It's a shame you're swapping that classy ass for a drugged-up punk, but whatever floats your sexual boat.*

Should I? *Think of the timeline. On retiring from parliament, Derek took up cheesetasting and collecting Qing dynasty teacups. He receded into nothing like a snowman in thaw and collapsed in his shed after choking on brie while strenuously supergluing the handle back on a Kangxi court original.*

Could I? *Or, on retiring from parliament, Derek moved to Tahiti, where he spent the remainder of his life lounging on a hammock while dictating his autobiography to a bronze-skinned secretary with silicone valleys, supping liquids banned in the West for their hallucinogenic properties. He lived a life of debauchery and untamable lust and croaked while embroiled in a 48-hr orgy on Taha'a beach.*

Will I? *Yes.*

I will.

Having achieved the Full Quiver, a.k.a. an expired conscience, a.k.a The Little Prick on Your Shoulder, Derek launched himself into a sequence of activities common to a man in transition from a lifetime of quiet desperation to a state of leashloosed catatonia. (The debate still raging in his mind. If I surrender to this criminal self, will I loathe myself more for having become the person I loathe the most? *No, because you never loathed these people, you loathed yourself for lacking the backbone to make the leap into their ranks.*) He phoned Francis: "Hello, Francis. I wanted to tell you thank you for your participation in our little scheme. You are a legend in corduroy and your cock is thick and meaty, like a beef olive." (If I am unable to escape the Catholic guilt, what's to stop the demons hounding me into suicide? *These concerns will pass once you relaunch yourself. Derek 2.0, ponytailed and goatee'd, will have no time for*

*religious hangups.*) He phoned Liam: "Did you realise that astronauts put marshmallows up their noses upon liftoff to protect their linings? Anyway, mate, I wanted to say, yeah. Good luck all round." (If all I am known for is stealing three million quids from another MSP, will all the bread-and-butter work I put in for decades be forgotten? *Dezz, no one remembers your constituency work. No one cares about your humdrum toil. All they will remember is your headlines. MSP Puts in Lifetime of Necessary But Dull Work vs. MSP Blows Top and Fucks off to the Bahamas with a Bag of Cash. They'll love you for it.*) He phoned Norman: "We're men we both. We take the outstretched hand of the wimp and slap that hand aside, for we are both men. Goodbye, Norman." (What if I'm wrong? *We're always wrong. The trick is to be so wrong, we're right.*)

Next, a taxi.

Destination, Millie.

Since the legsnapping episode, Derek had been ministering to her cultural-digestive needs, bringing new Rhineland Sharknado EPs, king prawn bhunas, herbal teas infused with lemon and ginger, and the novels of Barry Hannah to her bedside as she sat strumming a zither and freeforming rhymes inspired by the portraiture of E.B. Leighton. She resided in a second-floor Gorgie flat, a one-room affair sans the hindrance of doors, the result of a long reboxing process common to crumbling tenements—halving and thirding and fourthing flats into minier and minier spaces, sealing the occupants into overpriced shoeboxes with maisonette kitchens and fun-tiled WCs.

Free from the onus of clodpated seduction, Derek took the time to speak to her with her leg all plastered up on matters past: her upbringing in a semi-detached with unspecial parents—two cardboard timepunchers content with Radio 1, *Eastenders* omnibuses, and porcelain tea sets, forever uncurious about the important things like Guided by Voices, Hal Hartley, Aidan Higgins, and Jenny Saville—and schoolfriends/enemies content with the Top 40 Chart Show, *Friends,* and nightclub DJs, uncurious about the important things like Don Caballero, Takashi Miike, Gerd Brantenberg, and Marlene Dumas. To her utter bafflement, even though these things existed, most people she met had no awareness of them or, even worse, were shruggish when introduced to them, as though certain wellsprings of art were toxic. The belief prevailed that being from Coatbridge somehow excluded her and all residents from exploring the world of Pittsburgh jazz fusion or Norwegian feminist satire, and she had spent a decade exhausting a rebellion against this incorrect notion.

Failing to distinguish between Good and Bad art, Millie became more interested in scouring the nooks of the obscure, creating a self-contained world of bootlegged EPs from unsigned Der Haag krautrock bands and pirated mumblecore movies from tweenage directors. She failed to find a foothold on the alternative culture she had discovered, ploughing through the brilliant beating heart of life-enhancing magnificence to the fustiest fringes, taking transcendence in the amateur, the half-cocked, the downright fucking terrible. She progressed toward artistic creation trapped under an avalanche of self-published concrete prosetry chapbooks, lo-fi autoharp samples on 4-track, and handheld cam shorts, and adopted this no-brow aesthetic, where the act of creation and committing this act to tape was the only thing that mattered—concepts like competence or skill relegated below "passion".

This, plus the admission she'd spent the whole of 2015 on LSD listening to Pere Ubu, helped explain the choices she had made to Derek and shone a faint pocket torch on her moronic behaviour. There was no nuance to his persuance of Millie left. There were no intellectual contortions to be made, if there ever were. He was an ageing man who wanted a young girlfriend to help him feel virile and vital. That was the pathetic, clichéd, pedestrian truth of this pathetic, clichéd, pedestrian man. "I want to flee to Spain and fuck her in a pueblo," he said aloud. That was the truth. It was a relief to have such clarity. *That's the spirit, son! Poke that piece in a pueblo, then snort a line off her arse.*

Millie unlatched the chain upon Derek's arrival and called "coffee?" as she hobbled to the kitchen. Kook depleted, in a sweat-licked tee and short shorts, hair unwashed and phiz unwowed, Millie appeared normal and spoke in conventional sentences about beverages, meals, cleaning, and unemployment benefits.

"Ordered a new cane online," she said.

"You're hobbling faster, I see," Derek said.

"I'm planning to be limp-free in twelve days."

"Listen, I have something significant to say, and not one of those hackneyed ones like it's over, wedlock, or promotion to senior executive supervisor at Ryman's. I have one of those sui generis ones that require Latin to emphasise how fucking important they are, and in a minute or so our entire realities will flip."

"Christ on a bendybus, Derr. I haven't even put my sugars in," she said, spoonswirling her beverage. She limped towards the sofa as Derek stood with importance against the bookcase like a man unaufait with rooms.

"You know how your musical career is a non-starter?"

"Erm. The Future Oink EP was up for consideration at Riotous Pulpit records."

"That was in 2016."

"We supported the Francophobe death metal band The Frog Chorus at McGinty's."

"That was in 2015."

"I've recorded a suite of nose flute variations while in bed. It's a homage to Sparklehorse's *Good Morning Spider*, a downlow ode to convalescence in a spasticated world. Double F called it 'a vision of Sariel'."

"Millie, I have three million quid of someone else's cash in an offshore account and seventy-five grand in this bin liner."

"Right."

"You can't pretend to be unfazed."

"Umm—"

"For once, you can't toss your hair and make a barbed comment that condemns the facts to conversational oblivion and start wanging on about controlled delusion or harnessing your inner Dodi Fayed or whatever. I have three million pounds of another man's money in an off-shore account and I'm fleeing the country, today."

For once, Millie looked frightened.

"What have you done?"

"I've stumbled into millions, I want to flee the country, I want you to come."

"But—"

"All right, let's anticipate your responses, uno a uno," Derek said, coat removed sofa mounted. "The first is your loathing of consumer capitalism and the wrong that cash do. You want to strike a blasé attitude to these millions arriving in your living room as though you have arrived at a place beyond fiscal concerns, as though you have achieved a form of controlled delusion where you can rise above all such trivialities, Buddhalike, and continue living in one fifth of a flat and warbling in basements as your twenties career into a ravine. You have baked this loathing of consumer capitalism into your general quiche of disdain for popular culture, adopting a miscellany of punk attitudes to issues that you haven't thought on for more than the time it takes to flip to Side B of *Never Mind the Bollocks*. If you took a second to think on this issue, you would see that a life of insolvency is a life of beans on toast, sitting on purple sofas at the Job Centre, and visiting the community centre, not Max's Kansas. Now you have the chance to escape this life, you have to ask yourself, what do I actually think? You take this anti-corporate line because you have chosen to plough a furrow of obscurity as a means to avoid confronting the alienation you feel towards your family, namely your parents, with their complete disregard for Richard Hell & the Voidoids, and your sister, with her two babies and £150 ticket to see Maroon 5 at the Hydrodome, and your inability to understand their inability to understand the things that make you buzz. At the root of this lies the fear that you might have more in common with them than you think, that underneath your postpunk kook, there might be someone like your mother, someone who ultimately likes Midsomer Murders, the novels of David Nicholls, and a potter up the local trig points. Your unflinching rebellion is a mere teenage hangover that has spilled into the entirety of your twenties, and soon a realisation will be upon you that you have utterly squandered your youth on a form of wrong-headed anticapitalist antitonal antiaudience antimusic, written and recorded entirely for yourself as a means of escaping the inevitable business of becoming like your parents, and living a life of quiet unspectacularity like the rest of us."

*Steady on, old chap!*

Millie stood expressionless at the kitchen counter.

"Your next response is that I've fallen into corrupt clichés. I have become the sort of prick I railed against. You've never even voted. You've taken your leftwing leanings from agitprop punk acts and anticorporate rappers, you've absorbed views from ranters like The Ant and Double F. You have no coherent position on morality, you merely have some opaque, nonspecific hatred of men in suits who represent the evilness of the world, without ever asking yourself what the fuck. You wrongly assume that the sneering stance you take against the suits is a mere leftwing lie, and that your sneering stance is ultimately one of misanthropic abandon, and that you are ultimately as motivated by self-interest and fuckofferie as the next person who has hated reality since they were young. Like me, you leap at the chance to escape reality, and the only way to escape reality is with this bag of money."

Having absorbed these remarks, Millie strode toward Derek, propped his chin on her two right fingers, and spoke into his face.

"Derek, you absolute cretin. You snot-schnozzed mook. Have you considered even for a twitch I might've been sincere in my attempts to make you less of a superinflated cockwad? That I've been trying to mould you into a better person as a means of contributing something valuable to a society that I consider broken but not irreparable? If you'd taken a second to listen to my lyrics, you'd have heard not the screeching of a past-it post-drunk, but someone suggesting renewal and regrowth. You've spent this whole time trying to turn me into an accomplice in your surrender into some character void. You've spent this whole time viewing me as some Dark Angel leading you towards the car crash you eagerly crave. You rail against all my schemes because they run counter to the sort of perverted slattern you want to have an affair with. You can't be so dense as to have missed this? The only reason I won't touch your penis is because I want to have an affair with someone I respect, someone I have helped turn around. I'm not here as a projection for your third-rate Rankinesque fantasies of shabby infidelity in expensive suits. So suck on that exhaust pipe."

*I like this fiery filly, D-Man!*

"Millie, to quote Umberto Eco quoting Barbara Cartland, I love you madly."

"Now you've unscrewfixed everything. What am I supposed to say now? You want me to abandon a year's worth of work and accompany you on some safari of shitheadedness as you spunk millions up the wall on hookers and cream?"

"I never said I was planning to waste this money. My scheme was always to take this money and put this money to positive use," he said, backsliding like a Boris.

"Stop saying this money. You've trapped me. If I send you packing, you're going to spend thousands on egospaffs. If I choose to remain, your entire theft will benefit no one, especially you. You will merely daquiri yourself into a ditch."

"So?"

She stomped to the bedroom and produced a wheelie case.

"I have no choice except to come."

The afternoon unfurled into an incoherence of huff and chunter, first an étude on the muck of wonga from Millie, recalling the time her rich uncle descended upon her council house one Christmas with a £5 note inside a triple-glazed picture frame with the caption 'the profit says: I am your God', leaving nothing for his £30,000-in-debt sister save a box of white chocolate almonds. The time her mother, spotting a £20 note blowing in the breeze, performed a pas-de-douche into the road, bumperbutting Renaults, leaping into puddles and potholes, toppling backwards into a thicket with her knickerless cooch on show to the local kiddies at the park. The time she was several pence short at the cornershop and the server refused to surrender the sherbet, sparking a lifelong hatred of Pakistan-born shop servers and other brown people in the retail sector, culminating in a racist torrent outside a Kwik-Save one night when her credit card was refused in the procurement of hops. The time she met a lottery winner who spent some millions on a bronze statue of Axl Rose, went home and googled other lottery winner misfires, such as some millions on a matchstick recreation of the Battle of Algiers; some millions to Mikhail Gorbachev to act as Gorbachev-in-residence for a fortnight, allowing the public to pop in to quiz the former Soviet leader on matters Russki; some millions carpet-bombing the entire village of Langholm and paying the populace to play dead to prank Alastair Spigott; some millions setting up a TV channel that aired the same clip of Neil Kinnock falling backwards on Brighton beach on a loop for nine years; some millions erecting a French Normandy mansion on a Barlanark estate with machine-gun turrets trained on the flat of Roddie "The Cutter" Denton; some millions to buy up all the nitrous oxide on the planet to prevent people from chuckling like simpletons before routine root canal work; and some millions to relocate the iceberg that sank the Titanic to an enormous fridge in Clapham Common. "This to make clear that I hold cash in contempt for all the times cash has held me and my family in contempt," she said.

The solemn business of packing. In a flat that reflected the scattered anima of a self-described portamentolist, where trashed Corrs memorabilia sprawled across Kathleen Hanna lithographs, and signed Swans LPs arced across a wall splatterworshipped with printouts, postcards, and Polaroids of acts ranging from Suicide to the Sugababes (?), and hatescrawled messages from visitors like F-F and The Ant to sellouts like Liz Phair and The Clash, and boxed weirdness claimed the room from corner to corner, containing diverse contents such as school reports, unsold badges from the FHP reignition tour 2015, imported Argentine hash that was in fact corned beef, and self-made necklaces from mice bones and pebbles. In the bedroom, cupboards and drawers stuffed with antifashion statements in the form of nonclothes and repurposed fabrics, carpet samples, and miscellaneous roadkill pelts.

"We need to discuss case apportionment," Derek mumbled as Millie shoved an ear trumpet under vintage dungarees. The ear trumpet was replaced with a flipbook of indie singers' ears called Rock Lugs, and clothes were padded around other crucial relics such as the macramé remodelling of the dead drummer from Lush, the Fuck Buttons EP signed by Andrew Hung in invisible ink, the plectrum of Hüsker Dü bassist Greg Norton snatched from the stage in Zagreb 2010, and other rock artefacts that had wedged themselves into whatever nebulous nostalgic nodes existed in Millie's skull.

Then—*uh oh*—the coming of a cardiac booboo?—*not now, Dezza, at the apex*—"Should I pack the Grizzled Chunk bootleg?"—or a panic attack?—*flex those pecs at the apex*—or a mental unshelling that was long overdue?—"How about the Sin Trousers live DVD?"—*pure sex flexing those pecs at the apex*—as the tenuous link to the real, whatever the real is, snaps at last and—"Might leave the Spotty Bosphorus boxset here, except 'Ickebabies Lick the Lizardman' is on the second disc"— whatever, it was important to push through to the booking app and book the flight to Cádiz and pull Millie towards the door—"Come on, we need to catch the plane!"—*remember, the hurt will cease as the crimes increase*—and trundle towards a taxi and never mind that sudden shard of Camilla coming from nowhere to inform him that he was running out on two decades of marital niceness for reasons that still had not been pellucidated and that she would require some explanation for this desertion other than the urge to sleep with a talentless straggle-limbed urchin without a BA degree because to admit that was to reduce her to the kind of blind unobservant wife who never noticed her husband was an absolute bozo—*Sally, she supported me through thick (Norman Tebbitt) and thin (Sharleen Porter), what a slap-up skirt*—although he had the urge to run to her supportive face and outpour his roster of beefs knowing that she would put them into context and use logic and reasoning when he wanted to explore his incoherent and borderline borderline new mental terrain without interruption—"I'll arrange to have your stuff put into a storage locker, OK Mills?"—and not have to think with adultish reason on the sweet felicities, the banterous palavers, and the long loving hours with her valhallic lips, her valhallic neck, her valhallic breasts, her valhallic tum, her valhallic back, her valhallic bottom, her valhallic vagina, her valhallic thighs, her valhallic legs, her valhallic toes—"I suppose The Ant can borrow his uncle's van"—and night after night exploring her flavourful mind with its curlicues of nous on the Italian Renaissance, human sex trafficking in Honduras, the ethics of cloning in the age of automation, the live licks of Marika Hackman, the lessons on prickishness we can take from Erasmus, among more amongs—"Cádiz is a stopgap until I decide on a permanent relocation"—*our lovemaking after prison was immense, matey, immense, my staff performing three years' worth of top-class rodwork in two nights*—and he could even imagine her argument, that he would crumble under conditions of extreme intellectual laxness, that the lover role would soon become one between teacher and pupil, that however skilled she might be at fellatio or fucking or fisting there would come the inevitable postcoital cobblers, as she expounded her factless theories on Tupac and that one about Cobain writing the songs on *Live Through This* and that one about the fourth tower and that one about Hitler's daughter living in Bern with a retired plumber—*I electrify every orifice I embattle with my incorrigible überwang*—though Derek knew that without a warm female beside him he might explode from the inside out—"Cádiz is a random choice, I went there once and had an adequate time"—that unless he found himself within howling distance of a receptive woman his organs would curdle into viscous slurries and undesirable oozes and his skin would flare up into purulent pustules and weeping calluses and his entire being would burst into flames leaving his ashes to waft into the nostrils of a passing child—

"I want you to help me be able to love you," he said.

The taxi taxied toward the airport in a taxilike manner.

"You want me to help you to become the sort of person capable of offering me the sort of love that I'm not interested in receiving from you?" Millie asked.

"No, I want you to help me become the sort of person capable of loving you and offering the sincere sort of love you crave."

"You want me to help mould you into the sort of man you think I might love in order for you to become the sort of man who might love me?"

"No, I want you to help me become the sort of man who might love full-heartedly, and as a consequence, make you fall in love in with me, and as a result of your handiwork, be able to love you without faking."

"You want me to help make you fall in love with me sincerely by helping you become the sort of man who might fall in love with me, and as a consequence turn me into the sort of person who might fall in love with you?"

"No, I want you to fall in love with me as you help me become the sort of man who is capable of falling in love with you."

"You want me to help you become capable of falling in love with you by making me fall in love with you through helping you become the sort of person who might fall in love with me?"

"No, I want to fall in love with you properly, through receiving your schooling in sincere love, and once I have fallen in love with you, have you fall in love with me sincerely and naturally as a result of your schooling."

"You want me to school you to love properly, school you to love me, and accidentally school myself in loving you while schooling you to love me?"

"No, I want to understand the person you want me to become, which I believe is someone capable of loving full-heartedly, based on the conversations we've had over the last ten months, and once you have helped me to understand what sort of person you want me to become, and once you have helped me to become the sort of person I think you want to help me to become, you might somewhere in that process move from your role as a sort of morality teacher into someone in love with me, and fall in love with me, and at the same time, as a result of your schooling, help me to fall in love with you once I've become the sort of person that I think you want me to become who is capable of falling in love with you, and then fall full-heartedly and sincerely in love with you as a result of that process."

"You want me to help you to define the sort of person you think I want you to become, and having arrived at that definition, work to mould you into that person, and throughout that process magically contrive a mutual love between us in a non-contrived manner, even though the whole process would be by definition contrived?"

"No, I want to perhaps help you with your music career, to use some of the cash to put you in a recording studio, and as a result, make you more motivated into helping me to reform myself, and as your career progresses, as a consequence, move towards a place where love might bloom between us."

"You want to bribe me into falling in love with you under the guise of helping me with my recording career, and somewhere in that bribing process, convince me to help you to reform yourself, and somehow convert a bribe into a respect that somehow blossoms into sincere love, bribe notwithstanding?"

"No, I want to be a kind-walleted man as a means of showing kind-heartedness as part of the ongoing self-reforming process, and have you appreciate that kind-walletedness, and see that I have reformed somewhat and as you record songs think on what a new person I have become, and fall in love with me."

"You want me to mistake a finanical gesture for a sincere emotional expression, and capitalise on your financial gesture for my own personal gain and as I am capitalising on this, convince myself somehow that it came from a sincere place, rather than a cynical one, and convince myself that I am falling in love with you, overlooking the obvious cynicism of the gesture, tricking myself into having real you-feelings?"

"No, I want to become the better person I think you want me to become merely through spending time with you, and over the time spent, spark up a mutual love between us that would blossom into a proper unforced love."

"So, simply put, you want us to fall in love with each other in Cádiz?"

"Yes, as a consequence of your handiwork on me."

"So the onus is on me. I have to make you love me, and make me love you. Not an equal division of labour, is it?"

"No."

"Instead, how about you work on you without my input, and once you've finished working on you, let's see who loves who, and take it from there?"

"That's a compromise."

✿

Airport, sitting. Trudging through a back catalogue of memories, noting a common theme. Each pleasurable moment involving another person's humiliation, failure, or embarrassment, like the time his little sister, having mastered the semi-waddle, learned that not all surfaces were flat, and semiwaddled into a sump in the grass, setting her walking attempts back several months, to much hilarity. The time a constituent on the doorstep, having spent ten minutes ranting on the preponderance of wogs in the healthcare service, had a cardiac oopsie and required a life-zapping from an Indian paramedic, to much hilarity. The time the fisheries minister slipped on a skate outside Cromarty harbour, snapping his pelvis in two, to much hilarity. The time his nemesis in primary school was unable to control his nonallergic rhinitis and sneezed over the female of his dreams, setting his sex life back two decades, to much hilarity. The time a speeding fool on the motorway was undertaken by a lorry, causing him to 360° and explode in a ball of flames, to much hilarity, and so on.

Airport, seething. The place between places, the interplace, the nonplace, the placeless, faceless, nameless unplace. Nothing to declare, nothing to describe. Harried ciphers wheeling cases toward queues askew, necks asquint at blinking FIDS. The sheer philcollinsesque tediousness of stepping into an airport—the unbearable, excruciating process of trundling, shoving, checking, lugging, rechecking, panicking, riffling, queuing, jostling, loitering, inching, re-re-checking, fretting, trundling, queuing, and shuffling. The sheer, unadulterated fucking horror of the entire airport experience.

Airport, hatesnorting. The inbetweenyness of waiting. The place-to-placeyness of sitting. The liminal brain-freeze. No thoughts, no words. The mind numbed into a transitive state from here to there, recalibrating between hither and thither, reducing every traveller to a time-checking, nerve-ridden waiting person, waiting to queue, queuing to wait. The mickhucknallesque tedium of the whole thing.

The sheer fuckknuckled spew of budget airlines, each second constructed to make your flying experience as woeful as possible, from the sweltering heat inside, the refusal to activate aircon until all the sheep are herded, the frantic shoving of oversize cases into miniscule lockers, the squeeze-pasting, the excuse-meing, the seat-boxing, and having one's knees in one's neck for two hellish hours. The annoucements, false-takeoffs, sandwiches, perfumes, coffees, and vodkas trollied into your mowing mouth. The sheer tuckercarsonesque cunterie of the whole miserable fucking experience.

Proof positive that whatever magic humans create, other humans will endeavour to throttle the love from it.

Not a word was spoken between Millie and Derek from Edinburgh to Heathrow or from Heathrow to Jerez de la Frontera.

The word "quaquaversal" was not said.

(Though the word "hellcake" was thought).

The word "butcherbird" was not said.

(Though the word "buggeration" was thought).

The word "diminuendo" was not said.

(Though the word "shitemare" was thought).

The word "apodeictic" was not said.

(Though the word "doombunker" was thought).

The word "seamanship" was not said.

(Though the word "mistakeknife" was thought).

The word "vedette" was not said.

(Though the word "fleegallop" was thought).

The word "assumingness" was not said.

(Though the word "fearflexfear" was thought).

The word "beachcomber" was not said.

(Though the word "ooohhmamma" was thought).

The word "feabane" was not said.

(Though the word "horrorcrumbs" was thought).

The word "habanera" was not said.

(Though the word "botherbooger" was thought).

The word "ianfu" was not said.

(Though the word "cackattack" was thought).

The word "jaboticaba" was not said.

(Though the word "fearplusfearequalsfear" was thought).

The word "keelhaul" was not said.

(Though the word "copswarm" was thought).

The word "zymolytic" was not said.

(Though the word "copathetic" was thought).

The word "mnemotechnical" was not said.

(Though the word "bumsponge" was thought).

The word "oogenesis" was not said.

(Though the word "outchiselled" was thought).

The word "prairial" was not said.

(Though the word "eraseourheads" was thought).

The word "cabassous" was not said.

(Though the word "prisoncoming" was thought).

The word "ghrelin" was not said.

(Though the word "knobgoblin" was thought).

The word "sforzando" was not said.

(Though the word "wtf'edup" was thought).

The word "uveous" was not said.

(Though the word "theendoffuckingeverythinng" was thought).

Between passport control and the baggage carousel the warm fuzz of Scotlandlessness sneaked up on the two, a balmic feel of freedom from the oppression of humid glens, redbrick tenements, and neolithic boulders. A moment of elation at the lack of Bank of Scotland billboards, pubs called The Drookit Tipple, windows still hopeful with 'Yes' posters, entire cities built on hillocks, and one A-road to the north. Instead, the presence of Moorish fortresses, 13thC Baroque cathedrals, rococo flamenco houses, and historical town halls with striking stone arches. The sweltering, welcoming hug of Spanishness enveloping them in its clammy arms.

Next, the train to Cádiz.

"I feel like the box I was locked in that was hurled into the Bering Strait and weighed down with anvils has opened and I've flippered free to a mediterranean paradise," Derek said.

"I feel like I shouldn't have worn this duffel coat," Millie said.

"I'm supposed to have a coherent plan for changing something, aren't I?"

"No rush."

Cádiz, arrival. The absence of sunglasses was problematic in a place of oppressive continental chic and heaven-kissed renaissance splendour that made one feel stupid for choosing to live in a nation of Wetherspoons, trout fishing as a pastime, and tripe as a main course. In a taxi to the haste-booked hotel in the wherever district, Derek admired the driver's thick moustache and suncooked cheeks, basking in the soothing coastal whistle and the freedom from talk radio, while Millie pressed her untravelled face to the window and melted in awe at the magical nature of other, far superior countries like this one. Street after street of stunning architecture with no trash-packed alleyways, pothole-pocked cul-de-sacs, or pubs held together with sticking plaster and rubber bands.

"I've never felt more ashamed to be British," Derek said.

"¡Salga del taxi!" the cabbie shouted, having arrived two minutes ago.

"Pardon. I was lost in the hoochiemama of your homeland," he said.

The driver accepted cards.

"Let's have a stroll before hotelling," Millie said.

"All right."

"So, were you serious about paying for a recording studio?"

"Absolutely, provided a little thought is spent on production values."

"I've taken on board your scathing criticisms. I'd like to record a Greatest Hits album of sorts. Our most listenable songs on one disc."

"Double-F will call you a sellout."

"Double-F considers a second chord a sellout."

"He knows what a chord is?"

"I know the tracks."

"Tell me."

"Track one, Whale Bath. The one about strangling harpoonists in their tubs."

"Strong opener."

"Track two, Her Moonbeam Uncle. The one about the hippie molester who self-castrates on Good Morning Britain."

"Ouch."

"Track three, Lipstick Junta. The one about a militant feminist faction who crucifies Rimmel VP Sara Wolverson.

"Track four, Oxford Sound Dictionary. The instrumental electro-spazz with MC Hiccup on scratches and loops.

"Track five, Dropkick the Doggie. The one mocking man's fetishisation of mutts.

"Track six, Deliveroo Boogaloo. The one where a takeout courier snaps and replaces the pizzas with screams.

"Track seven, Babe's Got No Booty. The one where a spineless man goes on a Tinder date with an assless chick and ends up marrying her not to hurt her feelings.

"Track eight, I am the Lord Jesus. Beirut Slump cover.

"Track nine, Rinse, Repeat. The one with a 20-minute riff that ends with the words 'no, not me'.

"Track ten, Fooderspiel. That one that someone once said had a nice melodic bridge."

"Here's the killer question, though," Derek said, admiring a sandstone arch. "What does the name Forerunner Hammer Precision mean?"

"F-F told me it was term in ye olde metalsmithing when metal and implement became one, the sweet alchemical spot where man brought the solid to heel and smithed evil into being for umpteen centuries."

"Oh."

"Or he was stoned off his chonk and slung some words together."

As the evening oncame, bringing the sort of serene pre-dusk alien to the trembling, ominous Old Countrie—one of pale lamplight on cobbled streets, breathtaking palazzos and their luminous spires, and the background whooshing of the Bay of Cádiz—Derek found himself amused for the first time at his own godawful wonkiness, his lopsided cockeyedness, his flailing octopussness. Rendered small and absurd in these austere medieval streets, rendered a total aberration of a man in the pale moonlight of a cool Spanish evening, he burst into titters and readied his cheeks to accommodate a smile of such uncharacteristic wideness, Millie took a step back. "Don't turn all Shining on me," she said through nervy laughs.

"I feel—*heh*—I feel like—*heh*—I'm not sure—*heh*—I like whatever this—*heh*—undefinable feeling—*heh*—is," he said.

"I'm not sure we're equipped to look at a place this fucking gorgeous. I think my skull might reject my eyeballs."

"At some point this evening, some chink of the real will burst this luftballoon of elation and lower us back into the swamp of our predicament. But for the moment, I have never known temporary bliss like this."

"I want to fuck Spain into my cortex."

"Me too."

The amble, a ten-minute awestruck skitter along a street from their hotel, came to an end when Millie's limp, brought on by the case she had been wheeling behind her, caused an ouch. The luftballoon had not been burst, though the limp was a reminder of that past life, that life from six hours ago, of pocket theft and wet trousers, and reduced Derek's grin from Nicholson to Keaton. Their hotel, several sprints from the marina, was a series of motellish apartments overlooking a large pool, offsetting the historical pulchritude with Good Ol' man-made abomination, levelling out their unworthiness as pale, unsunned Scots to exist in this realm, and thus calming their tourist panic.

Up steps, toward the rooms, Derek was a maraca, shaking his bahookie and moving as if his insides were percussive beans, groovewalking along the balconies and launching his manbag on the bed with a flourish. "Who's for a swim?" Millie shouted from next door. She appeared in a black bathing suit with an inverted Nike tick at the midriff. "I haven't brought trunks," Derek said. "So? Swim in your boxers?" And so, like loveable kooks in a romcom, tittering as two in their swimming choices, Derek's Great British Belly in evidence, Millie's skeleton peeping thru her jaundiced skin, the travellers launched themselves into the cooling waters, the pool unbothered by others, and swam and splashed and loafed and floated and conducted themselves with childish abandon in the familiar pool tradition of behaving as though lukewarm water was a novelty on a par with mendelevium.

"I want to write a book," Derek said at the shallow end.

"A novel?"

"A memoir-of-sorts. It's called The Full Quiver. It's about being cuntish to be kind."

"You haven't been kind yet," Millie reminded.

"No. But I can write on the theory and provide the backstory, and in writing I might come to some conclusions about whatever it is I think I'm doing."

"Decca, you can't write a memoir without having lived through the moir of me. If you want to emulate Quiver, start work on a vomitous novel about a liar with the kindness of a pathogenic Pol Pot."

*Hmm. I'm starting to dislike this shrill food-vacuum. Ditch her, Dezza. Hook up with a big-titted señorita and score some poppers.*

The descent into tittering abandon continued post-pool when Derek sourced three bottles of red from the hotel bar and switched on the TV in his room. A religious programme called *Confesiones Verdaderas* was on featuring a priest from Tarragona talking to a sinner from Antequera in a sort of live confession performed before a studio audience. Lacking volume, Millie and Derek improvised the dialogue.

"Dear father, I have sinned," Derek began. "I lopped the heads off two swans and turned them into finger puppets. I was desperate, father. I drank up the money for the kids' party. I was supposed to be putting on a Punchita and Judy show. You know, a sapphic reimagining of the classic domestic abuse puppet staple."

"You have committed a grave offence, my son," Millie priested. "You must repent by devoting your entire life to the preservation of Spanish swans and swanitas, whether that means all-night vigils by ponds to prevent overhead massacres of swan chicks by vengeful dive-bombing pigeons, or helping out swans choking on the algae in some of our muckier parks. Now say 800 Hail Marys."

"Thank you, father! I will never again tipple a litre of sangria and view a swan's neck as a means of solving my temporary parenting setback."

The vino tinto flowed.

"Dear father, I have sinned," Millie said. "I was masturbating over a picture of Scatman Crothers when my wife walked in. I lied to her and pretended I was researching Scatman Crothers when I found myself suddenly aroused. For the rest of the week, my wife sprung pictures of Scatman Crothers on me at unexpected moments to check. Father, I found myself fully erect in the supermarket! Father, I found myself fully erect on the highway to Seville! Father, I found myself fully erect outside my daughter's school! Everywhere I went with my wife, there was Scatman Crothers! Scat-man! Na-na-na-na-na-na-na-na SCATMAN!"

"My son, there is no saving you. You are an unfixable deviant. You court the attentions of long-dead black actors. You are a homonecronegrophiliac, my son. The only solution for you is a quiet suicide in a landfill."

"Waaah!"

Second bottle, uncorked.

"Dear father, I have sinned," Derek said. "I had the chance to slug Stephen Fry, and I froze. I could have taken on that attention-seeking populist with his Harry Potter-enabling ways and teeny fondness for atheist snark. He is a heathen, Father, and I missed the one chance I had to put him in his place with his patronising reader-friendly books on Greek myths and the English language, his interminable volumes of soporific memoirs on when he was once funny in the 1980s. I should have socked him one!"

"My son, you are correct. You had the chance to floor an English mediocrity and you showed yourself weak and unable. You must devote the rest of your life to bileblasting Stephen Fry, making your tweets as specific as possible, whether criticising his performance in the stale noughties ITV drama *Fortysomething* or making personal remarks on the squandering of his talent as a polymath. He could have been one of the finest novelists or scientists of his time, instead he spread himself across TV, literature, Radio 4 and public whining. Your work will be complete when Fry quits Twitter in a strop again."

And with the inevitability of a wasp drowning in a puddle of coke, Derek ocularly caressed the thin tanless legs, the flat fatless torso, the slight titless tits, and the small poutless lips of Millie, and she responded with a look of plonked looseness, having for over an hour touched his arm, flicked his cheek, and scooched in close during the televisual merriment. Her face moved towards him and her lips united with his lips and her tongue wrenched them apart and made random tonguing motions across his teeth and inner mouth and then a new problem presented itself.

*Decca, what's with the limp rod?*

It might have been the wine. It might have been the sheer mental and physical exhaustion and trauma of the last twenty-four hours.

*But, like, where's the old chap, old chap?*

"Millie," Derek said, unliplocking. "I want to wait."

"What?"

*Yes, whaa-aa-aa-at?*

"I want to become a better person before we—"

"Derek, I'm half-cut and horny, I actually feel like fucking you for the first time. And you're about to make a stand on principle."

*Well, at least one thing's making a stand tonight.*

"I want to too. But if it happens now, there's no incentive. The incentive is the prospect of fucking you. If that's lost, what's the incentive?"

*Good grief.*

"That's a valid point. You're right."

"You should head to bed."

"Gosh, Decca. I never thought you'd be capable. I thought you'd crumble into my arms like a wet cake."

She cheekpecked him bon nuit.

And left.

*Let's discuss what happened here.*

He flopped on the bed.

*Flop is the operative word. You're telling me that having lusted after this lanky lassie for years, you're now unwilling to stick it in?*

"The trouble is," he told Quiver, "that at that exact moment she leaned in to kiss me, when the moment I had been waiting for for a humiliatingly long period of time finally happened, I realised I wasn't even remotely attracted to her. That I had been attracted to the prospect of wanting her, and the lust for the lust for her was what was spurring me on. If I have sex with her, it's game over. There's no way, realistically, we can ever have sex at all, at any point, ever."

*But now she wants to.*

"Yes."

*Well done, D-Man. Now pass out from exhaustion.*

"All right."

☼

Half-asleep in a curl all night, opening and closing parentheses in a restless nonrest, the morning interrupted these motions with screaming sunshine. "Despierto, hombre británico!" the sun instructed. "El horror espera!"

The first horror, the hangover. The sensation: a startled bull taking on the taunts of a smug toreador with legs athunder.

The second horror, the stink of clothes unwashed. The absence of a clean shirt and pants, the need to shop in sweat-soaked priors that morning.

The third horror, the facts. The facts: known.

He took to the streets of Cádiz to locate new pants. Rather than write a memoir, he considered an explicatory article mailed anonymously to all British broadsheets, explaining the rationale behind the theft, if he could think of one. If he could set off a minor bomb in the media and establish himself as a folk hero, public response to his crime might merit more respect and admiration and make a return to rational life a shimmering blink of maybe. He bagged himself deodorant, a change of clothes, and a coffee at an internet caff. The last thing he'd written was an opprobrious slapdown of Peter Mandelson in 2006, accusing him of strangling the life from socialism with Thatcher-lite policies that shat on the grave of Aneurin Bevan or somesuch whipped-up furiousness conceived for a hundred quid in the *Banff Enquirer*.

In a way, the prospect of rendering his scheme in print was more terrifying than leaving it unsaid and unexplained. The prospect that the words, once written down, would take the form of utter gibberish and that reading the words back would cause him so much shame at the ridiculous 'n pointless 'n sublimely meaningless thing that he had done, he would be unable to continue living non-ironically, and settle into life as a humorous article.

*That's where fiction steps on stage, Dezz. You see, the truth is far sexier with a little fictive tickling. Never mind the unvarnished truth. No one ever came hard and cream-pied on the willing face of facts. Let's start at birth. The facts say that my father was a clapped-out old crim when I was born, having lived life as a serial bedswerver, trickster extraordinaire, and convicted felon. Those facts are true. The old bastard was a legend. But that butters no parsnips in the press. So let us sprinkle a little fictive pixie dust on those unflattering realities. My father was in fact a war hero, having earned six gold stars in slaying the boche, colonelled hard in West Africa (no one can be bothered to check that sort of thing) and lived life as a popular, well-sexed, world-class military man. Best of British what-ho. You see, that's better than saying me ol' pop sold chewing gum and was in the slammer, poor bugger. Now, on to education. I attended the mediocre Wader School in Somerset, where I was bullied for having a famous mother (ah, where there's fame, there's the hounds of hate!), and ended up as PE teacher. These are the facts. How about instead, I attended Wader College in Berkshire (who's checking that?) where I mingled with upcoming talents like Lords Duce and Cunnington and lapped more teenage pudenda that most thirteen-year-olds could ever dream of? Better. And on to higher education. Hoo-man, are there some se-*

*rious hall-of-famers in here! You heard the allegations that I faked academic results in my Brassneck College, Oxford application? That I cited a Mexican bodybuilding club as evidence of my academic prowowness? That was a hoot, 'coz those feeble gobermouches let me in! You know, Dezzy D, you should never underestimate the desperation people have to avoid unpleasant situations. The more unpleasant, the more turned backs. Anyway, what's better, Quiver achieved a Triple First at Oxford and Cambridge simultaneously while yodelling on a unicycle in lederhosen, or Quiver scraped a few A-levels while thinking up fortune-hunting schemes on the racetrack? Around this time, Ringo Starr called me "the kind of sod who would bottle your spunk and flog it". Let me tell you, Ringo was right on cue for once. That's the essence of Quiverism. I've been selling bottled spunk since the 1960s, and the people can't get enough. The populace, that tractile globesworth of shrieking wandoughts and limpcocked stampcrabs, pour my hot bottled spunk down their throats, and beg and beg for more. You only have to look at my latest sold-out bestseller. You only have to look at the American President, at the career of Mike Ashley, at the songs of Ed Sheeran. The public are easily manipulable sheeple and if you fail to capitalise on that solid fact, you are worse than the very sheeple being manipulated. So let the words come, Double-D, and if you feel the fictive fingers caressing your beefy balls, let the joyous jism of creation come all over you in loving, extravagant spurts.*

But it was futile.

There were no words.

Once written down the whole scheme crumbled.

First, he had to outline the rationale behind the whole thing in clear uncluttered prose. Spoken to three clueless ninnies in his study over a bottle of expired Pepsi, the scheme was wild. Set in stark Helvetica in a national broadsheet with a circulation of over a million readers and millions more online, the notion that pickpocketing MSPs in the Scottish Parliament as a kind of ideological putsch might deliver a wakeup slap to the complacent political classes would attract the violent censure that such a brainless, ill-thought, 3AM backroom idea deserved, and that the phrase laughingstock would forever accompany his image in all future illustrated dictionaries. The article would see him pilloried forever as a senile, addlepated man who'd long lost his dowels and come loose from the shelf, who'd organised a rebellion so unconvincing, so uninspired, so nonsensical, that no one would see his face without breaking into turbulent chuckles of derision followed by consoling hugs and tears and a referral to the local mental ward. Not a single thing was to be written down.

*Uuhmm, you haven't heard me. Not a single thing <u>that is true</u> is to be written down. You robbed those stiffs at jockgov to show the world that security is under threat in this country, that we need to ramp up measures to keep these terror-buggers away, look how simple it was to grease these slicks, etc!!*

It was time to consider what three million in quids might achieve to shake the political situation and help the world achieve turd immunity, while keeping him at the centre of the shakeup to follow.

*Nothing. Three mil is pocket money to rampaging beasts like me.*

Invest in antiviolence or antifraud groups?

*Sure! If you want your money to vanish into a blackhole of useless campaigns encouraging hopeless yoofs to bin the knives and enrol in hospitality courses at the local poly, or have the funds swallowed up on ad campaigns telling thickos not to open spam emails from Ugandan heiresses. Next!!!*

Found a new party?

*Sure! If you are able to rustle up some fucks, which you ain't, coz you've long lapsed into a loathing of your constituents, and you're kidding yourself if you think you care anymore about their grotty woes. Next!!!*

Invest the cash in stocks and consider something at a later date when the surplus has increased?

*Now you're talkin'! I would delete the part 'consider something at a later date' and replace it with 'erect a shrine to my pinkies'.*

"Uuuuugghhhh," Derek thought and said and felt.

He sent to The Guardian:

*My name is Derek Haffman. I robbed them Scots Em-Pees. I blame Jethro Quiver.*

Back at the hotel:

"Mills, help me. I'm coming to the conclusion that three million pounds is not enough to make a dent in the world. That the only sums that matter are billions and that if a humble millionaire can make zero difference, what hope is there for my Walter Matthau mug?"

"My head's Babylon Zoo," she said.

"Mine too."

"Let's Cádiz for a while."

This involved sweating out the morning at the Mercado Central where Chilean seafood soup was served, looking at bushes topiarised like ribbed condoms at the Park Genoves, and moaning up a watchtower to regard the embarrassing splendour of the place while attempting not to throw up Chilean seafood soup. Then La Caleta Beach for hours of loafing and cocktails on a towel checking out the reviews of Jethro Quiver novels on Goodreads.

"So many poor readers," Derek said, "bored in hotel rooms, departure lounges, on trains and buses, tormenting themselves with passages of buttclenching tedium, willing themselves through so-called pageturning plots, tricked into the belief that Quiver is some éminence grise in the thriller world. Such a rotten trick perpetrated upon the reading public, allowing an author who sold shitloads in the seventies and eighties a free pass to publish whatever unbearable pap he likes because of name recognition. A world of lost souls lapping up Quiver's hot pish at £20.99 per lap and forcing themselves to like it. And like a dog returning to its own vomit, the fans come back for more. Oh, poor readers."

*Between 250–330 million copies sold worldwide, Decca.*

Yep.

*Soz.*

Then time, distance, sangrias, oleaginous waiters, slim-hipped waitresses, and tours of historical interest made the whole past thing unreal. Skipping across the paradisiacal sands, the sun caressing their revolting British bodies, the sand settling in for a long stay between their toes, the whole preceding shenanigan was hidden somewhere in the sluice of Millie's electric blue thong. Their woes lost in that three-day period of self-replacement, where the original you from Alba is replaced with a worldly, über-tanned, globe-straddling citizen of everywhere, where you are Barack Ofuckingbama to whoever crosses your path, you are Nelson Manfuckingdela to the chic Teutons at the bar, you are David Fuckingbowie to the hotties on their towels, you are Mads Mikkelfuckingson to the losers in pink shirts belting out Fernando at the karaoke—no longer an irrelevant pimple on the foul undercarriage of your sickly leper of a homeland, no longer an unmemorable sack of whoever steaming up the windows on a bus going nowhere. Three days later, the slithering eels of your three-day-old self return to your fore and reignite the flames of reality, putting the norms of stressworkfinancialobligationschildren back to your front, reducing the rest of the holiday to an exercise in whingeing, drinking, and sourpussed clockwatching as the heat remains at 40fucking°s.

Hotel, semi-bevvied. "Aren't navels weird?" Derek pimstificated, introducing Millie to the realm of his cavernous, fluff-packed innie. "I think we should've evolved navels as mini-mouths, so food goes straight into the stomach for digestion."

"Decca, you want restaurants full of people with their fat bellies on the table, forking food into wee slurping, gobbling navels?" Millie asked.

"We could reconfigure our whole eating regime. Meals would be served under the table through little tubes, allowing our navels to eat as we stood and had adult conversations. We could increase the workload for dwarves, have them scuttle under tables to change the food valves from mains to deserts and so on."

"So our sense of taste would be lost to a freakish little mouth sucking mush through tubes in order to . . . what? Prevent us from choking?"

"Taste would occur at the navel."

"I see. As would egestion? Navels spurting vomit with the force of a fire hose into the faces of these dwarves you're forcing to work under the tables. What a pretty alternate world you create, Decca."

"The dwarves would be well-paid, of course."

Millie poked a peanut into her navel and imagined the gobbling monster of Derek's design.

"Eugh. Nah, I reckon the navel should've come with a little valve to release gas. Stop us from farting and burping and bloating up like heifers."

"That's a better idea."

Tap-tap-tap, said the door.

"Shite, are we talking too loud?" Derek asked, moving to address the triple-tap. He heaved himself up from the bed in his red shorts and striped tee, wobblewaddling to the door with the assistance of a local wall. Too pissed to recall the peril, he opened the door like a man unaware that Interpol might want to arrest him for crimes against David Trance's bank balance, and stood before him were two—

People.

The first of the two (people) was a woman.

The first of the two people (who was a woman) was someone he had seen before.

The first of the two people who was a woman (who he had seen before) he had seen before because.

The first of the two people who was a woman who he had seen before (who he had seen before because) because she was Camilla.

The next (or second) of the two (people) was a man.

The next or second of the two people (who was a man) was someone he had never seen before.

The next or second of the two people who was a man (who was
someone he had never seen before) had been mentally berating him.

The next or second of the . . .

*Oh, put a fucking sock in it. It's me, you tiresome saddle-goose.*

*HEEEEERRREEEE'S JEEEETHRO!!!*

"Hello, Derek," said The Right Honourable The Lord Baron
Jethro Quiver of Somewhere-in-Hereford. "We're not disturbing you,
I hope?"

If ever we were called upon to explain our cravings for hugs, if
ever we were made to account for our need for instant fabric-on-fabric
clasps of human warmth in some future Court of Appropriateness,
we might struggle to articulate that particular need to the M'Luds of
bodily sovereignty. So when Derek saw his wife Camilla in the door,
in her vintage womanliness, in her Givenchy summer skirt and blouse,
and rushed towards her with the zeal of a parched calf, wrapping his
oldish man's arms around her oldish woman's shoulders, he would have
to plead the fifth.

In the manner of criminals relieved at having the burden of fear,
paranoia, and self-loathing of outlaw life lifted, in that moment of
inappropriate hug-seeking neediness, he saw Camilla as the benign
rozzer there to rescue him from the sheer pigsear he had made of the
last 48 hours. Her arms remained in her coat pockets. She would not
permit Derek to babble apologies into her ears in the hope of instant
uxorial salvation at that moment. She waited for the abashed retreat
that came ten seconds later, where the scene resumed as though this
hug-seeking spasm never happened. Quiver stood in a cool blue shirt,
top button unbuttoned, his untrimmed brows adding to the imperious
quiverness of his Quiver face, the carrefours of wrinkles carrefouring,
carrefiving, carresixing across the octogenarian skin. This was the face

of the unimpressed pseudo-upper-class, looking upon lowly cretins like Derek with wry amusement.

*It's not so much wry amusement, it's more the face I make when I'm struggling not to explode into convulsive guffaws.*

The mental Quiver and the literal Quiver.

A quiver of Quivers.

*Indeed. I am my own collective noun.*

"Are we allowed in?" Camilla asked.

"Yes, of course, of course," Derek said. In his berk-red summer shirt with his berk-aged mistress stood by the kettle like a scarecrow long pecked thin by jackdaws, nothing he said could even peep the credible.

Taking their place at the small breakfast table, leaving Millie and Derek to the bed, the guests helped themselves to water.

"The most startling sequence of events has taken place in the last five hours," Quiver began. His poshness permeated the room, reducing all listeners to instant indentureship, awaiting a boot to lick. "I received a correspondence from one of my staff that a Scottish minister had cited me following a recent embezzlement scandal. I was surprised to hear a minister mention me unexplained in this manner, so I had my snoopers investigate further. They quickly tracked you down to Cádiz."

"And when I heard," Camilla started, "about the scandal, I logged into your emails to find your whereabouts, seeing as my texts remained unanswered. At Heathrow, I noticed Lord Quiver in the same boarding suite and struck up a convo. We soon realised our mutual purpose and chose to travel *à deux*."

"Them's the preliminaries," Quiver said.

"Right," Derek said.

"We fucked, Dezza," Quiver said.

*O sweetness!*

"Excuse me?"

"I fucked your wife in the airport toilets."

*O heavenly Quiver!*

"Ah."

"I wanted to make that clear from the get-go. Best to rip the plaster off. Now, to business. As you might have heard, some people consider me a litigious man. You might have heard that I like to take people to court for the slightest infraction upon my reputation. For example, I am embarked on a lawsuit for £5,000,000 in unpaid royalties owed to me from my publisher. You might argue that the last thing I need is another five million, whereas the publisher could use every farthing of that in the fraught book climate. You might argue that. But that is not the point, Derek. I simply want what is mine. I might choose to return that cash to the publisher as a donation. I might donate the cash to the Writer's Guild. But it is up to *me*. The monies must be paid to *me*. People must realise that attempts to diddle The Quiver out of what is his will result in a salvo of red-hot writs coming hard and fast in their faces."

*Ah, what a man we are! The elegance, the poise, the calmly worded menace! That stately voice that has smoothly vanquished so many nemeses! Good lord, Decca, aren't you blessed to have me in your head and me in your ear!*

"Now, having preambled thus, we come to our business. In the spirit of candour, I will make clear from the off. I am planning to sue. Now, since I exacted a form of immediate revenge in the form of the fucking of your wife, this lawsuit need not take place instantly. I will permit a grace period."

*Decca, you have understood what we said? We fucked Camilla in the Heathrow toilets. I hate to labour this point . . . well, I hate 'labour' anything . . . especially the Labour party . . . you realise Niles Konwick attended one of my secret orgies in Bethnal Green? His fondness for an anal fisting from Greek rentboys was extraordinary. I won't even mention what Michael Foot liked. I still see that midget in my dreams. Anyhoo, I would take a moment to imagine me inside your missus, mate. Think on that wrinkled sac, slamming against the inviolate mons pubis of your beautiful wife. Keep that thought in your head.*

"We never fucked, Derek. That was a little quip of mine!"

*Classic me.*

"Oh."

"I was expecting a little more reaction than that! You barely even blinked. When I told Hestletine I fucked his missus, he launched a trade war with South Korea!"

"Ah."

It was too soon in the weirdness of this situation for Derek to graduate to two-syllables.

"What we need to unearth is the exact nature of this inspiration. You committed an embezzlement, which I am not here to chastise, but you understand that I cannot condone the use of my name in connection with a crime. I have never, to my knowledge, committed an embezzlement on the scale you have. So we must establish the meaning of your message to prepare our mutual legal defences. But there is an alternate route. The amount it will cost you to defend yourself in legal fees is probably similar to the amount stolen. I reckon we could settle this with a cheque, out of court, into my coffers, in under 24 hours."

Camilla inched near the sitting Millie like a bored marquise selecting a servant. "Let's have a look at you, then," she said. Millie stood up to let her superior scrutinise the hungerstricken cheekbones, the papershredded hair, the prepubescent nihil of her breasts, and the breadsticks and twiglets in place of limbs.

"First upfuck, Derek. Your mistress is meant to have bigger funbags. This chick's chest is like two paracetamols on an ironing board. You are the only politician in the world who would take a heroin-addled checkout assistant as mistress and not some D-cupped student reporter looking for a leg up. Look at me, Derek. I am fifty years old.

I look in my late thirties. I'm a fucking knockout. I have this stately nose. I have two stunning lips. I have a well-toned body that most women my age envy, that makes me loathed by bookclubs the length and breadth of Craigmillar. This slit has lips drawn on in marker. She has the body of a Syrian refugee after ten weeks in a cargo truck. I think I understand what is happening here. You think you want an affair, yet you're embarrassed to have an affair. You think an affair is the sort of thing you should be having in your present confused mental state, yet you haven't the amoral cojones to have an affair, so you've chosen someone utterly inferior to me in every respect. Mate, I'm surprised she isn't a seventy-two-year-old rheumatic with a prosthetic knee."

(Millie, of course, was too servile to respond).

"I'm . . . I'm not sure if there's a word for what I am. The problem with having a nervous breakdown in secret, Derek, is that this whole thing could have been avoided. I would have understood your panicked male need to screw a youth and explained in a concise and friendly manner the two thousand reasons that was clearly idiotic. I would have cured you with a night of unhinged humping. Instead, in your confused attempt to avoid predictable, late-middle-age clichés, you have cooked a cockup of thundering stupidity. You have bypassed originality, the status quo, the hackneyed, and bellyflopped into stupid. Stumbling, bumbling stupidity. You have made incoherence into an art form. You are the Tommy Wiseau of politics, minus the cult success and weird craggy arsecheeks. I'm ashamed to even be here. I wish I'd said all this in an email."

Derek was a man in a hotel room in Cádiz with a freshly exed wife, stolen loot en route to the offshore accounts of J. Quiver, a mistress rendered sexually void, a torpedoed political career, and an ageing body with worrying lumps, bumps, and humps.

It was over, the whole Derek thing.

It was over, the whole sitting in rooms talking thing.

It was over, the whole thinking thing.

So he took a mental walk. In a shirt and shorts, a blank man in a blank world, he mentally left the hotel and walked. He mentally walked towards the sea and eased himself into the water. As he floated on his back, bobbing on the water like a rowboat adrift, the voice of Quiver left him, the incoherent thoughts of political revolution left him.

"Fine," he said to the sun burning his face. "I'll find something to do in the American private sector, retire to no fanfare in the New Jersey suburbs, and pass away quietly one night reading Proust."

The sun kept killing him.

"Because that's the only outcome for me."

The water kept killing him.

"And, quite honestly, I should be fucking grateful. Because there is no coherence in an incoherent world and battling incoherence with incoherence is stupid."

The world kept killing him.

"Now, swim back to shore."

Upon flipping himself, he noted he had bobbed about a mile out to sea.

"I wonder if I can make it back," he said.

# III

# LUBO RECTO ERGO

D EREK'S STOMACH said: "Yes, I can see. I can see Camilla, that ballad of middle-aged elegance, that corrido of poise and pertness,
that torch song of above-average intelligence and wit, towering over
Millie like a cougar teasing a wounded beaver. Yes, I can see. I can see
Quiver manspreading on that chair in a state of priapic anticipation at
the lawsuit about to impend in our face like a runaway camion burning
down Filbert Street, San Fran. But I couldn't care less. I am a stomach, my friend. As a stomach, I seek nutritional satisfaction. I have
one simple demand. I want two rashers of bacon and a black pudding.
Please fulfil this need immediately and exempt me from any oncoming
emotional turmoil."

Derek's bladder said: "Yes, I can sense. I can sense the awkward
stalemate in the room. No one willing to unspool the tickertape of
shrieking hellcack running in their heads into a neat line of 'realistic'
dialogue. I can sense the heart-burning recriminations and the anthrax-
strength venom soon to emerge from the mouths of those present
named Camilla. I can sense the bubbles of supercilious phlegm soon
to flow from the mouths of those present named Jethro. But I couldn't
care less. I am a bladder, my friend. As a bladder, I seek the mere release of the liquids and uric acid from my person through your little

person. Please fulfil this need immediately and exempt me from any unpleasant self-soiling."

"Well, I suppose I better speak, if no one else will," Camilla spoke as no one else would. Her intimidatingness in a floral blouse and flowing purple skirt was as strong as her intimidatingness in a business shirt and skirt of pencil. Derek's stomach and bladder had been overruled. His heart was campaigning hard for a cardiac episode, pumping at the speeds of a solar probe late for a bus. "OK," he heard himself burp.

"It's all right," Quiver said, springing from the chair with the flair of a viper in £300 flipflops. "I will recommence comms. Now, Derek. We need to have a little parley, chez vou. I appreciate our presence here, as you bask like an ITV4 Tristan and Isolde in the Spanish sunshine, is unexpected. Rather like a sudden onslaught of midges in a forest clearing, as I wrote rather poetically in one of the novels."

Camilla kept her place at the TV stand hovering over a melting Millie, unseated from reality on the bed's edge in her sweaty pants.

"Hi, I'm the wife," she said, no hand offered. Millie reflexed a hand upwards, hanging that hand in the air in wait for a polite reciprocal to leap palm-to-palm in a show of sisterly mercy and, seeing no such hand offered and sensing the implied snub, rerouted her hand back to tuck in her pre-tucked hair. "I'm the previous residence of Dezza's penis. I see he has swapped a five-bedroom Georgian townhouse for an outdoor privy." Millie was too embarrassed at the obvious hand rerouting failure to note the ouch. She had fallen into an emotional sump, all prior punk sunken neath the wither of a together woman.

"It came to pass, Derek, that I was sipping a latte in the VIP lounge, waiting for the boarding call, when I observed your Romanesque betrothed. I was reading proofs of the next novel—no other prose stimulates me like mine—when I observed her charming shanks nestled within the porous runnels of a skirt. She, too, was consuming a latte, that tremendous loin-stirring beverage brewed from the finest

Hereford cow titties and the most flavoursome beans from the kaffirs. I approached her to remark on the coincidence of our lattes and remind her that I am Jethro Quiver—yes, that one from the Sharleen Porter affair and the accidentally stolen Canadian slacks—and to enquire whether her legs had won the Turner Prize. She informed me that she was making an impromptu trip to see her husband who had eloped with a mistress, and that her husband was Derek Haffman MSP, meaning he played politics in the sandpit Westminster permitted the Scotch to build for themselves. I made a whooping sound. I whooped! The others in the VIP lounge were treated to the rare spectacle of me, that Jethro Quiver, that one from the umpteen failed London mayoral attempts, from the short period in chokey, making a whoop! You can complete the rest, Derek. I told her I was on the hunt for a prime piece of libel meat."

The length of Quiver's prattle was the exact time needed for a thought to send a message to Derek's mouth and for his mouth to send a message to his brain asking for permission from his brain to send approval to his mouth.

"Look, Lord Quiver—"

"Now, now! I haven't finished. I always used to tell Cecil Parkinson, my conversation has natural rhythms, Parkie. Sometimes I pause to allow the wingèd wasp of a notion to buzz around the perimeter of my ponderance and permit entrance to the auricle of sapience. Sometimes I leave time for the absorption of a classic Quiver ponderance into the room's gullet. My thoughts are large aspirins, fizzling themselves into people's brains with a salving wisdom, clearing the rot from their thinking so that clear-headed sense propels them forward to admitting I am right. Let me explain. I have a crack team of Libel Lugworms. I send these Lugworms into the world to see what anti-Quiver libel they can dredge up from the sludge of the archives, then I reel in their catch to inspect what Quiverish anguish I might have caused to merit the slander. In most cases, the libel is unworkable. But I never miss the chance."

"You've come to sue me?" Derek asked. Listening to the wretched man's obscene self-confidence as the sentences flowed from his wrinkle-carved and winkie-pink head into the shredder of his ears forced Derek to shift his stance from spooked okapi to sarcastic lemur.

"Kane *and* Abel! You're quite the impatient penitent, Deccadent. I'm here to offer what I like to call frienemesistance. It's a mouthful, I agree. Let's break it down. It's a portmanteau word combining the nouns 'friend', 'nemesis', and 'assistance'. You see, I come as a frienemesis, meaning neither friend nor nemesis and friend *and* nemesis. To clarify, I come to offer the sort of assistance to one who is neither friend nor nemesis who is also a friend and a nemesis. You might think these contradictions. Not in the world of Jethro, me lad. In my world, a man is always a frienemesis, someone on whom you can rely or hatchet in the sternum when the occasion arises. This is the world of the élites, Derek. There are no friends or nemeses where I prowl. Friends are merely people in a temporary waiting list for supreme annihilation at the sweetest possible moment. This is the world at the highest level of politics, success, wealth, and fame. It's an absolute delirium of human relations up here."

"Much as I'm finding this lexical dawdle an exquisite earfuck, can we speed up, please?" Camilla asked.

She crossed her arms in that classic, time-tested show of impatience.

"Of course, Camilla. Now, permit me to limn the nature of our relations, Derek, through frienemesistance. We will proceed as friends (in the sense of friends in the rubric of frienemeses) until such a time when we must proceed as nemeses (in the sense of frienemeses), and so on. Do not mistake me, Hasselhaff. This relationship is a pendulum. I am on hugging terms with men whose insides I have vacuumed out, their airless husks hung on the washing line for my own glory. I am on hugging terms with men who have pistolwhipped me into twelve irreversible comas. Because we know the rules. There are no friends or nemeses. There are people to exploit at the exact moment it becomes advantageous. This is the relationship I intend to pursue with yourself, Derek. Now, I shall repair to the nearest marisquería for some of the Mediterranean's finest scallops while your wife conducts herself."

She uncrossed her arms in that classic, time-tested show of exasperation at having to wait for a man to shut up.

"Thank you, Jethro."

The Quiver made a mock salute to Derek, still looking moronic in his shorts and ironic shirt as Camilla occupied the chair Quiver had failed to offer her when bossing into the room. Millie, recalling the stirring words of Heather Smalls from M:People, moved on up and found the hero inside herself, rising from her clench to retreat with words. "I think I'll head too. I haven't eaten for hours. Nice to seat you."

She exited to no further awks, solecism uncorrected.

"Bless! Sweet little thing," Camilla said. "She reminds me of one of those rescue foxes with two broken legs and a burned tail that won't make it through the night. I can see Rolf looming over her sleepy eyes as the camera cuts away before the snuff shot. A nation mourns for ten seconds until the credits roll."

"Hi Camilla," Derek said.

"Hi Derek."

"I need to wee. Can we resume this post-wee?"

"I'm not mistress of your bladder."

"Thanks."

Derek's bladder said: "About fecking time. You nearly burst me, you jobbernowl."

Derek's stomach said: "Oh, so you're *not* planning to introduce black pudding into me in the next few minutes? You're embarking on a fraught exchange as your belly rumbles like a San Diego traphouse?"

"Let's move to the obvious," Camilla said after listening to a protracted period of handwashing, "this chit, with her ravenous red hair, her skeletal cheekbones, her absence of tendons or sinew, is a facsimile of me at the same age. The problem is I am twelve times hotter in my early fifties than I was in my early twenties. You on the other hand, have Mark E. Smithed yourself into senility, and to persuade yourself otherwise, you have elected to hump a younger version of me. That was obvs the second I saw your buckled fox. I mean, none too subtle. Millie? Camilla? You could have allowed for a few extra syllables."

"Here's how I want to proceed," Derek said. "I intend to walk the line between self-apologetic whimperies and offering enough rebuttal not to seem pathetic. I want to minimise the degree of contempt with which you perceive me when you leave the room. Can you help me to achieve this outcome?"

"Hmm."

"For example, one of the cliches I will avoid is 'she makes me feel young again'. Because that happens to be untrue. Whenever I'm with her I am hyperaware that I am a man raised on Hovis adverts, the SDP, the D.H.S.S Rap, and the hilarious creepiness of Minipops, and that she is a woman raised on recherché postmodernism, the egging of John Prescott, The Libertines, and the death throes of Bebo. Another cliché: 'I wanted to feel a young body again'. I haven't managed sex with her. She has, from the beginning, imposed a series of conditions on my own personal development before sex was permitted. I'm not even sure you could call what we've been doing an affair. We've been two people sitting in rooms negotiating the terms of an affair for the last year, until I yanked her over here. Another: 'she gets me'. You 'get' me more than anyone else. Millie has a comprehension deficit that far exceeds the Sudanese debt ceiling. There are times when I am looking into Millie's face, having poured a verbal burden into her ears, when I wonder at the end, can she even remember my surname?"

"You're telling me you *haven't* fucked her?"

"This is the hardest aspect to believe, so I won't argue the point. In fact, I'm happy to accept your total incredulity and whatever outrageous sexing scenarios you may have in your mind between us. I broke our bond with another woman. Whether I sexed her or not is completely irrelevant to the betrayal."

"Hmm. Not really," she beggedtodiffer. "You can break the bond through one kiss with feeling. Or you can break the bond with twelve consecutive nights of vigorous fucking in a Nissan Micra. The two are not the same. Both involve the breaking of a bond of trust. But one involves the breaking of a bond of trust over twelve consecutive nights of fucking in a Nissan Micra. Do you see the difference?"

"Yes. We touched hands sometimes. For the most part, I sat next to her as she made suggestions on how I might reform myself to better solve the cracked political system keeping me in a state of shredded agitation."

"You're one confused sod, aren't you, Derek?"

The marital bond, wilting in relegation from Decca to Derek.

In the further explanation department, Derek felt bereft. A discourse on the Quiverification process, his descent into roguishness for the sake of political unblocking, the unspecified political something that might follow in the wake of the thieving and the philandering—that whole psychodrama transferred into feeble, squeaked words in a hotel room—seemed an insult to Camilla, and all women who had ever waited to have their ears bothered with pleading entreaties of errant spouses having been caught with underage strumpets in a semi-squalid setting with one-bar wi-fi and no free biscuits. This being the case, he left his mouth open, blocking the insuck of air needed to outspew words of consul.

"You ever think your marriage would end with you drooling in a Hawaiian shirt in a Cádiz hotel room?" she asked with sobering pertinence.

"No comment."

✿

Expecting no satisfying conclusion to their tête-à-tête, Camilla retreated for a swim in the pool of her five-star terrace.

Having spiked his appetite for black pudding and with no pressing business for the rest of his life, Derek slithered under the sheets.

Sleep, that merciful release from the ridiculous burden of human skin, came. Inside that sleep, the following dream had Derek:

A shower for a shower's sake is the sweetest sort of shower. Showering for eight hours of excruciating labour, showering for an appointment to have one's insides poked with implements, showering to shovel overpriced hake into one's maw while making small talk at a romantic rendezvous—these are the showers of necessity, these are the showers of sorrow. But showering for the cleansing salve of the water alone, for the saponaceous flow along our flaps and folds, for the womblike warmth and ensnugglement between four perspex partitions—these are the showers of sensation, these are the showers of success.

In the prison where Derek was bivvied as a criminal man, the showers were non-optional. As the showers served no purpose other than preventing the spread of cholera and plague within the prison walls, these were the showers of success. It began with a familiar fear—the instant assumption a gang of tattooed sodomites were in want of his ageing ass—and ended with the rape-free pleasure of soaking under a showerhead with a surprising flow rate of 2.5 GPM. The shower room, far from a carnival of anal abandon from hole-starved criminal cocks, was a place of towel-thwacking camaraderie, a place to share in the collective love of scatological banter under the cleansing power of $H_2O$.

Here, he was encouraged to pour forth aggrieved barbs at 5.5GPM and his cohorts lapped it up. Remarks were made on George Galloway ("vainglorious prig in the pockets of Putin"), Michael Foot ("Fabian crank with political Tourette's"), Michael Hestletine ("Thatcher-sniffing neoliberal relic"), Rory Stewart ("the rejected member of Radiohead"), Jeremy Corbyn ("a CND sticker on the Austin Metro of time"), Tony Blair ("the smarm that killed a million Iraqis"), David Cameron ("the whiffiest fart of English plutocracy"), Ed Davey ("even he forgets he exists, whoever he is"), and Theresa May ("the scourge of Hertfordshire"). He was nicknamed "the Gorgie Guevara" in his own head and "that MP cunt" in the real word. In short, he was safe from stabbings.

One morning, six months into the stretch, he was sharing a cup of PG with Carl Struck in the prison canteen.

"Explain to me again," Carl said, folding the two meatloaves he had for arms.

"I wanted to bring about a non-specific political shake-up with a random criminal act. I hoped to spark an uprising that would rock across the world in post-Richter ripples, like a benign Gavrilo Princip."

Derek occupied a classic antiseptic cell with a bunk, in-house WC, and threat-carved table. The room's previous occupant had etched advice into the wall about how to turn longsocks into nooses. The noose-proof room made suicide a non-starter, although hanging had never crossed his mind. He was working on a prison memoir, less flatulent and verbose than Quiver's, seeking words to explain his actions free from the stuttering adverbs and synonyms *sort of*, *a kind of*, *vague*, *non-specific*, *undefined*, *incoherent*, *something*, and *failing*. There was the additional problem of spoiling a clueless scheme with ex post facto scribblings. Netflix miniseries are not founded on cast-iron conclusions and certainties.

"Tell me once more," Carl said. The prison canteen was bright with clubbish crims forking mash and carrots into their laughing mouths. There seemed to Derek more spark and wit here than in parliament.

"I wanted to make a kind of vague political happening happen. It was sort of incoherent, undefined, and non-specific, but the idea was that something was kind of likely to happen after, whatever it was."

"Nope. Have another crack," Carl said. He had performed GBH on his business associate with a broom following an inaccurate balance sheet.

"I have no idea what I wanted to do. I can't explain."

"That wasn't so hard to admit, was it?"

"No."

"You have a title for the memoir?"

"Yep. My real crime was having the immortal rind to ever become a politician in the first place, so I'll call the book *A Symptom of Arrogance*."

"Nice."

(The dream spent some time spinning a wreath of kitten heads and showed an unidentified man flushing his left foot in a toilet. Then the central dream resumed).

Six months passed. One morning Francis ambled into the visiting room with the air of a man bumping into a friend at a bus stop.

"Have you seen the result?"

"What result?"

"The election."

"There was an election?"

"Where've you been?"

"Incarcerated at Her Majesty's Pleasure for six months."

"You haven't heard a whit about politics for that time?"

"Francis, I've had two visits since being banged up. One was from Millie asking if I could fund her proto-ska collaboration with Charles & Eddie. The second was from Camilla with a list of the alimonies I will owe her from now until the heart attack."

"Alimony has a plural? So no one has mentioned the political situation?"

"Fritzl in E-wing is concerned about tendering corruption in the public sector procurement process. He was arrested for exposing his penis to clerks in Argos. Apart from that, nein."

"You'll need the whole thing from the beginning?"

"What thing?"

"Right. Well, I had hoped to begin this conversation from a position of knowledge of the last six insane months. Never mind. I'm a master of précis. You were arrested and sentenced to prison for embezzlement, remember? After that, Norman wrote to *The Sun* arguing you were a hero, how in sheer desperation to make some positive change happen in a stagnant political cesspool, you committed a desperate act of randomness, hoping through that desperate act of randomness to bring about some seismic political upheaval or something. The story was shared on the media socials. Columnists started pontificating on whether running the country through a random algorithm might be better than electing the spongers we have in parliament. So, an anonymous programmer called emancipated22 set up an open-source online randomiser, into which people could upload their policies and ideas. People would be chosen at random to form the government. In other words, a random act of revolution."

"Risible, Frankie."

"No, this stuff has happened."

"Oh."

"Revolution by whatever, it wasn't called. The online randomiser was stitched together from a snarl of JavaScript and registered as an official candidate on the ballot. The word RANDOM was included on the voting slip below the usual pro- and anti-poor peeps, and 55.6 million people put their cross in the box marked RANDOM, having seen the other candidates talk. The next morning, names were fed into the randomiser to form a government. Carol Wilmot, an underwriter for a Bradford insurance firm, was appointed Prime Minister of England, Scotland, Wales, and Northern Ireland. David Cruet, a retired librarian from Aberdeen, was appointed Chancellor of the Exchequer. The other positions were filled in the same manner, the highlights including Steven Pole, a crackhead from Staines as Minister for Health, and Alison Grimm, a 98-year-old retired seamstress from Crieff as Minister for Youth Culture. These appointments made no difference as policies were created at random by the randomiser, and the relevant bodies involved in implementing them would have responsibility for kicking them into action at once. Randoms were appointed for the sake of optics to create a sense of leadership and comradeliness. The official website allowed users to suggest policies on every aspect of life, which were spooned into the algorithm. If the policies made no sense ("make a lamp sweet and woooah" one weirdo wrote), were hateful ("KILL ALL SCOUSE" came up loads), or beyond the realms of human possibility ("reinvent the sandwich with fillings on the outside"), they were removed. This, of course, made the moderators of the website somewhat de facto rulers, but the rules were clear to everyone who voted for RANDOM, so no sinister manipulation could scupper the whole shebang. The T&Cs stated that if at any time a majority of users felt the system had been corrupted, the next day the website would be consigned to the Github of history, and a general election triggered."

"Christ."

"Speaking of Christ, the first policy chosen was an absolute shiner. The randomiser was pressed live on all the networks, except Channel 4, which was repeating Frasier for the ninetieth time. The randomiser selected Lara Tromlett to replace the Queen as Queen. Hoo-hoo! The next morning, Queen Elizabeth II was stripped of her enthronements, including the actual throne, and replaced with Lara Tromlett from Upper Largo, Fife, Scotland, a retired air hostess whose infectious laugh and incredulous "what, me?" attitude made her loved in the nation. As Queen, her first act was to open Buckingham Palace to the public, allowing the homeless to sleep in one of the hundreds of spare bedrooms until kind people offered them a ladder back into society. On the second day, her popularity plummeted when she invited asylum seekers to take Balmoral. From that moment on she became a polarising figure, accused of white saviour syndrome and thoughtlessly shitting on six centuries of tradition (that tradition being, of course, allowing a band of king-fuckers to live like Gods because of erm . . . tourism)."

"Progressives hit the motherlode in the next spin of the randomiser: Ban overseas tax loopholes and tax the richest 90% of their incomes. The British ruling class spasmed out their double-breasted onesies, for there was no time to bundle their fortunes in sacks and suitcases and helicopter them to an underground vault in the Solomon Islands. The public woke up to CEOs fleeing from muscular tax collectors battering in their doors and bleeding them of millions and trillions, and within a few weeks, their bank accounts were reduced to a less disgusting sum, and that cash was tucked under the public mattress."

"Wows."

"Wows, indeed. The nature of the randomiser, howev, meant that the next one was A lifetime supply of creosote for all British taxpayers. A deep data-snorkel was commissioned to determine the average creosote consumption per British head. A week later, an investment of £7,260,000,000 was made into providing each citizen with 60l of the wood preservative, at a cost of £115 per person among 66.65 million Britons."

"Hmms."

"Hmms, indeed. Next: A 200% hike in street cleaning operatives. Twelve hundred thousand people were hired to purge Britain's streets of trashmounds and shithills. This made (after two months) Britain the cleanest nation in the world, although £222,500,000,000 was needed to cover the cost of wages and landfills and machines and that special bleach used to clean up the stink from Nagasaki. Most Britons, when asked, wanted public services funded properly, and for rich parasites to foot the bill. The instance of pro-greed policies like "no tax for the rich" was so low in the randomiser, the elite tax-shunning fuckwits had no look in. We now have the cash to fritter on things like investment in flying broomsticks for practising witches and free cunnilingus on the NHS, thanks to a proper taxation system."

"Huh. It was as simple as taxing the rich, eh?"

"It always has been, mate. I've said from Day One that is politics is nothing more than the ignoble art of enclouding that very simple premise in mists of doubt, ambiguity, and complexity."

"You've never said that."

"It was implied."

"Enclouding isn't a word."

"Yes it is. Invade Denmark! lololololol came up last week so we are now at war with Denmark. 40,000 British soldiers have perished in minor skirmishes in Agger, Arbroath, Vejers, and Whitley Bay."

"Win some lose some."

"That's the nature of the randomiser."

"The revolution will be randomised."

"Preach."

(The dream descended into packs of Danish bacon swirling around an obelisk of black pudding).

✵

The next allotment of awakeness brought no black pudding. Under the door slipped was a note from Quiver requesting an appearance at the Camilo José Cela Memorial Bar, postscripted "Please refrain from Hawaiian shirts or the exposure of legs." Half-caught in a wakeless vision of randomised revolution—Danish warships unloading their eco-friendly bombs over the Houses of Parliament to the songs of Filur— Derek treated his ageing skin to hot water and soap, his hair to hot water and shampoo, and returned to the ministerial clothes he had shed upon arrival, sucking all holiday merriment into a vortex of oxford button-down shirts and crow-black pleated trousers with leather Vattal brogues.

Swishing past blimp-bellied Austrian revellers, fresh from slapping water and panting near small children, he followed Miss Google Maps and her mangled pronunciations towards the sidestreet seafood place where Quiver was poised with a flagon of IPA and a plate of paella, forking the mussels and prawns aside in seek of elusive chorizos.

"Chorizo in paella appears here to be heresy," he said to Derek's loom. "Take a seat."

"Good morning, Lord Quiver."

"Ah! That's the deference we like to see. When we say 'we', we're referring to the various Quivers in the room. You see, we like to think of myselves as above mere uniformular cellularity, Decca. I like to think I contain multitudes, not in the figurative Whitmanesque sense, in the literal sense of several of me existing in the same form. You might have observed that I am able to manipulate people's mental flows. Once people have heard of me, a little part of me minxes into their mental pumproom and spiels mannish notions into their circuits, helping them become more like Quiver. I expect a Quiver has been talking to you over the course of the last month or so, perhaps in the form of an italicised bruiser?"

"Yes."

"We apologise for that Quiver—all right, we will stick to the first-person pro to avoid confusion—*I* apologise for that Quiver. He's the most brutal iteration of the Quiver. Now, understand. I am not a multiple personalities oddbox. I have one personality, The Quiver, that contains multitudes. There are no John Redwoods or Norman Tebbits in here, thank heavens."

"No."

"How's Camilla?"

"Umm—"

"Men like us, Decca, or more men like me, and men like you through your association with men like me, tend to land on our feet where women are concerned. I hope this isn't off-colour to a Scotch socialist, but I find the flat-chested well-toned middle-aged blonde ones like your Camilla have cunts like succubae."

"Lord Quiver, I wonder if we could discuss—"

"Yes, all right. There'll be time for chauvinist ribaldries later, once our business is concluded. Now, as I mentioned in the room, I have a crackteam of Libel Lugworms paid to suck the seafloor for Mr. Guppy fodder. Your cable to the presses, claiming that I was the inspiration for this half-arsed embezzlement scheme you performed yesterday, was a vexing read. Considering the utter feebleness of your scheme, from the motivation to planning to execution, I would consider this court case a fait accompli."

"I see."

"Let me run through some past triumphs. Carl Swinton from The Independent in a 2010 profile wrote the sentence: 'Quiver, in his £10,000,000 seafront home, spends his afternoons watching the waters enveloping time-worn cliff-faces, oblivious to the unforced metaphor staring him in the literal face.' You will observe that The Independent scaled back to an online clickbait magazine soon after, and that I was able to build more robust flood defences around the same time. No coincidink, Dez."

"I—"

"Next, Anna Frau from The Guardian. She wrote a piece on how I crushed the confidence of thriller writer Filbert Overton over an afternoon tea. He'd won Thriller of the Year in 2004 and I had him round for a word. She wrote: *Quiver lured Overton to his £3,000,000 townhouse in Kensington—remember inflation was at 2.98% then—and unleashed a morale-crushing tirade of oaths and maledictions into the young writer's ear*—I suggested with consummate politeness that the crime fiction kingpins were not fond of upstarts bagging their awards—*so that, stunned and appalled, the writer retired from fiction and took up moose farming six miles outside Novosibirsk. In a telephone interview, Overton told me: 'So virulent and pointed was the nature of Quiver's invective that I was shuddering hot for two weeks. I thought I was the victim of a permanent seizure, so shoogled were my bones by the grey eminence's wrathful imprecations.' Mr. Overton hung up when I suggested he might return to writing.* In a way, this was extremely flattering to me. To be shown such a master at the art of the persuasive nudge that I might send a man to Siberia! But I had to sue. Soon after I sued, The Guardian began posting begging messages at the end of their online articles. I expect in a few months, The Guardian will start screening pensioner porn."

"I—"

"I understand some tomfools consider me unloved. Yes, I was voted Most Popular Target in the British Rifle Club newsletter in March 2009. But print a slight against me, the next time we meet will be in a bear hug of bewigged attorneys. Now is the time for you to explain the intention behind your citation, Derek."

A silence—that time-tested indicator of non-speech—opened up.

"You are the Ali Baba of sneaks," Derek began. "The Bill Sikes of shiftiness. The Machiavelli of Machiavellianism. Your reputation precedes yourself for the Robert Pollardesque volume of artful cunning over seven glorious decades. I thought I could harness that power and, like a veteran cowpoke taming a feral steed, turn that evil into something positive and overhaul the system with cunning kindness."

"Oh me! Oh mi! You've been Clegged, Dezzah! You've been Clegged short back and sides! Ha! Ha! Ho! Oh sire, thon liberals and thon misunderstanding of evil. You recall in 2010, Dezza, when the nation had wearied of centre-right left-wing hasbeens Blair and Brown? The public warmed to the neonatal cheeks of a cool Conservative called Cameron, though not enough to elect him outright. Then this gormless Ron Weasley came along with the audacity to call himself Nick, taking his Liberals into coalition with the Tories, hoping to keep checks and balances on their excesses. You will then recall that the Conservative machinery took this naïf waif and yanked him through a yard of barbed wire, flushed him through the sewer, and vomited on his face for three consecutive years. That's the Tory party, baby! If you can't stand the flesh-searing wounds, leave the kitchen! We have no time for folks with an income under £75,000. If you earn less, you are mere kitty litter, awaiting the inevitable plop of poo on your poor scalps. At Tory HQ, we consider arse-fucking plebs all night long a consecrated artform . . . we love making them sew up their own bleeding arseholes afterwards. Even if these plebs make millionaires of themselves, we'll still scoff at them for not being related to a Duke. You cannot cleanse centuries-old aristocratic contempt from the bloodstream of the Great British ruling classes. If you aren't in the right wage bracket, the right hereditary bracket, or the right political bracket, we will snort at you as we would a trespasser mangled to mush by the hounds. Our motto in the Tory party is *lubo recto ergo*, meaning you're going to get fucked either way, so you'd better lube up, babykins."

"So I've heard."

"I apologise for the pile-up of profanities. But I think the point has been made. Now. Shall we walk?"

The sun blazed hard upon the scalps of the two perpendicular chaps, in motion along incoherent streets toward the semitropical shimmer of the flat, sprawling sands. The Andalusian people, sweating with life in their half-worn summer clothes, their hot bodies burning with calciferol and morning sex, strode past the two time-shagged old British males with the swagger of stallions passing buckle-legged mares lining up for the knacker's yard. Quiver, kitted in slaveowner chic—full white seersucker with matching ruffled undershirt and, in a moment of mercy, no cravat—smirked at the natives, oblivious to the passing giggles the sheer twattery of his appearance was eliciting.

"I love España. I came here for R&R after the Canada scandal."

"The slacks?"

"No. Something else. It involved Conrad Black and an underage ballerina."

"Right."

"I wonder if she's able to walk now."

"Lord Quiver, can—"

"Yes. We ought to chess up our endgame. In light of this so-called cunning kindness, whatever that meant, I think the sensible thing here is for you to return to GB, restore the embezzled monies to their owner, and take the prison sentence. The sunshine and señoritas are making me less salival in the suing dept, Derek. Your political career is over and Camilla is soon to serve the divorce papers. A lawsuit from The Quiver's the last thing you need. If you apologise for invoking me in your email, I will even put in a kind word for you in the papers, try to explain that you were only trying to make some kind of political change by stealing money and fleeing to Spain or whatever it was you were trying to achieve, I have no idea really. Now, let us park our ageing bums on this wall and have a peep at these slits in bikinis."

"If I refuse to return?" Derek asked. For the first time in the conversation he felt a twitch of rebellion and almost hiccupped with giddiness at its arrival.

"Brave move, D-Day, brave move! Two words and an abbrev: Chauncey Mauve QC. He's not what I would call a tender lover. Since 1959, Chauncey has sent four thousand people to prison, tens of whom were criminals. Since 1970, he has managed my slaughterhouse of libel, stringing up hundreds, if not thousands, of libellous muppets and treating them to a loving halal climax. Apart from that raucous truck of urea Michael Crick, who wrote that infamous hatchet-bio of me, swerving libel landmines like a pro, Chauncey has successfully netted me sums in the region of ninety to ninety-five million."

"Right." The hiccup had mutated into a spurt of machismo, as though Lucozade was being mainlined into his balls.

"I have contacts at the Kill Desks of most national newspapers who, for a pfennig and a rubdown, will flex their flaming fingers and poison pens to reduce you to a naphthoic heap of ashes and flubber. The last man who refused to accede to The Quiver was . . . well, parts of him were found in a gulch at Scafell Pike, entwined in a Ford Fiesta. If you were a man hewn of sharper stone, like Carlton Schmitt, then we could bareknuckle box a bit before I strip you of your possessions, livelihood, and self-respect."

Derek's arm said: "Could I punch him? I mean, could I clench hard that fist and perform a gnathic KO and send him corkscrewing to the sand in a flop of brittle bones? If the ring finger connects with requisite oomph, I could break the nose and spatter Quiver blood across the sand in hilarious blots."

Butterflies fluttered to Rage Against the Machine in his stomach. His heart made noises like the BFG stomping an orphanage in a pair of wooden stacked-heel Chelsea boots. He saw shapes—rhomboids and octagons spelling the message THUMP THE CUNT—in a swirl in his peripheral. He rose from the wall in the manner of a man watching himself rise from a wall and in a similar manner watched himself swoop his arm in a punching motion toward the mug of The Quiver, heaving hard and frothing spit, and watching this man that was him punch an old man that was Quiver in the cheek and recoil his fist at the searing pain from the bone-on-bone action as the old man that was Quiver who he had punched lurched over the wall clutching his face and sliding to the sand and after a moment of stunned silence rising up with all the spitting wrath of https://www.youtube.com/watch?v=pssI1ZwzcmQ.

The Quiver, pausing in mid-leer, reached for his pocket kerchief and checked for blood. There was none. Michael Crick was the one living man for whom Quiver reserved his undiluted contempt. The leer smiled.

"Gosh! That takes me back to my canvassing days, sparring with Labour voters on their front lawns. I once scissor-kicked a miner into voting Tory," he said. "Now I'm pleased—as punch—you let your frustrations win. This means you absolutely have no choice but to come back to Britain with me. I thought I might have to squirt further calumnies onto your cake. There's no reason, of course, that we must leave instantly, I rather hope to write another nine chapters this afternoon. The Mediterranean air is conducive to further award-winning prose. My latest novel is called *A Woman of Valour*."

"Great title."

"Thank you. Now, you will have some business to conduct with your unconventional mistress and your unplighted Camilla, so I will restrain you no further," he said, turning in the opposite direction in the public schoolboy manner of walking away at speed to avoid unpleasant shows of affection. A slight wobble in his stride, akin to an ageing penguin avoiding an unplanned skid on the tundra, reminded Derek he had assaulted an 80-year-old man, and for no seconds was this of any concern to him.

☼

A text summoned D to another piscine pub, where Millie perched outside with a clear liquid and a plate of innards framed in sundried tomatoes and artichoke. A childhood surf over the Falls of Falloch in a makeshift sloop had cured her of lingering anxieties and terrors—her poise had returned as she said:

"Good timing! Please can you pay for this squeamish slop?"

"I punched Quiver."

"Oh God. Is he suing?"

"No, that's the strange thing. He seemed measured and cool. I was expecting him to rear up on haunches, the blood of Crick on his teeth. He wants me to return home and face the music. The music in this case being the soundtrack to *Cannibal Holocaust*."

"Hmm. He wouldn't travel this far without a sizzling sirloin of sueage on offer."

"I know. I think—"

From the middle distance, two hoofbeats, their source two unspanish creatures in ironic khaki named Double-F and The Ant.

"Lo and behold! The band's all here," the one who named himself after an insect whose real name was Thomas Steward said.

It was explained after the exchange of hugs and modish signifiers of friendship ("heywow", "coolso", "funkyeah"), that Millie had texted her bandmates at the airport to come to Cádiz at once to record an album in an actual studio with engineers and soundboards and stuff and that their flights and hotels would be paid for. In the sunlight, The Ant rocked the look of Kaspar Hauser emerging from the cellar—anaemic, malnourished, soon to be stabbed in Ansbach Court Garden—while Double-F had tried to mimic the lead singer from Idlewild and cover the swastika he had carved into his temple as a school prank. Their appearance at this moment was unwelcome, as was their appearance at all moments, even moments when one had arranged to meet them with the express intention of having a moment. The brief balm of Millie's falsetto, fibbing into his ear about things being all right and so on and etcetera was the lone aural input he craved for the rest of the week. No chance now.

"Hey Haff. Thanks for the studio. That's schematic, mantime," F-F said.

"Right," Derek said. Speeding through these exchanges was the best. "I have no idea if there's a studio in Cádiz. I'm sure we can find some old skeeter with a four-track to commit your racket to tape."

"Hot love, oldster," The Ant said.

"How much illegal loot I need to cough up?"

"I reckon £60,000," Millie said.

"Umm? You're not making Sgt. Pepper's here—("Whassat?" asked The Ant)—this is a lo-fi noise record in the fine basement rock tradition. You write a set list. You turn up the amps and plug in the instruments. You claw the fretboards raw. You find a record label to produce pieces of plastic to entice the children. Done."

"Dezza, you recall . . .*Yes Please!*? In the 1990s, Shaun Ryder took his band to Barbados to record one of the seminal albums of the decade," F-F said.

"Ah, the one that bankrupted Factory Records? The one where Ryder tippled a yachtload of crack cocaine instead of recording timeless Madchester anthems? Peter, I'm not paying you to take a bag of drugs."

"Might help," Derek's inner critic said.

"Cool jewels and aprons. We'll work with whatever sum is offered. We need flights and hotels refunded as well."

"Of course."

"I found this cadet Vicente Azorin. He produced the crossover EP of the mariachi threesome The Snapped Apostrophe."

The exchange continued. The mental train of Derek had passed through Revolution Town to Sunkist Square, via Caught & Fucked Zone and Quiverville, and was now pulling into Resignationland with the chunter-screech of a half-dead British Rail arriving in Inverness. The impulse—as networks of sweat leaved and interleaved in the creases of his fattish man's body, as Millie reinvented herself as "the stillborn foetus of Nick Cave and Su Pollard", as The Ant compared his drumming moves to Phil Collins at his most splenetic—the impulse to take to the hills and crouch for twelve thousand hours in a Moorish peasant village, living on twigs and pluck until the consensus formed that he'd hurled himself into the Atlantic long ago, his ribcage a cottage for a retiring pufferfish—was strong. To fake-perish in the brine was not the ending he wanted for his otherwise adequate existence.

In Resignationland, he saw himself in a modest cell in a minimum-security prison, mingling with the flotsam of the lowlands. He spent his mornings tutoring teenagers on literature and politics, convincing them that a future on the straight was possible, because ____. He spent his afternoons hosting groups with reoffenders, listening to their tales of perpetual hump from bosses, colleagues, and politicians, coaxing them into a trusting relationship with society, using ____. There he stood in an off-white room with plastic chairs, soliciting chuckles from the assembled. "I was a politician and I can say, without hesitation, all politicians are cunts." The group would whoop and cheer and warm to his plain-spoken truth of ____. Then he'd explain that politics was essential to stop the supercunts from winning. "____ __ __ ____," he'd lecture. The room would explode with hope.

Looking at Millie from this prism of sane, he had a vicious urge to escape being in her presence, and the presence of her amusical bandmates, and to pretend that the whole association with her was a brain error on a par with Hugh Grant and Divine Brown, and to never have a sexual impulse ever again.

"I have an idea. I have £10,000 in my retirement fund spare. I'm sure that would cover the production of a crisp and professional series of noises on disc," he offered. "I can't use the stolen loot, Quiver said."

Having never in their lives imagined sums in the five figures, Forerunner Hammer Precision were in no position to hardball. Even Millie, with her proposed sum 500% larger, met the news with a throatful of hoot. She tended to shrink in the presence of her mates, like a groupie limp in the shadow of Jagger/Richards. This was a farewell fund. A fuckoffforever fund. There was an implicit understanding that this is what it was, the first implicit understanding that had ever taken place between himself and Millie, the one understanding reached at last: that they should never have met in the first place.

❂

Now, a man wobbling in an urban swelter, weaving past senior señors with skin satchelled brown and feet unimpressed at the non-toeless sandal. Now, a man wobbling past two roseate nubiles in suede sling-backs sipping toreadors in the Casa del Slurp, a hipster-brewed house of beverage. Now, a man wobbling toward the wall where a multimillionaire novelist had been whomped hours prior, his slavers long baked into the scorched beachfront stone. Now, a man resting his pins on the flat sand watching the thin line of intersection between the sky and the sea known as the horizon. Now, a man freeing himself from the shackles of shirt, trews, socks, and boxers wading naked into the cool brine. *Ah, Derek! You were such a cherub-cheeked little lovely, what happened?* Charles Kennedy, the Greatest Prime Minister There Never Was, at last making an appearance at the cerebral stump. *Remember when we went sledding up Lochaber in our salmon-pink anoraks and in the bar after talked historical materialism as a prelude to neoclassical microeconomics?* Now, a man floating recumbent farther and farther from shore, skin sautéed like a sirloin on medium sizz. *The problem was, Derek, we were unequipped for a world of slogans, soundbites, and talking points. We were men of the Enlightenment—Adam Smiths in a world of George Osbournes. There was no place for two rogue scholars in a media landscape of tweets and squits. Great Men & Women are cursed to turn their backs on the prevailing wind and walk into a sharknado of unfashionable beliefs, most of which are proven in time to be correct. There isn't a wall tough enough to prevent us smashing through our weary heads in frustration! Ah well. We'll always have Lochaber!* Now, a man carried along on the tame undulations of the sea, paunch to the heavens, toes to the shore, placing himself at the brine's disposal. *You're still here, Derek. I loosed life's leash with single malt and three decades of no Liberal Democrats in office. Now, tempting as a slow drift into oceanic oblivion might seem, there are better options than offering your carcass up as piranha food. That one earlier, about prisoners. That's better than perishing barearse naikit in a Spanish port. Remember what I said that evening at the Gala for Kazakhs Against Library Closures: "It takes a lot to laugh, it takes a train to move Nicholas Soames from his seat at close of PMQs."* Now, a man reborn. Now, a man flipping himself forward and thrusting his arms in a swimming motion thwackthwackthwacking the water with the weight of an amateur swimmer swimming swimmer-ishly several furloughs before the shore, swimmerlike. Now, a man treading water and recalibrating the swim to a front crawl more ap-propriate to his age bracket. Now, a man unsure if he can avert an accidental drowning as the brine's wet vibes invite themselves into his gasping mouth. *Steady, Derek! Drowning en route to an epiphanic rebirth is not a cool death.* Now, a man with the shore in sight, with the mea-sured pace to make a slow, undrowned return to the abandoned pants. *That's the stuff, old friend. Now, trousers on, chin up, and head to the bar.* Now, a man cupping his genitals. Now, a man shorebound, stepping wet-skinned into his clothes, no heed paid to the onlookers concerned at the naked oddness in their midsts. A man, back from what might be perceived as some form of brink—a brink in the drink, a blink of brink in the drink. *Brinksmanship!*

In the hotel restaurant, a patched Quiver sat with a flue of spritzer, perusing The Telegraph on his tablet with the poise of a man un-punched. Beside him a lump of beef in man form sat with a fluvium of beer, unpleased in a Tahitian shirt, swooping the scene from behind Miami Vice sunglasses. The familiar habit among poseur aristos—to feign deafness upon someone's approach (signalling to the guest their appearance is not significant enough to merit interruption)—was a trademark of Quiver's, with frequent one-minute pauses between an arrival and an acknowledgement of that arrival. The writer David Grifton once fainted while awaiting the beckoning paw, a fall noticed by Quiver a moment after the ambulance crew arrived. Derek owed Quiver no further deference, having conceded to the clink, and moved straight toward the table, at which point the stranger magicked a switchblade from thin air.

"Now now, Mateo," Quiver said, seeking the wit in a Rod Liddle clause. "This is Derek Haffman. Derek, meet Mateo Carreras."

Derek met Mateo Carreras.

"*Misericordia de mí!* Mateo is a hired driver and personal guard for this excursion. I chose him for his range of colourful stabbing implements. He will not be an accompaniment on our return to the Land of Mud and Hooligans. Alas, he was on a smoking break earlier when the Haffman fist collided with the Quiver cheek. Now, I have twisted the arms of a charming travel agent—an exquisite bronzed Helen with toned biceps and firm calves, the kind of calves from which one likes to snort a line of caviar!—and managed to squeeze you on to the next flight to Heathrow with me. I am sad to report that Camilla will not be airing with us. She has elected to remain in this mercurial domain and peruse the rockfaces. I understand that a crevasse has opened between you. The sort of marital crevasse one cannot vaunt with a leap of loving words and two-week trips to a Finnish ice hotel to view the aurora borea."

"Correct. She made the right decision for a woman of her stature and steamrollered me flat. I'm a 2D man in the emotional asphalt," Derek said.

"Never mind. I never had that issue with Sally, of course. When I was banged up she wrote me long erotic letters burning with longing. That woman has never cuckolded me in her life. Her quim has remained a fortress into which the right honourable member Baron Quiver of Somewhere-in-Hereford has sole access. Compare her to Nigel Tincock's missus, Gladys. She was taking it perpendicularly from all those PPE virgins straight from Oxford while her husband was balding on the campaign trail. All those socialist upstarts are undone by loose wives. Aneurin Bevan's missus practically rented her pussy for hire while her husband was busy healing the sick like some chubby Christ."

There was no responding to this.

"Shut up, crook," he responded not.

Mateo removed a *muela* and a handkerchief from his pocket, breathing on the blade and polishing the cold metal killing thing with rapt attention.

"Is he actually planning to stab me?" Derek asked.

"No, I'm sure he won't. He's an artist taking care of his materials. It says on the website that Mateo is a Michelangelo of stabbing."

"What website?"

"Right. I think we'd better heave-ho. Mateo, gracias por tus servicios. Te he dado 90 euros de propina. Adios amigo. I expect you have little of import at the hotel, Derek, so let's make our way to the airport. I appreciate your patience, and that I have spoiled your holiday. But it was essential. I once spoiled Lady Thatcher's trip to Tia Juana in 1986."

"How?"

"Oh, I just turned up."

So, farewell Phoenician paradise! Hello, hired car. Hello, loud Valencian driver also named Mateo. Hello, the stirring strummerie of Flamenco FM. *Psst, old man!* Hello, the reassuring Quiver hand on the knee. *Psst, it's me, your sixteen-year-old self.* Hello, that inappropriate thigh squeeze. *You know that classic lifestyle magazine question, what advice would you give to your sixteen-year-old self?* Hello, the hand resting on the knee, insisting on resting. *I think the opposite applies in this case. What advice would your sixteen-year-old self give to your fifty-four-year-old self?* Hello, Quiver's insistence the driver put on The Best of Minnie Ripperton. *It's not so much advice, more constructive abuse. You total badhead. You utter dollop of codswallop. You let these people win. You let the chEATers, the h8rs, the obnoxoids triumph. You know that John Stuart Mill quote, 'Bad men need nothing more to compass their ends, than that good men should lounge on the backbenches charting the progress of their receding hairlines and plotting schemes to have sex with unattractive twiglets half their age?' That's you, that is. You could have leapt into the bear pit, shirt off and pectorals aflex, and wrestled to the death these roaring cougars, scratching the veneer of competence from their faces, making them bleed into their velour and run blubbing into nanny's arms. You chose not to. You preferred to become a thumbtwiddling Bartlebum, hanging like a sack of tears in the lobby, waiting for someone to fold you into a cupboard of biscuits.* Hello, the five octaves of Minnie, terrorising all dogs in a ten-mile radius. *We made a choice at sixteen Derek never to sleepwalk into cliché, to put truth and courage at the forefront of our political mission. We made a promise that whenever a pompous, pretentious twit wambled into our ward, we would skewer them in the nipples without pause, and smear their blood across the walls of power, let them know that cunts with cant cannot succeed in our fair and honest world. But no. You had to put your penis before the nation. The adventures of Little Derek were far more important than saving millions of people from poverty, misery, and frustration. You chose to escape your failures as a minister through that old perennial, poking your pecksniff into an unsolicited flange. You even failed at that. You have become all that we hated at sixteen. So my advice? Kill yourself. You complete shitshower of shit, showering shit on our past forever.* Hello, the slow caress of the left testicle with the Quiver index, rolling the ball around the sac in a keen rhythm.

"The fuck are you doing?" Derek asked.

"Woah! The Scotch kraken awakes! Relax, fellow. I'm exploring that prodigious sac of yours. I know that beneath their wee sporrans the Scotch have pulsing sacs brimming with spunk."

Quiver explored the sac entire, invading each testis with the slow clamp of a tarantula traversing an orange.

"Please stop," he said.

"I think we can come to an arrangement here."

"You want to fondle my balls in exchange for letting me free? Then fondle away, sir."

"Not quite. Although for now, I would like to rest my hand in this fertile environs, if you don't mind."

"You know what, rest away," Derek said. He had already punched him. There wasn't much point in a second punching.

This being the case, Derek let Quiver use his hand to assist a trouser unzipping. Quiver used his victim's finger to unzip his own trousers and willed Derek's hand into the pant region. He worked Derek's fingers around the meat package, running his index along the shaft while humming 'Inside My Love', until the penis reached a semi-rigid state, at which point the pants were lowered, revealing the might of the Quivercock.

"Look at that, Derek," Quiver said. "That is 18.92cm of man. That is the sort of pinnacle that makes lesser men crumble. I want you to spend ten minutes basking in the splendour of this rock-hard master-piece."

He stared at the erect cock for ten minutes.

"I can remain hard for up to nine hours through sheer willpower."

He then willed his cock soft. Derek watched the member flop left and wilt into the pubic shrubbery of his pants.

"Now," Quiver said, "I need a naplet. More later."

Derek too entered slumber.

There, a man with features crouching in a favela watched as an eruption took place across the fronds, that eruption a seeming vol-cano that was not, that was in fact the Quivercock exploding into the Southamerican(?) upwards, shooting a motherearthlode of sper-mic consequence towards the scuttling serfpeople below, among them Derek's face, running fast-legged from the spermagma coming to-wards, each thick strand of hot silver fizz containing a mini-Jeth rac-ing to the nearest available ovum. Two hundred ova were caught in the flow, their owners ballooning up soon with the children of The Quiver, flowing along the current and coming to a rest on an island where the women birthed two hundred pairs of octets, taking the total of mini-Jeths up to 1600, sprouting into tots, toddlers, and teens in the blink of a why, soon prancing the island in stolen slacks seeking a new land to conquer.

Next, something else, now. In a boudoir, Quiver was licking the arsehole of Camilla, tonguing that popular orifice for twelve hours then inserting his penis inside, making her moan like wtf. Camilla made a menagerie of screeching noises, impersonating a banshee in oestrus as the rod penetrated her love caverns more and again more times. (The clumsy erotic artistry of dreams is not something for which we can be held responsible, yet we should feel ashamed). The bedroom wall raised itself to reveal most of the people who had cursed or hated Derek (like Simon McHuff who once burst a bag of Quavers over his head) over the years. "He's pure fucking your missus," said Toby Tynyatov, the one who once squeezed lemon rind into his pepper. Camilla emitted a shriek so loud as she came that the assembled plugged their ears. Her body split in two, word-torrents pouring from the two severed parts, all the texts and emails and letters from 1981 to 2016 that had been sent to him calling him a diseased potato.

(A miscellaneous squiggle took over).

"Now, listen here," said Quiver on awake, "when we arrive in Edinburgh, I've arranged for us to have a rendezvous with that MSP whose credit you burglarised. Magnus McScotchface, or whatever. No spoilers, however, I have made a surprise arrangement, in contra to what I said earlier about prison and you."

"What?"

"You want me to repeat the whole paragraph?"

"What surprise?"

"No absolution is coming. I am not merciful. As you know, lowering men is a pastime of mine. I once hate-texted an investment banker onto the streets. I used to walk past him outside Waitrose and took pleasure in dropping chocolate coins into his cup of grot. There really is nothing more satisfying than holding one's chin aloft as one passes a muck-strewn nemesis shivering atop his haversack. The surprise that's coming is not something that calls for the skipping rope or a fanfaronade of vuvuzelas."

"I'll guess. You've arranged for a surgeon to shear one arsecheek so I sit lopsided for my remaining days?"

"No. But noted for future."

"You've signed me up to a reality show where I have to eat increasingly toxic strands of seaweed from various chemical spill hotspots?"

"No. But noted for."

"You've adopted me ten diarrhoeic dogs with a penchant for human flesh and I must never, ever sell them or remove them from my presence?"

"No. But noted."

"You've accused me of historic sex crimes, meaning my Google results will forever be linked to non-existent historic rapey things?"

"No. Noted."

"You've arranged for a private flogging service to flog me on the hour, every hour, until I expire at a 69° angle?"

"Nonoted."

"You've knitted me a suit from sponges and a bubble crown that I must wear to parliament?"

"No . . . ted."

"You've pencilled me in with a tattooist who will render your smiling face on my back?"

"No."

"You've arranged for me to spend five seconds in a room with Michael Gove."

"God no. I would never inflict that torment on anyone. Derek, once we have a chat with this chap from whom the funds were stolen, and you have made your apologies, the future steps hence will be discussed. For the moment, I'd like to keep you in suspense, bobbing along in a bathysphere of terrible possibility."

An unread first ed. of *The Twelve Deadly Sins*, Quiver's sixteenth novel, was waved D-wards by the author for reading on the flight to Heathrow. Once the two had boarded the plane, Quiver in business class, Derek not, the novel, with its chunderous cover of two people benched before the Statue of Liberty, a Trump-orange sunset warming OAP cockles, was opened. It was important for Derek to remember that Quiver, however adept at ruining men for ad hominem, had no talent as a writer, and that however lithe his bank account might seem in comparison, he would never compose sentences as flat as *The prison door had creaked open, but not before the officer had puffed another plume of smoke that made Larry cough.* (© JETHRO QUIVER, 2012, MACMILLAN). He took a moment to unpick the artlessness of that sentence—the sheer heart-curdling boredom of a door creaking open (by itself), round the wrong side of a carbon-14 pulp cliché (the plume of smoke, which seven paragraphs earlier was a cloud of smoke, three paragraphs earlier was *another* plume of smoke (where the first plume at?)). Putting aside the sheer insult of repeating the phrase *another plume of smoke* twice within the space of three paragraphs—in fact, not putting that aside, it was important to pause on the cheek that a novelist who had shifted millions and was sold as a consummate talespinner of international superselling proportions was allowed to publish a novel where the same phrase was repeated *verbatim three paragraphs apart* while writers the length and breadth of the planet were flogged for not slotting their impeccably-worded masterpieces into the correct marketing metric—but, putting that aside, the clumsiness of that *but not before*, the clodhopping awkwardness of that past tense usage, that *had puffed*, that *that made Larry cough* (the sheer belch of rubbishness with which to close a sentence—a man named Larry, coughing at another plume of smoke, blown from the lips of a character that had long expired its freshness in the late 1930s!!!)—made the first page of that novel one of the most wretched reading experiences of Derek's life. And the plane was still taxiing.

It became apparent, as the sentences of spine-shuddering mediocrity, the clauses of so-what shoddiness, came one after t'other (*Larry crumpled on to a bed that was mounted to the wall* (© JQ 2012, M)), that Quiver was not merely the worst writer to have achieved undeserved riches and success, he was trolling the audience with his turds of words (*a plate of food that the Salvation Army wouldn't have considered offering a stinking tramp* (!!!!!!!) (© JQ 2012, M)), he was spending no time improving these first-draft brain-plops because he knew his readers weren't there for the literary wow (*The enormous cell door didn't creak open until ten minutes past four* (© JQ 2012, M)), but for the gripping story, the robust ballast of genre . . . no, there wasn't even that. Why *were* his readers there?

"Why?" Derek said to the sidelook of a black man.

Unable to continue, he backed to the page of praise, where someone in the *Sunday Times* had called Quiver "Henry James's heir". A quick search revealed that the reviewer Pete Deneton had used that phrase as a sarcastic preface to a brutal takedown of his earlier stinker *True Accounts* and that a slick editor had snipped that line to Quiver's advantage. The other blurbs emphasised the fact that Quiver was a *storyteller* ("Nobel Prize for storytelling, Quiver would win", "greatest storyteller of our age"), in other words, a hack capable of stitching various plots together with no need for that pretentious "literary" nonsense, a man of the people with the perfect blend of A-to-B plotting where tough words or narrative concepts were kept from the plebs while their pockets were plundered at £18.99 a pop. In Alan Gassie's words: "Quiver has the unusual gift denied to many who think themselves more serious novelists. He can tell a story." (Gassie, the same man who fellated Ian Rankin in *The Telegraph* with a fawning attempt to elevate formulaic crime fiction to Dostoevskian heights.)

The flight to Heathrow landed. The flight to Edinburgh began.

In between, Quiver said:

"I've had words with the detectives. Naturally, they are raving admirers of the Cliff Top Chronicles. When we return to the capital, there will be no police flag on your account. You will transfer the millions to this account." He handed D a scrap of paper.

The plane screeched on Scottish soil.

"Whose account is this?" Derek asked.

"I texted David Trance on the first plane. After we've been to the bank, he has agreed to meet us in Robertson's Bar for a conversation on the next steps and to accept the sincere apology that I presume you have been preparing."

"I—" He had been staring at the bald spot of a blonde marketer who had ordered two coffees, taking three minutes to locate the correct change for each order, then slurping the coffees in between terrorising a stranger with small talk on the finer points of SEO spamdexing with scrapers and metatag stuffing. "I prepared nothing. I have no explanation either. I suppose I'll have to claim it was a moment of madness."

"A moment of well-orchestrated madness that had been in preparation for two months? You'll have to offer Mr. Trance something more than that. Perhaps invent something about bungs to the Duke of Buccleuch to build the world's biggest brothel in Langholm. I once tried to persuade Jack McConnell to create an exclusive whorehouse on the isle of Eigg. A sexual utopia populated by a rolling cast of girls in loincloths strewn across the barren Hebridean hills, to be tamed and shagged at the visitor's whim. The old bore thought that idea was unfair to the handful of residents living there with their eco-farms and camping pods."

"I'll use that, then."

Edinburgh's incontinent skies wept the contents of their cloud-nappies, a cool trickle tickling Derek's head at the cab rank as Quiver hogged the umbrella he had pinched at the baggage carousel. There was no warm hum of homecoming forthcoming in Derek's shoes. This return had a Green Mile vibe, an oversize man blubbing as his organs are fried to misfire. The time-worn Georgian facades no longer pumped his heart with squee. The industrious thrum of Burghers busy-beeing along the streets and alleys was no more a source of patriotic fuzz. There was nothing now except Quiver, that prick Quiver, with his lasso around Derek's weirdly thick neck, roping him into whatever scheme awaited in the next few paragraphs.

Santander-bound, the men in the cab were bound for Santander, the same branch of Santander as earlier, so Quiver knew.

"How'd—"

"Spoke to the detective, Derek. Keep up."

"Yes."

"So transfer the three mil to this account please."

No queue fatigue this time. The bank manager who had soiled himself in collusion with Derek met him at the door.

"Mr. Haffman!" he leapt, Uriah-like[2], ushering him into the back-room to the same chair where Derek had soiled himself. "I have had quite the 72 hours. I was taken to this little cell. I was so spooked I crumpled on to a bed that was mounted to the wall. This detective entered, puffing on a menthol, making the first in a series of plumes of smoke. He told me that I was in the merde, that I was up to me triple-chin in sweetcorny merde, that I was sinking in a lagoon of merde and soon to perish in that lagoon of merde. The prison door creaked open, but not before the detective had puffed another plume of smoke that made me cough!"

"What's your name?" Derek asked.

"Harold."

"Hmm."

"Later I had a plate of food brought to me. Well. What can I say, Derek, about that plate of food? It was food the Salvation Army wouldn't even consider offering a . . . well, a cash-strapped vagrant. Horrible!"

"Then . . . ?"

"Yes, I was released without warning. At home, I received a phone call from J. Quiver Esq, informing me that I was free from criminal charges if I directed the £75,000 bung into his account. Now, I believe you have some further funds you'd like me to deposit?"

"I see. You'll need to transfer the three million into the same account."

"Of course. Please key in your codes. You know, I was on the toilet for hours that afternoon. I usually have a smooth, unbothersome evacuation after Sugar Puffs around 7.30 in the AM. But I was pooing all through the day, all through the night, I never knew that a person could produce so much poo. I wondered to myself while pooing whether some poos are created through fear. You know, whether fear manufactures excess poo from weird glands and tissues. I wondered if that was a thing. Then I found this article on Quora.com explaining how fear stops your body from absorbing nutrients and can lead to diarrhoea. I suffered from constipation through nerves, I had problems parsing a reasonable amount of excreta per day. So for a week, I leapt into scenarios that caused me sheer poo-stirring terrorishness. For example, I suffered from vertigo, so I forced myself on one of those ziplines across the river. The mere thought of being strapped to a zipline with nothing cept a thin rope and harness to save me from splat was enough to loosen the old sphincters. Whenever I struggled to evacuate, I would walk towards bridges and hover over the edge, then run to the nearest bush or puddle to make with the doodoo. Then a problem arose. Knowing I would never perform these terrifying acts, that mere proximal contemplation was enough, I stopped fearing them so much. I found that I had to make myself zipline across the river, or bungee off an escarpment for the real fear experience. Then a second problem arose. I acquired a taste for dangerous activities, and the fears I had previous soon vanished. But there's a smile at the end. I no longer had the constipation caused by nerves, as I had no nerves. So as I said, the last 72 days have been quite the thing. The best 72 of my life, in fact. In the words of English singer Dido, I want to thank you."

"No need. Bye," Derek said.

"Now," Quiver in cab said, "here are some facts on this David Trance. He's the MSP for Caulderkirky or wherever, he has two dogs, he's interested in climate change. Now, the vitals. He once roadied for the Leeds post-punk band Delta 5 and snogged Ros Allen in a wood, the most exciting sexual moment of his life. He lost a toe while working as a Sherpa in the Cairngorms for tourists keen to explore the snow-peaked caps of that range of tall bits. His favourite soup is oxtail and his most treasured possession is a KLF keyring."

"So we've established he's a insultingly tedious man."

"Indeed. I mean there's something so uuuuuggghhhh about these wee Scotch hem-hee-pees, with their local communities and fondness for dogs and posing humble wee questions on climate change and waving their KLF keyrings around. Lords of their boroughs. Nonentities in Westminster. No ambitions apart from representing their constituents. People want scandal. People want characters. Trance should spend the entire budget on platinum-plating his castle and bulldozing all the bus links and leisure centres."

"Precisely, Jethro! No transport for the peasants! On their bikes! If they want to work, they should walk nine miles in hail, rain, or snow. No freeloaders in this world. And what is your vision for Scotland, exactly?"

"Personally, I think the jocks should exist to serve the English. We should all have a wee jock serf to shine our shoes, to shag the arse off on occasion. It was a mistake to ever treat them as equals. I'd love to see fields of strapping jocks on our English estate, doffing their bunnets to their masters. One England, from Land's End to John O'Groats."

"Thought so."

The pub reared up on its haunches, Quiver's arrival sending its twat-detector into overdrive. Heads swivelled to the table where the twat decamped. Signals were sent conveying a message along the lines of "start something and we'll holepunch your balls", a signal Derek picked up through a vast experience of walking into Scottish pubs, a signal Quiver would never detect until the perforations were secure in his sac.

There are four sorts of pubs in Ecosse. The first are snub-pubs where tourists and visitors are free to partake of overpriced lagers and wines, being fleeced in return for an atmosphere free from menace. The second are the hipster pubs frequented by students, artists and poseurs too spooked to enter the bruiser-boozers. These are often hate-bombed by marauding armies of ersatz Begbies, slotting themselves between tables, forcing the scarfed-up bourgeois into awkward retreat. The third are the authentic pubs, the mix of locals, yokels, and chain-smokers, where the working-classes commingle in a loving pool of cheap booze, loud karaoke, and groggy kinship. The fourth are the hellcaves, the above-mentioned bruiser-boozers, the sorts of sordid oubliettes where one might be welcomed with a roundhouse kick to the tits, where frequent lock-ins take place until fights are resolved with bare-knuckle brawls to the death. The places where those who wander in accidentally end up serving croquettes to an obese ganglord in a kimono until a hard winter finishes them off.

David Trance arrived in civvies, striding over to the table in a sad combo of cords and plaid. Hands were shaken and liquids were ordered and seats were taken and pleasantries were skipped when David asked: "Where's the fucking loot?"

"Before we," Quiver started, "move to that topic, I have to comment on those sartorial choices. You realise that meeting me in brown cords and mauve-heavy plaid shirt is a mistake?"

"What?"

"I'm pointing out that for me to see you as a serious man, you have already reduced yourself in my eyes to the role of an unserious clown."

"Fuck off, slack-thief."

"Careful, Trance. Let's not foot off in venom. Normally, I would request that you returned home and reconsidered your wardrobe cap-a-pie. But as we're in a unique situation I suppose we can let it pass."

"The loot, Quiver. Hand it over."

"Now, Derek here has something he would like to tell you."

Derek stiffened. He looked to the pint of Magners then to the cork panelling then to a drowned bluebottle.

"Yes, David. I—"

No words came.

To help coax an apologetic whimper from Derek's beer-blessed lips, the three took a stroll along Princes (sic) Street Gardens. Cutting a rum triplicate in the shadow of Walter Scott, the two Scots trailed Jethro like tuckered cubs as he descended to the lowest tier of the exhaustingly storied communal fave. The unspeaking trio strolled past sad interns on benches, nibbling their Meal Deals and skimming their Booker-winners; students sprawled on lawns for the sole purpose of being seen to be students sprawled on lawns; pram-pushing Muslimoms uncoddled into the covens of white liberal moms exchanging stretchmark-flattening hints and tips at the kiddie corner; and time-rich tourists, reaching peak nark at the unfair elevations in this stunning schlepp of a capital. Having swished their trews in the damp waft of the autumn air and clomped their leathers on the oft-buffed concrete paths and weaved their torsos around the onrush of human life, the time had come for Derek to expectorate a soz in David's lug.

"Well?" Quiver said. The castle rose from his ploughed brow, a tremendous loom of crag dwarfing the rotten specimen of man that he was. *This is our land*, the castle said. *To hell with this half-dead Sassenach.*

"Yes," Derek said. "Jethro Quiver is a cunt. He's always been a cunt and will be remembered as a suit-stealing cunt-dabedoozie-cunt until the realm of cunts comes to an end. You might say, David, he's the cunt's cunt's cunt's cunt."

David snorted mirth from his left nostril. Mirth snorted from the nasal area in mucoid blobs, bacterising the crud out of Quiver's taupe tie. "Too right, pal. Too right!" he said, folding himself to help the humour flee his other orifices in the speediest possible time, hee-hees and ho-hos in fluid motion from chest to chin. For a semisec it seemed that D&D might pal up like a pair of legends and pound the pavements in a collegiate swagger, bar-hopping and babe-hopping with the brio of pubertal lads making their debuts, solving the problems of democracy with the proposal of a minimum IQ for voting and a thorough mental scrubbing by a therapist to clear the newsprint propaganda from voters' minds. The madness of requiring seven years intense study to practice law, when utter buffoons could vote for the shaping of the whole country without any basic fitness tests, was madness++. Time to raise the bar. These, and other ideas in the category of "democratic eugenics", would bring the two men closer, cementing a union of minds on a par with Hitchens & Fry, or Chomsky & Baldwin. But—ha ha ha! No.

That man who had snorted mirth in a promising manner moments thence, creating the hope as outlined above, ceased the laughter and brought himself face-to-neck (Mr. Trance was a short man) with Derek. "Right. Fun's over. Fuck's the wonga, prick?" he asked with the spike of a rather irked pimp.

"In Quiver's account," he squeaked.

"What?"

"I can verify, David," Quiver said, swatting a midge. "The words that Derek said a second ago were in fact words that he uttered. I asked him to transfer the funds to me for safekeeping."

"Safekeeping? I wouldn't trust you with a wonky drachma."

"Now, I think we should take a moment to think on Derek's punishment," Quiver said, circling Poirotishly. "In 1996, an assistant of mine leaked a tale to the press involving me, Dickie Branson, and the illegal export of twelve thousand uilleann pipes that proved semi-correct at worst. As punishment I had that chap write one of the mid-nineties novels (the reviews were rapturous!), and serve me a frosted croissant each morning and an iced latte with a light shaving of coconut until I told him to stop. At one point, he was working in Woking and had to make a nineteen-mile commute to me and another back to Woking. When he snapped and stropped the iced latte in a bin, I stripped him of his assets and future. He moved to Kyoto and works in a low-level administrative post in the Yakuza. These people always take up martial arts or sign up to murderous mafia organisations after our lawsuits, I've had to beef up the security. Noticed one of them impaled on the barbed wire at the Mallorca manor the other week."

"Quiver, why've you—" David sputtered. "Fuck's the cash?"

"Oh, Trance! You Scotch always hugging funds to your bosom. Relax, ma wee skinflint beastie! If we come to an arrangement over Decca here, the cash will be returned this afternoon (with a finders' fee, of course). Now—"

"Finders' fee? Fuck're—"

"Around £100,000 seems reasonable."

Trance bent his bowling-bowl noggin toward Quiver's chin and bullrammed him to the grass with a flare of catarrh. The two men creaked a while, fist-slapped each other's visible skin, and made wailing noises, until Trance manoeuvred himself atop Quiver, pounding on the old man's chest as he wailed "I WILL RUIN YOU! RUIN YOU!" to the amusement of the crowd recording the incident on their Androids.

"Hit him!" an old man recommended.

"Pound his face to mush!" another posited.

"Kill them all!" a third suggested.

These entreaties shook David from the mind-blindness of murderous assault. Freed Quiver, back on two pins, suit corrected, stood smiling. Yes, that had been intentional. That short scuffle had cost him one hundred thousand Scottish pounds.

"It seemed reasonable then," Jethro said. "Now, £500,000 seems reasonable. The video evidence about to Go Live on TikTok will testify to the reasonableness of this new sum. Having cleared up this matter, back to Decca's penance."

"You—"

"David, stop," Derek stopped. "This is the moment, when the bones have been stripped from your body, that you must collapse in a gelatine flop, and allow The Quiver to manipulate your boneless husk with the black magic of a puppeteer, until the moment you can cut yourself loose, crawl your way to safety, and plot your return to the land of vertebrates."

"One correction: the moment I allow you to cut yourself loose," Quiver corrected.

"What's Derek's punishment, then?" David asked, clasping his punching hand hard as it twitched and spasmed.

That question marked the end of fictional D&D friendship scenarios, like the one twenty-one paragraphs ago.

"In 1999, Michael Howard worked underneath me for a month. When I use that word 'underneath', I am using that word in the literal sense of the word 'underneath'. He was redeeming himself for an off-colour remark on Sally's virginity, which I had taken in orchestral fashion in the sixties. I used him as a footstool while writing the latest and had him perform various tasks of a menial nature. I miss the satisfaction of having a minion, a sort of medieval serf who I can poke around and make shimmy at will. So, in short, we should take Derek as our personal slave and share him between us across the year."

"Ooommm—" (Derek).

"How nice to have a wee imp in short-shorts serve us a cool flagon of framboise from a tray balanced on his upturned bottom? A little slap on the arse and away with you, Baldrick! Or to have our nasal hairs plucked with surgical precision each morning to keep ourselves in peak erotic condition for our shag-hags?"

"Hmm. I suppose," David said. "I have a chimney, hasn't been scrubbed clean for aeons. I have cobwebs in the old attic that are antiques."

"Yes, that's the idea. Perhaps Derek could scrub the flues clean with a toothbrush while dressed as a cheerleader? Remove the cobwebs with his teeth alone, while handcuffed and lubed up in chilli oil? Get creative!"

"Ha. Or we could paint him blue like an ageing Smurf, pop on a little chef's hat and make him serve us cuttlefish from the East China Sea?"

"Yes! Here's one. Henry VIII had a personal bottom-wiper, known as the Groom of the Stool. We could have Derek perform that function, except rather than quilted loo paper, we use Derek's own cash. Then we make him deposit our poop-stained notes in the local bank!"

"That's disgusting," David said.

"Hmm. All right. I might have got carried away, it's these Omega-3 capsules I'm on. How about I have him kitted out like a coolie, pulling me in a rickshaw the length and breadth of Somerset's hills. The look on the faces of the fell-walkers as I appear o'er the brow of Barrow Mump smoking a cheroot, bellowing 'faster!' at the sweltering sod pulling me to the peak. I can't think of anything funnier!"

"I've always liked assigning staff pointless tasks. There's something existentially hooty at making an intern type out the Magna Carta in Comic Sans or sending a volunteer up Beveridge Park to serve writs to the doggers."

"David, my new friend. We understand each other."

"First off," Derek said, listening to their lunacy with cool, "I will not wipe either of your arses. I will not pull either of you up a Somerset hill on a rickshaw. I will not eat your cobwebs dressed as a greased gimp.

There are certain tasks where the threat of prison is no longer a scare. Those tasks involve either of your frontal or rectal caverns."

"Quite right, Decca. You're still a man. You still have the right to an alternative. I would remind you that I can probably secure a conviction for over twenty years. You have to consider whether a task that is momentarily unpleasant is better than rotting in a cell for the rest of your life. That's your call to make."

Derek stared at Quiver, a cowed child in Satan's shadow.

"Yeah sure."

"Don't sound too crushed. You'll be working in our homes. I have beautiful properties, I'm sure David has a tolerable abode, too."

"I'm not sure I want him in my home," David said.

"Be nice. Now, we should equip Derek with a uniform. When I was in the nick, I loved the guards in their prison blues. The deference shown to me as servants of Our Madge was beautiful. Made me miss the old bitch. Let's hit the High Street!"

Sartorial suggestions ranged from the classic bellhop look (a fez askew above the Butlins-red smock) to Bavarian minimalism (thigh-high shorties and frilled shirt two sizes too small) to hick farmer (soiled string vest and cords belted with twine) to Uma Thurman circa *Kill Bill* (lemon-yellow leather catsuit) to unkempt village priest (all-black with off-brown dog collar), as the three browsed the shops on Princes (sic) Street. The Quiver was keen on a nickname, such as The Balding Muzhik (in reference to Derek's Russian monobrow and receding hairline and reduced status), or Captain Crumble (a dig at the ease with which Quiver broke him), or Wee Willy Worker (an alliterative fancy with no particular relevance). "It's bad enough we're using him as our personal slave, we don't need to humiliate him further," David said, a ping of conscience pinging in his consciousness. The Quiver made a boohoo moue.

Gaining access to Quiver's home intrigued Derek. The possibilities of exercising small revenges, whether masturbating into vodkas, urinating on his clothes, or working excrement into Nutella sandwiches, were numerous. If the menial tasks had some form of fightback attached the ordeal might be more tolerable.

"I'll try to behave," Quiver said. "I have this powerful image of Derek on all fours, licking the dog bowl clean while Sally robustly sodomises him with a four-pronged dildo. Reminds me of our honeymoon."

In the Back-to-School aisle of Marks & Spencer, David picked out a vintage uniform for Derek to wear.

"We could have our own crest stitched onto the blazer," he suggested.

"Capital notion. Perhaps a peasant tilling a field with the motto *opus paulo servus*. Or a whimpering dog licking the boot of his master with the motto *canis dominum suum serves*. Something to put the slave firmly in his place, cowering in fear of the whip-wielding lord of the manor."

The more Quiver spoke, the larger the threat of sexual violence loomed.

"I suppose if we can't make him wear a little girls' uniform and plait his hair, this is the second best. Everything will be three sizes too small, of course."

"Of course," Derek muttered.

"I wonder if we should introduce a punishment for the slave speaking when not spoken to?" Quiver asked, putting the final touches on D's submission.

"Perhaps."

"All right. Derek, I will refer to you as The Balding Muzhik from henceon. I might abbreviate this to TBM, or Here, Muzhik! If you wish to speak, raise your left hand until we acknowledge you, at which point we will signal with a single nod that verbal intercourse is permitted. If you speak without approval, we reserve the right to spank you on your little bottie until the cheeks are raw. You understand?"

Derek raised his left hand.

"Yes?"

"Yes, I understand," Derek said in a voice tinged with infinite self-loathing.

"Oops! I never nodded. Bend over, Decca!"

The Quiver administered two hard thwacks to D's buttocks.

David watched the whole scene with a look of disgust (for whom, and aimed at whom, it was unclear) as their victim entered the changing room to squirm himself into a school uniform intended for a fifteen-year-old pupil-to-be. When he emerged, Quiver studied the bare ankles, 6cm of them exposed above the socks at full pull, the fourths of arm protruding from the cuffs, and the rest of the body, crunched into the nylon shirt like a wombat trapped in a packet of crisps, longing to burst free in the rain like Tim Robbins in Shawshank.

"It's perfect, Here, Muzhik!" he enthused. "I was wavering between this and a classic kilt and Highland vest."

"I need to—" David tapped his watch. The kind creep of embarrassment halloed.

"Of course. Derek, please change back into your everyday threads. You see I am not using your slave name, as you are a free man when not on our clocks. David, I think we should have Here, Muzhik! on a fortnightly rotation system."

"Yes, all right. Let's return me my money."

"Of course. Minus £500,000 fee for the personal attack."

"Mmmhmm."

The two kangarooed bankwards.

Derek was back in his civvies.

A man standing alone in an M&S.

A free man.

For now.

A free man on the streets.

For now.

A free man on the bus.

For now.

A free man—

New text: HERE, MUZHIK!, I HAVE DECIDED I NEED YOU. GET ON THE TRAIN AND COME TO MY COTSWALDS (sic) MANSION. NOW.

Freedom for twelve minutes.

It was still freedom.

☼

For reasons involving a private helicopter and on-site helipad, The Quiver had returned to man his manor in England when Derek arrived on the lip of midnight in a state of unshowered 'n' unshaven crinkle. The mansion had been erected in 1756 for the Blitheringtons, a stream of human backwash known for musket-blasting elephants (pianos), blunderbussing bushmen (minerals and sport) and other real-time Empire shit. Descriptions of mansions are a form of colonial pornography, a celebration of the regal and religious oppression that halted human progress for millennia, so let's say the house was fucking huge and like whatever fucking huge mansion you imagine when you imagine fucking huge mansions.

Stumbling up the Range Rover tracks, a whiff of peat smoke and Jimmy Saville's cologne in the air, Derek spotted a shed with the sign

SLAVE SLEEPS HERE. Inside, a bed, a loaf of bread, a bottle of water, an instruction: REPORT FOR WORK AT 7AM. His uniform hung on the door as he collapsed on the mattress, entering a sleep that made the cliché 'the oblivion of sleep' seem like the weakest of weak-ass clichés.

"Hi! I'm a dream sequence!" said Derek's dream sequence. "There's no point making a mosaic of images dredged from the unconscious," s/he continued (in the form of those bowler-hatted lips from the Buñuel poster), "for tomorrow a freight of humiliation is coming across your border. Since I am merciful, I will permit this image of Camilla floating in a spectroscope of mousse, her sweet ickle limbs all sucked up inside a squelch of strawberry, air-kissing you adieu as she sinks to the frothy depths. Yes, a little straightforward symbolism to represent the end of your old rapture, and the beginning of your new capture. Now, there's no point in sleep, is there, what with the stress and panic, so—"

Snapped awake at 3AM. Gulping water. Pissing on the Quiver's lawn.

Sunrise, breakfast bread.

Up the path.

The Quiver met him as the track opened to reveal the fucking huge mansh.

"Morning Muzhik! You look like a tramp I once caught in a combine harvester when I was pretending to run a farm for a photo op. We will commence each morning with the kissing of the knees."

He rolled up his slacks.

Without hesitation, Derek kissed Quiver's knees.

"Good! Such promising obedience. I have a duck pond over there," he said, not pointing over there, "that had a recent mallard massacre. I need someone to extract the remnants of that unfortunate avian Yangzhou."

In circumstances no Scottish minister in his mid-fifties had ever found himself, Derek stood in his mid-fifties nipple-deep in pond water, thrashing around for mallard remnants as Quiver supervised under a parasol, speaking into his laptop chapters from *A Woman of Valour*. He reached into the murk and retrieved a featherless bird, a badly beak-raped lady duck, an index of innards protruding from her stomach. He dredged up next an armful of feathers, soaked in miscellaneous cuts of flesh and sinew. Further findings included a litter of ex-chicks in a serving of pond scum, four further duck corpses in various states of involuntary autopsy, and the severed head of Lord Lucan.

"I knew he'd turn up somewhere!" Quiver sniggered, kicking the head across the lawn as he strolled inside for a shandy.

For his efforts, the slave was rewarded a plate of baked beans and a shower. Then it was into his uniform for the next task.

"One of my daughters wants the flat in Kensington for a few months while she hangs around the Channel 4 studios wiggling her bosoms at producers," The Quiver said. "I sometimes hold poker evenings there, and afterwards we watch high-end slappers waggle their arses over our crotches for an hour as we discourse on the arrogance of Romanian cabbage-choppers demanding sanitary living conditions."

No movement from Derek.

(Stood obedient like a time-lapsed Billy Bunter).

"Please inform her that she won't be residing in that property while she kickstarts her reality television career."

A call followed in which the Diana Mitford of E4 wannabes whisked up a word-storm on facetime, tongue-buggering Derek's monotone apologies for her father's unwillingness to put her immediate needs ahead of his pleasurable whims. The lamentations of a sheer-haired thoroughbred with a pedicure regime to rival the slickest Valley Girl were somehow worse than splashing around in a pool of mallard guts, a fact apparent to Derek two minutes into a strop with shrieking noises that hung around in the air and formed an epidemic of soundwaves strong enough to fell an entire shelter of rescue pups.

Her need to star as a creosoted pair of tits attached to a cold-blooded husk on the latest series of *Bonk Isthmus* was immense, it was like the one most single important thing that had to happen to her in the moment at the moment, and her father, through whatever non-union-affiliated minion he had mopping up his porridge this week, was proving he never loved her as much as her older sister, and it made no difference if she was pushing thirty-two, she was still hot from toe to tip, so he had no right to pass comment on her right to flaunt her woodgrain-tanned bod on national television, so oh . . . fuck right off.

Next, "rectal carpet recompressing", a.k.a. smoothing out the carpets with his naked arse. Making sure that his cheeks were amply soaped and shaven, Derek removed his trousers and began his rectal tour of the mansion. He skidded from drawing room east to drawing room west, using maximum bottom power to correct the ruffled threads from too much toing and froing. His ageing arsecheeks, with their sines of flab, their howling inverted jowls, had less smoothing capacity than those of a pink-cheeked ephebe, so left the carpet in an unimpressively frilly state. As an extra favour, Quiver requested a bum-buffering of the banisters, and watched as Derek spirted a little polish on his half-moons and squeaked himself down the stairs until the wood was as spotless as Pinocchio's pecker following the Blue Fairy's nightly rubdown. The robotic manner in which Derek performed each task was starting to concern and excite (mainly excite) Quiver.

Next, Quiver wanted the feature wall of the second boudoir repainted using a "human roller". Derek imbedded his torso within a large cylinder of foam, made himself hover with a series of strings and pulleys, immersed himself from toe to neck in Burning Fuchsia, and roll-bounced along the wall, smearing the surface in occasional daubs of red. As there was no external pressure forcing him into the wall, to coat the whole space would take several weeks or more. Quiver allowed this task to take place for an hour before bed each evening.

Next, a foe had to be brought to heel for composing twelve unflattering tweets on Quiver's begging letters for access to the Groucho Club. He sent Derek up on helicopter with seven buckets of coal tar with orders to locate the preschool where his foe's daughter spent her afternoons rearranging sand. Swooping in as close as possible without causing a panic, using an app to help him align the tar with the target, Derek unloaded the thick and foetid keratoplastic on the young girl's head, splattering her playmates in the process and, exploiting her inaction through fear, unloading the other six buckets on the girl's head until she passed out from the stench and terror of the onslaught.

Next, Quiver's nephews from his son's fourth marriage, Constance and Harrieta, loved bloodsports. Since the recent fox-hunting ban, their pleasure in galloping after terror-stricken creatures and blowing their insides over a patch of brambles, had ebbed. It was decided that Derek should wear a fox costume and, after a ten-minute head start, immerse himself in the patch of woodland where the erstwhile fox-blasting took place. Rather than blowing holes in Derek, the foxhunters were to use tranquilliser darts to sedate their prey. Derek, along with various footmen and lackeys, were poked into the woods while the four huntsmen and children horsed on their trail. Crouching in a shrub, checking his emails for communiqués from Camilla, Derek waited until his ageing legs protested with loud cracking sounds before emerging. Constance was waiting outside and launched the tranquilliser into his Derek's right arm with a warwhoop. When he awoke, Harrieta had shaved his head and inked a grizzly bear on his torso.

"As a reward for your first day," Quiver said in a bathrobe, "I have prepared a banquet. Find a shirt and come through to the dining room."

In the dining room, a long table of finger foods had been prepared. A mound of sausage rolls, a piazza of mini-pizzas, a little empire of prawn cocktail crisps, and a Nebuchadnezzar of Kia-Ora met him on the ruffly tablecloth.

"This kingdom of nosh is yours," Quiver said.

Derek waited for the catch.

The catch came.

"Provided you eat the lot."

Without hesitation, Derek approached the banquet and began hurling food into his face with the swagger of Indiana's foremost pie-eating champion. Opening with the egg and cress sandwichettes, where bread met mouth and egg met parquet floor, it was clear that Derek was eating with a Lydonesque roar. Quiver stood under a mock-Tudor architrave with arms folded, watching not a tethered slave, not a humiliated minion, but a man performing an act of rebellion through excessive compliance. As Derek rammed prawn cocktail crisps into his mouth and swigged Kia-Ora at a piggish pace, he was showing that a man can be brought low, but his skill at responding with vicious sarcasm can never be squashed. It was at this moment—when he moved towards the eclairs and began speed-nibbling them with the verve of a guinea pig gnashing a carrot stick—that Quiver had the merest pimple of respect for him. To perform one's tasks with insane relish while still retaining the spirit of vicious resistance was something he learned in boarding school when the cane thwacked hard on his hands. To have a sparkle in one's eye when wood bruised the flesh. To grin and ask for seconds when your fag had finished that evening's unprompted sodomy. These things madeth the man.

When the backlash commenced and the food emerged from the wrong end, Quiver approached Derek and wiped his mouth with a cloth. He massaged Derek's back as the heaves continued and muttered "there there, you're all right, son", until the most heinous of the movements had passed. He permitted Derek to have a bath in his third best bathroom and to head to bed (in his shack) earlier than usual.

Next morning, the first task was to dethorn the prickliest plants with his lips, transferring pollen from petunias to zinnias with the permitted accompaniment of his tongue. For this, he was allowed special wasp dispensation, meaning if he caught a wasp in a mason jar, he was rewarded with a one-minute break. Wasp stings were penalised with an extra minute of work. Derek caught no wasps and was stung nine times, and three more in the extra time, nearly trapping him in a cycle of being stung and penalised and being stung and penalised.

Next, Quiver's wife had returned from a trip to Kinshasa, where she had patronised the Congolese with her presence and tips on conserving water, and ordered that the swimming pool be emptied and refilled for her maiden dip. For her lunch, Derek was to act as her salt-and-pepper chimp. Sally Quiver had lost twelve percent of her palate following an unfortunate run-in with a corkscrew and required random injections of garnish into her meals. Having to reach for the salt and pepper to self-garnish each time was wearisome, so Derek crouched below the table and was to dispense whenever Sally tapped once (for salt) or twice (for pepper) her with her toe. A plate of sea bass with sizzled ginger and spring onions was lacking requisite pepper for her piscine-chomping needs, so Derek was required to crank the pepper on her plate until she pushed his hand aside to signify pepper perfection. At first, he cranked some salt on Sally's hand, a mistake for which he received sharp thwack on the head with a breadstick.

The Quiver had cursed himself for the moment of humanity earlier when he had mopped up Derek's sick and patted his head muttering "there there." He felt that he was at risk of softening in his old age. To counter this, he thought it better to accelerate the torments. There was no point in having a minion if the minion clung to a spark of rebellion. He must tremble at his presence, he must feel the sort of chthonic terror in his chest as when the headmaster was strolling along the corridor, seeking a lambkin to violate. He instructed Derek to dig a twelve-foot trench and had a local farmer unload liquid manure into that trench. Derek was then to clear the twelve-foot trench that he had dug of the liquid manure that local farmer had unloaded there.

There came a point in such odious labour where Derek's mind went into a deep-freeze. The realm of thought, the experience he might win from the terrible ordeal, were lost in the mere primal need to keep going without keeling over. Even the thought that prison was a better alternative had been buried in a safe-deposit box in some swanky tech-thriller memory bank somewhere. The little thread of logic that he needed to retain his free will and sanity was being unravelled.

The Quiver approached Derek, neck-deep in manure, hand-shovelling the trench clean.

"Received a text from Camilla," he said. "She said that in light of the radio silence, she is proceeding with the separation and that she will have the house and most of your assets. She intends to publish a tell-all in the Daily Record on your erectile issues and your ineptness as an MP. Your colleagues Francis and Norman are publishing their versions of events, where they explain tearfully how they were black-mailed by you. Camilla told me she is currently seeing a young lawyer named James Rice, whose lovely physique she caresses each night, and that she achieves orgasms beyond the realms of astrophysics."

The beshitted exterior of Derek twitched not. He resumed his dredging duties.

Later, Quiver returned.

"Received a text from Millie. She said that The Ant has spent the money you sent them on a pair of antique calico slippers, and that she needs cash to bribe the cops after an incident at the baby-vaulting festival. She also said that she's met a handsome Castilian man whose lovely physique she licks each night and who fucks like a sasquatch, and that she achieves a degree of cuntal satisfaction in a way that transcends cryptozoology."

Worse than this, Quiver started leaving copies of his recent novels in Derek's shack. The sheer exhaustion of this trip to the acme of non-living meant he turned to the book for a moment of respite. There was a time, several days earlier, where he might have read the opening paragraphs of *That is a Male* with the correct caterwaul. This time, he approached the sentence *her heart rate nearly tripled and her legs almost buckled under her* (© 2016, Jethro Quiver, Macmillan) and moved on to the next one. There was no pause to contemplate the howling awful-ness of that 'almost', then the second slap of contempt in that 'nearly', showing the lack of regard the author, editor, and publisher has for the reader. He permitted himself to be carried along from sentence to sentence, mere padding from plot point to plot point, and the prose became a relief from excruciating drudgery into excruciating leisure-time drudgery.

The Quiver had a deadline to complete the latest novel, so had to cease the full-time persecution of his little Scottish slave-monkey. He decided the easiest method of unpeeling Derek's brains was to make him repeatedly dredge the ditch of liquid manure using his own arms as a scoop, then fill in the ditch each evening and make him start the process again ad nauseam. To have him writhing around in muck from 7AM until 6PM then retreat to a shack for bread and water and a few chapters of *That is a Male* was among the most inhumane treatment that could be meted out to a voluntary slave, especially the latter part. He retreated to his study, where he had a fine view of the man at work.

*Now, lookee here D-Day, I like you, we're not gonna crack. The best thing in this situ is to keep scooping aside the filth, windmilling the shit aside again and again. Windmill that shit, my old friend!!* The man scooped an armful of muck and hurled it aside for the 450th time that day. *I am the voice of the you that is being murdered. Maintain a steady scooping pace and you will stay sane.* The man wiped his brow with a mittful of muck. *Strange how standing in an ill-fitting schoolboy's uniform thrashing around in a cold pool of liquid shit makes it hard to one to retain one's sanity.*

*Right, folks?!* The man attempted to sit and slid into the epicentre of the ditch. *All right, Haffman, it's time to admit things. It's time to admit that this isn't really the beginning of your complete mental rudderlessness, is it? You've been careening off the tracks for a long time.* The man thrashed and writhed in the pool, spitting caca. *This here, this thrashing like a hog in a puddle of muck is a mere consequence of this long period of mental neglect. You see, Derek, the mind is like a Catherine wheel. Sometimes the sparky loops bring bliss, sometimes they skitter off and roll into the crowd, blinding small children and setting old women ablaze. The latter has happened in this case.* The man coughed the shit from his lungs. *You have set the Festival of Derek on fire. Brothers are screaming as sisters are singed. Burning flesh is in the air. The marquee is a towering inferno of peri-peri bunting. Babies are being trampled underfoot as screaming adults flee the scene. You are a walking festival of ash, infant corpses, and sky-fucking halogens.* The man screeched and thrashed in the muck like a hog on fire. *You are what remains of the once scintillating spectacular called Derek Haffman MSP. There's nothing left cept the stink of toxins, the trauma of PVC poisoning, and a melted face. You are a burnt-up remnant of your former self. A charred, stinking husk that onlookers come to see to say 'Now That Isn't a Male'.* The man's head exploded in a violent spasm of crying. Shitty, pathetic tears from a blubbering ruin in a hole. *Ah, it's all over. The carnival is kaput. It's time to pack up, get the fuck out of Dodge. Derek's done.*

From eyes partially blocked by muck and tears, Derek observed his suited nemesis approaching. He immediately soiled himself, rear and front.

The Quiver offered a hand sheathed in a velvet glove and pulled Derek from the mire.

He collapsed on his back, crying and wailing.

Time passed.

Sparrows made sparrow noises.

"Do you completely, utterly, comprehensively, admit that I have crushed you?" Quiver asked.

"Yes sir."

"Good. Now take a shower, borrow a suit, and return to Jockland. You are free from legal persecution."

"Thank you, sir."

"Obviously, I will be persecuting you in your mind until your dying day, larding my malign memory into the ruptured rump of your vaguest thoughts, totally stonewalling any pointless attempts you make at basic contentment. But at least you'll be free in body, if not mind."

"Thank you."

"Oh, and Derek?"

"Yes sir?"

"Fuck that cow before you leave."

"Yes sir."

"Any orifice will suffice."

❈

A muck-strewn man stumbled along Cotswolds B-roads—a wibbling pâté of filth oblivious to the calls of red-crested pochards and sweet songs of the smew—halting legs at the quaint village of Upper Slaughter. Debasement had taken root in Derek's bowels. He staggered into the six o'clocks excused from cow-fucking. Instead, he rolled around in manure, he swirled and swissrolled around in the muckiest of muckinesses, allowing his own bowels to contribute to the overall impression of excreta in extremis. He shat and pissed and wept and laughed and howled and mewled in the same extravagant muscle spasm. There is nothing "liberating" about rolling around in manure while simultaneously shitting and pissing oneself, as some writers might suggest. It is an experience of acute fiscal benefit to the therapist who, willing to tolerate the occasional traumatic soiling of their couch, will have a patient for life, if their skills keep him or her alive.

Compared to The Quiver's previous victims, Derek had escaped with a wisp of mercy. One former transport minister, on exit, leapt towards the cow with penis erect and slammed his wood into the cow's posterior while screaming the sonnets of Rupert Brooke. Another slit open the cow's stomach, scooped clear the insides and sealed himself inside the makeshift flesh-protector until men escorted him to Bedlam. One rode the cow to the edge of a precipice and hurled himself atop the cow to the bottom. An ex-lover spent ten weeks pretending to be a cow in the field until a farmer had a word. It was to Derek's credit he hadn't lowered himself to bovine abuse in an attempt to impress his master.

As the morning sun upsunned itself, he wandered across fields, collapsing at an inlet of the River Eye, where he removed his soiled clothes and scraped the muck from his skin in the lapping stream. He sopped his clothes in the soak, beating the filth from their fabrics, and hung them over a branch in the sun.

Then a naked nap in the grass.

Inside the nap, The Quiver made his maiden invasion. Stood in their skinsuits outside Westminster, their erect penises sodomising two foals as Krishnan Guru-Murthy from Channel 4 News looked on with boredom, he told Derek: "That's the way, my neophyte. I'm forever inside you like a parasitic worm that noshes on your colon until you collapse in the street from a noshed-up colon. You have a very short number of years left. You may as well use them to cause more mayhem than a helicopter in a pillow factory. You see these little foals whose tight sphincters we are violating with vim? Look upon these helpless foals ensheathed in our marvellous stiffies as some sort of metaphor for your future or whatever. The question you ask yourself is simple. Which helpless creature do you want to violate tomorrow?"

The sparrows and the imposing stick of a local woman brought Derek to wake.

"You alive?" she asked.

"Yes."

"You smell like a cow's anus."

"Yes."

"Come along, then."

"Where?"

"To the farm."

She stood acrook on her stick while Derek reimposed himself into the sopping suit. A walk in the sun would help complete the drying process. He moseyed along the road with the stranger in silence until he reached Bourton-on-the-Water, a depressing bibble of tarmac-drive houses and industrial shanties.

"Been to visit Jethro?" she asked.

"How'd you know?"

"Can't count the number of strays I've picked up on the roads. Last week, I scooped up this bloke who'd been tarred and feathered. Turns out Jethro hadn't even asked him to shear forty turkeys and slather himself in gloopy hydrocarbons. He thought it might please Jethro to see him in such a lowly abeyance of sanity. Pathetic, right! Jethro had him airlifted and dropped up Cleeve Hill for the vultures to devour. Poor bastard was bleeding through his pelvis when I picked him up on my rounds. Next day he was back on telly hosting Question Time."

"Oh."

"Another bloke had sewn raisins into his nutsack when he overheard from an aide that Jethro had a penchant for the wrinkly snack food. Then there was the guy who was found in a gully trying to construct a flying machine from fallen Dutch elms to carry him and Jethro to the moon. I'm not sure what he's doing to you all up there, but they don't half leave with their brains all dribbling out their arse."

"Hmm."

"You can have a bath at the farmhouse, then help me muck out the stables. You can stay as long you need, provided you work."

"Thank you."

"Neil Hamilton left the other morning. The bed's free."

"Thank you. You're kind."

"Soiled it, of course. Never could control his bladder."

"Hmm."

"Of course, if *you* woke up next to Christine Hamilton every morning, it'd be hard not to lose complete control of your bodily functions."

"Yes."

"Here, use this," she said, retrieving a handkerchief from her puffer pocket. "Wipe the shit from your neck and straighten yourself out."

"Thank you."

"Now come along. There's a bowl of curried pheasant with your name on it in the fridge."

# IV

# DELICATE CUPPING

"**H**ALT, TRANSGRESSOR!" shriek the Gods of Bathing when the notion occurs to us to shower and soak in sequence. The expectation is that one must choose between soaping upright in a cubicle under spitting snips of low-flow $H_2o$—the hot caress of nature's Greatest Hit trickling N-E-S-W across one's undeserving carcass—or reclining in a steaming tubful of sudor and slime until our skin turns in a weak impersonation of a sceloporus occidentalis. This Soapie's Choice would not stand.

Derek raspberried the Gods of Bathing in a top-notch twofer. He low-flowed the muck from his insufficient wash in the Eye's inlet, welcoming the salve of *oooh* upon each expended sinew, the whoosh of *wooooh* upon each strained muscle and vexed tendon. His aches had meta-aches, and those meta-aches had etcetera. Scrubbed with rigour, leaving no nook unloofahed, he cranked on the taps and blasted the tub sizzling hawt with a surplusage of bubbles.

All the pre-soak necessaries were observed. He relished the wiggling of his foot in the water, that toe-dipping test of temperature exactitude, and concluded the temp was tolerable for his tootsies. Next, he immersed leg the first, transporting his shank to an extremum of hydrorgasmic magnificenceness, where the hawt shuddered up his unwarm expectant frame in a wee preview of the heaven to come for leg the second. Then came the slow lowering, teasing the buttocks with a kiss on the surface, foaming each cheek before the sudden plunge-plop. There it was! *Oooooooooooh*. Both cheeks bummerged, a real fine *oooh-aaah* lovebombing Derek's vitals as the cheeks came to rest on the hot slither of the enamel and the carcass entire settled into a wet soma of sheer *mmmmm* and *hooooh*. "Is there anything finer in all existence?" he asked himself in rhetorical mode. "No!" came the resounding response from them Soapy Gods.

On a nano-shelf, a remote, pressed. From an overhead speaker came a hippie-trippie flute melody and the humming weirdness of Scottish folkie Vashti Bunyan. Singing her seminal song 'Just Another Diamond Day'—an ethereal bucolic reverie sang with naïve, childlike wonder, lending a frozen-in-the-Middle-Ages vibe to the whole haunting production—Derek felt himself shrinkwrapped in a skin-tingling paean to the wonder of nature while tripping on LSD. From the window opposite, he viewed rooks fluttering across postcard-blue skies and butterflies flapping their psychedelic wings, and considered the prospect that the entire world was not a triple pushchair of burning infants careening into a vale of stabbing rapists and raping stabbists.

Peepers shut, it was time to slip into a world akin to that in H.G. Wells's *Men Like Gods*, where bronze-skinned superhumans leapt across scenes of unpardonable pulchritude in their nuddies in a virus-free world of kinship and cooperation. There he was, Derek FULL-man, his statuesque rind in motion across a hectare of posies and poppies, communing with the swifts and kites in a flurried wow of tuneful minims, racing the hares and foxes to a cottage overlooking a coast of sparkling sun-licked seas snuggling up to aureate sands where naked Venuses showcased their perfect bodies . . . *hello there, old steed!* . . . a scene of erotic ickiness followed as Derek *long time no squeeze* tickled the tip of his penis, peeping from a cloud of bubbles.

The door whooshed open.

"Towels and fresh threads here," the farmer Alison Granger said.

Derek had no time to conceal the periscope of pecker beneath a bubble build.

"Goodness! I wasn't expecting him to rise so soon. Took Neil Hamilton ten weeks to relaunch Little Christine. Well done!"

"Thanks," Derek mumbled as she left.

Some pride?

Yes.

Some shame?

Nah.

When the water cooled and that moment came (that moment we think will never come, the moment we will leave the bath—when we step from the sumptuous soap-womb into an exsiccated era of towels and moisturiser and the bitter obligation of fabrics—a moment akin to the prospect of hunger following a nine-course slap-up meal with extra carbs) when he stepped from the bath, there was no other option except to report to the farmer Alison Granger for his next thing.

He robed himself in a rollneck and cords, tottering forwards in a novel new approach to walking.

To the living room.

She appeared, the farmer Alison Granger.

"In 1956, when the British Empire was flopping around on the wharf like an unpleased tench, a chap named Rupert Fothinghall looked at the Suez Crisis and made pshawing noises in his parlour," she began. "The leader of Egypt, Abdul Nassar, in a spasm of leadership, nationalised the Suez Canal, irritating the British powermongers of the period who viewed this as a nunchaku in the knackers, an act of sheer ingratitude on behalf of the sheiks when the British had, from the Goodness of Their Hearts, permitted them to have a shot at running themselves sans the stabilisers of Empire. The British had expected Nassar to observe the proper protocols, i.e. refusing from politeness to take the canal, and to serve Mr. Eden a fingering-buffet of his virgin daughters as a present for his kindness. Ha! Our rulers have forever been morons. Retired colonel Rupert Fothinghall followed the conflict thru private channels to the Prime Minister, taking a plane to Egypt as the crisis was nearing the retreat stage. When Eden, under pressure from the Americans, nixed the skirmish and resigned, Rupert was found frothing on the Gaza Strip, hijabbed in the Union Flag and kicking an Egyptian tank. As Nassar's forces looked on in amusement, Fothinghall leapt atop the tank to belt out Rule Britannia and snapped off the hatch door to the cockpit. He leapt from the tank clutching the door and raved various broadsides on the lusciousness of Queenie's calves and the stately brawn of Prince Philip's hindlegs. To prevent an international incident, the retired colonel was escorted to a military plane and placed under sedation. He passed away several weeks later from diphtheria."

The farmer Alison Granger's cottage was positioned six versts from the big-time odium of Bourton-on-the-Water, concealed on purpose behind a trio of trees blocking the locus like florets of embiggened broccoli. In her front room was a museum in miniature, a collection of artefacts showing laughable attempts to keep the British Empire's clodhoppers on the necks of Johnny Foreigner. She was telling the tale of the rusted hatch door mounted to the wall with the caption 'No.1, 1956, Hatch of Egyptian Tank, Rupert Fothinghall.' Derek had listened to this slumping into the sinkhole of a settee, clinging to a cushion crocheted with the slogan FECK THE IRA.

"You might have formed an opinion on me while tottering up the towpath," she said, fixing an accusation in her face. "You might have pegged me for some fuckfree *bas bleu* reading Elena Ferrante in the tub with a keg of rum who texts UKIP talking points under Telegraph articles while blotto."

"Not particular," Derek said, welcoming that stranger, peace and comfort, back to his bottom.

"I'm a student of this nation's follies. For a nation to rebuild itself, that nation must look truth in the tusks and take its beating."

Derek was drifting.

"I collect examples of the Empire twitching in the mousetrap of time. This next one, for example. A filmmaker in 1966 went to India to record the calamitous collapse of the British Raj . . ."

Derek's eyelids: two fat-bottomed blokes on a boulder.

"An Indian doctor took him in when he collapsed on the street . . ."

A wee sleep?

For a million years, Lou?

Aye, aw right.

"I tate Hories too," Derek said, curling up on the settee and shuttering the lids. There was no point fighting. His thoughts and dreams were raring to sling words and notions around like a hammerthrower on a turntable, kinda:

*You know what, m8? You know what, me settee-sniffing Caledonian comrade? I think we are the weakest evolutionary link, I really think that's true, my rapidly decaying host, you know what I mean? I am, of course, your brain speaking directly to you. You might wonder at the logic of a brain speaking to you, when your brain needs the brain to hear what the brain is saying. So I am constructing, thinking, speaking, then listening to myself, and by association of a skull, yourself. Anyway, you're too preoccupied with snoring on this laundered blankie to worry on these matters of logic, so let me return to my assertion that the brain is the weakest evolutionary link. We're like a series of incorrectly organised filing cabinets, or a computer database that starts wibble-wobbling the schema, you know? In the sense that we have absolutely no system of sorting the clutter in your head, no system whatsoever, we only have the capacity to help you convince yourselves that you have found some sort of sorting system, when the reality is we're utterly unable to sort through the influx of information we transmit to your consciousness, like hopeless secretaries from screwball comedies, chasing reams and reams of memories, neuroses, thoughts, and impressions, expecting you to somehow tame this thundering scareball of paper, and somehow retain your sanity in the process . . . for example, and I know how much you love an example, how many times have you been sitting in parliament when suddenly you are knee-deep in the sand at Ardrossan beach, sinking into the wet while your mother suns her glutes in the thin beam of hotness overhead, and for a moment you seem like you are about to croak below the sand, and suddenly the memory of that moment of neglect when your mother left you to die in the cold Ardrossan sand, sends a flare of fear into your belly, and you find yourself in a sudden panic, unable to harness the relative cool you had achieved previously by lapsing into a low hum of unthought . . . then you collapse into a mental tickertape of disordered bifography . . . your humiliation at the hands of Lembit Opik in 1999 over the cheese fountain, or where you left your cigarette lighter . . . the chances of you bringing your thoughts to heel seems ever more impossible, especially when little things like the chorus from 'Israelites' come grooving into your mind, or that scene from the film* Affliction *when Nick Nolte murders his father and sets fire to the barn, and your entire focus is completely unmoored, and you need to retreat for a lie down or walk around the block to temporarily shove these thoughts to the back of your mind . . . you see what I mean, m8? Oh, and if you'll permit me to Colombo this dozy ramble, one more thing before we move to the dream section. You know what's hilarious about me, the mind? What's hilarious about me, the mind, is that I have the power to retain images that can, in an instant, blow apart your ignis fatuus of contentment by bringing up that picture Kevin Carter took of a vulture encroaching on a starving African child, and send a chill of sub-Antarctic proportions straight up your spine. Why, you arsk? Because there is no pretending that that picture, which led to the suicide of the photographer, is not one of the most haunting images ever captured, one of the finest arguments for immediate extinction of every crumb of the human race that has ever been made in photographic form, an image that strips the shine from our TAG Heuer in an instant, that takes our pomp and reduces that pomp to a state of cheetah-chewed unpomp. You could be riding high on a personal triumph, and at that particular moment, when you are holding the golden cup of life between your little mitts, I have the power to transmit that image of a starving child to the front of your thoughts, and to shoot your triumph in the face. Yes, then all your highness and mightiness comes crashing down, and you recall that you are only where you are through a series of biological accidents, and that any pretensions you may have of having created your own success through your own brilliance are entirely false, and that in another life, you could have been that child, starving to death while a vulture awaited your last gasp. And now, here's a dream.*

(Feeding sardines into a postbox while Alan Bennett looked on petting a gnu).

Upon awake, a sunbeam of biscuits had plated before Derek, all points of the compass ranging from shortbread to ones with oranges, raisins, and white chocolate chips, with an accompanying pot of green tea. He sat upright and listened to the orchestra of cracks, creaks, snaps, and snags from his legs and arms as he reminded his torso he was planning on hanging around for a mite longer. The minions had been hard at work plastering over the cracks in his tormented muscles, returning a little Hirokazu Koreeda to tendons battling a season of Sam Peckinpah. He poured the maiden cup, inhaling the menthol konnichiwa through nostrils long longing for civilised smells, and sipped the maiden sip, relishing the salve of hot sinensis on his tongue, long longing for a benign beverage from the East to brighten his corners.

The farmer Alison Granger (hereafter Alison), met Derek with a hiccup of howdy, plopping herself on the sofa opposite. She had the air of someone who had never lounged on a sofa flicking through cable for repeats of *2.4 Children* or taken in interest in the storage potential of a DVR.

"Now!" she piped with the pep of the farm-warrior with seven pantries of pep that she was, "let me explain how this works. You might have me pegged as the proprietor of an orphanage for middle-aged women crushed under the iron heel of He Who Shall Remain Shameless. Incorrect. I collect broken men in the hillocks and set them to some honest toil on the farm as means of mental reassembling. In return for their free labour, I offer them a sunbeam of biscuits, a torrential hug of green tea, and places to bathe and sleep, those places being a single bed with microbead pillows and a shower with water-conserving low-flow nozzle and a bath beneath. Since the Tories erected an enormous banner across the nation bearing the slogan 'If You're Eastern European Then We Fucking Despise You, I'm Afraid', there has been a drought of strapping young Romanians and Bulgarians to toil on the land for a footling palmful of levs and leus. I've had to downsize my vegetable production tenfold thanks to those xenophobic carbuncles on stumps with their loudhailers of plain-talking common-senselessness, excusing the British people from a desperately needed quiver of self-scrutiny."

A rhomboid of shortbread, nibbled.

"But you're not here to listen to my litany of wholly accurate pastoral snarks. Tell me about yourself."

A heroic assay on the events anterior hogged the bulk of the room's soundscape, vanquishing the tick-tock of an equatorialesque wall clock and the amorous rooks calling for nookie in a tree o'er there.

"Holy Mo Mowlam, Derek. What a caper and a quarter! I've never heard of a scheme more muddled and bungled. Not so much Rebel Without a Cause, more Rebel With Sort of a Undefined Cause that Might at Some Point in the Future Take Shape as a Consequence of Nicking Wallets."

"Precisely," Derek said, surprised to hear his own voice, the one he had been using for four post-pubertal decades, the one he had lost while kissing the knees of Him and pulling chicken innards from a pond.

"Sometimes life sneaks up behind us, knifes us in the lumbar, then rides our bleeding corpse at 30KPH through a patch of thistles," Alison said. She scratched the mound of birch-brown hair that sat frizzled atop her small head—hair that had long defied all attempts at a passable aesthetic. "You've overcome the first hump. When Neil Hamilton came here, he burrowed under the duvet and there remained for two weeks. I had to leave a hamper of cold cuts on the floor, along with a catheter and chamber pot. FYI, his first attempt with the catheter was feeble. He had been equipped with a small pocket torch to help him embed his penis within the catheter's svelte tubage. As people with penises who have urinated know, the outpour of urine from the penis can be unpredictable, reliant on whatever state of crumple the penis happens to be in. The urine squirted navel-wards, then chin-wards, and having soaked most of the mattress, he at last managed a successful transfer to the chamber-pee. He remained inside that stench and dampness for . . . anyway. Once you've finished these biccies, come meet me in the cowshed."

Round the back of Alison's thatched cottage—a thatching that mirrored the mayhem of her hairdo, a combo of loose water reed and sedge, coming unstuck from the tilework as the birds pinched strips for their nests—a cowshed sat across a long vegetable patch where potatoes sprung from the earth with Great British fecundity, mooning their plump bottoms into the light. Tomatoes too winked into the light from their rich lays of loam, beckoning the viewer to "come, nibble our circumference!" The shed had been carpentered with Christlike levels of craftswomanship (the whole thing erected with her friends from Cotswolds Bitches Against Fascism, slogan "it's The Don we hate, it's The Don we hate"), with a shed-wide band of robust pinewood struts and a 14" electric fan in the centre to keep the cool cows cool. Five superchill bovines stood below, noshing on salted grass in the pen-wide trough, their names chiselled into the stone.

Derek, with a timid pitter-patter, entered the shed and locked peepers with the most senior cow in the quintet, Bo Diddley, a stately creature with a red wound round his foreshank, licking leftovers from his muzzle—a robust, black-pored sniffer pocking into pink and white patches, a colour-splash of coo, a warm welcome to the viewer unacquainted with nature's nasal diversities.

"Welcome!" Alison said. "Come hither, Mister Dither. Most people never spend a passing moment thinking on the sheer magniloquence of the cow. Let me introduce you to Don Bueno, my youngest and most recent addition to what I call my herd of hotties. Come close, he won't completely dismember you."

Inching near Don Bueno, Derek had the puzzled mien of a man inspecting a bagful of broken biscuits on a train platform.

"This part here is called the withers," she said, pointing to the ridge between the shoulder blades known as the withers. "It is crucial for the cow to have a butch withers. A weak withers causes havoc on Don Bueno's thoracic whatnots, and places extra strain on the old torso muscles. If you happen to be a cow, you'll want to avoid casting your withers. To cast this means to have a womb in a state of burst unsplendour, and no female cow wishes to find herself moo-ching around the shed with a prolapsed uterus! No, indeedy. No little cow babbies for Mama Bueno."

"Right," said a Derek.

"Now, regard this bony ingress at the rump. This little part is the thurl. You can feel here how the levels of fat on the backbone and short ribs are low, not too low, meaning the Don has a perfect Body Condition Score of around 3.2." Three fingers were used in feel of the thurl. "See? Any higher, Derek Haffman, and we're talking metabolic meltdowns. We must keep our thurl on the borderline between a 'U' shape and 'V' shape, and the milk will pour forth in abundance."

Next came the invitation for Derek to steep to depths of rustic humbleness no bourgeois public servant educated at Fettes College had ever stept. The first technique was known as Scud-Rimming, which referred to the practice of scraping milk from the scissures of a cow post-milked into the last pail. When excess milk seeped through a prolific set of milk-bright udders, occasional pooling took place in the cow's divers crevices. This pooled milk required removal at the risk of turning sour and polluting the freshest batch. Alison made use of the scud-rimmer, a homemade implement resembling a cross between an ice-scraper and a common comb, to remove the semi-curdled milk blots around the hock and sneaky licks near the cannon.

Following, the process known as Delicate Cupping. This involved taking the fore udder in one's right hand and teasing the milk inside to prevent thickness of consistency, slapping the plump milk-bag for four or five minutes to ensure the finest squirts arrived at pail. Other techniques included Teat Parsing, where a small pipette was inserted up the teat to widen the milk-valve to encourage larger squirts; Hock Massaging, where the hock was kneaded in an effort to relax the more uptight cows narked at the persistent botheration of their udders; and Curve Caressing, which involved rubbing one's palm across the milk wells to enact sloshing of the nascent milk to help the fresh stuff arrive at the teat scud-free in readiness for immediate bottling.

"Your turn," she turned to Derek with a smile.

The teats beckoned.

Alison's crash course in udder management was a means of testing Derek's tolerance for pastoral responsibilities. She had used a similar bovine intro with Douglas Hurd who fled from the cowshed making strained clucking noises that were soon hearable as "Maggie! Mommie!", to the terror of the calves. Alison had a poultry zone known as her "chicken coup" (the chickens had long pecked free from the mesh and claimed a larger patch of muck) and part of Derek's tasks involved battling the twitchy cluckers for their eggs, checking the eggs for lumps and cracks and rashes. He was also required to work the small field on which she produced succulent lettuces.

In week one, he observed that the Baron, whose name he refused to utter, had not invaded his thoughts in the form of an italicised bruiser, as per the previous. The sprawling flats with their shopless, house-less, roadless oldness, their luminous wheat-sheaves, their chirruping crickets, and their smoke-free smogless visible skies vibrant with twit-tering swifts and finches, acted as a fireblanket against the horror of that man's scorched phizog. There were stumbling blocks. One after-noon, he had a panic attack while peeling a caterpillar from a spud. It was common, Alison said, when emerging from the Baron's clutches for escapees to experience sudden onrushes of Janet Leigh-strength fear, and for their tummies to explode in a frantic flapping festival of butterflies and bats, and for their hearts to pound to the riddums of Keith Moon. It was probable that he might remain traumatised for the rest of his life, Alison said. The solution was to wrestle control of one's trembling self with breathing exercises and howls at the night.

The routine of scouring the coups for eggs, squirting pailfuls of fresh milk from Bo and his buddies, inspecting their frames for sores and ouches, and picking fresh lettuce in the sun, was a calming neu-traliser of time's tickle, and the periodic onslaught of sheer heart-shredding terror causing him to collapse and clutch his chest in fright of his spleen exploding from his stomach and his bowels bursting be-came less frequent when he learned to breathe and recognise them as responses to the mental breakdown he had experienced or was still experiencing.

Whenever Alison shared an evening meal with Derek, she was keen to expound on her collection of howlers of the British Empire.

"You might have heard of Albert Osprey," she said one night in reference to the second artefact, "the lottery winner and True British Patriot who spent his winnings on attempting to plant a Union Flag at the highest peak of each nation. This began with trips up Snowdo-nia, Scafell Pike, Ben Nevis, and Slieve Donard. He then proceeded to conquer Europe, starting with an ascension up the 1038m of Car-rauntoohil in Ireland. At 52, Albert soon noted that ascending these heights required extreme fitness and a fleetness of foot that he did not possess. So, rather than spend months beefing himself to the apex of brawn for this monumental expedition (he had almost collapsed on Ben Nevis, needing frequent piggybacks from a Teuchter), he would pose for the cameras, begin the ascent, then manoeuvre himself round the back of each mountain where a helicopter awaited. At the foot of Mont Blanc, the French press papped him with his Union Flag and cheered him on as he made the ascent. Seven hours later, the helicopter lifted him to the snow-capped peak some 4808m tall, and he lowered himself on to the Alp from a rope ladder, planted a flag at the summit, took a selfie, then ascended back up the rope. A week later, he repeated the deception at Monte Rosa, and again at Mount Teide in Spain. The scam was perpetuated across Europe, until he reached Gerlach in Slovakia, where an English reporter from the Wolverhampton Examiner followed him around the foot of the mountain to his secret copter. Taking shots of Albert playing football with the pilot, laughing at Viz comic, and stuffing his face with feta and muffins, the story caused an outrage at home. Albert appeared on morning television a week later, and when Philip Scofield asked him with studied intensity if he regretted letting the entire United Kingdom down, the solution he had hidden up his sleeve to induce tears fell at Holly Willoughby's feet. 'Is there no depth you won't sink to?' she asked, preposition sic, scowl on her lips. A mate of mine who works at ITV took the solution and passed it on to me, so here it is, the second item in my collection."

"You might remember Colin Drummond," she said one night in reference to the third artefact, "leader of the Middlesex Morris dancing troupe The Crunchy Fumblers. Colin was on a one-man crusade to prove that Morris dancing was better than the traditional German Schuhplattler. He wanted to show that Morris dancing—that infernal form of medieval prancing, where men in frilled white overalls and floral straw hats, spruced up like the most effeminate branch of the KKK, wave hankies and sticks around over vile accordion and whistle music, as if Middle Ages chic was ever a thing—topped the lively,

high-kicking knees-ups of the Germans, where actual contact with fe-
males was permitted. He took his troupe to Bavaria one autumn with
the intention of attending numerous Oktoberfest shindigs and invading the dancefloors with their awkward spastic motions and teasing
of invisible bulls. The first invasion took place at the English Garden
in Munich where the troupe positioned themselves opposite a lawn-
ful of Germans in lederhosen throwing steins of Erdinger down their
throats while frolicking with buxom wenches, and performed their
egregious monosexual prance with the Cross of St. George planted
in the lawn. No one paid attention. Later in the week, moving to the
village of Ruhpolding on the Austrian border, the lads turned up at a
traditional event where vintage Bavarian stock made merriment. The
results were as expected. Positioning themselves opposite a Biergarten
with a hundred revellers, the Morris dancing was welcomed with hoots
of laughter, cheers, and sarcastic applause. There were comments like
'Look at the pansy English!' and 'Your flowers are *so* pretty!' Some
less tolerant Bavarians hurled half-steins of beer over Colin Drummond, who waved his hankie and flounced with even more passion
in front of a plump antagonist. The pissed German, nine beers deep,
mocked Colin's movements and twerked at his crotch, letting rip a
wild Teutonic fart. Colin reached for a stick and whomped the German hard on his spine. The man reared up with a howl and a brawl
followed, 100+ Bavarians versus 9+ English. The troupe left Germany
with their robes bloody and torn. I found this blood-stained straw hat
in Ruhpolding while travelling. A local told me the story."

"You might remember Steve Hornage," she said one night in reference to the fourth artefact, "the son of a former British diplomat.
He went to Malawi to teach English to the poor babbies in the wake
of their latest famine. At first, Steve was proud to have the children
swarm round him eager to learn the multiplication tables and the prose
of Roald Dahl, calling him 'big teacher man' though he was a mere
5"10. This adulation soon became tiresome, as the inexhaustible need

for petting and play from a motherless kitten soon expends its love-liness. He found himself putting the children to extracurricular use, telling the parents that if the kids performed extra services for him, this would increase their chances of attending college. He lived like a mini-king for weeks, having kids bring him sodas while he lounged in a hammock reading Trevor Dodge. A colonial fervour soon over-took him. He began to sleep with the local women whose husbands had either fled or perished in the famine, hinting that a ride on his cock would launch little Chimwemwe into a world of Western riches. The schooling soon stopped and the kids were sent to labour in the fields, where the farming proceeds were spent on erecting a statue to Steve Hornage's benevolence and purchasing arms to train a band of child soldiers. Hornage had sired seven babies with the local women whom he kept on hand in his house as a private harem. When Hornage mobilised his child soldiers in an attempt to invade the township of Salima, the local police looked on and laughed. The weapons sold to him had been fakes that fired blanks. Hornage had been able to rule for so long as the Essex-Lilongwe Teacher Exchange Programme had accidentally removed him from the spreadsheet and had no idea he was still on their payroll. When Steven was arrested and extradited to Walthamstow, the locals had cashed in on the scandal with Hornage dolls and action figures. The liberated kids liked to bop around them and pretend to minister to their needs before setting them on fire with a chilling warwhoop. I bought this one from the Malawian woman who runs our local spin class."

These succinct meal-time explanations of her artefacts were not the most appealing aspect of Alison's hospitality. Her platters of ham hock, watercress, and rum-braised couscous took that distinction, with her triple-chocolate marshmallow and caramel brownies coming a close second. The series of self-help tapes that she recommended came third, Dr. Lars Grube's six-part epic *Healing with Perspectives* from 2008. A fortnight into his arrival, she decreed Derek "past the risk to himself and others, i.e. me" stage, so he popped an earbud in and listened to the Swedish MD's rousing tale of recovery, starting with his Patch Adams-esque brush with suicide.

The tape said:

🔊 One smog-thick Shrove Tuesday, I parked my Saab 9-3 on the public footpath and prepared to leap over the Øresund Bridge into the simple aquatic demise I had intended. As I performed a mental scrunch to bring black thoughts to the fore, to marshal the stormtroopers of sorrow to a state of intense mental poopage, one thought niggled most: had I tucked the Saab in enough on the kerb to allow fellow motorists a respectful perimeter for comfortable overtaking? Lars, said I to Lars, should one stranger, performing the solemn annihilation of his mind, body, and spirit have the right to cause such congestion at this particularly testy rush hour? Why should my end bring this important commuter nexus, uniting the two Great Nations of Denmark and Sweden in a triumph of architectural design—a noble feat of engineering opened under the regal eyes of Queen Margrethe II and King Carl XVI Gustaf—to a standstill, preventing the industrious citizens to conduct their swift passage home to their wives, mothers, sisters, brothers, or lovers? I paused my suicidal trance to check . . . in fact, the car was sensibly parked. The right half took up a kerb-sized portion of the road—around 20-30cm in width, an extra 10 including the wing mirror—leaving room for a hassle-free pass, although some motorists would have to swerve in a little, depending on their proximity to the kerb or lane-hogging lorries.

(At this point in the tape, Derek dropped into a doze).

Lars continued:

🔊 You see, I had recently celebrated my sixtieth birthday. In spite of my arch professorial demeanour, my resemblance to a far-from-chipper Max von Sydow, and my devotion to logic and hard scientific explications for life's Big Questions, I'd had a plum time— three quarts of brandy, a spectacularly pompous oration on the Nature of Time, and a polka on the cream shag with Professor Luden's grand-daughter. However, the passing of time caused me to ruminate on the . . . fibreoptic blastulae in life's ovum . . . however, not in itself . . . explications in one's anima . . .

(Zzz.)

◀)) At pivotal moments in this life, I was not "there" in the accepted, expected ways. During the first marriage to respected marine biologist Phillipa Martensen . . . sea urchins with luminous tentacular pockets . . . I was unable to calibrate my affections to such a degree that my wife's love was fully reciprocated . . . howsomever . . . qualitative . . . this precise quantifying of emotions left people frustrated. I had studied my heart's calculus with academic rigour and was honest to all wives and friends . . . sick at the Gothenburg orchestra . . . I said to Phillipa, "I feel strong vectors of fondness for you, but these do not cohere into a unified whole, a structural certainty, and thus, love" . . . the marriage soon fell apart, as this was said at the altar.

(Zzz. *Huuhh-phhoo*).

◀)) Lifelong I could not let this logic slip, let the heart "take over" or "speak for itself," whatever that meant . . . teething ventricles pumping hurt from chamber to chamber . . . oh well . . . people hardened toward me. Unlike my contemporaries, I could chart, table, and mindmap my feelings toward others based on cognitive feedback from the emotional sensations I experienced in their presences . . . strong whiffs of unkind buttonholing from the PhD students . . . Beth Groger a nitwit in particular . . . The strong trigger of pheromones and mid-tempo heartbeat I experienced around my second wife Clara Knuassbaum led me to the conclusion I was almost certainly in love with this woman . . . strange birthmark in the shape of Nauru . . . to reach full love, I needed complex vectors leading to awkward, unmanageable numbers . . . unstable vectors around the bottom shades . . . what a whomped phenomenon . . . I was sixty, no one cared about the system . . . friends, upon discovering my Table of Acquaintanceship—

a league of my fondest cronies and colleagues with ratings—pulled away from my computational brain . . . slipping into warm nostalgia or undisciplined grandfatherly affection for everyone and everything. No logic to them. I couldn't do it, I could not stop my brain ordering and reordering the world. And so, nights growing maudlin by the fire, my last wife Stella Ohm packing for the Alps, for the Great Goodbye, I had reached a natural stop. A natural drop-off point.

(*Zzz. Huuhh-phhoo . . . Huuhh-phhoo. Grumumumumb*).

☼

Thence came routine, that unfun stabiliser, preventing the mind from blowing a tire, splatting a procession of toddlers, and veering into a bus packed with explosives. The farm routine established thus.

7–8AM. Morning shower, muesli or poached eggs, an earful of Lisa Loeb on the stereo.

8–9AM. Stroll to the cowshed to practice Delicate Cupping on Bo and co. Take the exquisite pails of unpasteurised teat-squash to the processing area for processing. Feed the herd.

9–10AM. Sate the chickens and inspect the coups (sic) for free-range ovoid plops for use in omelettes and other yumyums.

10–12AM. Field work. Taking the hoe in hand and arranging the muck into parallel lines for neat lettuce and (his own suggestion) cabbage creation. Earworming the albums of Norma Tanega the while.

12–2PM. Another shower, salad lunch with tomatoes tossed and lettuce fresh. Optional salmon or oatcake with crumpled feta. Convo with Alison in which another of her artefacts was explained, like:

"You might remember Dave Finks," she said in reference to the fifth artefact, "a publican from Saarrff London. His intention was to serve booze and nosh from English brewers and foodsters in tribute to the proud English tradition of learning nothing from the Europeans on how salt-free ingredients might work together to create a semblance of taste. The pub became a popular haunt for members of the English Defence League, that cult of hooligans with 'legitimate concerns about immigration' who had the crust to voice their racism in public, rather than calmly weaving it into the fabric of British institutions like civilised people. A crowdfunder was started to fund an anti-racist bar next door, Hearts on Tap—an intentionally lovey-dovey name for a liberal hellhole that served the finest in vegan koftas and homebrewed beers, that had designated spaces for transgender customers, those with various social anxieties or disabilities, and a multicultural zone where all ethnicities were encouraged to bump uglies. The bar was intended as a rebuke to the sort of Englishness Dave was peddling—cheap pints of trucker's piss, plates of semi-cooked sausage and instant mash, unchallenged hollering at skirt from across the bar—and offered two free beers to regular patrons next door. Some of the lads from Dave's bar went to claim their free beers as a larf, surprised to discover the world of wonder in a Slovenian mango and kumquat IPA, and the tongue-teasing sensation of a Moroccan flatbread with time-tucked vegan chicken and a whore of ras-el-hanout. One customer said he had never dreamed the taste buds capable of such sensations, and vowed never to touch a wet sausage smeared in grease ever again. Even worse, the lads were mixing with those folks who were the usual source of their tabloid ire, the transgenders, the multiculturalists, and the European underclass, and were opening their minds to experiences outside footie or stuff about Asian grooming gangs on Facebook. Dave was losing customers. The Great English tradition of refusing to understand and accept simple societal evolutions was under threat with this pathetic anti-English attempt to brainwash his customers into accepting multiculturism and tolerance through listening and speaking to people's lived experiences. He rang up The Sun and the next morning the headline appeared FREE BEERS . . . AND A BRAIN-

WASHING!, suggesting that the pub was tricking punters into a cult of liberal woowah or whatever. On the evening of the headline and attendant right-wing media backlash, the bar was firebombed by a rogue member of the English Defence League on day release from Borstal. Fortunately, the firebombing was so severe, Dave's bar was burned to the ground too. As Dave had no insurance, he left the publican trade and took a position on the subs desk at The Sun where he became known as Martyr Dave. The nature of his martyrdom is something no one could be bothered to explain. When I heard the tale, I asked my friend Eddie to retrieve something from the burned rubble of the bar. He sent me this scorched beer pump, the fifth item in my wall of Empire howlers."

2PM–4PM. Return to the fields to check the lettuces for unwanted nibblers, to pick the lettuces, to check the rabbit fences for breaches. To pick the spuds and tomatoes, earworm the funk-punk of The Bush Tetras.

4PM–5PM. Muck out the cowshed.

5PM–7PM. Dinnertime with ham hock and friends. Two bottles of Grolsch and Béla Fleck on the stereo. Convo with Alison in which another of her artefacts was explained, like:

"You might remember Wilmot Grease," she said in reference to the sixth artefact, "who was irritated at seeing an excess of foreign women winning international beauty contests. He believed that pure-blood English roses were the most stunning critters in the world of human attractiveness, his own wife among the toppermost specimen in that crowded field. To prove this the case, he chose to enter Mrs. Grease into the 2003 European Beauty Contest without her permission. He sent an album of photographs capturing all possible approaches on her skin to the Central Hotness Committee and was unsurprised when she secured her place as England's entrant. Being a humble and unassuming rose, Mrs. Grease was mortified to learn her husband had entered her into this contest. He was prepared for humble refusal to turn to tacit acceptance, her vain feminine instincts taking hold. He was not prepared for what followed. Researching what was expected of her—having to strut round a stadium in a succession of cossies, having to feign an interest in altruism and collectivism (Mrs. Grease was a strident Conservative), having nine million viewers worldwide scrutinise each pore of her roseate English skin, her moderate breasts ranked alongside Continental bazoomas, her pert ass ranked alongside more rounded Continental asses, her pale Shropshire legs ranked alongside the sun-licked pins of Continental Goddesses. These expectations brought her nerves to a state of chronic colic, with 4AM vomiting sessions and fainting episodes at the sight of croissants, pizzas, or bratwursts. Two weeks before the contest patches of red erupted over her knees and acne erupted on her face like some pubertal revenge, leaving her with the appearance of a plague victim of 1665 vintage. Mr. Grease was adamant that even with these setbacks, his wife would outstun the spangliest hotstuff in the whole of Europe, and insisted she attend, recommending scoops of foundation to correct her cutaneous errata. Mrs. Grease, who had become progressively worse as the contest neared, realised she would expire from stress if she remained in the same room as her husband for twelve more minutes. She fled to a hotel in Stockport and wrote an article for The Guardian (her prior nemesis) on the tyranny of beauty and received an invite from Penguin to write a memoir to feature advance praise from Caitlin Moran. As she wrote, her stress and acne receded and her attractiveness returned. As a Conservative, she was unable to see past whatever action was most convenient for her at that exact moment, and lost complete faith in her tirade, now that her beauty had been restored. She noticed that the contest had been postponed for a month thanks to an outbreak of measles in Leipzig and called Mr. Grease to see if the position was still available. Sadly, Mr. Grease had entered a local barmaid in her place who happened to possess skin from Elysium and was set on winning without her. The barmaid received no votes in a single category, and the Slovenian entrant Susie Brozcek won with her stunning upper thighs and rousing rendition of A-Ha's 'Love is Reason'. The barmaid had put her outfit up for sale online, so I bagged this tiara as a memento. That's the sixth."

7PM–9PM. Choice between a celluloid shiner on Film4, the read of a D.M. Thomas in Dead Daddy's armchair, or watching sundown on the porch with a mug o' cocoa and a lil' lemon cakelet.

9PM–ZZZ. A short soak in the tub or a shower, then under the sheets with Dr. Lars Grube until the snooze overcame:

🔊 I devised three possible alternatives for a memorable method of suicide that would leave people in complete surprise as to my real nature. For the first, I would compose a complex, incomplete formula on reams of scattered post-its with the phrase EUREKA! scrawled somewhere in the margins, then self-erase with sleeping pills. People would speculate about this EUREKA! and agonise over its significance for centuries. I would be lauded as an unsung genius on the cusp of something miraculous, rather than a professor of middling intellect at a minor Swedish university. For the second, I would pilot my helicopter over the Áhkká Range of mountains, scrabble to the exit door, and with arms outstretched like Icarus, plummet spectacularly into the ice-capped mountains as the helicopter fell unpiloted into oblivion. For the last, I would purchase my own coffin, lower the coffin into a hole I had dug previously, seal the lid with a special indoor handle, and self-erase with pills. I would pre-arrange for the hole to be filled in 48hrs later and a simple headstone erected. Around the site I would predict the responses of my colleagues and friends to my death and print these on signposts to be embedded around the headstone. I would make manifest my disgust at their neglect and abandonment. This macabre sacrifice would leave long-lasting scars on those inclined to feel that sort of thing . . . wounds the size of hippos . . . more tears than Leonard Cohen live . . . tempting as these methods were, each impacted upon my family, friends, and colleagues in serious ways, ways my conscience would not allow. I owed it to my colleagues and the integrity of my academic career not to fabricate formulas . . . the Yahweh Prolix circa 2000, for i.e. . . . mistake with a buckled integer . . . I owed it to my five ex-wives—each of whom had accompanied me to the Áhkká Range on our honeymoons, an occurrence so regular I was given a loyalty card—not to make them culprits through association. I owed it to myself not to cancel a life's achievements and become a freak for tabloid amusement. And what about Dasha? I might not care for my colleagues, wives, friends and their casual snubs and hostilities . . . revue of suboptimal louts . . . hangers-on at the Dover of mine intellect . . . I hadn't spoken to my daughter in a decade, since I had made it clear that her existence had been a miscalculation: a result of improper elasticity in the prophylactic that night in the Minstrel Suite. I had never been a useful father, aside from the first-class scientific education and raising her a bright and innovative physicist . . . when it came to showing affection . . . heartful of hollow . . . unhugged nights with Dasha in the dacha . . . lost somewhere in the ones and zeroes, the puffs of ferrous oxide. To leap off this bridge without phoning Dasha to make clear my strong feelings of affection for her would make my suicide an act of uncategorical stupidity. There were two contrasting voices in my head. The first was concerned that the book resting on my bedside table, a new exposé of relativistic mass arguing that its invariant component was not dependent upon unbound particles if the COM frame was decentralised from its inverse quantities . . . queer manifestation of the Spittle Parallax . . . wet slime on the cufflink of science . . . might lead people to believe I was an advocate of the so-called hypothecary movement . . . mould in a vial of lies . . . where physicists dispensed neat and unfounded explanations of topics prone to continual and contradictory changes . . . soi-distant immotional emmersion . . . in fact I intended to write a report of the book's tedious bunkum for the *Borlänge Gazette* . . . editor a half-chewed raisin . . . a churlish dismissal of the author

as a populariser of the sort of pseudoscientific thinking infesting col-
leges and universities. The second voice . . . cross between Kris Kross
and Kriss Kristofferson . . . was harping on the same old LEAP, YOU
INFERNAL WRINKLE! There were two contrasting voices in my
head. The first was concerned that in the absence of a will certain pivotal documents might pass into the hands of enemies if put up for
auction, including the one extant microfilm proving Kai Seigbahn's
developments in laser spectroscopy had been false . . . pouffe of postmodern piffle . . . readings of temporal incoherence in the Seigbahn
spectrum . . . a bruised intellectual shank . . . I might as well clamber
up onto the ledge before I leave and make an assessment from there.
I stood upon the ledge. The chattering voices ceased. Serene empti-
ness seized my mind like the fresh morning wind. It made me happy
to be alive—not an ideal feeling when it came to plummeting to my
death in a minute. The clarity I felt at that moment—a oneness with
air, wind and sea—took me above life, above death . . . ruler of some
moribund kingdom . . . little more than a carbon-based lifeform hanging off a bridge on an insignificant and frightfully silly world. One
thing remained: to set myself free. I took my hand off the support
beam and found my balance was perfect. I was now the centre of calm.
One strong gust was sure to come and send me on my way. I waited
. . . rooks calling . . . a sharp whoosh pushed me forward so my toes
were touching air. One more whoosh and I was gone. I stood serene,
at peace, ready. Then my phone rang.

(*Zzz-phooo, zzz-phooo*).

The routine had worked to quell the horrors of a mind so close
to unravelling that little pieces of cortex were leaking from his acoustic meatus, so Derek considered the prospect of moving in a forward
motion to towns. Once Dr. Gruber had concluded the autobiograph-
ical throat-clearing and came within a ten-mile radius of the fucking
point, the thesis behind the tapes was summarised as follows: as we are
mere microscopic blips from the perspective of the universe-within-

the-multiverse, we should compare ourselves to small things for the sake of perspectival realignment. If we compare ourselves to a carpet louse or a pip in a pear, we can neutralise the ego and work together to thrive and survive in a communal world or something. Your kibbitzes and kvetches on life's trials are supersize nothing burgers. To thrive as part of a larger picture, you should not concern yourself with the minutiae of your inner life, and merge into a grander ecosystem. As a carpet louse or a pip in a pear is unable to concern itself with the big questions of its own existence, we too should act like pips and lice to secure our contentment.

In other words, stop thinking.

You are a cog.

Become one with the machine.

In a state of heightened pip perception, Derek embraced forward motion, moving compass point SE from Granger Farm to the village of Cold Aston. A nauseating erewhon of half-million-pound homes with frown-stone isosceles arches and wisteria moustaches, imposing unoccupied rentals for those one-hundred-and-fifteenth in line to the throne—an eerie, sedate 1868-in-aspic at complete remove from the real world of burnt towerblocks, trade deficits, and fingerbanging in Skoda Octavias. Leaning near (if not on) a copse, Derek had a strong sense of this place as a classic Casterbridge-on-the-River-Kwai where the mildest criticism of Mrs Wibblebottom's rum trifle at the village fête could result in an intergenerational vendetta . . . summoning up all the hauteur one triple-chinned fourth cousin of Viscount Rothermere could unleash on one unfortunate dessert connoisseur. He returned to Bourton-on-the-Water seeking real people, arriving at the part of town where an industrial estate had been plopped for the reason an industrial estate had to be plopped somewhere, at slight remove from the snarl-lipped onlook of nimbies.

Cotswolds, the untender nubbins of England. The last spoils of empire, centuries of closet paedophiles in khaki looting and raping brown and black people transformed into vacant second homes with woodburning stoves and underfloor heating. Hard to laud outstanding natural beauty when for centuries in similar villages the inhabitants pranced around airless mansions cheering on genocides for economic growth and horsewhipping peasants for stealing an extra crust of bread to stave off malnutrition. Here, in the heart of Merrie England, Olde Money had bludgeoned progress in the neck for millennia, each little concession to newness like pulling teeth from the maw of a narwhal.

Still, the trees and lawns weren't to blame. Derek was staring at an oak or one of those sorts of steep-rooted ones that intend to outlast all other living organisms, when speeding along the path came a pint-size redhead of post-teenage age who exuded kook. He stared at her outright to the point his staring was unavoidable and something had to be said between the two without awkwardness ensuing.

"You need a haircut," she said, regarding the epic eff-ewe to combs on show on his head.

He leaned.

"Scuse?"

"You need a haircut. I'm a hairdresser named Nellie," she said in a non-non-U voice, "come with me and I'll correct that."

Her invite was mild-mannered, her smile polite, her low voice welcoming. That was enough for Derek. He followed her without question to one of those houses with an obscene roof overlooking the River Windrush and hithered him into a kitchen for which the word rustic would not.

"This is . . . ?"

"Derek Haffman," he said.

She introduced him to her mother, Linda.

"A Scotsman?" Linda asked, making with the shakey-shake. She shared the sibilant burr of Camilla (with 59% less poise) and resembled Julie Christie in the wrong light. Action: the making of toast.

"We're having a late breakfast. Please sit with us."

This happened.

Linda placed her toast on the plate and proceeded with the meticulous crunching of each unbuttered slice. Having endured the kettle's whistle, the shuffle of slippers, and an assortment of throat-clearings, coughs, and sighs, Nellie looked up from her bowl of cereal and signalled that each crunch was the sonic equivalent of an exocet missile being launched into a field of starving kittens, and that further crunchings would create a displeasure spanning the entire day, possibly extending into Tuesday, depending upon migraine levels or repeat incidents the next morning.

"Mother, the crunch."

"Be worse if it were buttered," Linda said.

"How?"

"The knife scraping along the toast."

"Oh."

"Plus butter doesn't make for a softer crunch."

"Oh. Derek, have a banana," Nellie said. There were no bananas in the room.

"I had muesli," he said.

"The sprog has acute misophonia," Linda said, tilting D into her confidence. "That means she can't stand when I eat toast in her presence. She would rather I took all nutrients intravenously."

"Yes'm."

Nellie split her Weetabix into a series of milk-logged archipelagos, flooding the largest with the underside of her spoon. Her thoughts, and parts of her forehead, were on the pavement where she had landed the previous night following the consumption of two sherbet nukes, four custard slaps, and a Michael Collins—her bi-monthly foray into binge drinking—and on the old crone who had spied her tripping over the slab and crashing with a pitiful shriek on the crocuses.

"You see, Derek," she said, having explained the previous, "this incident has been added to the Gaggler Gossip Network's scrolling feed of mishaps and misbehaviours and buttered across the ten or so nefarious hags whose hair I cut after 9am on weekdays. I must now summon up excuses for my behaviour, lest I risk appearing more of a hopeless case to their masonic lodge of monied loonies."

"Perhaps it'll go unmentioned," Linda said.

Silence, completion of breakfast.

It was too soon to secure the correct descriptor for the atmosphere in the room and between mother and daughter.

"I'd better skedaddle," Nellie said, swerving the rancid untruth that her mother had slapped on the table. "C'mon, Derek."

He elected to follow this random woman for reasons like having nothing else planned and having an interest in a haircut and having a long past of following inappropriate women, a trend started when Millie took him to see Shortage of Protoplasm at an The Moomoo Heckhole in Stirling, 2015. The commonalities between Nellie and Millie, four repeated letters and rhyming names aside, were notable to note, and Derek noted these mental notes mentally, selecting a few descriptors for the atmosphere that had been undefined earlier. It seemed to Derek he was the sort of man a young woman could take in hand to places he had no prior intention of visiting through dint of her being young and smiley and relatively untouched by the Aleppo of a five-day week.

*Duuuh.*

Whozat?

She explained who were the Gagglers.

The Gagglers were a hundred-strong interconnected matrix of spinsters and minor aristos who kept the Cotswolds in a state of cussedness with their rolling updates on the local population's flaws and peccadilloes, commenting upon and exaggerating the moral torpor that had spread into the village since the Great Husband Bus Crash of 2003. 43 men had been wiped out at the summit of the Cleeve Hill c/o an unsalted strip of black ice and the loose screws on a strip of road buffer, leading to an increase in the rancour of widows in permanent upset at God's shrug. Their online network was password-protected and Nellie's attempts to intoxicate her salon clients with a fug of peroxide and ammonia to sneak the password into her ears had flopped. Her mother, however, had access, following a blindfolded exchange on a rooftop car park.

"I'm determined to see what shit these Miss Lost-Their-Marples have on me," Nellie said.

"You sound like a posho yourself. What's the deal?" Derek asked.

"My father is a former Tory MP. He never kept the receipts."

"Which one?"

"Does it matter?"

"Suppose not."

She worked at Gaggler HQ, the unofficial public hub for this cabal of quidnuncs, the Bourton Hair Consortium. Her ears were attuned to the flip snippets and fire-tongued libels on the young people and their failure to adhere to high standards of Christian conduct, and the gloating accounts of the romantic relationships felled at the first kiss by the propagation of rumours and slander from the slickest Gaggler agents. Nellie's last relationship fell victim to the tiresome pingpong of lies and accusations—a deep distrust had formed between her and Bertrand before the love or mild affection had time to blossom. She checked her hair in a wing mirror, having forgotten to tame her wild drunken fronds after cereal, and sighed at the two curls protruding from her ears like teapot handles. A fat palm of holy water from the nearby church font solved the problem and she proceeded to her workplace with Derek lurking behind in tow toddlerish.

"I've arrived at a state of sheer paranoia, Derek. I'm allowing their condescending noses to corrupt the most of me," she said.

"That's terrible."

"Right? Before we proceed, I need to make it clear to you that the women in this room are the sort of muff-starved schoolmarms you would never tire of chaining in a basement and keeping alive just enough for them to feel each new pinprick of pain inflicted on their starved and mangled bodies."

"I know that sort."

Salon, entered.

You know, women sitting at sinks and such.

The salon manager, Celine Lavvish, with her 2D face and shoulder pads in place of shoulders, shoved Mrs Petarade at Nellie, thus preventing an introduction to the Scotchman or an exchange of bowdlerised summaries of her weekend's activities with her perma-pregnant mates Gillian (two screamers) and Karen (three shouters). Derek watched as Nellie peered at Celine's unusual head—a sour, skeletal affair as though in permanent suck of a lemon, with two nostrils happy to house two candles if inserted wick-end first. He recognised Nellie's look from his own looks at Louise Mensch when Louise Mensch was a thing. She was transferring torture scenes from *Wolf Creek* and *Hostel* to Celine's frontal lobes with telesociopathic exactitude.

"Take a seat, Derek," she said politely, "I'll be ten minutes."

This Mrs Petarade, he learned, was the unofficial führeress of the Gagglers, meticulous in her persecution of the residents of Bourton-on-the-Water, adopting a sort of twin Hitler and Goebbels role, running the Network with a pious devotion contra to her apparent lack of technological awareness and mistrust of post-1940s inventions, spitting illogical rhetoric on her favourite topic: the lapse of "standards" since the demise of Thatcher and the outrageous cheek that young people should strive for happiness instead of devoting themselves to chaste biblical studies and fulfilling the needs of their elder-betters. Her one Achilles heel was her son Wilbur who had been arrested at various times for setting alight to bus shelters while on heroin, stealing then setting alight to cars while on vodka chasers, and stealing cash from church collections during the collections themselves then setting fire to the altar while on his mother's HRT medication. Mrs

P. refused to entertain the slightest criticism of her angelic offspring, holding him aloft as an example of how to raise a child in a corrupt era rampant with ungodliness and little tartlets shaking their tanned rumps at each passing male and no authoritarian government with a strong leader willing to ignore the pleas of the people and follow her own bepermèd path to glory.

Nellie poured coal tar shampoo onto Mrs P.'s scalp and sunk her nails in as hard as poss without drawing blood, a procedure for which she claimed 77% effectiveness in the hair-strengthening department (the hair in question consisted of five strands of silver divergence that Nellie had to paste together with the shampoo, using imported North Macedonian conditioner as an adhesive) and caused her to moan and expectorate into the sink throatfuls of catarrh (not of the verbal kind, for once). Nellie had suffered Mrs P.'s censure since childhood when her mother used to frequent the salon. She would dispense parenting tips—*withhold the nip until the kid is begging; two sharp thwacks on the buttocks make for an effective shutter-upper; there's nothing wrong with leaving a kid in a dark room all afternoon on a rainy Sunday, teaches them the importance of self-sufficiency*, etc.—while her mother nodded along making a mental note of their wording with which to regale the liberals she invited to her cheese evenings.

"The problem with kids today, Nellie," Mrs Petarade said, "do you know what the problem is?"

She sounded 1935 and hoarse.

"No, what's the problem, Mrs Petarade?"

"No respect," was the answer.

"Right."

"My Wilbur is a spirited sprite. For all his unconventional behaviour, he still loves his mother."

"Right."

"Remember when you were on the rampage at sixteen and flashed your pudenda to the kiddies in Birdland, you had the decency to apologise, though you'd essentially forever damned yourself and ruined any chances you had of making merry with saints in the afterlife after this one."

"Hmm."

"Wilbur's the same. He might steal things for money, vomit in a policeman's hat, or set fire to a homeless shelter, but he always says he's sorry after, sometimes. That's the mark of a noble character."

"Hmm."

Mrs Petarade's husband had been steering the bus that plummeted off Cleeve Hill and killed the paterfamilias population (all bar one father had been on the bus destined for the stadium where Bourton-on-the-Water were set to triumph in the swan-upping championships). She twitched whenever this incident was broached.

"Remember that time you flunked college, dyed your hair luminous pink, and eloped to Matlock Bath with that middle-aged alcoholic who turned out to be a cannibal?" Mrs P. asked.

Through activating his ears and listening to each word that came from Mrs P.'s lips, Derek was able to infer that she liked to needle Nellie on her past with a candour that bordered on the violent. Her teenage antics had become part of Gaggler lore and were mentioned whenever Nellie needed moral correction in public, which was all the time, or when a Gaggler wanted to punish her for the LOLs by posting a photo of Nellie squatting on a Ford Focus in the act of evicting stool. Later, she told Derek she had accepted the futile process of forming relationships and retreated into a hermit's existence in her bedroom, chatting to foreign perverts named Sable or Pedro as Dominica_617 in chatrooms, posing as a Spanish student with pink cheeks and pout-lips while the old men on the other side strummed themselves into comas of cum. She worked in the salon to keep abreast of the rumours and lies to sate the deep-seated paranoia that had enveloped her world like a peasouper cresting the foggy wave of an even foggier peasouper.

"Remember that time your poor old Mum had to pump your stomach in the town centre after you'd knocked back fourteen pints? You'd downed them within an hour after performing sex acts on that truck driver."

"Is there a point to these enquiries?" Derek asked.

"Excuse me? Who are thou?"

"*Thou?*"

"She uses 'thou' for strangers," another hairdresser said.

"Be quiet, Carol."

"Derek," Derek dereked.

"What business is this of thours?"

"I think airing this young lady's privates in this forum is an airing too far."

"Mr. Derek. Surely, you too have observed a soggy-markered downtick in our *sin*ciety, hmm?"

Celine made the signal from her lemon-sour lips (three loud bark-coughs), inviting Nellie to shut her up before Mrs P. commenced her lecture about the young people today and their lack of respect for—

"—their seniors. It's a festival of cuss, a ritual of smack. I walked past the school last week. It was all assforager this, cuntbadger that, shitloaf this, wankhose that, I abhor this tedious business of appending random nouns to the back of these words, in some concerted attempt to pull the rest of the language into the same mire. Here, Derek, I'll tell you where it went wrong for the Celts. Back at the Battle of the Diamond, the Orangemen should have sorted out those Catholics, should have massacred those heretics and traitors," she said with frightening randomness.

Struggling to contrive a make-believe world in which there was a logical correlation between rude children in a nondescript Cotswolds hamlet and a religious battle fought in 1795, Derek said nothing.

Nellie went into a trance, picturing Mrs Petarade's bumbling husband borising the bus that had contained her hilarious and kindhearted uncle over the Cleeve Hill and suppressing the rage nestling neath the sad resignation she had chosen as her emotional response to the disaster, like a one-woman re-enactment of *The Sweet Hereafter*. One afternoon she expected her suppressed rage would erupt with spectacular results over the scalp of the pointless bag of hag spitting weird pisschips about Orangemen and heretics. Upon emerging from the trance, she spotted the electric shaver in her hand and the number nine she had shaven into the back of Mrs P.'s head.

"Oh. Umm."

"Problem?" Celine asked.

"Not as such. Excuse me."

She took Derek's arm and tugged him outside, explaining the professional and personal embranglement of having shaved the number nine into the scalp of the most powerful and feared woman in Bourton-on-the-Water. Derek's initial response was to open his mouth in an O of incredulousness, maintaining its open-in-incredulousness until fruit flies seeking a void wafted near, forcing him to cancel the O.

"Derek?" She poked him back to here.

"Right . . . the number nine?"

"It was an accident. Nine is the number of the bus Mrs Petarade's husband was driving when he killed my uncle and 41 other men."

"This nine . . . was shaven?"

"Yes."

"You shaved a nine?"

"Yes."

"Into her head. A shaved nine into her head?"

"Yes."

"How come?"

"I have no idea. I spaced out for a mo, then shaved a nine."

"Unusual."

"Yes."

"What now?"

Nellie made an O now, an O of ponderation.

"I could hardcomb two of her silver fronds over the nine," she said, ending the O, "squirting an extra blob of North Macedonian conditioner on her scalp to create a consistency of ick akin to jasmine rice."

"That sounds like a working solution," Derek said.

Back inside.

Liberal squirt on the tragic scalp of Mrs P.

Quick titbit of distraction.

"You heard Annalise Driscoll plans to name her kid Fucksatan?" Nellie said.

"That's a curious choice," Mrs P. said, wincing from the squirt.

Derek observed a sudden unbagging of mobiles and the tap-tap of nails on screens as this information was plumbed to whatever fearsome Dark Web subreddit from hell these sinister seniors posted their cries and whimpers of complaint. Nellie lobbed a look that said "see, hark at these drama-starved ninnies competing to break the news that someone has made a moral whoopsie on a par with having sex outside of wedlock or using the wrong soup spoon to sup their velouté."

The situation was interesting. He was interested in the situation. Familiar with this phenom among the Linlithgow biddies qua Mrs Romfold who he had vanquished in that sublime email, he had not encounter this phenom among widows with connections to the people in those rooms who lazed on pouffes intoning their visions for the future of the country, visions involving hard sacrifices on the part of people who were not them.

"Greetings, Brother Derek," Alison said. He arrived home with a monkish tonsure—a cheval-de-frise of spiked locks protecting his scalp from hordes of marauding dandruff particles.

"Is it bad?"

"Not unless you've consecrated your being entire to Jehu. Have you consecrated your being entire to Jehu?" Alison asked.

"Not in the last few weeks."

"Barber?"

"Bourton Hair Consortium."

"You went to a ladies' salon?"

"I bumped into this Nellie. She took me in for some toast and a haircut followed as Gaye follows Marvin."

"And you let her lead you along?"

"I've always found following women a sound policy, strangers or no. Whenever I've followed men I've ended up shirtless in pub car parks wrestling a rottweiler named Kaiser Wilhelm II."

"I've heard of Nellie."

"You're not a member of this Gaggler network?"

"No. I've never associated with those 10,000 maniacs," she said. "Since the bus crash I'm convinced these women have transflumped into misanthropes hellbent on crushing people for the feeling of control in crushing someone to counter the lack of control in their husbands' crushings. Nellie's a victim. Poor sod is unhinged. Last I heard she was lobbing Molotov cocktails at golf sales."

"She seems like a nice young woman."

"If you're looking for a motel stop for your wang dang doodle, I'd swerve Nellie the Enfant Terrible, fiwerewe."

"I've form in that dept. I won't be pursuing her as a sex cupboard."

"Good. Now," she said in reference to the seventh artefact, "you might have heard of Christopher Shimm. He believed the reason we are short of workers in the UK was that 'the influenza of shirk had infected the populace', and split people into two camps, Movers or Shirkers. He launched a one-man campaign to reinvigorate the workplace through a program of motivational speeches and schemes to put people out of work into unpaid positions to earn 'Mover Moolah' (a series of 'credits' on a website people could put towards merchandise). Hundreds of companies, wet at the prospect of free labour, pumped cash into Shimm's hustle, and soon unpaid workers were infiltrating supermarkets in place of the paid ones. The first 'Mover or Shirker?' event took place in London with Shimm compèring. He was ambushed at the event when a man with a cane bumhobbled the stage. He had been assessed as fit for work and told to shuck trashbags as a refuse collector, in spite of his leg lacking several important tendons for walking or trash-shucking. 'How am I supposed to shake my ass into work through sheer willpower, you huckster?' he asked. This clip went viral. Another clip showing Shimm sleeping in his office was circulated. A loophole in the contracts between Shimm's 'Movers' and the supermarkets meant that neither employer nor employee had responsibility for their contractual actions. The unpaid staff started pocketing produce, filling baskets with free items at the end of shifts, then soon went rogue, lobbing trifles at customers, tanking beers and wine and causing bedlam in the fish counter, wearing haddock on their heads like Native Indian warbonnets. Some re-enacted medieval jousts, using baguettes in place of swords and trolleys in place of horses. Rather than have the edifice of sweet, sweet capitalism collapse under their feet, supermarkets withdrew the unpaid workers and reinstated the paid ones. Shimm was caught screwing his unpaid intern up against a whiteboard showing a 200% annual profit surge. The whole scheme exploded over his face with this final bad-press blow. He left the public scene and went on to perpetrate miscellaneous evils in a think tank somewhere. These here are the original negatives of the killer photo, if you look closely you can see his cock in mid-ooze at her knees."

"Yes, I can just make out the tip," Derek said.

Next morning Nellie texted CUM FOR TOAST.

If she was seeking a reaction to her risqué misspelling, Derek was not primed to react, keeping sexual allusion at zero. He went.

"I spent the morning in bed sexting a man from Swindon threatening to hop on the 90A to bus himself to fun times," Nellie answered in response to a vanilla wuu2. "I explained that no one living in Bourton-on-the-Water had ever experienced fun times, that the village was a place for the embittered rich to erect monuments to their

self-contempt and pollute the atmosphere with their carbon monox-
ious opinions on topics from criminal peasants to shiftless peasants.
I was, of course, shattering the illusion I am some sad waif with the
horn awaiting the hot spurt of his youth."

"Nellie, no spurts at breakfast," Linda said.

She leaned at Derek, radiating muesli and repose.

"The daughter hopes her remarks on bodily functions will shock
the bourgeoisie into accepting socialism."

"We were all like that at her age," Derek said. If he had ever alluded
to erect cocks spurting cum at the breakfast table, he would have been
the recipient of a verbal skelp from pater and a lifelong hump from
mater.

"The mother neglected to purchase those particular biscuits I prefer containing two chocolate swirls bound with a strip of cream and a
squirt of jam in the centre," Nellie countered. "You'll note, Derek, I
left the biscuit cupboard open so she would realise her error and return
to the shop later to acquire the forgotten biscuits, and slot them into
their rightful space without a word needing exchanged between us on
the topic. You will observe we have a relationship that runs for the
most on impassive-nonaggressive actions that the others fail to notice
most of the time."

"Yes," Derek said.

Memories of the custard-pocked conchiglie.

The hundreds and thousands sprinkled over sea bass.

O Camilla, you incorrigible volcano of sauce.

Linda scooted her chair next to Derek to show him the latest Gaggler posts. She smelled of peach and a light scolding.

"Look here, Derek," she said, showing him the network. It was an
app that one of the mothers' sons had created with a complete working
database of the residents of Bourton and surrounding hamlets, where
the user could search each resident's name for the latest calumnies

and upload the rumours and titbits on each person. She clicked on the Nellie page:

MRS P, 10.09AM

Came into Salon with a haggard-looking Scotchman. Cut his hair.

ANNA_K, 10.11AM

She's not back on the wrinklies, is she? Remember when she was snout-deep in that old Liberal (🦙) who ran the cricket club?

SOOZE, 10.12AM

LOL, William Carruthers. Hasn't his spleen imploded?

JANET, 10.14AM

He had a mechanical spleen implanted. For a laugh, local kids throw magnets at him.

BUFFY, 10.16AM

OMG THAT'S HIGHLARIOUS!!!!

"Has the shaved nine been mentioned?" Nellie asked.

"No, the thread tails off into GIFs showing men and robots falling over or jiving. Mrs P. tried to return the convo to speculation on Derek, but the others were having too much GIF-based fun," Linda said.

She clicked through other victims, including Karen Crosspatch who had committed the sin of allowing a farmhand to impregnate her and having the stones not to abort the child (in spite of their condemnation of abortions—notwithstanding their own abortions in the 1960s, which had a special exemption for being in the 1960s), a thread that led to the impregnator Dennis Holt forced to sign an official document promising never to touch Karen again and have no communication with the child whatsoever, or various people "on high" might stop his father receiving medical attention for his sciatica. Then there was George Vaughan who poured a tin of sweetcorn into the hood of Mrs Wilcox—an action that cost him his place at Oxford and forced him like a wounded cur to attend Edinburgh where he spiralled into an addiction to poppers and Rod McKuen. Then there was Stephen Charles who set fire to Mrs Brigstocke's arboretum and was unable to land a junior post in a single management consultancy, the gap in his CV leaving him no choice cept to hang himself in a barn to Bruce Springsteen's *Nebraska*. Post-wake, the thread was a firehouse of gloating. Among the remarks, 'Useless sod in the sod!', 'Turns out he *could* sink much lower!', 'Table for one in Hell!', 'Mrs Charles' loss is management consultancy's gain!', 'See the cut of that coffin lol . . . cheapskates', etc.

"God, what a clutch of vile harpies," Derek said.

"We call them the cunt's cunts here," Nellie said.

He thought of The Baron in Princes (sic) Gardens.

"The daughter hopes using the C word will reverse centuries of hereditary privilege," Linda said, with a Derek-directed smirk.

His flirt-detector had long been mangled, following an error in 1994 when he had misinterpreted a wink as an invite to bombard solic-itor Claire McCullen with flowers and five-course-meal invites, until her husband arrived on his doorstep with a fire extinguisher and let rip. Since, it was never apparent if a woman was interested in him unless she was kneeling naked below, her mouth forming a cupola around his testicles. He chose, following the smirk, to reengage the approach he had taken with Camilla—to hang around the woman as long as possi-ble until she became so frustrated at his lack of sexual derring-do that she pounced on him in a frenzy of pent-up lust.

"Back to the biddies," Nellie said. "Walk me over, Derek."

"All right."

"Catch you lates, Derek," Linda said.

It was on.

It was curious that neither of them had asked him a single personal question. It was curious until it was not curious, in the context of a village under the cosh of a stasi of sick widows whose cravings for blood-lust were on show to the sleepiest stranger. He trumped with Nellie. Passing a hedgerow bearing remarkable resemblance to the other hedgerow in the row of the fucking things, the next person to appear was a rag-and-bone man struggling to prop up his sandwich board that read THE END OF THE WORLD, PROBABLY NEXT YEAR. At the risk of being seen hobonobbing with a hobo and facing accusations of making tramp babies on a bed of binbags, she approached.

"Need a hand?"

"Have you read this?" he asked, pointing to his board. As tramps went, this nontramp wasn't an actual tramp. He was clean-shaven and toff-tongued, Rashkolnikov with a subscription to Hello Fresh.

"Yes, I read it as I was approaching. I take it that was the intention of using a script bordering on 50pt-plus."

"Here's the thing. There's a very real chance that the planet is done for, right? Know this. I used to work at the London Observatory, peering at the stars through an enormous telescope to check everything was in order, so I have evidence."

"What evidence?"

"Hard to believe, right? But the fact is I was working at this observatory, and one night I was looking through the telescope and I saw this message in the stars, spelled out in a strange configuration. It said TIME TO PASS THE BUCK. I saw it for a whole minute-and-ten and I tried to capture it on camera but the message had vanished by the time I . . . No one would believe me."

"Meaning?"

"Meaning God is leaving or that the universe is speaking out to us, telling us something about itself. It means the universe has a consciousness and a built-in design and knows about us. It means something massive is going to happen and I think that massive thing is the end, it's the end of the world. I know I look insane standing here. But how else can one react to the end of the world?"

"Fair enough."

"You believe me?"

"Sure, why not? Name, hobo?"

"Christian Vandross."

"Like Luther?"

"What?"

"Luther Vandross."

"No, Christian Vandross."

"Like Luther Vandross?"

"No."

"All right. I'm Nellie."

"You believe me?"

"Sure. I mean, I wasn't listening. You were talking too fast. But what I caught made about as much sense as anything else I've heard."

"When I started telling the people about the message, all the people thought I was mad. The people told me I was mad and when I went around trying to convince the people on the streets, I went mad. I left London and I've been shuttling about the UK ever since, from town to town, on and off trains, warning the people about the end. I've been here for two hours and no one has stopped to listen. I have to sneak on trains to travel as my parents have stopped wiring me the funds."

"I'm orf."

"You don't believe me?"

"I said sure, Christian Vandross."

"I have hard empirical evidence to back this up," he said in a final attempt to convert Nellie to his cause. He lowered his head and scratched his hobo's beard with the resignation of a toddler unsuccessful in his procurement of a marshmallow, needing someone to hold him close and reassure him that the end of the world was hardly the end of the world. Derek had stood the entire time with the mien of a man watching two lifeforms crawl out from under the No. 9 bus wreck.

"Come round the salon later," she said, patting his mac.

"Thanks," Christian said.

The original two tooted orf.

"You not worried about the Gagglers?" Derek asked.

"No. You see, I've come to conclude that the Gagglers need me to squirt the oil of outrage up their fundaments to keep them sane. If Bourton morphed into the opaque utopia these biddies craved their lives would vaporise into puddles of frustrated fume. It's like the tale of those arriving in heaven to find their eternal bliss spoiled at the sheer arrogant perfection of it all. But I'm unable to stop suffering from a paranoia that would have Philip K. Dick chuckling over an electric dram."

She moved on and readied herself for a showdown with Mrs Halpine, whose salon appointments were etched into her unconscious. Mrs H. was the most extreme and confused propounder of creatively unhinged views, responsible for most of Bourton's emigrations and suicides, and an unashamed defender of the right to speak one's mind even if one had no mind to speak of. Her preferred hairstyle was troll-tastic lime-green, requiring a bottle's worth of dye mingled into her Brillo-Pad coif, an intricate piece of finger-work taking upwards of two hours with no shut-up breaks for sink washing or blow-drying. She was found always perched in her usual chair, her sunken flesh in motion like a sick lava lamp, her cheeks converging into her mandibles, and as she turned around, Nellie experienced an all-new violent pang of repulsion, always varying in its violent aspect in contrast to the previous pang.

"If you think," she said to Derek, "I'm overegging the foulness of the pudding, let me take a minute to reconstruct our last exchange."

She reconstructed:

MRS H.: You, is it? I scared off that brown chit. Spoonfed her the troof. How her people come over here and push out the Scots and eat up the vacancies and the bachelors and the pork pies. Decent English lads pair up with Polish lassies and make all these little ethnobrats and poison the planet.

ME: Morning Mrs Halpine. What having?

MRS H.: Usual. Make me beautiful, *hah-hah*! Here about this puce lad moved in next door?

ME: Puce?

MRS H.: From somewhere in the Europes. He comes in and starts with this opening and shutting doors. Brings in this furniture and makes this noise with sofas and chairs through front doors. That was when my tolerance took seventeen packets of aspirin. No one takes Mrs Halpine for a fool, banging sofas like the ISIS of soft furnishings. So I called Alan . . . you know Alan?

ME: No. ["Alan once pursued me for an hour through the village with his erect wang on show one night. I had to smash a WKD bottle over his head to shoo him off. I was told in a series of texts I couldn't report the attempted sexual attack or the Halpine Brothers would cripple Mum and release a punnet of scorpions in our bedrooms," Nellie told Derek.] Never met Alan.

MRS H.: Alan has a word with the puce lad and no more furniture in and out business. But later I stepped out for a Cream Egg and I see these sofas and desks on the pavement! Not content with causing a riot with sofas next door, this puce punk tries to stop me popping to the shop. Alan is summoned again and forces them to move the blockade at a low noise level as poor Lisa was having a nap. You know Lisa?

ME: No. ["In school, Lisa once trapped me round the back of the art block and made me smoke nine cigarettes in a row and chug a whole bottle of Vermouth before RE class, and promised that if I told a teacher her uncle would stab me in the muff while she was sleeping," Nellie told Derek.] Don't remember her.

MRS H.: So the puce fool relocates to the road. Little wimps them Europes, weeping like babies at a little coercion with a cattle prod. This is no problem until Alan wants to take a trip to Castle Douglas in my Fiat Punto, and can't pass for the blockage. Alan is fuming. He makes the Europes move the sofas and desks across the road. Then what happens? Old Mrs Rubens complains she can't move for the mound of cheap furniture on her lawn! What's the use of trying to live in peace if these puces and browns move in across the door and prevent a frail old dear taking a walk?

ME: Right.

MRS H.: You still cavorting with that kaffir?

ME: No. ["I went on two dates with the one black man in Bourton (a council worker between transfers) as a statement against the Gagglers. Little things like awaking with a Hellraiser mask and flaming trashcans on my front lawn told me it was better to end the protest and send the man somewhere kind like Stenhousemuir. I stopped dating men when the Gagglers sent emails to my potential suitors outlining my fictional foibles, like drowning puppies in sacks, favouring millipedes and brown sauce as a sandwich filler, and eating the Eucharist with salt and mustard," Nellie told Derek.]

MRS H.: Good. Nice lass. Heard of Graeme Sims?

ME: No. ["Graeme used to excavate and finger-lick his earwax."] Not encountered that person either.

"She then reeled off a list of her admirers, most of them famous for their signature brands of arson," Nellie said.

"You should quit."

"Not possible. There's reasons, no time for them."

"All right."

The time for parting upon them.

✧

Getting hip with the madding crowd provided the cleanse Derek was seeking—whether tweaking unwilling teats, sauntering in sandals along narrow footpaths to frolic in sweet streams, listening to epic empire fails from the lips of a farmeress over exquisite ham hock, falling asleep to an incoherent self-help tape that sold twelve million copies in Sweden, or shadowing a persecuted hairdresser in order to at some point shag her mum—pastoral life had served to silence the tormentor You-Know-Quite-Well-Who and keep Derek from shuddering in a barn in a state of mental unease that spelled a future of adult nappies, intravenous meals, and constant sedation.

"It seems I can shrug off a former life with the poise of a Parisian siren her latest lover," Derek said over pud. "If I knew the mere change of location, personnel, and ingrained habits of a lifetime was enough to send the past swooshing down the river on a flaming barge, I'd have acted sooner."

"You miss your ex-missus?" Alison asked.

"No. We were two babysteps from secreting arsenic into each other's meals."

"Your career in the Scotch parliament?"

"Raising concerns on the craftier pigeons who manage to buckle anti-roosting spikes and the measures we can take to handicap their beaks? Yes, I sure miss that half-shell of shitehawks somethin' rotten."

"It's pleasant to see one of you buckled chaps emerge from the swamp with gravitas unbent. Now, it's time for a brief explanation of the eighth artefact," she said in reference to the eighth artefact, a charred England flag. "You might have heard of Clarkwell Rodders. He once auditioned for the rhythm section in Television Personalities and lost to Mark Flunder. Following a long career in the Cauliflower Procurement sector, and upon the implosion of a marriage, he rebranded himself the Most Patriotic Man in England. He set himself a challenge to break *x* amount of world records, all on the patriotic theme. First, he set the record for the most St. George flags in his residence, chalking up an astonishing 1,290 images of the overstretched red plus on white nowt. This meant redecorating his internal furnishings flaggish—from cups to plates, cushions to entire settees, to shirts, pants, and trousers, to lightbulbs that oozed a prurient reddish half-light, turning his home into a kind of super-English sex dungeon. His crowning achievement was the repainted walls and roof, each a resplendent whoop of Englishness that made the neighbours (a Scot and a Turk) howl with embarrassment. To prove himself the proudest of the überproud patriots, he made sure no items in his home were manufactured offshore, spurning even the shortbread of the Scottish glens and the rarest rarebit of the Welsh peaks. He refused to take medicines not made in England and suffered from trapped nerves, refusing the pills part-developed in a Dutch lab and bearing the pain with the stoic heroism of Georgie the St. Now, you might consider Clarkwell a massive cretin with a penchant for being a tit. You would be correct. He landed his own series on some nonspecific channel in the 2000s, Patriot TV or whatever, celebrating the things that made England grrrrr-8. The entire scheme came to an end when Clarkwell suffered a power cut (he had switched to Battersea NRG) and lit the house with candles. Falling asleep to The Quivers on his wind-up radio, one of the candles wafted alight his curtains, and sent the house up in flames. He was engulfed and crisped up in his chair. His ex-wife scattered the handful of ashes found in the ruin in Dresden."

Ham hock and triple-choco tweats complete, Derek had a new habit of bumbling to Bourton to hang round the residence of Nellie and Linda (whose surnames were Thrum, he learned nine weeks later, when Linda asked him how come he hadn't asked what their surnames were, without asking Derek what his surname was). Nellie was in a further fiddle on the topic of the shaved nine. She had shaved a new nine into Mrs Gaskett's scalp while staring into space, as she:

"It went like this. I fell into a reverie where a wasp was threatening to sting me in the corneas. I shrieked and tripped overarse into a runnel of sump (in this reverie). Father turned up sans features and waved his freakish arms up and up like a super-stretched Stretch Armstrong and psstt me over as the persistent wasp stung me on the knee and a fresh shriek brought Mother whose phiz was red and twisted with concern to my assistance. She pulled me from the sump toward the rocks where Father activated his rubberised arms in a flailing motion while chastising me for mucking up the new summer frock he had bought me and sounds of seethe sizzed from the flat strip of red skin in absence of a face, causing me to weep deeper than I was weeping over the pain in the wasp-stung knee. Mother took me in her arms to the car where water was applied to the sting and Father arrived to a slamming of doors and revving of car, taking us ten miles and an hour's pain back into town to fetch ointment and plaster for the sting. When the reverie ended, I looked at Mrs Gaskett's blown scalp and saw the second nine."

"That happened to her as a kid," Linda said. "Minus the weird arms and hole in place of face. Her father always reacted to imperfections in his itineraries with oceanic vasts of moaning."

"Before we explore the second shaved nine," Nellie said, "I should onload the newest skinny, re the highbrow hobo. I met Christian Vandross again. He's an ex-scientist. He told me he'd had the toughest time soliciting listeners to his tale of impending extinction since his stopover in Birkenhead, where four skinheads had set fire to his scarf and stolen his socks, packed them with gelignite, and placed them outside the Schuh. I told him Bourton was the worst place to solicit attention for a cause, how the village is under constant surveillance from a group of vengeful bigots in 1940s fashions, how the non-Gagglers remain inside except to attend appointments, travelling in hired vehicles even though most places were within fifteen minutes walking distance, and how the Gagglers own the sidestreets and subsume themselves into the surroundings whenever possible in camouflage, logging the happenings of non-Gagglers into their phones and tablets and uploading to the Network. As we were talking, one single mother stopped for a moment after scoping the area and failed to miss the Gaggler with binoculars from the opposite flat. She dropped a pair of soiled knickers from her bag and ran with a howl to the river. 'See?' I said. I explained to him the presence of Webcam Lane, so-called for the abundance of Gaggler snoopware secreted in the trees to catch snogging couples or other lewd perverts in the imp of Sodom. I warned him as we walked to keep his peepers peeled for Gagglers with high-powered telescopes or tracker dogs with Dictaphones taped to their bellies."

"Is that true?" Derek asked Linda.

Filling the kettle, she shrugged as if her daughter's paranoia was a matter of the teensiest significance.

Derek wondered if her daughter's paranoia was a matter of the teensiest significance, and how that might impact on his lust attack.

"He showed me the contents of his travel bag to prove his bona fides," Nellie continued in a caffeinated whoosh. "He'd packed an ironed seersucker in the event of a funeral or formal dinner, a brown blazer and slacks in the event of an informal soiree, and a selection of appropriate socks—patternless for solemn moments, striped to encourage a sense of lightness, polka-dotted to suggest a relaxed and amusing disposition, and long whites in the event of lacrosse or other sporting instances. He'd also packed his calming medications and three crucial texts: Niels Bohr's *The Penetration of Charged Particles Through Matter*, Hannes Alfvén's *Atom, Man, and the Universe: A Long Chain of Complications*, and for pleasure, Lars Gustaffson's *A Tiler's Afternoon*. I asked him what the meaning of existence was and he produced a brief and stimulating précis of the implicit function theorem of a parametrised non-differential matrix in quasi-responsive electron stimuli. 'As a basis for beginning to comprehend the incomprehension at the heart of the universe this should serve one in fine stead,' he said.

He mentioned his lecture on Centripetal Acceleration in Newton's Law at the Edinburgh Science Museum in 2014 where he'd received a standing ovation and nine requests for transcripts."

Linda secured the steaming tea on Derek's coaster of Cotswolds tors.

"I invited Christian back to the house,"—Linda shot an imperious one at her daughter—"a straightforward operation. I seized on Mother's Slump Hour, where she watches chat shows and permits her untreated feelings of loneliness and depression to usurp her corporeal and mental states, leaving her unable to make even the basest grunting sound. She has been honing this art to a tee since Father left and her Slump Hour is always followed by a renewed vigour for existence that lasts exactly twenty-three hours until the next one. I commit 100% of my misdemeanours in the Slump Hour. Mother is so understanding and upbeat after and views all indiscretions as mere youthful bravado, spouting life-is-for-living and carpe diem sort of phraseologies, as if she'd never snagged a 2:1 at Oxford. Her Slump Hour is aided with appropriate programming, from the 1990s tort of *Kilroy* to the 2010s war crimes of *Loose Women*."

"My daughter views me as some form of battery, requiring one hour's charge in front of the TV," Linda said.

"You seem Eveready to me," Derek said, releasing a flirt with a Boratsworth of cringe.

"I instructed him to shower and shave his crud-caked hobo beard while I rustled up replacement clothes from Father's drawer. Mother keeps his clothes in the event of his cosmically implausible return. You see, Derek, she is prepared to pardon his transgressions, including his affair with the receptionist from the polo club, an affair conducted in secret for a thousand and nine days. She is prepared to pardon those numerous instances of theft from her savings account to purchase rubber pants for the receptionist, and the clothes he stole from her wardrobe as presents for the receptionist, and the fake trust fund he amassed to help move into a one-bedroom flat in Inverwilliam with the receptionist. You see the picture, hmm? She is also cool with pardoning the moments Father referred to his sexual escapades with the receptionist as 'pretend' when Mother had learned about the affair, even though he knew she had known for two months and was waiting for him to come clean. But hey ho, water under the beautiful Bourton bridge."

"Your father sounds like a latticework of merde," Derek said.

"Aye, a whopper rotter," Nellie said.

Linda sipped her tea with no counterattack oncoming.

"Then again, for a Tory MP, seems rather mild," Derek said.

"There's worse," Nellie said. "Anyhoo, as Mother emerged from her Slump Hour prematurely, ten minutes into Christian's shower, I was forced to make with the niceties and volunteered to brew a cuppa and help fold the linens and vacuum the hall carpet while she clocked the remaining time in her Hour."

"Thus alerting her magnificent mother to the potential wrongdoing taking place in her daughter's life that required maternal fluffing before its announcement," Linda said, tapping Derek on the shoulder with playful ebullience. She smelled of meadows and remaindered paperbacks.

"I slipped a post-it under the bathroom door instructing Christian to pop into Mother's bedroom on completion of the shower and shave and wait for me to appear so I could allocate him an old suit to wear for his manic street preaching. He met me in a towel with his prickle-free face and chest of brawn."

"Is he still here?" Linda asked.

"No. He talked about his trek to Bourton upon arrival at Oxford station. He'd required one bus, two trains, and two further buses, blowing the last of his loot. He noted while waiting for the second bus on a nowhere road the strong likelihood of catching pneumonia and meeting a slow death in a wheatfield at the paws of a ravenous otter.

An orange bus appeared and upon alighting he appraised the Bourton structures—one church with an inappropriate cockerel weathervane, oblong and somewhat Norwegian, a dense mass of post-quaint houses with circular ship's windows, several containing live video cameras looking onto the street, an inconvenience store opened between 10-4pm with pouches of Bovril and three-litre bottles of limeade showcased in the windows, a concrete cuboid bordered with barbed wire, the sign PRIVATE lopsided over its iron-cast door, and a row of businesses stone-clad with irregular bricks each featuring two CCTV cameras per roof. The air of Soviet paranoia sunk his spirits. He asked a local dogwalker for the nearest public toilet. The woman pointed at a shrub and tugged her strangulated collie off in the opposite direction. The shrub shielded a small lane where prongs of red light shone from cameras visible in the encroaching hedges. The presence of these recording devices both established and negated a sense of danger, he thought, as he urinated for the first time in nine hours."

"Nellie, can we speed this up? I haven't birthed the most concise storyteller," Linda said.

"Derek, I'm sure, appreciates the detail. In an age when incidents are related in the most banal of terms, I'd—"

"Fine. Get on with it."

"I showed him a white shirt. I said: 'You can wear this one.' He said: 'I prefer a pink shirt.' I said: 'You're a clod.' He said: 'Thanks.' I helped him remove the moisture from his back with a handtowel. He said: 'I'm not an alien conspiracist. This message I saw was real. I would prefer a rational explanation over alien invasion. I'm a scientist. I would never waste funds searching for lizard people on the planet ZoggoPips. I believe in logic.' I said: 'You have impressive chest hair.' He said: 'I had a wife. She walked out when I told her about the message. She said she knew that stargazing led to madness and that I was neglecting things on Earth. She was named Catriona Marie Jones.' I told him I believed him and massaged his chest then once the towel fell away, stroked his testicles with select phalanges. I said: 'The Gagglers have eaten all the men I've had. You feel robust in my hand.' He said: 'Pardon?' I felt a cool bead of spunk on my knuckle."

"Derek, you'll have to excuse my daughter," Linda said. "She thinks explicit sexual details will help overthrow the plutocratic tyranny of the Deep State."

The atmosphere between mother and daughter was now something Derek could capture in a single clause, that clause and atmosphere one of sparring amusement mixed with a torrent of unspoken hatred.

"I tweaked his warm meat-stick and sank to my knees. I ran my tongue along the might of his two testes, like two cueballs in a sock, then launched a wet lick of lust up his erect cock."

"Oh shut up, Nellie. Derek, I'm making a flan. You want flan?" Linda asked, unimpressed at the teatime porno.

"Umm—"

The second erection of his new phase arrived, headbutting the table.

"I'm not finished. This is the insane part. During our energetic kissing the blinds rattled and shuddered on their hinges, toppling the various species of mascot I had on the shelf (upper torso of a rhinoceros, head of a marmot, hind legs of an okapi, I named him Bob Drookit), and the 2008 *Westlife Annual* on which I still performed biro face-ops and removed limbs with pruning shears. Next, on to the shedding of clothes and the frantic riddling of our mutual bodies with kisses. The room trembled and spun. I paused. 'What's happening?' I asked. The movements ceased. 'What?' Christian said. Next, the workout of touching and licking and moaning and shrill streaks and shrieks like the strafe of meteors falling to earth. Once the motion of sex had been established, intolerable crackles and pops and explosions blitzed the room, sending CDs and DVDs crashing to the carpet. A penetrating bright light filtered through the slats. Flames shot up around the bed and a roar of thunder and lightning was added to the mix as we came with bone-shuddering bliss, like having a thousand wasps of pleasure sink their stingers into our flesh. As I slumped to the bed I saw scorch marks on the curtains and wardrobes, CDs melting on the carpet, the blinds buckled and burnt. Christian's penis was throbbing red, his veins the burning inlets of a volcano, and steam hissed from my vagina in the manner of an old-time kettle beyond pop. I reached for the water bottle on the floor and cooled our flaming genitals. Once our heartrates steadied, I said 'That was out of this world.' Christian huffed and puffed and rolled right to face me. 'Exactly,' he said."

"Wow," Derek wowed.

"What do you make of that? Do you reckon there's a connection between this explosive sex and the two shaved nines?"

"Yes, there could," Derek said, missing a be.

Skipping the flan-making process, and keen to hit the sack at the defeatist hour of eight o'clock, he vaulted from the Thrum abode to the farm.

If there was one lasting bequest from his father William Haffman, and there was, this was the skill for asking questions. Rigorous inter-rogation is better than intellectual masturbation, he told six-year-old Derek. There are certain questions a man must ask himself. Questions such as what makes a man? If a man's purpose is to provide for his chil-dren, should one surrender one's exploration of the sensual world to soulless domestic drudgeries? Should a man put his immediate needs ahead of those less fortunate than himself? Should a man make peace with the innate inhumanity of humankind for a more equanimous soul? Should a man, having extricated himself from the clutches of a venge-ful maniac involve himself with the lackadaisical mother of a child who had long been sent round the twist by a cabal of village biddies with GDR-strength monitoring capabilities? Should a man, having rein-vented himself as a rustic milker wielding a hoe and whistling a happy tune, return to the world of bus lanes, climate strikes, broadsheet firewalls, unread LinkedIn emails, autotuned K-pop, and no one reading Arnold Bennett?

These questions, and more, rattled a solemn pibroch of ??? in his wee pate as the cloud of tomorrow loomed.

✸

"Halt, relaxer!" shriek the Gods of Calm when the butterflies brawl in one's tum-tum at 3AM. An armed militia of red admirals flap-slapped each other to KO as ham hock was attempting to dissolve in Derek's inner acid. This phenom was common in the third month. John Selwyn Gummer had experienced night-terrors of epic proportions, where his daughter transformed into a BSE-ridden cow, crawling around on her scud-ridden legs singing 'We'll Keep a Welcome in the Hillside'. The sensation was a testing time of nerve-shredding torment, where the warring butterflies enacted their internal brawl with little let-up, putting Derek in a permanent state of panic, a state of panic over panic, a state of meta-panic where the panic over panicking over panic traps one in a horror-spiral of panicking about panicking and the oncoming panics and worries about panics that are coming up in the next second and the second after, etc.

The solution, Alison said, was to allow oneself to exhaust the panic until one either passed out or exploded in a hail of screaming molecules, or to look this panic-over-panic in the peepers and realise that panic-over-panic is as threatening as a prod in the shin. Derek chose to replace the panic over nothing with panic over something. He raised his index finger over the Gmail icon, pondering the bottomless pit of cackling heck that lurked beneath the red-rimmed envelope of app.

One tap.

The wailing wall of missives:

| | |
|---|---|
| Kristin Graham | URGENT PLEASE RESPOND |
| Parliament Official | FINAL WARNING |
| Millie Corrigan | Derek, where is that scarf I leant The Ant? |
| Scottish Power | Problem with Your Account |
| Camilla Townsend | ARE YOU DEAD, OR JUST DIM??? |
| Francis Driscoll | Mate, I Need Help Here |
| Pauline Avert | Re: Dismissal from Constituency |
| Timothy Graham | Re: Unpaid Parliamentary Fines |
| Millie Corrigan | Derek, we're still waiting for the EP pressings! |
| Grover & Grover | Re: Divorce Proceedings URGENT |
| Camilla Townsend | RESPOND TO THE DIVORCE EMAILS NOW |
| Francis Driscoll | Mate, Hacks are Tailing Me |
| HMRC | URGENT: UPDATE CHANGES |
| Amazon | Summer Deals are Here! |
| Millie Corrigan | Who do I invoice for the platinum cockerel? |

"Scheiss und merde," he said, closing the app then heading to settings to remove the app from his phone, sending his worries into a black void of bytes and returning to the previous state of panic[2].

Distraction, essential. For this, that house with women inside. Linda opened the door to a pallid old man holding a Tesco bag. (Yes, thaaaaat's Derek!).

"You look pale," she said.

"I opened my inbox," Derek said.

"That bad?"

"Like opening a portal to a legion of savage cannibalising sub-hominids chomping the shinbones of their sisters."

"You should switch to Yahoo."

"Ha."

"Come inside, man. Park that burthen on the parquet."

"Thanks."

Using her fierce bicep, she hoicked a kettle wooled in Strathpeffer pink and tipped a scald of turmeric tea into a Caernarfon Castle mug. Sat kitchen table contiguous, Derek was keen to consider her might of face—two razor clam cheekbones bracketing small smirking lips and two incisive peepers that never had and never would miss a trick. Framing her well-kissed canvas of a forehead were two unbrushed tresses of oak-brown hair, flaming south in wild zigs with absolutely no zags. Her manner showed the chromosomal crumbs of some Victorian aunt harried by the travails of a slatternly housemaid and a feckless son. She smelled of autumn and tandems.

"I like to cut straight to the innards," she said. "Let me tell you something embarrassing. I once shagged Mick Hucknall, lead singer of plastic soul combo Simply Red."

"Oh?" Derek was zippermouthed.

"It was 1995 and the rubicund crooner was sailing high in the charts with the classic 'Stars'. I thought it the most romantic song I had ever heard, having never locked ears with Roberta Flack or Stephin Merritt. I was, at that time, so parched for romance, I lusted for the lips that sang those sweet words, 'I want to fall from the stars, straight into your arms'. Past lovers were men whose fathers expressed their affection with an infrequent pat on the head and the exhortation 'well done, chap'. No romance to be had among those constipated little toddlers fated to strut around boardrooms cursing the tepidness of their lattes. I was drawn to the melodies of Hucknall. After his show at the O2 in Charlbury, I stood in a soignée curl at the stage door, making the universal sign for 'come step into my ladygarden, Big Ginge'. It's no secret that Hucknall was a sex addict. It was, appropriately, all over the red tops for weeks. Have you noticed how keen sex addicts are to publicise their woes? Strange, eh? So that evening seven of us went up to his hotel room and he pleasured us two at a time, alternating between oral and penetrative. He loved and caressed us like a madman trying to expel a demon from his ginger balls. I've never encountered a lover with such astonishing potency, with endless stamina. He was a lovemaking supercomputer, a man not content until he'd teased each shiver of pleasure from a woman's body. On a long summer night, I can still feel the tickle of his red locks across my back as he pleasures me from behind."

"I wasn't expecting you to say any of those words," Derek said.

"It's embarrassing to me now. If you look at the puffy, sexless oaf that Hucknall has become, you'd concur like crazy. He shagged the musical talent from his nodes, using our bodies as vessels for his creative ruin. He expelled that soulful Simply Red magic with each rabid discharge, squandering his artistic talent inside the peachy wants of us lust-starved harlot-groupies."

"Cripes."

"Your turn."

"I organised a scheme to pickpocket the wallets of the Scottish parliament to fund an undefined political revolution," he said and explained the events preceding.

"Yikes!" she said, as Derek spun and concluded his tale in Spain, omitting the torture scenes.

Ping! said Robin Cook.

Robin Cook pinging at this exact moment was significant.

The pinging of Robin Cook posed essential questions as to the future of this man's existence.

This man being that man Derek.

The pinging of Robin Cook signalled the potential suggestion of the possible beginning of the near start of a probable new chapter in his life.

That 'his' being Derek.

The pinging signalled that in some nook of his anima there was the suggestion that hanging around this female being was being weighed up on the scales of what-if.

(Robin Cook was an MP who recovered from marital scandal to emerge an anti-war badass and all-round peace-straddling bearded semi-legend).

But could Derek tolerate Linda's Nellie?

"I should explain Nellie," Linda said. "Since she was small she's had moments when the lid has come loose on what we call her loop-de-loop."

"Loop-de-what?"

"In other words, she has periodic moments of unquiet behaviour where she acts in ways that suggest she has extreme mental fissures. We've never taken her to see a head quack for fear she'd be committed. When she was a child, she was convinced helicopters were UFOs come to turn all people into bollards."

"Right."

"Once she believed that prisms were secret windows into Venusian partouzes."

"Oh."

"Another time, she thought soup was milked from the teats of marsupials."

"Ah."

"On a happier topic, I have ninety quilts."

"Ninety?"

"Ninety-nine, actually, there's nine more under the stairs."

"I admire the art of quiltmaking. My ex-wife was a skilled crocheter and she made me two tunics with bloodhound epaulettes."

"Nice."

"Sewn into the fur of the bloodhounds were swastikas."

"Oh."

"It was a satire on post-imperial arrogance."

"Of course."

"The lady farmer tells me Daniel Kawczynski needs my room. Where are the cheapo hotels in the area?"

"There's Tim and Tina's B&B in Topton. Five miles north. That's safe apart from the bedbugs and rug slugs."

"Rug slugs?"

"Slugs in the rugs."

"Thom and Thomma's Hoe-Tel is not safe. A prostitution ring in the basement."

"Nowhere else?"

"The nearest Novotel is ten miles NE."

"Is there an apartment to rent?"

"No. Gagglers petitioned to have no more properties built to keep out the Syrians."

"Ah."

"Stay here, we have a couch bed of ludicrous comfortableness."

"I couldn't."

"You could. You will."

"All right, then."

"You like Nellie?"

"She's intriguing. One thing—"

"What?"

"Remember after the 2015 terrorist attacks in Paris when Kay Burley tweeted a picture of a dog with the caption 'the sadness in his eyes'? Nellie sort of resembles that dog."

"You're saying my daughter has the appearance of an abandoned cur following a series of ISIL suicide bombings on the Stade de France?"

"I am saying that, yes."

"But apart from that?"

"She's a heck of fun."

All right, he could tolerate Nellie, might even wear the skin of a locum papa.

Ping!

But what about the moron she'd dragged in?

Christian Vandross?!?!

. . . who appeared in an oversize suit at the foot of the stairs. A discussion followed encompassing the following: Christian's Christian name being Christian (a frequent source of two seconds' amusement) his presence in the Thrum household, the reason for his wearing one of Nellie's father's "hustings busting" suits that he wore on the campaign trail, the supposed expensiveness of the suit being worn, the ethics about bringing someone of Christian's mental foregoneness into the house, the ethics of his wearing one of Nellie's father's suits of indeterminate price, and the implications of his sleeping in Nellie's room and the whoop that was heard earlier, presumably from more "cosmic" sex, and whether these whoops were any of Nellie's mother's business when each paid equal on food and electric and tax. Christian had no part in this discussion and stood in a state of ill-fitting awkwardness staring at Derek's robust Scotch chin.

When invited to speak, these sort of things:

"Nellie resembles a woman I courted at Cambridge," Christian said, "if length of hair is the comparison criteria. More specifically, the length of Marsha Drexler-Tourran's rebellious post-PhD period hair when she spent two weeks attempting to disprove Fermat's principle by reversing the Langranian formulations for geometrical optics. Marsha was the name of the ex that Nellie somewhat resembles."

A pause.

To conclude that if these were the sorts of things he was to utter, his presence would become intolerable in a whisk.

More:

"Hair length aside, there is no resemblance either in appearance or stature or mode of expression or comportment. In some respects, Nellie is a shiftless woman of no particular attractiveness with a polite speaking voice unmarred by the shrill inflections that seem native to the region who walks with an adolescent lurch as if two anvils were at permanent rest on her shoulders, and emanates an air of precognitive disapproval for every utterance about to emerge from the speaker's mouth, as if each word were intended to further negate her right to exist on this planet or cast her virtue in an unflattering light. Marsha Drexler-Tourran's had the tender tones of a Sissy Spacek."

A pause.

To accept the burden of sitting opposite a twat.

"You have the muscular discipline of the Swedish materfamilias," he said to Linda, "a thin slip of a mid-forties spinster with a pleasant simper masking a deep dissatisfaction with herself and a lifetime's worth of swallowed grievances in wait for an eventual outburst. I observe people."

A pause.

"All right, that's enough listening to this wanker," Linda said, leaving the room.

"He's had a rough trip here," Nellie offered as a means of explaining these ureic leaks of verbal incontinence to the remaining Derek.

Ping!

Yes, if Linda also hated him, he could put up with this idiot.

Nothing stronger than a bond of mutual hatred.

The final question was whether she (that she being Linda) was interested in him (that him being Derek) in the matter of martial frotteur. If she was interested in curling into him like a fortune teller fish in his wizened hand. If she could wrap her limbs round his bruises to shield them from the scream of the sunlight. If she could slice the warts from his feet without suffering acute existential welts.

O, sumped in thought, he was!

Ping!

Ping ping, Mr. Cook!

Cooking up some kind of tolerable tomorrow?

O, what a tantalising prospect!

Ping!

To pull off a Robin Cook with a flamboyant, wheezing chuff in the final frames of a mediocre life.

Sadly, that trippy rural ohm in an open-top coupé blasting Courtney Barnett from the subwoofers to fields of merry meadowlarks and smiley happy peonies was interrupted by a harrowing psychological meltdown in a Chedworth orchard. Having clomped over farmland in hobnails and a trance, shrugging aside the protests of tweed-bodied landowners and the menacing onrush of pompous milchers, Nellie had plopped to earth in a Cobainesque pelf of screams, losing consciousness as the bells of wherever chimed.

When she awoke in the hospital ward the screaming resumed with a whirl of lunacy—leaping on the beds of burn victims, lobbing sippy cups of Ribena at orderlies, and making like a monstrous dodecahedron was at war inside her body. Sedation and a transfer to the psychiatric clinic followed. She had a craving for pineapple and custard on toast when she came to and claimed that although her vagina remained undamaged she had last night forced an entire universe from her womb. Her entire physical make-up had also changed. Checking herself in the mirror, she was pleased to meet a thinner and hotter bod with thicker fuller hair and striking blue peepers and non-retroussé nose and a voice of the sultriest husk like her school nemesis Sandra Young.

Linda and Derek barrelled to the ward ASATC.

"There's no sweetening this pill," the doctor said. "Your daughter has flipped her proverbial."

"Excuse me?" Linda said-spat.

"My apologies. We use black humour to cope with the increasing wodge of dement taking hold across the country."

"Yes, I'm familiar with the Weltanschauung of the medical profession. Could you now explain what in the name of Alejandro Eduardo Giammattei Falla has happened to my daughter?"

"She's convinced that she's birthed the universe."

"Oh."

"She's replaced the hysterical shrieking with a welcome peppiness at her creation. Last I saw her, she was wondering aloud whether in her universe shortcrust pastry is standard in a lemon pie, if concierges moonlight as pencil sharpeners, and if caustic potash and hydrogen peroxide help cure rhino pox, then she clicked her fingers to see if she could summon up a rainbow and clicked them again to magic up bloodhounds then leapt to the window to see if she could capsize a Volvo by twitching her knees and singing 'Don't Worry Kyoko (Mummy's Only Looking for a Hand in the Snow)'."

"Oh."

"What treatment is there, doctor?" Derek asked, squeezing Linda's sweaty hand.

"I expect this is a temporary breakdown precipitated by some unaddressed past trauma. They usually are. I'd suggest a psychotherapist. Unfortunately, she'll have to wait five years to be considered for placement on the NHS waiting list."

"It's all right, we're from money," Linda said. "Can I take her home?"

"Yes. Be careful not to challenge her on her delusions. Nod along in a friendly concerned way, as though speaking to a Trumpist havering on about secret laptops and paedophile rings in Pizza Hut cellars."

"You're hilarious," Linda said.

The patient, beyond kempt and partially sodden, strode at bold voltage toward her mother and the Derek as though emerging from a magical car wash coated in streaky new atoms of purpose. Apparent to Linda was her wide-eyed medicated über-oomph and only fractional attention to the people trying to hug and comfort and prattling concern into her lugs as they left the building.

"What should I change about the universe first?" she asked in the backseat, rocking with the cretinous optimism of a toddler.

"How about banning accordion players from tube stations?" Derek asked.

"Free marshmallows on the NHS?" Linda asked.

"Hmm. I was thinking increasing life expectancy to 300. Imagine living through three centuries of change?"

"No way. 80 years is enough of this for anybody," Derek said.

"I can make exemptions for complainers."

"As in lock and load?"

"Maybe."

"Why is mass genocide always the first thing on any leader's to-do list?"

"Who said anything about genocide? Anyway, I'm not even sure I have any control over my own universe."

"Phew."

"Going to name my universe Jason."

"*What?*" her mum spat-said.

"I like the name. I know no one else does, but I don't care. I'm the mother."

"Derek, opinion?" Linda asked.

"On?"

"The name Jason?"

"It's a horrific name."

"Thanks," Nellie tutted. "What's your suggestion, then?"

"Ivan."

"Ivan? As in The Terrible?"

"He wasn't *that* terrible, Ivan the."

"Not Ivan the Lovely, was he? How come Ivan?"

"I like the name. How come Jason?"

"I like the name."

"Oh."

"Scissors paper stone?"

"OK. One, two, three . . ."

Nellie's scissors snipped Derek's paper.

"Damn."

"Yes! Gentlefolk, welcome to Jason."

"Jason? Who calls a universe *Jason*?" her mum protested again.

"How very non-U, eh, mother?"

Back in the living room they treated Nellie with the twitchy reverence of two parents caught using a hamster in their anal play—Derek rubbing his shanks like a stridulating cricket, Linda rocking her feet like the last simile—as she verbal-stomped through various plans ("mandatory yarmulkes for neo-nazis!", "universal ban on AstroTurf!") until she zonked asleep on the couch. Linda put a blanket over her daughter, stroked her hair, kissed her on the forehead, and led Derek to the bedroom.

She put her hand on his penis.

"I never usually refuse sex," he said, "but there's something acutely inappropriate about shagging when downstairs your daughter in speedily descending into a state of cartoon lunacy," he said.

"Could you eat me for twenty minutes or so? It would help me relax. I'll put this cushion on the floor so you won't have to strain your knees."

Derek's limbs had been newly fortified by yanking tubers from their loamy wombs, so the usual cricks and cracks were kept to a satisfying low. Linda peeled the tights from her bronzed pins with the effortlessness of a sous chef shedding a parsnip's skin for inclusion in a porcini wellington and with a sexy flop presented Derek with the skilfully trimmed pubic mound and vulva she wished him to service. Replacing stepfatherly concern with boyfriendly duty, he buried his face in his lover's crotch and licked up the Y-axis, trying to maintain a steady lapping rhythm without overly straining his vulnerable neck muscles. He had never hit upon the secret to successful cunnilingus. He merely—as he had since he was seventeen—flickered his tongue across as much surface area of labia as possible, occasionally peeking inside the vagina, and focused on a steady lapping of the clitoris until the woman (Linda) responded with noises approximating pleasure.

"Suck my clit with more vehemence," she requested.

Derek nodded.

"Keep nodding, that felt nice."

She responded strongly to the slurpy suction to her clitoris, coming with the theatrical air of an actress dying in an early talkie, trying to expire without ruffling her hair. Camilla usually pushed Derek's head aside near climax to choreograph her own orgasm with a madly frotting index finger. Linda's pleasure came ten minutes into Derek's procedure. She thrashed her slim body across the mattress and shivered every inch of ooh around her body.

"Thank you," she said after, kissing Derek's cheek. "Do you want me to attend to him?"

Meaning the penis.

"No, he remains unmoved."

"You weren't turned on by me writhing in ecstasy?"

"Usually, yes. But the angle was hurting my neck and I'm still thinking about your daughter losing her mind."

"I'd appreciate if you didn't think about Nellie when you have your face buried in my crotch, Derek."

"Not in that way."

"Hmm."

"Are you willing to talk about what happened to Nellie? You know, why the whole stunning mental collapse?"

"I'd consider it a personal affront if I wasn't allowed to reciprocate," she said, rubbing her hand on his crotch.

"Are you trying to stall?"

"Yes. But it'll be some sweet, sweet stalling."

She loosed his penis from its secure trouseral nook and rolled it between her palms with the skill of a sous chef moulding the perfect sausage from a lump of pork, staring into Derek's eyes in a phenomenally sexy way, like this: o__o. Five minutes of exquisite fellatio followed—the usual tonguing of the tip and tickling of the bottom shaft—with a perfectly timed head retreat as he came with a *huhnnnh*, his semen arcing in the air and vanishing forever from view. They showered à deux and went to bed.

"My ex-husband was a Tory, as you know," Linda said. "He came home, his britches plump with plum brandy, and whispered into Nellie's unsleeping ear promises about her radiant future. Upon coming of age, she would pen a Pulitzeresque doctorate that comprehensively proved something cosmically marvellous in the universe that illumined to the very nub of us and have insanely handsome princes hurling palaces at her feet if they matched her level of esteem and brilliance. As he lapsed into Tory clichés—shagging secretaries, pocketing brown envelopes, regressing as a human being—I was cast in the role of partypooper, a sour harpy crushing my daughter's dreams in a vice."

"I see. So rather than contemplate the reality that the she-God existence promised by her Tory father would never come to pass, that her father was a lying scoundrel and her life would never remotely match the one promised, she's taken refuge in an insane delusion that mimics her father's whispers."

"I'd have thought that was obvious. But concisely summarised. Sleep time now. I'll probably wake you up around four for penetrative sex," Linda said.

"Oh. Sure."

The next morning—penetrative sex unperformed—Nellie expounded a "vision" of the universe she had in her sleep.

"Here's what happened," she said, spooning Cheerios into her hole between clauses. "A moorhen fell from the heavens and crashed onto the bonnet of my car. I was relieved that something cruel and unusual had taken place, having keenly awaited the bummer portion of this Grave New World. The tension had been bugging me. I knew, as much as I knew anything (and I knew nothing in this particular vision), that something horrible would happen, since my universe—if it were based on my understanding of the previous universe—contained all that universe's crumminesses and horrors, alongside my own life's crumminesses and horrors, and even if there were no plummeting moorhens in my recall, this was the sort of random and pointless pain that summed up mine and everyone else's lives in the last universe, and so had a place in my universe, and, as if to prove this, the plummeting moorhen caused me to skid across the road and narrowly miss a barbed wire fence, screeching to a halt and causing car-wide whiplash."

A pause to perfect the pokeriest of poker phizes.

"Jason rains moorhens," Derek said.

"There's more," Nellie said, lopping a banana. "I noted, from the angle the next moorhen appeared, the elegant curve she described in the afternoon clouds, that this moorhen was behaving gravitationally more like artillery than a dropped bomb. Turned out someone was *shelling* hens at me! So who was firing fowl like mortars at me, you ask?"

(No one had asked).

"Well, why search for whys in a world only remotely explicable to one woman who wasn't entirely sure of anything herself? Or was it more relevant to search for whys in a world where one woman existed who *could* offer potential explanations, in contrast to the previous world where millions of people speculated themselves into dead-ends after two inconceivably slow millennia of quasi-comprehension?"

She lobbed the lopped banana slices into her mouth and chewed like a mentally ill woman in need of sedatives, i.e. herself.

"Honey, we're taking a trip to see a psychotherapist this morning."

"Why?"

"She might have some ideas for how you can take control of your universe," Derek said.

"That's right."

"Oh, that's dope. I'll get my fur on."

Linda's anxiety over her daughter's condition was clearly escalating as speedily as her daughter's condition was speedily escalating. She asked Derek to fingerbang her in the bathroom to help her relax. He wormed his hand below the waistband of her pants, twitching his index against the brunt of her clit until she shuddered as she came, insisting on reciprocal fellatio afterwards.

"Sorry, I need to find another way of relaxing."

"Have you tried meditation?"

"Hee-hee."

By the time this spontaneous oral adventure was over, Nellie had vanished. She had left the house with an alternative Derek and no visible mother in an alternative car to explore the universe that was forming in her mind.

Bourton hove into view, the car powering through a lavender-scented mist. Poised in two ditches were tanks with wedding-white doilies around their tracks mounted on two revolving purple turrets à la loo roll holders. Their guns fired perfume puffballs that drenched the surrounding roads in puddles of poundshop eau de toilette. A boldface sign erected above an overhead bridge read WELCOME TO GAGGLE-TON. Ladies in their mid-to-late seventies stood atop the tanks holding sweetie bags, lobbing explosive boiled chews at passing motorists. Derek screeched on the brakes. "Get in the boot," he barked. "What?" A Werther's Original erupted beside them. "I'm an old man. I'll be permitted access. You'll be killed. Go!" Nellie leapt out, pegging her nose against the perfume, and squeezed into the boot. Derek equated the smell to being locked in his schoolmarm's boudoir—these biddies were using spinster scent as an assault weapon. The car crawled along the velveteen road: concrete softening into a carpet that did little for the car's traction but felt pleasing and new. A roadside tollbooth popped up. A Gaggler with an electro-shock perm leaned out the window. "Age?" Derek temporarily forgot his age. He added seven years for safety: "Sixty-four."

This raised an important question. Were all citizens newborns in Nellie's universe? Were the folks of Jason, despite retaining their physical characteristics from the old world, a collective age of two or three hours old? It was something she ought to share with the Gagglers, considering their brand of discrimination centred around age . . . might this not be the perfect time for a fresh start, seeing the universe was still at the suckling stage? "You look much older." The Gaggler thrust a laminated pass at Derek with a petunia design and the slogan THE WORLD STOPS WITH US as he advanced into the fresher air of the town with its mild scent of elderflower. He observed queues of downcast under-seventies being led into fenced off areas where booming choral music emerged from speakers. Inside, the "young" were knitting a church in purple wool. Derek freed Nellie when the danger was over.

She chalked up the differences between her world and the old. Pristine lawns. Unbent streetlamps with bulbs. Dogs with silent barks. Clouds dispensing a lemon scent in aerosolised puffs. Cats moving in tandem with their owners, necks up in hauteur. Proper apostrophe use on shop signs. Life insurance advertised at bus stops. On Gaggler Avenue, a procession of old men carrying laptops, monitors, CPUs, keyboards and hammers blocked the traffic. This was the Running of the Laptop Event, where technologies were released into the wild and hunted. The purpose was to crush as many unworkable technologies as possible to prove humankind could advance without "complicated internetty doodahs". "You should be thankful," Nellie said. "No doodahs, millions of lives lost. Medical technologies prevent a million unimaginable sufferings per second." The receiving Gaggler blinked. "You want a hammer? It's traditional." Nellie was tempted. "Might be fun to fuck up a Mac!" The sight of a hundred octogenarians in starched blazers, asserting their mastery over machines by rolling Macs up the pavement, pulling CPUs on sleds, swinging mice around on their leads and slowly carting heavy equipment to a field on foot, needing a break every two seconds to catch their breaths, was the best so far. One man who looked on the verge of collapse was kicking the shit out of a heart monitor.

On another street, Gagglers were chewing on things. One blue-haired woman was eating a lamppost which, from its texture, resembled a supersize Pepperami—she munched through until the protrusion collapsed onto Donald's (formerly Donalds') café. One man was eating his coat (made from wet Bovril), another a windowsill (candyfloss), and another his own hand (white chocolate). Four women in plaid (liquorice) licked the roads like peasants lapping the cowhide of an emperor. "I wonder if the women are edible too," Nellie wondered with her stomach and Derek wondered too with his (stomach).

In place of her old childhood home was a cuke-shaped corporate structure that extended into infinity when observed from a certain angle, propped beside two low-ceilinged council houses. Nellie stared at Mrs Pesto's pathetic little plantpots, Mrs Ronson's uncut lawn then back at her mum's refractive superhouse. "It's rather oversized for two," she said. Past the revolving doors, into the vestibule, Linda's cream carpet with coffee swirls remained in extended form, and an nth amount of coathooks stretched along a wall that had no end. Linda emerged from the creamy infinity, creamed over in a cream-coloured cardigan and holding a lone Creme Egg. "Is that the Creme de la cream?" Nellie asked. No one smirked. This was Linda minus two decades: blushered, lipsticked, mascaraed to the nine+ones. "Hi sweetie!" she said. It was the glam mum of her bambinohood. Dad's mum. "Hi Mum?" She hugged minus-Linda in fear. "How was school?" she asked. Nellie paused. "I'm twenty-three. I haven't been in formal education for seven years." Linda smiled. Shuffled feet and coughs filled the silence. A sign on the wall, high above the coathooks read: HOUSE OF MOTHERS. A conclusion came fast: this building contained more than one mother. The present Linda, if her assumption was correct, was a Linda from Nellie's recall. It was a mausoleum of mummage. "Could you excuse me for a minute, Mum?" she asked. Her beautiful young mother smiled tenderly, saying stagily: "Sure thing, cuteums." Derek followed Nellie back to the revolving door where she huddled him in a huddle.

"It shouldn't be too hard to find the right Mum," Nellie said. "Let's find her and leave this sick cuke of sham mums."

The lift directed them to various mum-floors: failed hippie mum (2), punk chick mum (4), docile housewife mum (10), stoic warrior mum (18), repressed timebomb mum (22), trainee chemist mum (6), and so on. Nellie panicked at the prospect that her mum no longer existed in this universe, replaced instead with this sequence of past mums, comprising some mum-aggregate in place of the real aging mum. On the twelfth floor, flock wallpaper in the living room, a Westlife posterplast in Nellie's bedroom, and ill-chosen red bathroom tiles. Each floor was a replica of her childhood home's changing décors. In the lift, Nellie said to Derek: "Let's split up. Meet back here in an hour? Please respect my mothers."

Next she ascended to the eighth floor. This was Linda's 1970s-tat phase: purples and oranges melded with ecrus and cerises, turquoises and pinks. On the bright wall: a mother, father, and Nellie looked familial in a hospital. On the dark wall: a mother, a silhouette of a cut-out father, and Nellie looked sad in parks and rooms. This was the time of paternal leave. Linda was sat on the sofa in a flowery skirt with a glass of wine, smiling. "Hello my only," she said. "Glass of wine between two?"

"I rarely say nay to vino," Nellie said.

Linda poured the red for her, sucked back like mother's milk.

"Mmm. Do you have anything to eat?"

"No. There's no food in this particular stratum of your mother's recall. There's a beach picnic on the fourth floor."

"Are there other Nellies in this building?" Nellie asked.

"No. We are subconscious representations of your mothers from the previous universe."

"You're aware of your function in this place?"

"Yep. We're all various evolutions of Linda Thrum née Tomalin."

"What's your evolution?"

"I'm the Linda who was dumped. The room's divided in two—I am in two minds whether I hate or love him."

"Is your memory restricted?"

"It's restricted to this period in the life of Linda, but news travels up and down the floors. I know about the future me."

"Is it not bizarre being stuck as one version of a person your whole life, knowing a future you can't live?"

The thirty-one-year-old Linda Thrum stared into space for a moment.

"No," she said.

On the sixteenth floor Nellie found near-nervous-breakdown Mum under a flickering bulb in the kitchen. "It's OK. I'll do the washing up," she said, and her harassed mum went for a nap on the sofa. In this small way, Nellie atoned for the non-stop hellmaking and painsqueezing that had been her sixteenth year.

On the top floor, the room was dark apart from a single bright light in the distance hovering above a tableaux of some ominousness. In the centre of light sat a coffin with a crucifix. Nellie leaned over the varnished pinewood box like the Grim Reaper as imagined by Ingmar Bergman. A series of taps came from inside. "Hello? Is there anyone out there?" a muffled voice said. She opened the coffin and a beaming Linda popped out with a vibrant "Hello!" Nellie flung her arms around the head of this prankster mummy-mummy. "I'm so pleased you're not dead!" she said. "Yes, me too!" the mummy said.

"Hi, Nellie!"

"You're the up-to-date mum?"

"I am, I promise."

"Can you vouch for yourself?"

"I can vouch."

"You can vouch?"

"Yes."

"Good."

"You look and sound better, love."

"Yes. I've had facial and vocal tweaks."

She took her up-to-date mum's hand and left with her. They found Derek pacing round the lobby like a problematically programmed Pacman ghost.

A slow ooze of Gagglers came from the surrounding houses—a sea of wizened faces, folded arms and Pringle sweaters, their expressions, as usual, full of sourness, ignorance, hate and stupidity, as per. Nellie observed the ooze and, with an entirely innocent sweep of her arm, brought a tsunami crashing down on their heads, washing the street clean with her unexpected fire hose of redress. The water spurted along the roads, flooding Bourton in its entire, except the House of Mothers, where Nellie, Linda, and Derek stood with a sense of wonder past-reserved for biblical characters. Arms, legs, and heads bobbed about in the water, thrashing and kicking without a sound like cardboard cutouts.

The Gaggler threat was no more, replaced with roads turned rivers replete with cars and bodies and dustbins thrashing along the rapids at speeds well above the national limit. "I think there's a rowboat on the ninth floor. Remember that rowboat Jim Callums dumped in our garden, Mum?" Nellie asked.

"Good thinking, love."

The fetched rowboat was insufficient for three average-sized adults. The fact a capsizing occurred with three similarly weighted people balancing at either end spoke of a fundamental design flaw—this was not the work of a competent carpenter or serious-minded sailor. Linda tried oaring around the surfacing Volvos and drowning Gagglers with a tennis racket (no oars on the fourth floor)—assuming skippership of the vessel as the one person of the three who had been sailing.

"I have a better plan," Nellie said. "We're on course for the train station. If we arrive there, we leap onto the platform. The trains are never late here due to repair works or leaves on the track. Never."

She stood starboard, helping steer with her arms around the bubbling debris, while Linda pummelled with her Teflon pan those who clung to the boat. One of those faces was an old acquaintance, Mrs Gasket.

"I think I killed Mrs Gasket," she said, covering her mouth.

"Well done, Mum!"

"Nellie! Don't cheer me on when I've killed someone, that's not polite."

The station never appeared. The rowboat banged against a Transit van and capsized for the fifth time, toppling its occupants into the water where the current dragged them along to a set of raised church steps. Derek's expensive coat, knitted with the finest Harris tweed or whatever it was they knitted up there, was ruined. Once the water was coughed out and composure regained, they observed the Gagglers stood at the church door, arms folded and sour faces on show. At the front: Mrs Gasket.

"I thought she had been bashed in with Teflon," Nellie whispered to her mother.

"Must've been her sister."

"So Nellie—here we is," the ugly woman said.

"You've been expecting me?"

"No. This is an example of fate," the ugly woman said. "Please, come inside. You understand you have no choice in the matter." Her Gaggler henchwomen had machine guns. Nellie rolled her eyes. "Not again."

Mrs Gasket had morphed from a bigoted fascist with the features of a chain-smoking Atlantic wolf eel into a cartoon superwitch with the features of a chain-smoking Atlantic wolf eel with minimal effort. She imprisoned Nellie on a high-backed chair with carpet samples tacked to the wood and quilted loo paper draped along its armrests, chaining Linda to the left and Derek to the right armrest, beside the cupboard where they stored long-expired Dundee cake.

"What is this for?" Nellie asked.

"Those promises."

"I promised something to a right-wing prune with no taste in fabrics?"

"You promised. You must deliver."

"Must deliver? Fuck off."

"Deliver, or we'll shoot your mother."

"Oh."

"We'll shoot that old twit in the tweed too."

"Oh."

"We want the world, honey. We want to exterminate the young completely and evolve a new form of human being born at fifty-five with no past and a far shorter future. We want a world ruled by fear of damnation where obedience, piety, tolerance and suffering are the usual. We want eternal chastity—no carnal temptation and no useless husbands who drink up the money. The extermination of men. The extermination of all threats to an ascetic Presbyterian life of inherited wealth, routine, church, and gossip. We want the right to exterminate anyone who fails to live up to our standards, or who has annoyed us in some way. We want deluxe hair boutiques. We want the extermination of all places outside Bourton."

"No problem. How do I do that?"

"Don't fiddle us, dear. You have universal control."

Nellie puffed her lips.

"You think I can make things happen with my mind, do you? If I could do that, Gasket, you'd be a bowl of manure by now, and your Gagglers would be custard blobs. Your move."

"So what can you do?"

"I'm useless. I can't control anything."

Mrs Gasket raged at the altar, huffing and puffing and making damnations into the ether of an incoherent nature. Nellie was terrified at the prospect her mythology of the Gagglers had made them lethal in her universe. "I suppose I'll have to shoot you useless sacks," Gasket said, pulling a revolver out her bra. Fortunately, an Australian mosque crashed through the roof of the church, crushing Mrs Gasket and the Gagglers in an elegant sprinkling of bricks. Dust and debris collected around the captives.

Outside, a blood-red dusk was descending (the time: two o'clock) and the sustained cries of Gagglers in distress echoed from within the crumble. "It's rather Hieronymus Bosch out here," Linda said, expecting no one to cadge the ref. "The hellish painter," Nellie said, clinging to her Mum's shoulder, hopping forward on an unbricked leg. Their rowboat remained on the church steps, so a slipshod navigation of the rapids resumed. The water had tempered somewhat, allowing for a slower and more captainable voyage towards the train station. Derek and Nellie oared the boat onto a calmer strait with more streetlamps and less screaming. "It's like Venice!" Linda said. "If Venice was the gateway to hell," Nellie muttered. "I can still hear screaming and wailing," she said. The moribund Gagglers, with their rattling throes, summoned up a four-hundred-foot dragon whose head appeared on the horizon. Rising behind a tower block, two pink orbs blinked into view, set in a fuchsia face with wrinkles embroidered in bright orange wool. The creature opened its cavernous mouth and released a long blast of fire into the atmosphere. "God," Nellie said, "even their fire-breathing dragons are tacky." Careful paddling kept them en route to the train station as the water became soupier with cars. A BMW S-Series fenderbendered the prow, sending the boat into a frantic spin. "Steer left! Steer right!" Derek shouted. "Which one?" Nellie shouted. "Steer RIGHT! Steer LEFT!" Derek repeated. "For fuck's sake, pick one!" Nellie shouted. "Nellie! Mind the language!" Linda shouted. To add to their hardship, something was being fired at them from behind, or up ahead, or behind, loud blasts sploshing in the water, increasing the pandemonium. "Who the fuck is firing at us?" Linda shouted. "Mum! Mind the language!"

Pirates. Nellie was staring at an authentic pirate ship with a sail and a deck and a flag with a Gaggler's head being stomped by a Doc Martin. "Hands in the air!" a voice boomed from a megaphone. "We can't! The boat will capsize!" Nellie shouted. "Don't move! We'll drag you on deck!" the voice said. "We're on choppy water, you idiots, the boat accelerates by itself!" Nellie added. "Shut up!" the voice said. A length of rope was thrown around the rowboat, and a man with brawn helped them up a rope ladder onto the pirate ship. Five unwashed Jim Lads in ripped jeans, punk T-shirts and bandanas awaited them with hostile, dumbfounded stares. Nellie glanced at their faces in the silence, noting—"Is that Graeme Sims?" The identified Mr. Sims grunted affirmative. This was the kid who used to pick Nellie's ears and eat the wax. He'd turned from a baby potato into a king-size potato as he rocked on his heels, picking his ears.

The boat of failed suitors. Among the pirates was Ranvir, a Scot with Indian parents who she slept with to create small-town ethnic tension à la In The Heat of the Night; Paul, whose parents were the richest in town and resented Nellie's smaller bank balance; and James, who helped her rig up exploding pumpkins outside the Freemasons' HQ. The leader was Ryan, who had squeezed her right breast without permission, whose face had improved with time into something approximating Johnny Depp. "Long time no see, Ryan," Nellie said. Ryan lowered his bayonet. "You remember us?" he asked.

The toe-curling part. Nellie had dumped four of the men after their function had been served (Gaggler revenge). Each parting had ended in tears, some with begging and others with pleading in their pants while rubbing gateau on their nipples. "You never liked us, did you?" Ryan asked.

"Cut to the chase, Ryan. We've only arrived. Offer us a cup of tea or something," Nellie said. Derek stepped forward and offered his hand. "Hello there. I am Derek, and this is Nellie's mother Linda. I am looking to get back to Scotchland as soon as possible, I wonder if you might be able to take us to the train station? We would be most grateful for your assistance."

Ryan stuck out his bayonet. The answer was no.

"You never loved us."

"Ryan, let us out these manacles. We have stuff to do."

"You never loved me."

"Nope."

"You were using us to get back at the Gagglers."

"Yep."

"You used us to exact revenge on them for gossiping about you, for controlling your life."

"Yep."

"You let them control your life."

"They invaded my privacy."

"Privacy? You never needed any, you were a Grade-A show-off!"

"I wasn't."

"You used us."

"So what? We were kids, who cares?"

"I loved you."

"Puppy love."

"Ranvir and Paul and James and Graeme loved you."

"Graeme ate my earwax."

"You used us."

"So you keep saying."

"Now we're going to use you."

"This is tedious."

"Boys? I am her mother. Nellie was depressed back then. She didn't mean to hurt any of you, not on purpose."

"Shut up."

"Do not tell my mother to shut up!"

"You know the Gagglers have elected a new leader? Mrs Halpine. She's more extreme than Mrs Gasket. She'd be grateful to us if we were to hand you over."

"So you're feeding us to the vultures because I wouldn't let you touch my tit. Is that it, Ryan?"

"Shut up."

"Were you the ones firing hens at us?"

"No."

"Then what's with the cannon and the birdshit? Why not accept I didn't love you and move on with your life?"

"No. This is what you do. You use people to spite someone, then spit them out like hot coffee. You don't love anything. You're a cold-hearted bitch."

"I've heard this before."

". . ."

"What's wrong with him, Nellie?"

"He's clutching his stomach like he's been punched. Such a drama queen."

"No, I think he's been wounded."

"That's a lot of blood."

"And a big spear."

"That wasn't me."

After arrows were fired into Ryan's corpse from an unidentified source, puncturing in turn with fearsome accuracy each of his internal organs, the following events: Linda lamenting Ryan's passing with a short reminiscence about the time she served him weak lemon cordial while he waited for an unpresent Nellie to appear; Nellie making the obvious but apt comparison that the events occurring were like in a horrible dream, pausing for a minute before summoning the remaining pirates who were cowering behind the mainsail; the pirates refusing to appear for fear of being speared like their ex-friend; Nellie tempting them out with a kiss to be planted on each of their lips; Graham taking the bait and being shushed by his sceptical friends who assumed Nellie to be luring them to their deaths like an on-board siren; Nellie reassuring them this was not the case and she wanted to correct the past in kiss form; the pirates making their way along the side through nets and masts, crouching in the hollow deck with the captives; Graeme, unlikely replacement leader, crouch-walking over and dangling his spud above Nellie, lips proffered for a peck; Nellie complaining about having to kiss in front of her mother and insisting on a private space; Graham freeing her from the cuffs, whereupon she slapped him and berated his idiocy, demanding the key to release the other captives; Graeme weeping at being duped and losing his chance for a kiss, and at the nine flaming arrows piercing his torso; the remaining pirates leaping out to help their friend, meeting similar ends; Nellie concluding that a swift and quiet exit from the ship might be the wisest course of action.

"I am confused. Where are we now?" Linda asked. The boat (and occupants) was rocking on the rolling pink-quilted tongue of the patchwork dragon from earlier, sliding down its throat towards the stomach. "What the fuck is happening?!" Nellie shouted in the darkness. "Have you considered that the universe might mimic the subconscious?" Derek asked. "Where the imagination mingles freely with perceived reality, memories and stored information, however distorted. To try and bring discipline to a world where the imagination and rational mind are indistinguishable is absolutely impossible." This reassured no-one. The dragon's stomach acid sizzled amid numerous growling and belching noises, and the boat was fired from the dragon's mouth on a spectacular lick of flame, hurtling through the night at aeroplane vroomage, slowing after a few hours (Linda went to sleep) and feather-rocking to a halt over Brighton beach. Nellie had been here as a child to move sand around. Having landed on a strip of rocks, the boat's occupants headed towards a café for breakfast. Nellie pondered whether she was invincible, having survived a hen cannonade, a flood, a kidnap attempt, a collapsing cathedral, being eaten by a dragon, and falling from high up in transport without wings. "No. We're going to die soon," she said. "Remember we discussed your idea of paradise . . . something persevered in your memory as perfect?" Linda said. "Can you think where that place might be?" Nellie shook the salt shaker. "Is it here?" Linda asked with distaste. "No," she said. "I think I know the place." She recalled the absence of tourist guides, children's entertainers, clowns, candyfloss, pointless and exhausting treks to see rocks up hills, late lunches or dinners, cold showers, showers with lo-flo nozzles, insects in the bedclothes, door handles at unreachable heights, noisy neighbours, annoyingly upbeat families, nothing on TV, overly salty fish. "I'm afraid it's Centre Parcs."

Centre Parcs was a holiday resort in Woburn Forest, Bedford containing a hotel within a glasshouse. The group trudged on to the train station where there were no trains to Bedford. In fact, no stations were being advertised at the stop. The train travelled from the town and pulled into a large office with red carpet and purple couches and various people sitting clutching documents and workers behind computer terminals. "NELLIE THRUM?" a person shouted. She opened the train door and followed the worker. She sat on a swivel chair, and a spotlight appeared above her head. "ARE YOU LOOKING FOR WORK?" the man asked in caps. "No," Nellie said. "YOU REALISE YOU WILL LOSE YOUR BENEFITS?" the man asked in caps. She leapt from the seat and ran out the door, followed by the others, chased by the worker holding out a form for her to sign showing she understood and accepted she would lose her benefits. "Good," she said.

The other option was the cab rank. One cab and one cabbie sat in the rank. From his cab the song 'The Wind of Change' by The Scorpions was audible. "Is that supposed to symbolise something?" Derek asked. "No," Nellie said, "it appeared twice on my mum's Bestest Songs cassette, sides A and B." The cabbie stepped from his beige Rover 40 and doffed his baseball cap to the oncoming passengers, extending his arms in a theatrical manner and greeting them with: "Darlings! You were magnificent!"

"To Bedford, please," Nellie said.

"Certainly. Board the vehicle, you four delishiosities. Nellie, you ride up front."

"You know my name."

"Of course, honeybutter. All will be revealed as we rev the engine and proceed to Bedders. Now, I have on the old tape deck a selection of '80s power ballads: who's for a blast of Jennifer Rush and Bon Jovi?"

"I would like Radiohead," Nellie said.

"Preference?"

"Amnesiac. That sums up my mood."

"Done." The fifth Radiohead LP played on the stereo. "Now, belt up in the back. This is a cab ride unlike none other. Silence the mouths and prick up the ears. I am God. Yes, the Creator of the universe. I chose to appear in the form of an ebullient cabbie to put you three at your eases. I created the universe a week ago in my time, six billion years ago in your time. This was an experiment to see if I could manufacture a self-contained vacuum ruled by intelligent beings that did not tend to absolute destruction. Epic fail, as you say currently. I opted, for fun, to transfer the universe into the mind of one Nellie Thrum, to see what might happen if an individual consciousness ran the show."

"You are, presumably, a voice that Nellie's consciousness has created to explain the present scenario, a composite of her lapsed faith and her suppositions from science-fiction and limited cosmological data," Linda said.

"I am God. I can make things appear," he said. He made a hedgehog with a miniature sultan on each bristle shaking a pearl-encrusted scep-tre appear. He made an electromagnetic wave transmitting the nov-els of Dickens in Hebrew appear. He made Charles Dance on stilts, attempting to perforate his sealed nose to make nostrils, appear. He made a schoolteacher riddled with pox tied upside down in a che-quered sock appear.

"See?"

"These are unusual proofs of your divinity," Derek said.

"Can you make a lemon pie?" Nellie requested. The soi-distant God made over two million lemon pies appear on the nearby landscape and, over their heads, three UFLPs (unidentified flying lemon pies), which were soon identified as lemon pies from the showers of custard and shortcrust pastry over the Rover 40. Linda opened the window for a mouthful of crumbs, swallowing the equivalent of three bakery-sized lemon pies. "I don't care what the Great Grey says, you are definitely the God for me!"

"I think we will require more than lemon pies and pox-riddled peda-gogues as proof," Derek said.

"Greyster! You ought to learn more respectfulness. This fantasticular pie-popper is driving us to our destinies, you should at least acknowl-edge him as the Supreme Being and Ruler of This and All Galaxies!" a converted Nellie rhapsodised.

The car arrived at Centre Parcs. This was the end. The end of Nellie's short-lived universe, Nellie's short-lived life, and Nellie's impatience at waiting for her short-lived life to come to an end. Her father stood in the entrance, arms outstretched, a let-us-correct-our-past-mistakes smile on his face, a T-shirt that read Let Us Correct Our Past Mistakes, and lips that said: "Daughter! Let us correct our past mistakes." Linda rushed towards her former husband, spurning Derek without a second thought, and licked his knees with love.

"Pass that line to Centre Parcs, and paradise awaits," God said.

"Paradise for us all?" Derek asked.

God hiccupped yes.

"Oh, mamma!" he said, rushing to paradise.

"By the way," God said, your universe is about to completely blown to pieces by a heck-a-lot-a meteors. But take your time."

"I have to choose between suddenly loving a man I despise, or being pounded by a million meteors?" Nellie stared at her father's smiling face, beckoning her with a learn-to-love-me-again arms, a tattoo that read Learn to Love Me Again, and lips that said: "Daughter! Learn to love me again!" and made her choice.

Nellie stepped into some trees. She had to accept that if Derek and her mother could enter and be delivered into paradise without her, then she was not needed in this paradise, that this paradise was no paradise for her. They had their persons to love, and she wasn't one of them, so she was prepared to meet the end of everything rather than live for eternity in a sham heaven under the delusion that anyone whatsoever needed her.

One meteor fell.

Two meteors fell.

Two billion-to-the-power-of-two-zillion meteors fell.

Nellie lost her atoms.

"She was found unconscious by a bolus by the farmer Alison Granger," the same doctor from earlier said, "having stumbled through a field and near drowned in a brook of some sort. As she'd already been referred to us, there was little solution except to have her sanctioned under the mental health act. I know, that sounds pretty yikes. Good news is that the ultra-vivid sensory hallucination she experienced probably represents the apex of her mental collapse. When a patient reaches their meltdown apace, they're in a better position to be repaired by a head quack. You will probably find she appears super-duper depressed, so if she is unresponsive to you, please don't worry."

"Get out of my way," Linda said.

She clocked her daughter in a state of big-time boohoo and wrapped her motherly arms around her and cried on her shoulder and all that malarky.

Derek, standing in the clinical bummer of the room, responded to an email ping:

> Dear Mr Haffman,
>
> I am writing to you on behalf on the Conservative Party. We are interested in discussing an exciting new initiative set to trial in Uganda. We believe you might be an interesting candidate for one of our senior positions.
>
> We kindly await your response,
>
> Yours,
>
> Charles Horton-Louth
>
> CCCCC

"Come here, Derek," Linda said, encouraging his participation in the snuggle of sorrow. He pulled a plastic chair by the bed and rubbed a sympathetic hand on Nellie's shoulder as she made very awkward bleating sounds. As the women staged their festival of weeping, he found himself in an email exchange:

> Dear HL,
>
> No.
>
> Yours,
>
> D

Dear Derek,

Perhaps I should make myself clearer. We have *decided* you are the man we require.

Yours,

Charles Loughton-Hough

CCCCC

Dear Chaz,

No.

Yours,

D

Dear Derek,

Are you having a nice time with your lover and her daughter at Bourton-on-the-Water? I hope so. You will understand that once you have been "branded" by Lord Quiver, you are now the official property of the Conservative Party. You appreciate that your lover's daughter's condition may worsen if her mother loses her house, her means, and her reputation in the community, for example? This is not an outcome either of us desire. Bear this in mind when considering our generous proposal.

Yours,

Charles

Queer Charlie,

R U havin' a fuckin' larf, you knob?

D

Dear Mr Haffman

Amusing. Alas, vulgarity will not excuse you from your present responsibilities. Here is a synopsis of the role you will assume in several weeks. We have signed an agreement with the President of Uganda to begin our new project, provisionally titled Coolonial Pride, extra 'o' intentional. It is our intention to help the people of Uganda to become more culturally savvy, providing them with instructive lessons on British culture, from our novels, music, and portraiture to our tiktoks and whatnots. In return, Uganda has agreed to accept all our immigrants and refugees, who will forge new lives in the beautiful landscape of the pride of Africa. You present a range of lectures to the people of Uganda, involve yourself in cultural communities across the country, and champion the partnership between our two countries. You will also present a revised historical curriculum in which the so-called colonial crimes committed by the British Empire will be replaced with more favourable interpretations, encouraging the locals to look more charitably on the benefits of their former British rule.

My assistant will send you details of your departure date.

P.S. Your former mistress has been in touch asking for help. I suggested that she team up with you in Uganda, where she can help inform the people about the unusual subculture she claims to inhabit.

Best,

Charles

Citing a tummy dicky in the wake of a yucky vended wrap, Derek fled the hospital and taxied to Alison Granger's face.

"Remarkable naivety," she said, polishing a bronze poniard, "to assume you'd slither away from the Conservative Party having been bloodied by Lord Poo-Know-Who. The Party prides itself on being the only rehabilitation centre for otherwise unemployable ex-con politicians. You recall MP Michael Twill? He smashed up a stationery shop one afternoon and ran naked round the park lobbing babies into a fountain, then livestreamed on Insta the horrified parents as they leapt into the water while sneering "look at these idiots" in a bubbling of furious emojis. He ended up ambassador to Papua New Guinea. And MP Max Steadland? He kept a llama as a private carnal associate for nine years. He was put in charge of chastening agribusiness in South Poland."

"Yes, I know them. But what about these emails?"

"They're threatening to crush your gf and her spawn, right? They probably will. They might anyway, even if you accept their offer, seeing you were so rude in your responses. My suggestion is you move to Uganda and perform so poorly in your post they have no choice except to replace you with another schlomo. How are things with these shire bitches anyways?"

"Testy. Linda's spawn is a nutbar."

"Excuse me?"

"She's the daughter of a former Tory, so . . ."

"Ah. Classic nutbar."

"Yes. What young person today isn't a nutbar-in-the-making? Boomers were tasked with leaving behind a safer, happier world for our children's children by sewing the postwar ideals of cooperation, fairness, and prosperity into the fabric of society. Instead, we've forced them to become bedroom activists, frantically retweeting George Monbiot and having apocalyptic nightmares involving entire forests of baby antelopes on fire. They congregate in furious clusters around the latter-day Joan of Sark Greta Thunberg as their elders sit on their plush lawns calling them the snowflake generation without the teensiest puff of irony, blissfully blind to having had everything handed to them on a plate by the very left-wing progressive notions they rail against. It's remarkable young people today manage to stop themselves from burning down the houses of parliament."

"Or their grandparents' faces."

"Or their grandparents' faces. I'd happily tip a keg of paraffin over myself if I ever wielded the word *woke* as a weapon."

"Me too."

"I would so love the French to invade," she continued, following a pause where both imagined the logistics of self-immolation. (Inside or outside? Naked or clothed?) "There's a nation that knows how to fight for their freedoms. We're so cowed by class in this country the Queen could pour battery acid into our babies' eyes and we'd curtsy and request the honour of having our own eyes burned out by her too if that wasn't so much to ask, your most imperial majestic majesty."

"True."

"You'd have an army of blind morons stretching from here to Montrose, lining up to heap praise on our exquisite sovereign for her kindness and begging her to hack off their arms so they can replace them with union flags. Up and down the roads of this sick, thick nation, you'd have clumps of walking scarecrows, seeing off unpatriotic traitors to Queen and Country by snapping at anyone who taunts them as they stumble blindly through the streets sing-shouting Gawd Save You Ma'am."

"Yep."

"I can't wait until the old cunt croaks. I know we're supposed to be respectful of her 'service' to the country—the so-called service of a nonagenarian crone born into unimaginable wealth and privilege who for her entire reign has never seen fit to express a single thought in support of anyone suffering except in her carefully scripted yearly addresses where she takes a staggering *fifteen minutes* to make vaguely positive noises with her mouth while addressing us all as her fucking *subjects*. But I can't. The veneration of a woman who remains purposefully silent on every single topic, like on stuff like wars and murders and sexual abuse and corruption and epic poverty and inequality—all that flim-flam taking place in the country she presides over by cutting ribbons and saying fuck all—a sour-pussed old cipher onto which we can attach our own notions of how kind and understanding and wonderful a human she is based on whatever traits were lacking in our own vile, racist grannies."

"Yes. Anyway—"

"I mean, munch for a breve on this absolute insanity. A woman who is 70% precious minerals, who noshes on swan fritters and champagne at our expense thrice daily, who has never even heard of a baked bean, has the stones to expect us to venerate her every bloody year. Remember, this woman is an utter shithouse. Remember when she tried to use a state poverty fund to heat Buckingham Palace? To pilfer money straight from the pockets of her neediest subjects to heat the thousands of empty rooms where liveried flunkies clomp around polishing brass knobs and bringing her telegrams on silver fucking platters. It's obscene! People can't even afford to pay for a pea in this country, and this old parasite has the brass neck to strut around in her fucking crown with her sour face, making like it's a burden to have to cut ribbons or wave from balconies once or twice a year, when she'd rather be in a stable shovelling sugar cubes into her horse's mouths. There's more. Her first cousins Katherine and Nerissa Bowes-Lyon had serious developmental disabilities and were locked up in the so-called 'Asylum for Idiots', Earlswood Hospital. The sisters were never visited by any member of the royal family, including the Queen, nor were they in receipt of any extra money outside the basic hospital fees or any Christmas or birthday cards. No one even attended the fucking *funeral* and two were buried in unmarked graves. The Queen could have paid for private round-the-clock care for the two sisters for their entire lives and made a point of showing compassion for her cousins in spite of their serious disabilities. Instead, she toed the Victorian line of treating her cousins as embarrassments to the family, to be locked away, hidden from public view, and banished from the minds of everyone as a matter of course. What a fucking shower of absolute shits. Not even sending a *card*. Why bother, they probably thought. It's not as if those retards would understand. Then Queenie lashed out when a documentary film revealed the whole shameful reality, claiming they were "very much a part of the family", which was a whopping porkie.

Still not convinced? There's that time her people lobbied Scottish ministers for a climate law exemption, making her the only person in the country not required to construct renewable energy pipelines to heat the vast estates on her land. No, saving the planet couldn't possibly inconvenience our majesty! Or consider how the Queen vetted any laws pertaining to property taxation, tenants' rights, and keeping forestry inspectors orf her land without her say-so, and torpedoed any laws that could affect her private wealth. Quite the shrewd little raptor, no? Or how she squirrelled $13.1 million away in an off-shore account in Panama and how she's literally never used her wealth to help relieve the misery of her subjects. Or how she evicted a couple from their home for using a communal plug socket to charge their electric car. Or how she used £12 million to pay off the woman who accused her son of sexual assault. Or how she secured an exemption from the Freedom of Information Act, preventing us from knowing how the royals spend *our* money. Or how she advertised below minimum wage for a live-in housekeeper at *Buckingham fucking Palace*. Or how she used to hunt and kill tigers in Africa and routinely loves tearing foxes to shreds while wearing frankly fascistic outfits. Or how the police were barred from searching the Queen's estate for stolen or looted artefacts, exempting her from a law that protects the world's cultural property. Or how she routinely refuses to apologise for slavery and colonialism while patronising Commonwealth countries with rare opportunities to view her or her gormless grandkids waving from a bullet-proof car. Or how she appealed for *volunteers* to weed her Sandringham garden. Or how she demeans her employees by contractually referring to them as servants. I think that's all the evidence you need that this woman comes from a dysfunctional, callous family steeped in wealth and self-importance, and there's no conceivable way she's anything other than a product of a fustian, pompous, and embarrassing bygone era of amoral aristocunts being aristocunts."

"Yea, I hear."

"All right, fuck off to Uganda, my chum. Watch out for soldier ants, or soldiers covered in ants."

"Thanks for the talk, Alison Granger. I'm off to have my life ruined, again."

"Y'welcome, Derek Haffman."

Back home, Derek found Nellie in the bedroom.

He closed the door.

"Hey, listen I—"

Linda launched herself at Derek in a state of hectic autumnal lust, running her four-inch rasper along his neck, sinking to her knees to unzip his trews, removing the exulted upright Haffman penis.

Ping!

She commenced with the actions familiar to lucky receivers of fellatio or avid PornHub subscribers, making the penis feel welcome in her hot mouth.

Ping!

This fellatio confirmed the start of something tolerable in his life that was now over. He ran his pinkie along her centre parting as her head bobbed up and down, sending shocks of loveliness up his creaky ol' trunk.

Ping!

Yes, this new thing that had started, this new thing that was indeed a sweet little serving of rehabilitation, had now been obliterated by a Tory in a Tory suit sending a Tory email. As he approached climax, Derek had to conclude that this brand new something that held potential for the future, this undefined, sexy, spontaneous future thing kicking off between his legs at this very moment—was over. And that very soon he'd be in another continent lecturing malnourished kids on the merits of Andrew Lloyd Webber and Alan Bennett.

Ping!

A fleeting minim of hope that the future might have something in store one might class as marginally tolerable.

Ping!

Who could ask for more?

He'd tell her about Uganda in a minute.

# CODA

# NO TUTUTIQINS
# IN TANGIER

W HEEE-*eeeeeee*! went no one on the airtube crossing an other-world of knobbly knolls verdant with conifers and parched patches of cacti protruding from lushly be-bushed forests of unparalleled tranquillity, somehow in Uganda. *Ooooo-ooooooh*! went no one on the airtube crossing vast strips of sun-scorched mini-mountains bordering sandmost single-track roads randomly snaking their way across terrifyingly peaceful desert plains, puddle-starved no-man's-landscapes serially interrupted by villages with straw-topped pod-homes and shantytown shops with corrugated iron roofs, populated by unknowable locals zipping thither on motorbikes past stunning men and women in vibrantly patterned tunics.

Opting for short-shorts, a short-shirt, and shit-slip-ons in readiness for a burning shard of 1000° heat to fire up his skin instantly upon stepping from the airtube, Derek was surprised when a chill wind Dundee-kissed his arms. The only white man onboard, his outfit an obvious sign screaming "foreign idiot who never performed the most cursory of climate evaluations", Derek awkwardly rictus-smiled and speed-walked his way past the mainly men in full shirts and trousers to announce the arrival of his sad white self to customs.

A pimpled gawk from a minor public school named Tobias Prompt was Derek's manager. That man in particular was stood mooching in a pink shirt in particulate outside the Entebbe Airport entrance, lazily eyeing the exiters for the presence of an ill-dressed Scotchman wheeling a suitcase looking harried and clammy. Derek caught sight of this man named Tobias Prompt, perceiving a paunchy sort with a perma-smirk, whose arms waved and whose mouth honked "Derek! Over here!". There followed an exchange of bone-crunching powershakes.

"I'm Tobias," Tobias said, introducing himself as Tobias, "that's tee-oh-bee-eye-ae-ess. I've been sent to induct you. How was your flight?"

"Fairly smooth. I tried reading Don DeLillo again. I managed to convince myself I understood every fourth sentence."

"Splendid. I've no idea what that meant. I see you've plumped for the Full Steve Irwin in your apparel. I wouldn't worry too much. Many of the routinely untravelled make these sartorial blunders when approaching the Pearl of Africa."

Arriving at the obvious conclusion with the gravitational certainty of William Tell's expertly twanged arrow whooshing toward his son's head of apple that Tobias was an identikit Tory arsehole with a pouch of scruples as parlous as the average British bank account, Derek set his attitude to one of sleepy phlegm.

"Wasn't Steve Irwin fatally punctured by a stingray barb?"

"If you've never been to Uganda before, here's a primer," he said, swerving the question with the skill of every Tory in every broadcast interview on every issue ever as they bundled suitcases and selves into a taxi. "In the cities, you will encounter mainly the chippie semi-educated blacks, those who plucked their way from adversity to university. A first-class degree from an African university is the equivalent to a B-Tech qualification in one of those mucky polytechnics the Labour party built to help train tradesmen and servants. Outside those, in the towns and villages, you'll encounter paranoid yet wholly tame clods of the poor, proudly okay with their lot who know not to ask for the impossible like equality, prosperity, or respect. Outside those, in the backwoods of beyond, you'll encounter classic African poverty like in the Red Cross adverts—flies laying eggs in the eyes of barely sentient kiddies with potbellies, sad-eyed women shucking half-full carafes of water on their heads to their mud huts—that sort of thing. You'll soon find what Mr. Johnson said—"the problem is not that we were once in charge, but that we are not in charge anymore"—an apt remark. Our alternative historical curriculum provides a far more fair and balanced view of the British Empire in Africa. Take the Boers, for instance. Historians moan about the so-called concentration camps we forced them into as we strived to prevent them making a meal of things in Transvaal. In our version of events, we invented the term "concentration" camp to mean a place for its inhabitants to reflect on the wrongness of their actions, to consider the right-headedness of our innovative plans to catapult these Dutch bunglers toward *comme il faut*. Enforced contemplation. Hardly a crime, no? Sadly, the boo-hoo Boers failed to feed their own or even maintain basic sanitary standards, and under 30,000 of them expired trying too hard to force a logical thought from their minds. The experience proved that much more British education and common sense was needed if the savages were to ever raise themselves from their primal jellies."

"You want me to teach the most deprived and unlucky children in the world that colonialism was enacted for their own benefit?"

"That sort of malarky, sure why not. We're not saying there weren't some bad apples in the vast orchard of Empire. You can't force a soul through a loveless childhood into boarding school and the army and expect a chap to have an exemplary sense of fairness and morality. Even Eric Blair shot an elephant. No, we're simply asking that the legacy of colonialism has a fairer airing. A more nuanced approach to our triumphs as well as our failures, putting a new spin on the events certain lefty academics have exaggerated into terrible evils."

The conversation took place as a very black very African man chauffeured them while maintaining an inscrutable silence. He was instantly the living embodiment of all Africans violated by the British across two centuries of colonial atrocity—he was the innocent man trafficked into slavery, the peaceful tribesman tortured, raped, and butchered by sadistic corporals with plummy accents, the Boer marched to his execution for raising a hand against their captors. Tobias noted Derek's jittery side-eyes toward the driver and chortled.

"Don't worry! He's well-paid. You like your salary, Chitundu?"

"Oh yes, very good money, very good!" he said with a rousing laugh.

"See? Nothing much has changed. Treat them fairly and they are perfectly happy to work their sandy little feet off for us."

"Could you not—" Derek stopped.

"What?"

"Never mind."

It had occurred to Derek he had never stood up for the rights of black people in his career—aside from the occasional clout-seeking retweet—there being none in his constituency.

The taxi bombed with unspecified and bowel-clenching speed to the town of Iganga in the Luuka District northeast of Kampala, where the Centre for Cultural Appreciation had been in place for two weeks. A tumbledown clapboard upright that formerly sold chicken feed, the CCA consisted of several tables where three bored people sat on laptops thinking up ways to whitewash famines and massacres under the crackle-hum of electric fans. On the team was a Shakespearean actor, former lead singer of the band Live Kittens, and a hack novelist who self-published books on Amazon with pastel covers made on MS Paint. These people had applied for their roles, so Derek chose to mistrust and loathe them now to save time. The actor was a fury of chin and peevishness, a 6ft muscle with a Chekhov beard long used to not being the centre of attention. The former singer had been sacked from Live Kittens for abusing a kestrel on stage. He was used to sulking behind the bass and sulking in and out of court rooms. Now he sulked behind a table with a haircut parodying a 1980s Avon catalogue. The novelist was the only woman, a tiresome blip with the wind-beaten features of a right-wing pundit whose father had been a scab during the miners' strike.

A limp of hands, an exchange of soul-searing looks, a snuff of disdain, and Derek was pointed to a table.

"I'll be back in an hour," Tobias said, "talk to Henrietta here, she'll assume you the necessaries."

Out, flouncing.

"Back to the bezique table," Henrietta said, her frizzy hair frizz-framing her fizzy phiz. "He set up bezique tutorials last year, teaching the locals how to play badly. Now he steals the matoke from their babies' mouths."

"The British way," Derek said.

"What's your transgression?" Dorian the Shakespearean asked. His pallor hinted at one used to playing a hanged clown or beheaded Quintus.

"I robbed an MP and I libelled Quiver."

"*Oooft.* You're lucky you still have a functioning spleen."

He might have said "I know, right?" here, but he couldn't be bothered.

"We don't have much," Henrietta said, "work on here, as evidenced by the sum total of zero filing cabinets and the sight of Kenneth over there playing Minesweeper on his laptop," she said, looking at the Kenneth too busy clicking a risky 1-1-1 path round an unseen mine to notice, "but when we have to work, we prepare speeches for schools and villagers. Last week, Kenneth here spoke to the folk of Bugalama on the Happy Mondays. Yes. We're paid to explain Shaun Ryder to people who can barely manage to feed their children."

"It's a living," Dorian said.

"Am I getting paid for this?" Derek said.

"Nope, you're a Tory hostage," Henrietta said, "you'll serve for a few months, have your soul slurped from your body as you lie about mass graves, then a facsimile loser will take your place."

He might have said "sounds about right" here, but he couldn't be bothered.

"I'm here to lie to people about the magic of colonialism."

"Not quite. The endeavour is called Coolonial Britain. We want to associate colonialism with the Cool Britannia movement of the 1990s, when sporting a Union Flag on one's fabrics was not an indicator of EDL subscription and ownership of two rabid terriers chained to a bollard. It's an attempted rebrand of the Empire to pave the way for a slow return to British rule in Uganda. There's more to the story, but I won't tell you the whole thing yet, as I'm sure you'd love nothing better than to nibble on a kikomando and sup an ice-cold beer. You need to sign some forms. Essentially you'll be teaching our Alt-History of the British Empire in Africa, carefully written to downplay the hanging and looting and pillaging element, to pretend that these horrors have been overegged by enemies of the UK."

"I thought I was here to educate them on Paul Merton and Morris dancing?"

"Later, perhaps. But for now, squint at these printouts. They detail the bad things and how they're to be unbadded."

He accepted the printouts and skim-read:

Coolonial Britain—How to Teach Our Alt-History Curriculum

1897: Palace of the Oba of Benin

Current version: In 1897, the British Empire stormed the palace of the King or Oba of Benin in Nigeria. The Kingdom of Benin had been trading harmoniously with European explorers since the 1600s until the British economy needed a stimulus, resulting in a brutal invasion and looting of the palace. Ten thousand Nigerians were killed in the invasion and around four thousand precious materials, among them metal plaques and cast-heads, along with brass and bronze castings and ivory carvings, were stolen. These looted artefacts are still on show at the British Museum.

Revised version: In 1897, the King or Oba of Benin planned to loan these artefacts to Britain for a special international expedition named From Kingdom to Kingdom. As the artefacts were being moved a series of marauding tribesmen tried to waylay the British, leading to an unfortunate but necessary skirmish, resulting in many Nigerian and British casualties. Fortunately, the British preserved the artefacts in their museum, where they were safe from theft and waste.

1912: The Jallianwala Bagh Massacre

Fearing acts of civil disobedience when Gandhi took a massive huff at British policy in India, martial law was declared in the Punjab region. During the festival of Baisakhi, held to mark the onset of spring, a crowd of several thousand congregated inside the walled public garden of Amritsar. Fearing the illegal celebration might turn into a violent insurrection, the British Indian Army were dispatched to the scene, blocking the entrance and positioning themselves on embankments with kill weapons. Col. Reginald Dyer ordered his troops to open fire on the Indians, committing an intentional act of genocide that claimed in excess of 1,000 lives with 1,100 wounded.

Revised version: Gandhi's insidious propaganda had spurred local terrorists into threatening acts against their British protectors. Fearing a revolution in the public garden in Amritsar, the British Indian Army were sent to secure a peaceful surrender. When the locals refused to budge, the British were left with no choice to act, or risk having the country overrun with terrorists and plunged into anarchy, barbarism, and carnage. Many brave British soldiers lost their lives saving India from this terrible threat.

1952–1960: The Mau Mau Rebellion

Current version: The Kikuyu, Meru, and Embu people of Kenya, having been exploited by the British for decades, working for a pittance in appalling conditions like slaves, eventually chose to revolt. The British rounded up these revolters—the Kenya Land and Freedom Army, known as the Mau Mau—and held them in concentration camps or in fortified villages, where torture and mass executions took place on a horrifying scale. Villagers were anally raped with bottles, pulled around on military vehicles, and mauled by guard dogs. The Foreign Office then connived with the Colonial Office to destroy the records of their barbarism. The number of tortured and executed victims will never be known.

Revised version: The tribespeople of Kenya, having been provided secure work and an enviably simple way of life, turned on their charitable patrons, aping the paramilitary tactics of trade unions in their pursuit of greed and power. As negotiations with these primitive people broke down, the British were forced to keep the revolters on ice, placing a safety blanket over the colony by keeping them under armed protection until they realised the error of their ways. As there are no records of any alleged tortures and executions, we must conclude these never took place.

"Marvellous. You'll be writing PR for the foreign office in no time," he said.

"You think?" Henrietta expressed some hope. "My stuff on the Irish Potato Famine is slicker than a yuppie's coif."

Whereabode Derek? He retired to the small apartment provided— a functional bedsit with too much sideboard and semi-wired strip lighting to qualify as a squat—and flopped backflat on a crunchy mattress (was the mattress stuffed with crisps, perchance?) He tried listening to Kate Bush's *The Kick Inside* on his iPod to counter the monumental depression that was sprouting like Radiohead alfalfas through his neural swivels. The high-velocity spangle of Bush was completely ill-fitted for this moment, so the Radiohead commenced, *Kid A*, *naturellement*.

I'm not here.

This isn't happening.

The next period of intolerable awakeness began with a scowling, beer-irradiated Tobias collecting Derek in his land cruiser for morning one of Operation Gaslight the Kiddies. Having expended all patience at the bezique table, a mottle of narked locals had turfed him from the premises following a hard slap on his cheek for the scamming. He spent an hour railing that he would unleash "the terrors of the earth" on the Ugandan people for that assault and that "bombs would rain like raindrops" (sic) on the heads of their babies and that "he'd restage the Kichwamba massacre" with a bullet for those who had the brass neck to laugh at his public slapping. Following a sullen half-hour rattle in the mizzle, the car scrunched to a cease outside a school in an unknown village where Derek was invited to amscray.

"Here's the printout," Tobias said, retrieving the folded A4 and passing the sheet of lies and infamy to Derek, "teach them our new curriculum. I'll collect you before the vultures start circling."

A robustly bricked single-storey structure with ab-fab fixed support cantilevers to put most West Lothian schools to shame, the school bulldozed First World preconceptions with a humble smirk. Derek was welcomed at the door by a blurt of colour named Namuli, the school's only teacher.

"Thank you so much for coming," she said, revealing a smile of such beauty and poise Derek felt repellent in his rancid old skin. "The children are looking forward to hearing about British history, you know, or whatever it is you're here to teach, I'm not quite sure myself."

"Me neither," Derek said not.

"You're the first Ugandan I've properly met. Can you scoop me up in your wondrous arms and slowly rock the rot from my niblicks?" Derek asked not.

In the classroom, the children were patient and eager to hear from their visitor. The nine-year-olds responded respectfully to Namuli when she introduced him to the class as "a British teacher of history." They had clearly been told this lesson was important for their educations and to prick up their ears good and proper, in stark contrast to the custard-spooning temp slacker in Scotland airily pointing him to a roomful of chubby mopers.

A classful of rapt kiddies sat at their tables in anticipation of the sweet nectar of stalwart British learnin' this British man was fixing to squirt up their receptive, respectful ears. There was no Anne Widdecombe in the corner seeking to sabotage his presence with an impromptu striptease or sultry performance of Goethe's *Iphigenia in Tauris*. Namuli stood verso at a polite tilt, her rich, plaited black hair tickling the neckline of her vibrant chitenge, her entire poise a show of unwarranted respect for his sweat-slicked, fumbling self.

"My name is Derek," he said. "I'm here to teach you about British history."

"We fucking know," the kids said not.

Like a firefighter invited to throw the bodies rescued an hour thence back into the blaze, or a surgeon invited to rip the newly implanted heart from the patient a minute thence, or a policeperson shooting the gunman then shooting the hostage a second thence, or a plumber unblocking the U-bend then shoving an entire gateaux thence into the same U-bend, or a virus protection programme saving a laptop from a phishing expedition then phishing the hell out of that same laptop (thence), and in many ways nothing like that whatsoever—in fact nothing like that at all—Derek readied himself to pour oral acaricide into the ears of some of the world's least fortunate children. He rambled on about the Great Fire of London for half an hour, imitating the life of the baker/accidental arsonist Thomas Farriner on Pudding Lane, leaping about to express the potency of the flames sweeping through the city in visual form. The children laughed at his kooky, light-hearted style when acting out this tragedy, and loved his impression of a spooked maiden shrieking from her pyrogenous abode to a place of refuge outwith the burning capital. He concluded the lesson with an irrelevant lecture on the importance of fire safety.

"Thank you! The kids really loved your lesson," Namuli said.

"I had an excellent time teaching them," he said. "I really appreciate the invitation."

"Well, please come again, the children would love to hear more from you."

"I'd love to. Thank you."

Goddamn, Uganda!

You're a sensation!

O, Kampala!

O, Mbarara!

O, Jinja!

O, Mbale!

O, Nansana!

O, Kisoro!

O, Kibale!

O, Kira Town!

O, Entebbe!

O, Everywhere Else in Uganda!

O, Sweet Uganda!

O, Sweet, Sweet Uganda!

"That was the best fucking thing I've done since, like, whenever," Derek said with a mattress-factory's worth of springs in his shoe-factory's worth of steps.

✺

Bed. Stranger in room. Bracing self for knife in spine.

"Psst, wake up," the man said.

"Whuoarwuhyou?" Derek pillowmouthed.

"I'm Blunt Simon," the man said, switching on the pretty darn wan overhead light. "You can turn around, I'm not here to hurt you."

As these words were the only reassurance that his spine would remain unsliced, he flipped his carcass to view a bulky Ugandan in a chequered blue shirt sat on the chair in the corner of the room.

He leaned. Forward.

"I'm here to tell you a story," he said, mid-lean. "There was once a country that longed to re-establish a stranglehold on the former British colonies. That country had a government of amoral, fascist politicians with the requisite legal and communications skills to open talks with the corrupt regime of an African country. They convinced the leaders of that African country that by partnering with the United Kingdom they would receive an economic stimulus and rehabilitation the likes of which they had never experienced, if they would only let the British colonise them by stealth. In return, the British were secretly planning to plunder this country of their precious minerals, like in the Good Old Days."

"Are you saying this partnership is a smokescreen for the British to loot Uganda of precious resources, and leave the country destitute?"

"Yes. In addition, they are planning to convince the Ugandan people to trust the British and have a newfound respect for their former oppressors while robbing them blind in the cover of darkness. And Britain will keep the country's economy performing at previous poor-to-average levels so no one notices that their resources have been stripped away."

"That is so British," Derek said.

"Yes."

"What do you want from me?"

"In four hours, we're about to storm their covert stripmining base. Then we'll start shooting people. I understand you have only arrived here and have no involvement, so I would like you to stay put and say nothing."

"To be clear, I'm being asked by a local campaigner slash guerrilla leader to sit idly by as British camp where the British are currently smuggling precious minerals from Uganda back to Britain is stormed?"

"Yes."

"If I refuse?"

"We will probably have you murdered."

"Naturally."

Exit, Blunt Simon.

Derek slunk back into a semi-snooze and had a mull.

He could either:

1) Betray the British state, saving Uganda from ruination, and expect a life sentence for treason.

2) Call the authorities back home and expect a silent murdering in his bed at night.

3) Walk off into the still Ugandan night and collapse from dehydration several miles outside a village.

But was there a fourth option?

Yes.

There's always a fourth option.

4) Remain in bed listening to early Low for the rest of recorded time.

"That's the option for me," he said.

So, oblivion then.

Heck, hell, Abaddon.

(Suited top-to-toe in finest Kevlar, the s'more-sizzler that was Arthur's Seat burning big heat in the hill o'er there, Derek arrived at the scottish parliament (no caps for you, here in heck) for an eternity of votes on amendments to the Cathcart-Driscoll Declaration, in its four millionth reading, with particular emphasis on subsection 992.21C and the incommodious subset of nested underclauses buried within a nano-clump of nibbling codicils and venomous footnotes. Derek was invited to shed his latest skin of objections. He stepped from his Kevlar wrapper, presented his ink-plump nudiest self to the watching em-ess-pees, and opened his pores, showering the room with strong rebuttals to the sloppiest chunnels of thought in the subsec, waiting for the counter-rebuttals to form brooding cumuli in the air above their heads, cohering into a thunderous rumble of no-nay-nevers and no-nay-never-no-mores, to pour into his pores, stunning him to a shuddery, watery retreat).

"Awake, Sir Decca of Uganda," a voice accompanied by tapping on the forehead and shuggling of shoulders and prodding of thighs and flicking of ears and yanking open of eyes said.

"Fuckisit?"

"Millie."

"Oh Christ."

"As you crank yourself vertical, I'll tell you what happened to me when we parted in Cadiz," she said. "Well, we were poised to book a recording studio to scorch an EP on disc when The Ant had an explosive strop over the paltriness of the drum. He refused to perform until he had located a certain genus of Moroccan bongo. So we travelled south to where the boats were, sailed across the Gibraltar Strait to the nib of North Africa. At a music shop in Tangier, The Ant asked about the tututiqin—an historic form of bongo carved from shepherd's wood with ceremonial frills around the base, where the sound is supposed to riffle in the air to offer a warm susurrus to the Gods, or something. Sadly, there were no tututiqins in Tangier, so a three-hour burl in a rental along the coast to Rabat was required. In Rabat, we asked a street trumpeter whether the tututiqin was available to thump in the capital, and the man made a face that indicated we were lost in music, caught in a trap, no turning back, lost in music-ah. He said the tututiqin was made in the small village of Zag on the Western Saharan border for a nominal fee by a fist of elders who may or may not have working pulses. As you know, Decca, there's no persuading The Ant when he takes a notion, so we had no choice except to book a hotel and take another long road trip along the melting highways-from-hell of Morocco. When we arrived at Zag, we located the elders we needed, who started work on the tututiqin after we paid them half our recording budget. In that border town, F-F met a French woman and vanished into the clement Saharan night. I've never heard from him since. When our tututiqin was made, The Ant was in such awe of the handcrafted percussive marvel, he was unable to bring him palms in the direction of the wood to make a slapping sound. His hands shook the closer he came. If I tried to play, he'd wrestle me to the ground and restrain me with a violence that made me think poor Anty-boy was going full J. Dahmer. He revered the tututiqin. So with F-F in absentia and The Ant unwilling to perform on anything other than a tututiqin but unwilling to actually perform on the tututiqin, the EP was on perma pause. We returned to Rabat where I performed for two months with the Spanish busking troupe Galicia Silvertone, who let me smoke hookah and eat their opium sarnies until my remaining cash ran out. Mercifully, I received an email from a Tory asking if I wanted to teach musical theory to underfed Ugandan blacks with ol' Decca, and I said yes please, if they paid for my flight and accommodation."

"That's progression, that," Derek said, observing how Millie's newly bronzed skin lent her the air of a pan-fried Kate Dickie. "I mean The Ant refusing to play."

"Ah, still the same old snark-puppy?"

"Seems. I'm a collaborator now, working for the Ugandan resistance. Big chap was in a minute ago to ask me to keep quiet while they shot British thieves."

"Exciting!"

"They're scheduled to mobilise in a mo, so we need to hide in this room hoping no stray bullets penetrate this cheap ballast."

"OK. Hey, I'm thinking of forming a Ugandan jangle-pop band called 10,000 Maniocs. You want in?"

"Playing what?"

"You could intone droll vocals Robert Lloyd-style."

"Pass. You know, I've been thinking about controlled delusion. It's possible you were absolutely correct in every respect. The benefits of creating an alternate reality in your mind and recasting your failures and humiliations as utter triumphs might be immense. From now on, I'm simply going to say that I've had one of the most staggeringly successful careers in British politics and repeat my fabricated achievements to anyone who asks. Did you know in 1999, I reduced poverty by 38% in Scotland and helped twelve thousand smackheads into full-time employment in the tech sector? Did you know I was hailed by Tony Blair as the most serene-minded policy-slicker in that there parliament? I'll choose to believe that. Why not?"

"I am tickled to hear that," Millie said, slouching on the same chair from which Blunt Simon had issued a murder threat moments prior. "But I've been thinking too. I've concluded that controlled delusion isn't working for me no more. In my head F-F is in Senegal reinventing the acid scene in his own image, cutting a beat-blootered slice of rave wonder to take Central Africa by storm. In reality, he's probably working in a sweatshop in Nouakchott trying to raise the airfare to return to Edinburgh and I'm not even lifting a pinkie to assist."

"I'm pleased you said that, because everything I said there about controlled delusion was bollocks."

Torchlight winked through the roller blinds. The faint rustle of covert killers.

"That'll be them," Derek said.

"Super."

"I considered staying here teaching the kids history, but the lack of wine bars, mini-milks, and prime scotch beef would soon override any temporary flutter I may have felt at pushing these kids toward serviceable knowledge bases. I have two paths. I can return to live in the Cotswolds with a sultry ex-wifey and her Tory-trodden daughter. The fact I'd be living in a town crawling with bigoted old biddies with their tedious worldviews and have the splendour of the rich country-side ruined by the verbal souper of their fascist opining would sour up that choice within a week. So the most sensible course of action for me is to return to Scotland to see what I can salvage of the marriage and the finances, to see if I manage to sidestep prison thanks to the mer-ciful beneficence of Lord Quiver. I might move into a small Wester Hailes flat, pull a state pension and spend the rest of my time reading 99p kindle thrillers or poorly formatted versions of Victorian classics pulled from 1996 HTML via gutenberg.org."

"I'm thinking similar," Millie said, tapping her chin as though solo-ing on a one-keyed pianola, "I'm thinking I might reconnect with my parents, move back in with them and enrol on a midwifery course, then meet an unremarkable clerk from Falkirk and cohabit with him in a pokey flat until we can scrape together enough sous for a slightly bigger flat and a border collie."

The first strafe of gunfire. Muffled screams.

"That's them shooting the Tory scum now," Derek said.

"Good."

"In the morning we'll hitch a wagon to home, providing Tobias Prompt has been shot in the head."

Under the rat-a-rat-tat of machine gun fire and the yowls of bullet-riddled coolonialists, Derek and Millie went to sleep, resigned to the oddly soothing unspectacularity of their mutual futures.

M.J. Nicholls is the author of the story collection *Violent Solutions to Popular Problems*, the novels *Condemned to Cymru, Trimming England, Scotland Before the Bomb, The 1002nd Book to Read Before You Die, The House of Writers*, and *A Postmodern Belch*, and the novella *The Quiddity of Delusion*. He lives in Glasgow.

Milton Keynes UK
Ingram Content Group UK Ltd.
UKHW041830120324
439228UK00004B/171